More Ghost Stories of the Estes Valley

Volume 2

by
Celeste Lasky

Write On Publications
Loveland, Colorado

Published by: Write On Publications
Loveland, Colorado 80537
970-635-1974

Disclaimer: The stories in this book are based on real experiences told to the author by local Estes Valley residents. The author does not attest to the veracity of the stories. In some cases, the names and places in the stories have been changed to protect the privacy of the individuals. In other cases, the names and places are real.

ISBN: 0-9643331-4-7

14   13   12   11   10   9   8   7

Printed in the United States of America by
Citizen Printing, Fort Collins, Colorado.

In Dedication to

my husband Ron
editor and typesetter extraordinaire
to say nothing of always being on hand
to encourage my muse.

Acknowledgments

The following people have contributed their stories, experiences, and input to this book. I am grateful for their contributions which helped each story to evolve to its present state. Many thanks are extended - in alphabetical order - to:

Kathy Durward

Dawn Hahler

Jena Harris

Susan Harris

Troy Heller

Heather Leigh

The Stanley Hotel/Paula Peat Page

Timothy Stolz

Stephen Storer

Carolyn Winey

Mary Wood

Michael Young

Introduction

I believe in ghosts! I have not had a verifiable ghostly experience, although at times I have sensed the presence of something from the "other world."

But, whether or not you believe in ghosts, the majority of people who contributed to this book do – or at the very least believe in "something" that allows the unexplainable to happen. As I gathered the stories for both Volume 1 and Volume 2, I made new friends and acquaintances who share the same feelings about ghosts as I do. It's been fun collecting all these stories and incidents and putting them into written form. It's hoped that you, the reader, find them fun too. Enjoy!

Table of Contents

An Evening With Rebecca 1

Girl of His Dreams 4

Grandma's House Eternal 7

Lost and Found 9

The Father's Day Ghost 13

Remembering the Flood 16

A Spirited Horse 20

The Table . . . the Beginning 24

And the Guests Stayed On 27

The Overseer 30

Room 237 34

The Lady in White - Room 17 37

The Connection 40

Music Appreciation 44

A Housekeeper's Dilemma 47

Under It All - Justice 51

An Evening With Rebecca

Michael lives in a small old house that is haunted! His Auntie can attest to that. The ghost in question is named Rebecca. She resides in the attic mostly.

Michael had told his friend Kathy about Rebecca, and Kathy thought it was really neat that Michael lived in a haunted house.

"Michael, can I bring my girls over to your place? They'd LOVE to tell their friends that they've seen – or even heard – a ghost!"

"Sure, but I have to tell you that I can't guarantee anything. Rebecca may or may not let her presence be known. I mean I can't cue her to do anything. She's very independent. We may wind up just watching TV and eating popcorn."

"Oh, that's OK. They'll love it!"

The next evening, Kathy and her two girls, Mary-Beth and Sarah, came over for the evening. Michael put on a movie and they all settled in – caught between watching the movie and listening for Rebecca. Midway through the movie, Michael excused himself to go make the popcorn.

Kerplunk!

"Michael, was that you," Kathy called from the living room.

"No, it wasn't. I heard something too. Thought it was one of you guys."

"No, it wasn't us," Kathy said, huddling a bit closer to her girls.

"Was it Rebecca," Mary Beth asked.

"It sounded like something upstairs. In my studio. Let's go take a look."

"Wellllll, . . . OK . . . if we all stay together," Kathy said.

The little group started up the small staircase. Just then Kathy noticed a framed newspaper article on the wall about Michael and his house. She read it aloud. The girls hugged each other.

"Yep, the newspaper people did that a while back. Here, come this way. Here's my studio.

"Oh, she did it again," Michael said, exasperated.

"Did WHAT again," Kathy whispered.

"See that spray can over there in the corner? That was on the shelf with all my other art stuff. I cleaned in here this afternoon because I knew you guys were coming and I wanted to show you some of my art work. All my paints and materials were on the shelves, including that can! Once before when I had company over, a similar thing happened. See my brushes in that bottle of water? Well, we heard a thud up here and came up to investigate and found the bottle in the corner on the floor – water and brushes scattered."

Kathy moved closer to Michael and whispered, "Maybe she doesn't like company."

"Could be, I don't know."

"Let's go back downstairs," one of the girls said.

As they started down the stairwell, Sarah screamed, "Get it off! Get it off!" She had a frightened look on her face. Whether it was imagination or real, something or someone had touched her hair. She thought at first that it was something hanging from the ceiling, but there was nothing above her head. The group went back to the TV and their popcorn, feeling no less uneasy.

By 11 p.m. Kathy and her girls were getting tired, so they decided to call it an evening. It was snowing, so Kathy went out to warm up the car. She came back into the house and visited a bit more with Michael as the girls got their coats and boots on. A few minutes later Kathy and the girls left. Michael made the rounds, turning out lights, checking windows, about to get ready for bed when . . .

BAM BAM BAM

Michael ran to the door. "Kathy! What's wrong?"

"My headlights are on and the radio too! None of that was on when I left the car!"

"Rebecca must like you!" Michael had to stifle a laugh.

"But I don't want to take her home with me! You keep her!"

"Kathy, I don't know what to do. This never happened before. I don't have a book on how to control my ghost."

"DO SOMETHING! Go out there and tell her she can't go with me! She has to stay here with you!"

Michael grabbed his jacket and stumbled outside. Kathy was right behind him, followed closely by two wide-eyed little girls.

Kathy took the initiative. "OK, get out, get out of my car!"

Michael reinforced Kathy's demand. "C'mon Rebecca. C'mon. You can't go. You have to stay here with me."

When Kathy felt sufficiently sure that Rebecca was not in the car, she and her girls got in and drove off. What convinced Kathy? Well . . . somehow the radio quit. However, it was a cold night, so . . . old cars do funny things. Right?

Girl of His Dreams

"Whew! I'm beat," the head chef said to one of his cooks. "These 18 hour shifts are killing me – to say nothing of my social life."

"Yeah, I know what you mean. Right now all I want is a shower and a bed," the cook chuckled.

The two men did their usual closing check list: ovens, stoves, appliances, door locks, a double check on the deep freeze, finally the lights. They made their way out through the dining room and into the lobby of the hotel where they parted company. The cook lived in one of the dorms behind The Stanley Hotel. The chef had a room in the hotel on the third floor. He decided to climb the stairs as the elevator wasn't at the lobby and someone would have to locate a bellman to bring the elevator to the lobby level. It was the original elevator for the old hotel and had to be run manually by a bellman. The stairs seemed faster to the chef.

He arrived out of breath at the door to his room. He juggled change around in his pocket and finally found his key. "Ah, that bed sure looks inviting," he said aloud, feeling a little . . . uneasy. "Think I'll shower and then go to bed," he decided, again talking out loud to himself.

Once the chef hit the bed he was suddenly wide awake. "If this doesn't beat all," he said. "I was half asleep on my feet before I showered. Now look at me! I'm wide awake. Well, I'll watch David Letterman for awhile. Maybe I'll get sleepy." He

4

turned on the TV and settled into the bed. Before long he began to hear a funny noise at the head of his bed. The noise became louder and more frequent. The chef thought it must be coming from the room next door. He picked up the phone and dialed the front desk.

"Front desk. How can I help you?"

"Ben this is Troy. I've got some funny noises coming from the room next to mine. Can you give them a ring and ask them to cool it? I'm really beat and need to get some sleep."

"Sorry Troy, but there's no one else on the third floor. Only you, good buddy."

A chill ran down Troy's spine. "Oh. Well, thanks anyway." Troy returned to bed, using the remote control to turn the TV down low. He waited and listened. It wasn't long before the same sound as before started again. He decided to concentrate on the Letterman Show – and at some point dozed off. He woke up and the station had gone off the air. He rolled over to turn off the TV and there she was!

The little girl – elementary school age he guessed – was dancing and twirling at the foot of his bed! She had on a frilly party dress and had shoulder length brown hair. Troy screamed and she disappeared.

The next day Troy discussed what had happened with several employees in the hotel and someone suggested that maybe it was the little girl that has frequently been seen in the halls by other people. No one could be sure. Still, Troy had an uneasy feeling about his own little girl about the same age. She was living in Florida at the time and he decided to call her. As it turned out, she was fine.

Sometime after this incident, Troy's father came for a visit and stayed in a mountain view room on the third floor. He had heard Troy's story, but he was sure it was just his imagination. His first night in the hotel he called Troy at 5 a.m.

"Hello," a sleepy Troy said into the phone.

"Son, I'm leaving."

"Dad? What's wrong? It's only 5 a.m."

"I know son, but I have to leave. There's something . . . strange . . . ."

Click.

Troy dressed quickly and raced down to the lobby just in time to catch his father going out the front door.

"Dad, wait! What happened?"

"It was . . . something. I can't explain it. I'll call you later," he said ashen-faced.

Troy stood watching his father hurriedly throwing luggage into his car.

Grandma's House Eternal

Caroline's house in Pinewood Springs – not far from Estes Park – was indeed unique. It was filled with a variety of ghostly happenings such as a ghost working on a repair job in the basement, a ghost named affectionately "Grandma" whose "baking" left distinct smells for Caroline and her daughter, and probably the same ghost (Grandma) who continually removed a picture and a clock from wall. (See Ghost Stories of the Estes Valley, Vol.1) This is another unexplained happening that does lead one to wonder. Caroline's house hummed! No it didn't hum any kind of known melody. It just hummed its own hum!

The hum seemed to center in the kitchen. At first Caroline assumed it was some type of electrical hum coming from an appliance or from outside electrical lines. She went outside and noted that the electrical lines were not attached to the house anywhere near the kitchen. She then unplugged all the appliances; still the kitchen continued to hum.

Not knowing what else to do, Caroline invited some people over to get their opinions. Some children who lived next door remembered hearing it too. They helped in trying to locate the humming. They checked the basement – even though there was no electrical equipment down there. Nothing. The hot water heater was gas, and besides it wasn't in the kitchen area.

Now the humming always happened when everything was peaceful and quiet, times when there was a feeling of contentment and happiness for Caroline and her daughter. She had learned that "Grandma" had loved that house and had lived there until she died of natural causes. Perhaps "Grandma" couldn't carry a tune, but maybe she could hum! Maybe "Grandma" was at peace. Evidently "Grandma" was quite a lady when she was alive. The neighbor children who had heard the humming in the kitchen told Caroline a lot about "Grandma." Apparently she was a caring individual – and quite possibly talented too!

Caroline's daughter, Joanie, was having trouble sleeping. She'd toss and turn and would doze off, then wake up again. This went on for weeks. Then one night, exhausted from lack of sleep, she got up and walked around her room. Something caught her eye, and she turned toward her bed.

Sitting there, on the bed, was a pretty young woman with a book in her hands. Joanie, as if in a dream, returned to her bed. The young woman opened her book and began reading poetry – beautiful poetry – in a soft gentle voice. Joanie drifted off to sleep.

When her daughter told her of the incident, Caroline assumed it was indeed a dream. She was soon to be proven wrong, however. Joanie's insomnia returned . . . and so did the young woman with her poetry book.

When the neighbor children heard about this ghostly visitor, they brought over an old picture of a pretty young woman. Joanie gasped! "That's her! I think that's my visitor! Who is she," she asked.

"That is 'Grandma'," one responded. Who knows. Maybe "Grandma" was putting one of the poems to music – and is continuing to work on it in her beloved kitchen – humming and waiting for just the right sound.

Lost and Found

The front desk manager, Raymond, answered the impatiently ringing phone.

"Registration, may I help you?"

"I hope so," replied the voice. "We were there a week ago – Jonathan Bascomb. My wife discovered that she left her bathrobe there. It's white terry cloth with her name – Barbara – embroidered on it. Has it been found?"

"Let me check our found list with housekeeping. Can you hold? Thank you."

Raymond called the housekeeping manager and learned that nothing like that had been turned in. Perhaps the woman left it at one of their other stops.

"Sir, I'm sorry but housekeeping says that nothing like that has been found or turned in."

"My wife is positive that she left it there. We came straight home. She didn't notice until yesterday that it was gone because she always wears a different bathrobe at home and saves that one for trips. Please call me if it is located."

Raymond promised to call, took Mr. Bascomb's telephone number, and hung up.

He shook his head. "That's the seventh call this week for articles lost that people are sure they left here. What's going on?" He added the item to his growing list: expensive sunglasses, a small camera – indicating the next picture to be number 12, a backpack containing a change of underwear (men's) and a light-weight water-repellant jacket, a pair of Indian moccasins, a silk scarf, and a woman's gold bracelet engraved "Forever, Brad," and now the bathrobe.

Later that afternoon Raymond met with the housekeeping manager. She was equally puzzled.

"I don't understand it either. I thought we were doing really well – no lost and found for quite awhile. Now suddenly we've got a list of seven items. Raymond, you know that we check every drawer and closet when we clean a room. There's been nothing."

"I know, I know. Well, it's a mystery to me. We've still got that old list of missing items – guess I'll just add this new list to it. I doubt any of it will turn up."

"I'm afraid you're right. Too bad."

*　　　　*　　　　*

As evening approached, guests for the night began to arrive. The front desk was kept quite busy. The eternal ringing of the in-house phone finally gained some attention.

"Front desk. This is Albert. How can I help you?"

"I'm in room 203. I'm Miss Duncan. There seems to be some mistake."

"How so," Albert inquired.

"Well, there's stuff in here."

"Stuff? What do you mean? Isn't the room clean?"

"Oh, yes, it's clean except for the stuff."

"Could you be a bit more specific, Miss Duncan?"

"Well, there's a backpack, a jacket, and a bathrobe in the

closet and a scarf in one drawer, a gold bracelet in another drawer, a pair of Indian moccasin in another drawer, and some men's underwear in another . . . and . . . "

"I'll send someone right up, Miss Duncan."

Albert immediately contacted Raymond.

"I'll be right there," Raymond said abruptly. "Look in my top desk drawer and find the lost and found list."

When Raymond arrived, both he and Albert went up to Miss Duncan's room. Raymond carried the list – with its recent additions – and Albert carried a large box.

Raymond knocked.

"Good evening, Miss Duncan. Sorry you are having this annoyance."

"Annoyance! You don't know the half of it! After I spoke to you last, I checked the other drawers and under the bed. There's the pile of stuff I found in addition to what I reported."

Raymond and Albert were stunned. They began to check the items against the list.

Every item was there! Albert filled the box and the two men returned to the front desk.

"Albert, you're new here. Guess maybe you don't know about our sticky-fingered ghost, do you?"

"What? I've never heard anything about any ghosts here."

"Oh, there are several. One moves things around a bit – nothing drastic – a chair here, a lamp there. Another one blows out candles on the piano – just little things. I've thought for a long time that we have a ghost that likes to collect things – guests' things specifically. Now I'm convinced of it."

"Well, why weren't these things found before?"

"Did you assign Miss Duncan to 203?"

"Yes, I did."

"I should have warned you. We avoid putting anyone in there – odd things have happened. Lights on and off, water running in the sink in the middle of the night.

Apparently our sticky-fingered ghost is in residence there. Housekeeping hasn't been in there in quite awhile. So, naturally they had no reason to check the closet or drawers. I'm surprised Miss Duncan didn't complain about it being dusty and unclean."

"On the contrary, she said it was very clean."

"Well, then we have a tidy sticky-fingered ghost in 203. Reassign Miss Duncan to another room. I'll get busy on this lost and found list and see how much of this collection of 'stuff' I can get back to the rightful owners."

Raymond was able to return over half of the items found in 203. Housekeeping was informed to always check 203 when something was reported missing. It saved a lot of time.

The Father's Day Ghost

It was a warm June evening. The Inn was filled to capacity. There were several honeymooners, people on a weekend for their anniversary, older couples vacationing, but there were no families. Generally speaking that was usually true. The Inn wasn't set up for families. There was no pool or play area, nothing to entice a family with young children.

One middle-aged gentleman had come in mid-June – Father's Day weekend specifically – for the past four years. This June was no exception.

"Welcome Mr. Henderson. I see you've joined us again this Father's Day weekend."

"Yes, it seems I just can't stay away."

What Mr. Henderson didn't tell the Inn's manager was a sad story that would never go away. Five years ago Mr. Henderson and his son Eric had gone on a fishing trip. Eric had begged his dad for months to take him out in their inboard motor boat. Mr. Henderson had asked his wife along, but she declined – fishing not being one of her favorite past-times.

The weather was clear. Mr. Henderson and his son left early in the morning, before daylight, to get to the boat's slip and get everything on board. Little Eric – 10 years old – was very excited. He couldn't wait to land a "big one!" He was convinced that this was his lucky day.

By late morning, Mr. Henderson noticed an ominous cloud

build up to the west. He thought about starting back then, but Eric begged to wait a few more minutes. He was still in search of the "big one."

Unfortunately they delayed a bit too long. Almost within minutes the weather worsened and the boat was tossed around in the turbulent water. The rain was blinding. It obliterated everything, leaving visibility to only 10 yards at most. Mr. Henderson sent Eric to the small cabin below.

Mr. Henderson checked his compass and believed he had the right bearing. He nudge the throttle forward to low speed, thinking they could inch their way back to the marina. Actually, he was correct in his calculations. It was the other boat's driver that had erred. Suddenly out of nowhere – and with little reaction time – the other boat was upon them, going too fast for conditions. Mr. Henderson swerved his craft to one side, but the other boat smashed into him.

Shortly after the boating accident, Mr. Henderson's wife divorced him. Due to the shock of the boating accident, the divorce, and being all alone, Mr. Henderson's doctor advised him to get away for awhile. Mr. Henderson chose the mountains of Colorado for healing. He had heard about a small town tucked away in the mountains and decided to try to find peace there. His first stay was on Father's Day five years ago.

"Mr. Henderson, I'm curious. You've been here for five Father's Day weekends. I'm assuming you are treating yourself to a holiday. Am I right?" the manager of the Inn said. "Of course we're delighted you've chosen our little out of the way lodge."

"Well, I do come here for a reason. I keep hoping I'll meet that little boy I met the first time I was here. As I passed him, I asked him how he was, and he smiled and said, "I'm fine, I am very happy." He looked very much like my son, Eric. As I was lonesome for my son, I turned around to talk to him some more, but he was gone - vanished. I inquired about him, but no one had ever seen him, and no family with a young boy was registered. That's why I come back – in case he comes back."

The manager was puzzled. "If seeing the boy made you lonesome for your son, why don't you bring your son to the Inn with you?" asked the manager.

"Well, you see," replied Mr. Henderson, "my son died five years ago."

Remembering the Flood

It came without warning – early one summer day about 7 a.m. Estes Park was just awakening, preparing for another busy day of visitors to the area. The sky was blue with a few puffy clouds. High above the little mountain town an earthen dam had just given way, unleashing the mountain lake behind it. No one in town had any idea of what was approaching.

The water rushed down the mountain, connecting with a small river, and gouged a path out of the ancient rocks, moving boulders the size of automobiles like they were toys and relocating them several miles downstream. Uncountable numbers of forest pines were destroyed. When the water finally hit a level area, it formed Fan Lake then went on through Horseshoe Park and down the Fall River into Aspenglen Campground just inside Rocky Mountain National Park's Fall River Entrance, and then on into Estes Park. The devastating damage was unbelievable. Water was three to four feet deep in places in Estes Park. Store front windows were smashed and the stores flooded out. Several trailers were washed away. Many motels were lost. Fortunately the loss of life was minimal. No recorded deaths occurred in town. However . . .

A woman and her two daughters lived in an apartment/motel near the Fall River that was re-built after the flood. Their apartment had a ghost. This ghost was a prankster. Where he came from, they didn't know. He was there when they moved in because things started to happen almost right away. For some odd reason they named him Mikey. One of the daughters saw him once and told her mother that he was a young man. The name Mikey seemed to fit him.

One happening occurred rather routinely. The woman had a special place where she kept quarters for the laundramat. When she'd go to get the quarters, they'd be gone. At first she blamed her daughters, thinking they had needed change for something and took the quarters. Both girls vehemently denied any involvement in the disappearing quarters. Then the mother thought that maybe the girls' friends had borrowed the money and forgot to tell them. Again both girls denied any involvement.

One daughter said, "Mom, you always leave money on the table. Why would anyone bother the quarters? The money you leave laying out is never gone, is it?" The woman had to admit that it was never touched. It was Mikey – it had to be!

"Mikey – enough! I need those quarters to do laundry," the woman said to an empty room. The disappearance of the quarters subsided, but every now and then . . .

Mikey also like to play with the shower faucets. He'd wait until someone was in the shower – water temperature set just right – and then he'd start. Suddenly the water would turn cold or, more dangerously, turn hotter. No one else in the apartments had any similar trouble with water temperature changes, so Mikey got the blame.

Once, when the woman was ill with the flu and fever, she felt particularly chilled. She mentioned to one of her daughters that she couldn't seem to get warm. That evening she suddenly felt a warmth around her – like a blanket or Afghan had been wrapped around her shoulders. There was nothing there – just a feeling of warmth. She was sure that Mikey was considerate and caring – just liked to be a prankster.

One of the big tricks that Mikey played happened to the oldest daughter. She had come to visit for a couple of weeks. The mother went on the evening shift to work, leaving her eldest daughter at home alone. They had an extra car but it wasn't running. It sat parked out in front of the apartment. Mikey liked to sit in the car. He had been seen in there many times. The daughter did not know about Mikey and his liking to sit in the car. Her mother had forgotten to tell her that little habit of his. So, around midnight that night, she looked outside – feeling a bit uneasy being alone. She saw a shadow in the car!

Fear gripped her! Her mother had told her the car was locked! How could . . . She decided to get her mother's pistol and confront whoever was out there. She put the pistol in her coat pocket and approached the car. When she got to one of the doors and looked inside, the car was empty. She checked all the doors and they were locked! She ran back into the apartment, closed and locked the door, and called her mother.

"Oh, honey, I'm sorry. I forgot to tell you. It's only Mikey."

Mikey got to where he would talk to the woman and her daughters. One thing he told them was that he was killed in a flood. They couldn't be sure it was the flood that hit Estes Park, however. But it did seem probable since they were living in an apartment/motel building that had been destroyed by the local flood. Although there were no recorded deaths in town, maybe he had been staying there alone and no one knew he was there. Mikey told them that the water carried him away and that it slammed him into a telephone pole and knocked him unconscious and he drowned. He described the area, but the woman said there would be no way to really determine exactly where it was.

The woman and her daughter finally moved from the apartment/motel but she doesn't know if Mikey left or not. Now there's no one to come home to and ask, "Hi, Mikey. What did you get into today?"

A Spirited Horse

It had been another warm and sunny Colorado summer day. The lodge was filled to capacity as usual with visitors from all over the world. The biggest demand from the visitors - as always - was horseback riding. The lodge had a large number of riding horses and ample wranglers to assist the visitors. Some had never even been close to a horse, much less ridden one!

Typical of a summer afternoon in Estes Park, Colorado storm clouds began to gather to the west.

Andy, one of the wranglers, voiced his concern over the darkening threat.

"Hey, Pat! Do you think that maybe we'd better cancel that three o'clock trail ride. I think we're gonna get rained out anyway."

"Nah. It can look like that and then not rain a drop," she said. Pat was a spunky gal from the panhandle of Texas. A few dark clouds didn't frighten her one bit.

As the guests collected near the corral after lunch, several kept eyeing the sky, pointing to the gathering storm. Pat and Andy tied yellow slickers behind each saddle.

"Ah . . . Miss, do you actually take people out on trail rides in the rain," one man from Boston asked.

"Yep, we sure do. Gives you the true cowboy experience," Pat smiled. She felt sure by the look on his face that he was becoming less and less interested in the cowboy experience.

"Won't the horses get nervous if it starts lightening and thundering," the Boston man inquired.

"Well, maybe some, but actually they're pretty used to it. And all of the horses we've saddled for this ride are pretty calm and laid back. It takes a lot to rile them."

The man from Boston walked away, not totally convinced. The dark clouds seemed to be a warning to him. "I believe I'll forego this afternoon's ride and take one in the morning," he told Pat.

"That's ok, sir. But there really isn't any danger," Pat assured him.

"Hey, Pat! I think we're gonna hafta cancel this group for sure. One of the wranglers just heard on the radio that we're in for some heavy rain and hail," Andy yelled over the first clap of thunder. The guests scattered, some heading for their cabins, others heading for the main lodge.

"Yep, you're right, Andy. Those clouds look like they mean business this time. Call for a couple of wranglers to help us with these horses," Pat said.

Another bolt of lightening and another clap of thunder began to unnerve the horses. It was all Pat and Andy could do to keep them contained. Finally a couple of other wranglers arrived, and they began leading the horses into their stalls in the barn.

"That'll calm 'em down, gettin' in out of this weather," Andy said. All the wranglers had their hands full, however. The horses were really nervous, more so than either Pat or Andy had ever seen.

"I can't get over 'em. Never seen 'em so jittery. They've all been out in storms before."

21

"Yeah, I know. No telling what's got them all spooked. I think it's more than just the storm," Pat added. "But I don't know what else it could be."

An older wrangler pulled Andy aside. "Say, have you heard the story?"

Andy was busy getting one of the bridles off. "What story is that?"

"About the ghost horse," the old timer said.

"Ghost horse? I've never heard anything about a ghost horse. Are you just trying to scare me or somethin'?"

"No, son, I'm not trying to scare you. Just thought that maybe he's around again. Maybe that's why these horses are so extra skittish right now."

"Well, I'm sorry, but I can't buy that story. Ghost horse? Ha, Ha," Andy laughed.

"You won't laugh when you see him. He's a big un, solid white. He's been around many times before. You'll get a glimpse of him someday. Just keep an eye out," the old timer cautioned as he headed out into the storm for the last horse.

Andy began talking to himself - maybe to ease his own jitters. "Aw heck, there ain't no such thing as a ghost horse. I mean I don't believe in people ghosts, so why should I believe in horse ghosts," he asked the horse in the stall. The horse pawed at the straw on the floor, his eyes bulging so that the white was showing.

"Now, looky here. You calm down. Don't go gettin' a notion that some ghost horse is around here," Andy told the horse. The horse continued to paw the ground. Andy looked around and found himself alone in the barn. The horses were all safely out of the storm and secured in their stalls. Andy caught some movement out of the corner of his eye. It was just a glance, but he knew it was another horse.

"Guess someone must have been ridin' by and the storm chased him to the lodge. Oh, well. We can tie up his horse in here for now. Andy went to the tack room and got a lead rope, planning to use it to secure the visiting horse. Only seconds had passed. He started for where the horse had been - but what he saw was the fading image of a big white stallion. Frantic horses in the stalls told Andy that he wasn't the only one who had seen the ghost horse.

Andy took off for the bunkhouse yelling, "Hey, Old-timer . . . . Old-timer . . . ."

The Table . . . the Beginning

Sam and Esther Stewart had come to Estes Park on a vacation – alone. The children, three girls and a boy, had been left behind at Grandma's house. What Sam and Esther found was as close to heaven as they could imagine. Estes Park was a small mountain town about thirty years ago. Yes, it had the usual benefits of a small community: schools, churches, a variety of small stores, a couple of grocery stores (albeit small ones), 2 gas stations, etc. Most of all it had friendly, warm people who took the time and made the effort to help with directions, suggestions on where to go and what to see - real people.

Sam and Esther weren't in Estes Park long when they jointly decided that this was where they wanted to raise their family. They would be away from the hub-bub of the big city and closer to nature, Esther's passion. Sam could start up a new construction business too, since a quick check at City Hall told them that the town was growing. They returned home, sold their house and business, and returned to Estes Park – this time with the four children in tow.

They settled quickly into a temporary home. Sam bought a lot down near the lake and began making plans to build a house there. Esther and the children settled into enjoying the beauty of nature in the area – Rocky Mountain National Park not the least of which became one of their favorite places. Finally, the home was ready, and they moved in. The children grew happily and

Sam and Esther fully enjoyed their life in the mountains. Then one night during a snow storm . . . .

"Mom, can the guys come over tonight? Thought we'd play some games and make popcorn," Dan asked his mother. "It's snowing too hard to go down to Loveland."

"You're right there, my son. I don't want you driving any-where tonight," Esther said. "I imagine the other mothers feel the same way."

"Tom's dad has volunteered to pick up Doug, Smitty, and Jason and bring 'em by. Maybe they could stay the night and you or Dad could take 'em home in the morning?"

Esther pondered the question. "Well, yes, I think we can manage that. Now Dan, I do not want you or your friends teasing your sisters. They live here too."

"Affirmative, Mom-o. They can even join us in the games. We're just gonna do like Monopoly, maybe Rummy, stuff like that. Hey, where are the games and cards and the Ouija board?"

"In the hall closet on the top shelf," Esther smiled. "I'll tell Beth, Lisa , and Carrie that they're invited too."

Beth and Lisa agreed, but Carrie wanted to watch a special movie on TV and declined.

"Wow, this is great fun! I've never won at Monopoly be-fore," Doug said. "Hey, what was that flash?" Within seconds a clap of thunder followed. "Waddaya know – a snow storm and a thunderstorm at the same time. Only in Colorado," Doug laughed.

"Thunderstorms spook me," Smitty admitted. "Never have liked 'em."

"I'm with you on that," Jason said.

"Try to ignore it," Beth suggested. "Hey, let's do the Ouija board!"

"What's that all about," Doug asked.

"Well, you use the letters and these different signs and the planchette to try to get messages from the spirits," Dan said. "Put your fingers on the planchette like this, then you concentrate and . . ." Dan went on to explain the fine points of the game.

Lightning flashed – followed almost immediately by a big clap of thunder. Everyone jumped.

"Ah . . . Dan, maybe we should play Rummy or something," Smitty said.

"It's okay, Smitty. It's just a game. Let's try it for awhile," Lisa said.

"Yeah, c'mon Smitty. Don't be a party-pooper," Dan encouraged.

"Ooh . . . all right. Let's do it!"

The group set the Ouija board on the card table. Dan proceeded to explain the rules and demonstrate again the use of the planchette. Finally there wasn't a sound in the room – except of course for the occasional clap of thunder.

Then it happened! The card table began to move! At first it was subtle – just a little movement. In fact Dan thought maybe it was somehow vibrating because of the thunder. What happened next dispelled all his theories! The table began trying to "walk" – but people and chairs were in the way. The teens leaped up knocking over chairs and stumbling into each other trying to get out of the way of the table!

Within a few seconds, the group was backed up against a wall. No one said a word. They just watched as the table waddled across the room! That was just the beginning.

And the Guests Stayed On

The Stewart house and the teens survived the night the table "walked." But that wasn't the end of the visits from . . . well, who knows?

The Stewart children grew up, married, and moved away, starting their own families. However, Esther always felt there was "someone" in the house – at different times and locations – from right after the table "walking" incident. Had some sort of "spiritual door" been accidently opened? She didn't know. She just knew that a feeling would come over her now and then like someone was "watching" her, but to her dismay she was never able to see anyone.

The TV had always been in the den at the back of the house. They preferred it there when the children were at home and just never moved it. Carrie always complained that she felt someone was watching her whenever she went in to watch a show. Also she complained that sometimes there was a cold "feeling" in there. Sam Stewart had checked all the heating ducts and windows. He couldn't find any kind of a draft problem. Carrie's complaints continued from winter into spring and then into summer. The cold "feeling" was there when she sensed someone in the room.

Some years later Beth and her family came back to the house to live temporarily until their new home was built in Estes Park. One evening Beth directed her young son to get ready for his bath.

"I'm running the water for your bath, Sammy. Get your p.j.'s and put your dirty clothes in the hamper. I'll be right in." Beth busied herself for a moment with one of the other children.

"Well, aren't you the big boy! You turned the water off and got into the tub all by yourself. You did check the water first though, didn't you?"

"Yes, Mommy. You told me to."

"That's right. That's so an accident doesn't happen where you might get burned by hot water," Beth explained to the 3 year old. "And . . . "

"Mommy, tell that hairy man to get out of here! I'm taking a bath!"

"What hairy man, honey," Beth asked, turning to look behind her.

"That man right there," he said pointing to just behind her left shoulder.

Beth looked again. She saw nothing. "There he is! Make him leave!"

By this time Sammy was becoming hysterical. Beth turned around again and said to no one, "You must leave now, please. Thank you."

"He's gone, Mommy."

Beth helped Sammy finish his bath. Nothing more was said nor did Sammy ever have another experience with the "hairy man." As an adult, Sammy has no recollection of the incident, but he doesn't doubt that it happened. His mother wouldn't lie to him.

Later, as all families must, the family gathered sadly to bury their mother, Esther. Sam Sr. had died a few months before.

Lisa was laying in bed and reading prior to going to sleep – as she used to do as a teenager. She was involved in the book she was reading. All of a sudden there was a voice!

"Good night, Lisa dear." The lamp by her bed went out.

Lisa glanced toward the door and saw a filmy movement. The voice was her mother's voice.

Thus, the Stewart house had a variety of "guests" over the years. Most of the children believe that it all began that night long ago when a group of teens decided to play with the Ouija board. The beginning of a series of ghostly visitors who, for whatever reason, chose to be "family" of sorts – friendly and inquisitive and forever there.

The Overseer

It was late for a storm to be coming in over Estes Park. Usually storms appeared in the mid-afternoon, stayed for awhile, then moved off – allowing the sun to dry away the water droplets. Not so this night. It was dark and it was stormy, lightening illuminating the western sky. Crashing thunder followed. The rain fell fast and furious. The young family pulled up as close as possible to the inn to unload. Just running a short distance soaked them all.

"Wow! That's quite a storm out there," the visitor said, shaking some of the rain from his hair and clothes. "We have reservations. It's the four of us. We asked for connecting rooms," he added with a note of hope in his voice.

"The name sir," asked the registration clerk.

"Aimsley – Jeff and Sarah Aimsley. The kids are Amy and Todd. Do you have connecting rooms?"

"Yes, sir. We've got you all set up for rooms 229 and 230. There's a full bath between them."

"Oh, that's wonderful," a tired and bedraggled Sarah Aimsley said. "May we be taken to our rooms right away. I want to get us out of these wet clothes."

"Right away," the clerk said as he tapped the small bell on the desk. "Our bellman, Tom, will see to your settling in."

Within moments a man resembling an old linebacker – large in stature but badly stooped – appeared out of nowhere.

30

"Good evening. I'm Tom and I'll take you to your rooms now."

Sarah looked at Jeff questioningly. Jeff saw Sarah's discomfort but pretended he didn't and followed Tom up the long staircase. Whatever Sarah was feeling had to be similar to his own apprehensions; Jeff was sure of that. However, he decided that it had to be related to the storm. Sure, that was it.

"C'mon kids, let's get some dry clothes on and come down later for some hot cocoa or something before bed," Jeff said brightly. The little family followed Tom single file to the second floor rooms.

When Tom reached Room 229 he said, "This is the room for the children." He opened the door and handed the key to Jeff. "Your room is through this here bathroom – see?" He pointed to the adjoining room but made no attempt to enter it. In fact he left Jeff and Sarah standing in the bathroom, holding their luggage. "The last call for a snack is in about fifteen minutes," Tom said and turned around and left.

"Daddy, can we get our clothes changed and go get that snack Tom talked about," Amy asked.

Jeff looked at Sarah. "Sure we can. Then it's off to bed for you and your brother. We've a big day planned for tomorrow."

"Aw Dad . . . gee whiz. We just got here," Todd whined.

"Not another word about it. Now hop into these sweatsuits. It's really rather chilly with this storm," Sarah said.

Within moments the Aimsley family was downstairs sitting in front of a cozy fire that seemed to erase all the chill in the air. Hot cocoa and cookies were served to several of the guests gathered around the fireplace.

Todd saw it first.

31

"Mama! Look! That rocker is empty but it's rocking!"

"Shhh, Todd. It's nothing. Probably just a draft from some-where. This is a very old building."

"Now isn't that odd," another guest commented. "I saw that same rocker moving this afternoon when there was no one here. Has to be a draft of some sort, don't you think?"

"Oh, definitely," Sarah answered. "There's no other expla-nation, is there?"

"Noooo, none I can think of," came the response.

"Well kids, time for bed," Jeff said to Amy and Todd. There was the usual "do we hafta" and the usual answer.

"Say, Jeff and Sarah. How about coming back down once the kids are settled in and visiting for awhile," another guest asked. "We'd like to get to know you better."

"Well, that would be nice. Yes, I'd like that," Sarah said, feeling better after the rocker incident.

"I'll get some more coffee ordered up," the guest said.

"Great. See you in a few minutes," Jeff said

After the children fell asleep, Sarah and Jeff locked the rooms and went downstairs. It had been a long day of driving and Jeff was ready to unwind with some coffee and friendly conversation.

"Okay now Sarah tell me the truth. Do you really think that rocker moved because of a draft," the guest asked.

"Oh, no of course not! I did some research on this old inn before we came. It is well known for having friendly ghosts from its past. There's one ghost in particular that loves animals and children. She supposedly lived most of her life here – raised a family and helped run the inn. She's always dressed in white."

"Oh, dear," the guest's wife said, looking around the room and jumping with a clap of thunder.

"There's nothing to fear, really. No one has ever been harmed."

The couples sat around the fire for over an hour, talking about the wonderful history of the inn and its resident ghosts. By the end of the evening no one seemed particularly bothered by the hint of spirits present. Finally, Jeff and Sarah said they had better go up to bed, considering all they had planned for the next day. The others agreed and followed them up the stairs, turning off at their own rooms.

When Jeff and Sarah entered their room – Room 230 – it seemed unusually chilly. Jeff went over to turn the heater on low.

"Jeff, did you bring a night light for the children? I totally forgot."

"So did I, honey. Oh well . . . hey, what's that dim light in their room coming from? Maybe the inn has them in the rooms."

Sarah led the way into the children's room, dimly bathed in a white light. Standing between the children's beds was a lady in white, looking down at the children. Jeff was frozen in his tracks. Sarah stepped into the room.

"Thank you for watching the children. You can leave now," Sarah said.

The lady in white nodded her head and simply vanished.

When Sarah turned back to Jeff, he was speechless for a moment. Finally he was able to get a few words out.

"I don't believe what I just saw!"

"Believe it," Sarah said.

Room 237

Mary Ann enjoyed her job at a local dude ranch outside of Estes Park. Actually she had several jobs – guest registrar, concierge, and trail ride guide. As a single parent, the job also afforded her the opportunity to have her son, Dan, age 14, come to the ranch and stay with her, working while there and earning some summertime money. He would come for two weeks, then go stay with his grandmother for two weeks, alternating like that throughout the summer months.

During one of his stays at the ranch, Dan was vacuuming on the second floor. He glanced up and saw a man coming out of Room 237 just down the hall. He nodded to the man and said hello, and the man returned the nod but said nothing.

"Gee, he's a strange looking guy," Dan said to himself. "Sure was different looking – dressed like that. Maybe he's in a play in town or something." Dan continued on with his chores and thought no more about it. He didn't even mention it to his mother that night at dinner.

Several days later Dan was again on the second floor. This time he was cleaning windows and mirrors. As he wiped the glass cleaner off a mirror at the end of the hall, he thought he saw someone behind him in the hallway. Dan turned in time to see the same man walking down the hallway in the opposite direction.

"That's that same guy," Dan said aloud. "Sure doesn't have

many clothes. He looks like he's wearing the same stuff as the other day." Once again, Dan gave it no further thought – until the next morning.

Dan was vacuuming again – about 10 to 12 feet away from the door to Room 237 – when all of a sudden, there he was! Right in front of him just outside the door, staring at him!

Dan couldn't speak. He looked at the man and noted that his black coat was a bit dusty, his vest was shiny looking, and he had a watch on a chain, the clock part tucked into a pocket on his vest. His white shirt had a strange high collar, and it looked wrinkled. He also wore a tall black hat. Dan mustered up his courage and finally spoke.

"Good morning, sir. Fine day out there."

The man stood there and stared at Dan. "Please say something, will ya," Dan almost pleaded.

The man from Room 237 nodded and walked away toward the stairs. Dan couldn't move. Finally after the man disappeared around the corner to the stairwell, Dan ran to see if he was on the stairs. There was no one there. He had disappeared!

After careful consideration, Dan decided to confide in his mother about his encounters. He knew she would believe him, but others may not. After all, he's not heard a single person talk about ghosts being around in the lodge or elsewhere on the ranch.

"Mom, I gotta tell you something. Promise you won't tell anyone?"

"Dan, did you break something today," his mother said, stiffening.

"No, Mom, honest I didn't. It's just that I saw . . . well, there's this strange looking man in Room 237, and he doesn't talk, and today he just disappeared!"

Not wanting to alarm her son, Mary Ann remained outwardly calm. "What do you mean, son?"

Dan re-told all that had happened. He needed an explanation! She decided to tell Dan the truth.

"Dan, that's one of our resident ghosts here at the ranch. The lodge has several, the bunk house too."

"Ghost? Oh, c'mon Mom. You're just kiddin' me, right?"

"No son, I'm not. Apparently the man in Room 237 has taken a liking to you since you've seen him more than once. I've only seen him one time, and he was dressed exactly like you described him. He's a friendly old gentleman. Never bothers any guests. Only a few of us working here have seen him."

"Wow! Cool! Think I'll see any more ghosts," Dan asked with enthusiasm.

"I really don't know, son. Maybe yes, maybe no."

"Well, I know one that I can keep an eye out for – that guy in 237. Mom can you fix it where I can work on the second floor of the lodge all the time?"

The Lady in White - Room 17

"She's at it again! The door at the end of the hall was open a couple of inches, and I closed it last night and locked it myself," Ann said.

"It's her heat war with one of the other ghosts," Beth added.

"Heat war? Who ever heard of two ghosts having a heat war?"

"Yep, it sounds strange, but it's been going on all winter. I wouldn't believe it either if it wasn't that I closed and locked that door almost every night because it's been opened! And also, I have to go into Room 17 and turn off that wall heater because it's turned all the way up. So, the heat is just flowing down the hall and out the door!"

"What's causing all this," Ann asked. "Aren't they friendly with each other?"

"You're new here. Wait awhile and you'll be able to figure out who's who," Beth assured her. "It all seems to center around the lady in Room 17."

"What lady? We're closed – no guests right now," Ann reminded her.

"It's the lady in white. We think she is the daughter of the man who had this ranch and built this lodge when he turned it into a dude ranch. She seems to be watching over things – sort of like a caretaker."

"What kinds of things does she do?"

"Oh, one night during a storm one of the wranglers was awakened by a banging sound. He thought it was the door on the barn. He looked out and could see the door banging in the wind. But he knew he had securely fastened that door with a lock. Yet, there it was banging. So, he got dressed, put on a slicker and went out to the barn. The lock was on the ground. He picked it up and for some reason slipped into the barn to check the horses. That's when he found a sick colt – who would have died if he hadn't called the vet right away. The lady in white loves the horses. That's not the only time she's given us a warning, so we always pay close attention when something is out of the normal," Beth said.

"Has anyone ever seen her," Ann asked.

"Sure, lots of times. That's why we call her the lady in white. She is always in a long white dress. Many of us have seen her."

"Do you only see her in the barn," Ann wanted to know.

"Oh, no. There was one time when I was upstairs alone. I heard footsteps but saw no one. Then all of a sudden, there she was – in her room, Room 17. That was the favorite room of the owner's daughter. So, we're pretty sure that's who she is. Sometimes, I'll fix up the room and come back later in the day and stuff is different. Things have been moved. And I've been the only one in the building all day."

"Gosh. You know, I've heard that animals – dogs in particular – are very sensitive to spirits. Do you think that's true?"

"Oh, sure. Without a doubt. I'll take King, my dog, with me sometimes when I'm over here alone, just for company of course. We'll be walking from one area to another, and all of a sudden he'll stop and the hair on his neck and back will stand up, and he won't go any further. He'll either whimper or give a low soft growl. So he definitely senses something different."

"Well, how long do you think it will be before I'll see the lady in the white dress in Room 17," Ann asked.

"Oh, not too long. She's around quite a bit. She keeps busy," Beth laughed. "Just be sure that if something is happening out of the ordinary, and you see or hear it, investigate. That's how she warns us of trouble."

"Absolutely! Oh, I can hardly wait!"

Beth laughed. Ann was going to enjoy working at the ranch. She'd collect stories to tell her children and grandchildren over and over! Beth made a note to herself to buy Ann a journal book the next day. "I may as well get her ready for the first encounter."

The Connection

It was a warm summer Sunday evening. The lobby of The Stanley was quiet after the usual hustle and bustle of the weekend. The desk clerk, Cecilia, was getting ready to go home. As she busied herself, she noticed a couple in their forties walking slowly across the lobby, the woman pointing to various areas of apparent interest. She spotted Cecilia and immediately walked over to her.

"Good evening. I am wondering about this grand old place. I've heard it is haunted. Is that true?"

"Well, we do get many reports of ghostly encounters," Cecilia answered smiling.

"Do they come from guests or the staff?"

"Actually both, and the reports are very convincing."

"I just heard about all this today. We're from Canada. A friend of mine lives in Denver, and she informed me about the hotel being haunted. At the moment, she didn't have time to go into any stories, just told me to find out for myself."

"There are quite a few stories told," Cecilia said.

"We'd really like to hear some. Do you give tours?"

"Yes, the museum gives them twice a day, but they are closed now," Cecilia said, checking her watch.

"Oh no. And we're leaving out early in the morning. Could you possibly do a tour for us? You see, I'm a psychic. I'm already feeling vibes. I'd love to go all through the hotel if possible. My friend did mention something about a tunnel some-where. Is there such a thing?"

"Yes, there is." Cecilia noticed that it was time for her to clock out. "If you'll wait here a minute, I'll go punch out and then take you on a quick tour."

"Oh, how wonderful of you! Are you sure?"

"I love this old hotel and the whole Stanley story. It's really quite a tale," Cecilia said. "I'd hate to see you leave without it."

Cecilia returned momentarily. The woman began to tell Cecilia about her other psychic experiences. The little group moved from room to room as Cecilia gave a modified tour, sprinkling in a variety of Stanley ghost stories.

"May we go upstairs? Something is drawing me there at this moment," the woman said with sincerity.

"Well, ordinarily we don't take tours upstairs during our busy months, but it's quiet right now, so I guess it will be okay."

When they arrived on the second floor, the immediate interest was Room 217. The movie "The Shining," which featured Room 217, is almost as popular in Canada as it is here.

"Can I go into Room 217?"

"I'm afraid not. It's occupied at the moment."

"Oh, I understand. Hmmm. I'm getting more vibes. There's some activity down at the end of the hallway! Oh my. There are many people laughing and waving and then going into their rooms. They all seem happy. Maybe that's why they come back here. Or maybe they never leave," she added.

Cecilia turned to the husband who had remained silent. "Are you a psychic too?"

"No, not officially. I didn't believe in ghosts or the paranormal at all. I'm a medical doctor. I deal with scientific data – you know, cold hard facts."

"You say 'didn't believe' as if you've changed you mind. Have you?"

"Yes, after I had my own personal experience with a patient."

"What happened," Cecilia asked.

"The man had died after a lengthy illness. I tried everything I knew, and he fought very hard to live. When he died, I had a feeling like I had failed him. I couldn't shake it. After several weeks of feeling like that, I had my first paranormal experience. My patient appeared to me in the Doctor's Lounge of all places! I was alone. He told me to stop fretting over him. He was happy now. That made a believer out of me!"

"I guess so," Cecilia laughed. " It would me too."

The woman had walked ahead while her husband was talking. Suddenly she stopped at the foot of the stairs leading to the third floor of rooms.

"Oh, goodness! Do you see her? Up on the landing! She's lovely! She's in a beautiful red dress."

Neither the husband nor Cecilia saw anything.

"The dress is making a rustling sound," she said.

Neither the husband nor Cecilia heard anything either.

"Oh! This is so exciting!"

The group stayed at that location for a few minutes after the woman in the red dress disappeared.

"May we continue up to the fourth floor?"

Cecilia agreed, since it was quiet at the time. She hadn't told them about the history behind the fourth floor.

"Oh, my! There is a lot of unhappiness up here. I don't see anyone, but I feel their unhappiness. What happened up here, do you know?"

"All I know is that early in the hotel's history this is where the servants of the guests stayed. There weren't private rooms for them, just little cubbyholes with little more than a cot of some sort," Cecilia told her. "And being the top floor, it was hot up here in the summer, I'm sure."

"That must be it then," the woman said.

As the group made their way downstairs again, both the woman and the doctor thanked Cecilia for taking the time to show them around.

"I'll never forget that woman in the red dress!"

Cecilia smiled. She had not told them about the woman in the red dress . . . and here she is again!

Music Appreciation

It's always rather sad when the end of the visitor season arrives in the Estes Valley. All the excitement is gone, signaling the approach of the long winter months ahead. The wind picks up, the temperature drops, and the days grow shorter. Such was the case many years ago as a local hotel began to close down for the winter.

This particular hotel had its own resident pianist, a Chinese man named Chang Fu. Mr. Fu was extremely talented; not only could he play any piece of music of the day, he also composed beautiful music of his own. But his duties included more than just providing entertainment for guests. He was also an excellent chef. Thus as winter approached, it became his job to assist the head chef in closing down the hotel's kitchen.

"Hey, Mr. Fu. I'll start working on the kitchen this afternoon. Are you with me," the head chef, Franklin, asked.

"Right you are, sir," said Fu in his surprising English accent. He had been born and raised in southern England. On his time off, Fu continued working on a new composition. He wanted it completed by mid-December when he left for a two month stay back home.

Around two o'clock, Franklin summoned Mr. Fu.

"Guess we'd better at least make a start on putting this kitchen in order, Mr. Fu. It's going to take us a while."

"Yes, indeed. Where shall I begin, sir?"

"Let's start with the pantry."

"Very good, sir. The pantry it is then," Mr. Fu said in agreement. The two men worked steadily, with only a supper break, until well after ten o'clock that night.

"Mr. Fu, I'm beat. Let's call it a night," Franklin said through a yawn.

"I'll agree to that, sir. I still want to practice and work on my new piece," Mr. Fu said.

" I don't know how you do that after working all day."

"Oh, it's quite simple. My music gives me such pleasure that I'm never too tired to play. Besides all that, they like it."

"But the guests are all gone now. Oh well, to each his own I always say. Good night, Mr. Fu," Franklin said, heading for his quarters.

"Good night, sir," Mr. Fu said smiling, knowing Franklin had misunderstood who "they" were. Fu turned off the kitchen lights and headed upstairs to a room at the far end of the building that housed an old but well tuned piano and three well-worn rocking chairs. He could have used the new Grand piano in the dining room, but he liked the privacy.

Fu entered the room and greeted "them" courteously.

"Good evening. Are you ready for some music?" No answer. There never was, but he knew "they" were there.

Mr. Fu began his nightly program, playing classical as well as popular music. Wonderful melodies filled the room. He played for over an hour. Then he set aside the music sheets and began working on his own composition. He worked for another hour. Finally he yawned, giving in to exhaustion.

"Time to close up for tonight. I'll play your favorite closing song first, however." When he finished, there were the usual happy and contented sighs from behind him. Then the two rocking chairs began to move. "They" were leaving for the night too. He always wondered where "they" were going. He never saw them, but he could always tell "they" were there. True music lovers.

A Housekeeper's Dilemma

In 1995, a group of international students arrived from a university in a neighboring state. They were eager to begin work in a hotel that they heard was haunted! All of the students were from Nepal, a country on the northern border of India. Their skin was dark, and they had jet black hair. Their religion was Hinduism, and all were ardent followers. The students were employed at the hotel as housekeepers – men only.

After their arrival and initial orientation of the hotel, the students were assigned to their beds in the dorm. The dorm was situated behind the main hotel. Each student had a bed, small chest of drawers, and a foot locker that locked. It was a Spartan environment, but they were young and eager for this new experience.

The day after their arrival, the students took to their assignments with gusto. All the young men were instructed in the care and preparation of a guest room. Bedmaking was of particular concern. Every bed had to be made up just so. Then each lavatory had special towels and soaps, and each bed had "pillow candies" to greet the guests at night. All these requirements were taken in stride by the new housekeepers. The guests began to arrive, and the pace of duties quickened.

Midway through the summer it happened. Rebellion! Threatened mutiny on land!

"I will not do it," one student was heard to say by the housekeeping manager.

"What is wrong here," she asked the gathering of students.

"He refuses to sleep further in the dorm, madam," one of the students said. "He thinks he is being smothered at night by a ghost."

"I am! It always happens after the midnight hour. I awaken, struggling to breathe. I must get up and go outside to get air."

"I think perhaps you are listening to too many ghost stories and your imagination has gotten the better of you. We've never had a mean ghost here," the manager assured him. "Now please, no more of this talk. I'll see all of you in the morning." The reluctant student and his friends headed off toward the dorms.

The next day a female guest came downstairs and approached the front desk.

"Excuse me. I was looking for a Bible in my room. Don't most hotels provide them?

"Yes, we do. It should be on your nightstand. Did you check the drawer?"

"Yes, I did. In fact I checked all the drawers. Nothing."

"That's odd. I'll check into it and see that you get one by tomorrow," the desk clerk promised.

During the day, the desk clerk called one of the housekeepers aside. "Do you know why the Bible in Room 332 is missing?"

"No sir. I never touch the holy books. It isn't good to do."

"Why not," the desk clerk asked.

"I am a Hindu," he replied, assuming that explained everything. The desk clerk remained mystified. He did, however, locate another copy of the Bible and took it to the lady in Room 332.

"Thank you, young man. Now my day will be complete."

The next day, around noon, the same woman stopped by the front desk.

"Young man, I hate to be a bother, but my Bible is gone again."

"Let me check into it again for you." He rang for the house-keeping manager, and explained the situation. He was astounded to learn that in several parts of the hotel other guests were also missing Bibles in their rooms.

The housekeeping manager arrived at the front desk with several Napali housekeepers in tow.

"I think I may have solved the mystery. Someone has been collecting the Bibles and stashing them away in closets behind blankets. I think I know who is behind all this."

That afternoon, at the end of the day shift for the house-keepers, the housekeeping manager called a brief meeting.

"For several days now Bibles have been disappearing from our guests' rooms.

"Madam, it is I who started this behavior," came the voice of the student who was sure he was being smothered.

"Why in this world would you do this," the manager asked him.

"Because we are Hindu," came the reply.

Thinking quickly, the manager replied, "But the ghosts aren't."

The student stood quietly, looking at her with a blank expression on his face.

Then there came a look of enlightenment!

"I will go quickly and put every book back, madam. Please extend my apologies to the ghosts."

"I will, and I think you may sleep better now," she said smiling to herself.

The next morning, the housekeeping manager saw the Bible-hiding student.

"How did you sleep last night," she asked with proper seriousness.

"Oh, very well, madam. Strange how a book could make a ghost angry," he replied.

"Yes, isn't it."

Under It All - Justice

In the 1930s, a local inn hosted the annual statewide quilting contest. Women came from all over the State of Colorado – some to compete, others just to get new ideas for their own quilts. Well over 100 women attended each year.

This particular year Matty Sterling decided that she was going to have some fun. She felt decidedly mischievous, and it was about time for some ghostly encounters! Her friend Emma Taggert was to be a co-conspirator. The two plotted and planned almost the whole way to Estes Park. They could hardly wait until the meetings got underway.

"Matty, there's Pauline. Oh, she'll be a good one to scare. She stays on the brink of hysteria anyway," Emma chuckled.

"And there's Lulu and her mother, Mrs. . . . what's-her-name. Those two must definitely go on our list," Matty grinned impishly.

"Absolutely," Emma agreed.

The first evening was a social, complete with ice cream. Everyone mingled as they brought each other up to date on the past year's happenings. Then it happened.

"HELP, HELP!!! It was poor Mrs. . . . what's-her-name. She looked as if she'd seen a ghost! Matty was missing, so Emma was sure that their game had started.

"Oh, Mama," Lulu said. "What's wrong?"

When she finally caught her breath, Lulu's mother swallowed hard and told of her encounter. "There was a man in the hallway. I thought it strange that he should be here since we've rented out the whole place. Anyway, I said to him, 'What are you doing here?' He just smiled and walked on. Then I felt guilty that maybe I had sounded rude, so I quickly turned to apologize, and he wasn't there!"

A murmur went throughout the room! The ghosts were here! Emma was delighted. She and Matty had planned something similar. "I wonder why she changed it?"

Later in the evening, the lights began to flicker. Then everything went black.

Screams erupted from almost every woman there. Within moments the innkeeper and several of the staff brought in lighted candles.

"Just a power outage, ladies. We get them frequently in this old building."

Matty looked for Emma without success. *Good girl, Emma! That was a good one,* Matty said to herself, stifling a giggle.

By this time everyone was a bit unnerved. One would say to another how there was a perfectly rational explanation for these things, and the other would agree. In this way, the group began to settle back into their social hour. Until . . . a lady asked Pauline a fateful question.

"Ah . . . my dear. Would you look casually at the little cart holding the punch bowl and tell me if it is moving?"

Pauline was anything but casual. She jerked her head around. To her horror she saw the punch bowl and table gently gliding by. She screamed then fainted.

Matty and Emma excused themselves to go to the ladies powder room. Once inside, the two burst out laughing.

"Emma, how did you ever get your trick arranged?"

"I was wondering how you did yours," Emma said. "I never got to do mine."

"Neither did I," Matty said.

"What?" they both said in unison. "Maybe someone else had the same idea and beat us to the punch," Matty said.

"Of course. That's it. Everyone knows there aren't any ghosts."

"I'd like to powder my nose," Matty said.

"Me, too," said Emma.

There were three stalls with doors in the restroom. One door was closed, already occupied.

Matty, being friendly, spoke to the woman in the third stall.

"What do you think of these shenanigans tonight. Isn't it a riot. How grown women can get spooked about ghosts?"

"Yes, it's quite humorous," came the soft voice.

Not to be outdone, Emma asked the third stall, "How do you feel about ghosts? Do you believe in them?"

"Oh definitely," returned the soft voice.

"Well, not me," said Matty emphatically.

" Me either," asserted Emma.

Immediately, Emma and Matty exited their stalls and went to the sink to wash their hands. Matty noticed the third door still closed. She tapped on the door.

"Are you all right in there? Hello?" There was no answer. Emma peeked under the door. The stall was empty!

"Matty, there's no way she could have gotten past us because we came out first . . . .

Both women bolted for the door, each shoving to be first out, and neither making it through.

"Olivia Gambelin has written an important and necessary book at a critical moment in AI. Her concept of the 'Values Canvas' is one of the few frameworks I've seen that makes Responsible AI more practical rather than more abstract. For any leader charged with ensuring AI is used responsibly within their organization, start here and return often."
Geoff Schaefer, Head of Responsible AI, Booz Allen Hamilton

"Diving deep into the practical realm of AI ethics, this is a beacon for organizations seeking tangible guidance. Backed by hands-on expertise, it delivers invaluable tools and insights for cultivating AI programs grounded in ethics in today's complex and dynamic landscape."
Alyssa Lefaivre Škopac, Head of Global Partnerships and Growth, Responsible AI Institute

"Olivia Gambelin has written the go-to book on Responsible AI. Beyond technicalities, the managerial and human aspects emphasized make this book required reading for all managers and AI practitioners alike. Even if you are new to AI and wonder how to embed it in your organization, this book will give you a framework to do it responsibly, ethically, sustainably, and economically. Read it, implement it, and reap the rewards."
Patrick Bangert, Senior Vice President for Data, Analytics, and AI, Searce

"This book challenges us to reflect on how we can use AI to make a positive impact on society. Olivia Gambelin offers a straightforward approach to ethical AI. *Responsible AI* is not merely instructional but also transformative, advocating for a shift towards an AI that is by people, for people, and about people. It serves as a crucial reminder that as we forge ahead in our technological journey, our ethical compass must always guide us."
Maria Axente, Head of AI Public Policy and Ethics, PwC UK

"Olivia Gambelin's insights apply the principles of enlightened self-interest to the complex topic of designing and deploying AI systems. This book is essential for anyone seeking to deploy AI thoughtfully to deliver positive societal impact while mitigating unintended consequences."
Anik Bose, Managing Partner, Benhamou Global Ventures, and Founder, Ethical AI Governance Group (EAIGG)

"This book is refreshingly action-oriented with an emphasis on real-world impacts. Olivia Gambelin builds on her academic background and hands-on experience as an AI ethicist to show that Responsible AI is more than compliance: it's a catalyst for innovation."
Milena Pribić, Design Principal, Ethical AI Practices, IBM

"Technology is only as good as the thought and craftsmanship that goes into it. *Responsible AI* is full of invaluable insights that every business leader, investor, and entrepreneur should know when building world-class ventures powered by AI."
Christopher Sanchez, CEO, Emergent Line, and Professor of Artificial Intelligence, EGADE Business School

"In a world increasingly shaped by AI, Olivia Gambelin's *Responsible AI* emerges as a beacon of ethical guidance for organizations navigating the complex landscape of technological innovation. With a masterful blend of practical insights and visionary foresight, Gambelin delivers a comprehensive playbook for cultivating Responsible AI practices within any organization."
Jesse Arlen Smith, Founder and President, Aiforgood Asia

"Presents a clear and reasonable approach to AI ethics from which every organization can benefit. Olivia Gambelin is no AI doomsayer, but instead offers a thoughtful discussion of the difficult and thorny work of striking a balance between responsibility and innovation. Her approach and guidance are practical, tactical, and tractable, which is deeply needed in the space, now more than ever."
Yoav Schlesinger, Architect, Responsible AI and Tech, Salesforce

"Ethics as a tool for innovation is one of the gifts shared with us by Olivia Gambelin in *Responsible AI.*"
Sandy Barsky, Executive Program Director, Government and Education, Oracle

"This book is a must-read for any business leader seeking to decipher the dynamic world of AI. This comprehensive guide clarifies the deep integration of ethics into AI and makes it an accessible and essential strategic priority. Olivia Gambelin brilliantly navigates the complex terrain offering a clear roadmap through the intricacies of people, processes, and technology. During a time of rapid change, this book is an invaluable resource for ensuring that integrity stays at the heart of AI strategies."
Benjamin Larsen, AI/ML Project Lead, AI Governance, World Economic Forum

"Olivia Gambelin provides an in-depth, specific, and pragmatic roadmap for any organization to implement a practical strategy towards the adoption of the comprehensive planning and buy-in required by all stakeholders to understand and safely utilize AI in the modern marketplace. More importantly, she reminds us that critical thinking, active listening, and above all, *bravery* are the key attributes needed for any responsible leader to navigate and bring value for all stakeholders utilizing AI systems now and in the future."
John C. Havens, Founding Executive Director, The IEEE Global Initiative on Ethics of Autonomous and Intelligent Systems, and author of Heartificial Intelligence

"This book is vital reading for leaders looking to implement AI in their organizations. Olivia Gambelin provides both a highly readable primer on the larger ethical questions that should be considered, alongside practical steps that can be taken to ensure AI is being deployed in a considered and responsible manner."
Mohamed Nanabhay, Managing Partner, Mozilla Ventures

Responsible AI

*Implement an Ethical Approach
in Your Organization*

Olivia Gambelin

KoganPage

First published in Great Britain and the United States in 2024 by Kogan Page Limited

2nd Floor, 45 Gee Street
London
EC1V 3RS
United Kingdom

8 W 38th Street, Suite 902
New York, NY 10018
USA

www.koganpage.com

Kogan Page books are printed on paper from sustainable forests.

ISBNs

Hardback   978 1 3986 1603 5
Paperback   978 1 3986 1570 0
Ebook   978 1 3986 1602 8

British Library Cataloguing-in-Publication Data
A CIP record for this book is available from the British Library.

Library of Congress Cataloging-in-Publication Data
Names: Gambelin, Olivia, author.
Title: Responsible AI : implement an ethical approach in your organization
  / Olivia Gambelin.
Description: London, United Kingdom ; New York, NY : Kogan Page, 2024. |
  Includes bibliographical references and index.
Identifiers: LCCN 2024010818 (print) | LCCN 2024010819 (ebook) | ISBN
  9781398615700 (paperback) | ISBN 9781398616035 (hardback) | ISBN
  9781398616028 (ebook)
Subjects: LCSH: Artificial intelligence–Industrial applications. |
  Business ethics. | Business–Technological innovations.
Classification: LCC HD45 .G295 2024 (print) | LCC HD45 (ebook) | DDC
  658.4/063–dc23/eng/20240402
LC record available at https://lccn.loc.gov/2024010818
LC ebook record available at https://lccn.loc.gov/2024010819

Typeset by Integra Software Services, Pondicherry
Print production managed by Jellyfish
Printed and bound by CPI Group (UK) Ltd, Croydon, CR0 4YY

To my fellow ethicists that I began this journey with back when no one would listen.

Stay the course, we have their attention now.

CONTENTS

Acknowledgments xiii

PART ONE

01 **Defining Ethics in AI: And How Values Will Shape the Face of Success** 3

How to Use a Hammer in the World of AI 4
The Silent Killer of AI 5
What Is Ethics Anyway? 8
What Is Responsible AI and Why Do You Need a Strategy for It? 12
How This Book Works 14
Getting Started 17

02 **Know Your Values: How to Find and Define Your Values for Responsible AI** 18

Breaking Down the Conceptual Blockers to AI Ethics 19
Is Ethics Really Subjective? 19
Whose Values Are They Anyway? 23
The Foundational Value Finder Framework 24
The Pitfall of Hyperfocused Value 30
The Blindspot of Undefined Values 31
Securing Buy-In for Your Values 33
Bringing Direction to Your Responsible AI Strategy 34

03 **The Duality of Ethics: Managing Risk and Innovation in AI** 36

The Dual Purposes of Ethics 37
Ethics as a Tool for Risk Mitigation 39
Ethics as a Tool for Innovation 43
Finding the Right Direction for Your Strategy 49

04 Calibrating the Compass: Aligning Responsible AI to Your Organization's Objectives 51

To Protect or to Promote? 52
Moral Imagination in AI 54
The Ethics Risk and Innovation Framework 55
Where to Next? 63

05 Five Reasons Why You Shouldn't Invest in Responsible AI: And One Reason Why You Should 64

The Five Reasons Why Not to Invest 66
The One Reason Why You Should 74

PART TWO

06 The Responsible AI Blindspot You Didn't Know You Had: And the Tool to Fix It 79

The Techno-Value Blindspot 80
The Three Pillars of Responsible AI 82
The Values Canvas 86
Learning Your Hammer 89

07 Who Is Building Your AI?: The People Driving Your Responsible AI Success 91

The Root of Responsible AI: *People* 92
Educate: Do your people know how to use ethics? 93
Motivate: Are your people motivated to engage with your values? 97
Communicate: Are your people talking about your values? 101
Bringing It All Together: Finalizing Your *People Pillar* 105
Risk Versus Innovation Approach in Your *People Pillar* 110
How Will You Know Your *People Pillar* Is Working? 111
The Human in Your AI Equation 112

08 How Is Your AI Being Built?: The Process Making the Responsible AI Engine Run 113

The Structural Support of Responsible AI: *Process* 114
Intent: Responsible AI policies 116

Implement: Governance and operational frameworks 120
Instrument/Tools 124
Bringing It All Together: Finalizing Your *Process Pillar* 127
Risk Versus Innovation Approach in Your *Process Pillar* 132
How Will You Know Your *Process Pillar* Is Working? 133
From *Process* to *Technology* 134

**09 What Are You Building into Your AI?: The Technical
Interventions of Responsible AI** 136

Best Practices in AI Development: *Technology* 137
Data 139
Document 143
Domain 146
Bringing It All Together: Finalizing Your *Technology Pillar* 150
Risk Versus Innovation Approach in Your *Technology Pillar* 153
How Will You Know Your *Technology Pillar* Is Working? 157
From *Technology* to Beyond 158

PART THREE

**10 The Different Phases of Responsible AI Adoption: And How
to Understand Where You Are Currently** 163

What It Means to Become a Responsible AI-Enabled
    Organization 165
The Journey of Responsible AI Adoption 167
What Happens Next: Advancing Through the Phases 175
Responsible AI Is a Journey, Not a Destination 178

**11 Becoming a Responsible AI Enabled-Organization: How to
Build a Strategy for Success** 180

The Burden of Choice: Overcoming Responsible AI Inertia 181
Do Not Pass Go 183
Laying Your Foundations 184
Designing Your Structure 189
Reinforcing Your Strategy 194
It's All Relative (to Size) 199
The Elephant in the Room 203
It's a Matter of Time 204

12   Who's Responsible for Responsible AI?: How to Bring About Responsible AI Change for Your Organization 205

The Pitfall of Responsibility in AI 206
The Roles of Responsible AI 207
Who Is Responsible for Change? 211
Understanding Your Organization's Responsibility Structure 214
Who Is Responsible? 219

13   The Responsible AI Professional: The Roles, Responsibilities, and Structures of Working in Responsible AI 220

What Does It Mean to Be an AI Ethicist? 221
The Responsible AI Professional: Variations of the Responsible AI
    Profession 223
Building Your Responsible AI Dream Team 226
How Responsible AI Teams Support Your Pillars 229
The AI Ethics Board 230
Moving Forward 232

14   In Pursuit of Good Tech: Bringing Your Responsible AI Strategy to Life 233

The Key to Responsible AI 234
Providing the Conceptual Structure to Responsible AI 236
The Two Things From This Book You Should Never Forget 238
In Pursuit of Good Tech 239
What Next? 240

References 241
Index 249

ACKNOWLEDGMENTS

As I sit down to write this, I am overwhelmed with an immense sense of gratitude toward all those who believed in me enough to make this book happen. When you spend your whole life hoping to one day reach this point in time, it can be quite humbling to find it has become a reality. My voice, my thoughts, my inspiration, everything that has gone into this book exists because of the people I am so lucky to have around me. Thanks seems too simple a word to express what I feel, but until I find a better one I will have to make do with it as I work my way through the long list of those who played a significant role in the making of this specific book.

To start, I must first of course thank the team at Kogan Page for their attention to all the details that go into publishing a book. Specifically I'd like to thank Charlie Lynn for his talent in finding the right balance between focusing my thinking and allowing me space for my thoughts to wander, and Isabelle Cheng for her impeccable timing, incredible patience and for being the first to believe in the potential of this all.

I am forever indebted to Michelle Zamora, Kirsten Collins, Armando Somoza and Yves Louise for their dedication to bringing the Values Canvas to life, and to Justin Lokitz for bringing us all together. Without your work designing and developing that Canvas, it would be nowhere near the tool that it is today. Thank you, truly, for helping me let go of the terribly drawn pyramid in order to unlock the full potential of what the Values Canvas was originally meant to achieve.

I am incredibly lucky to have parents who have not only been supporters but also collaborators to my work over the years. Thank you Mom for all the doodles I have on the corners of my notes as you helped me visualize how the concepts I was navigating through were intricately related, and thank you Dad for the hours spent on the hiking trails listening to me repeat myself as I worked out how to communicate those same intricacies.

To my godparents, Ray and Anneke Dempsey, for the many hours spent editing all shapes and forms of my writing, all the way back to final essays in college. Thank you especially to Ray, my special person, for all the love he has poured into reading every nook and cranny of this text.

Sorting through five years of research and experience to create a constructive narrative is no simple task, and I am deeply appreciative to all those who dedicated time to helping me get my mind wrapped around it all. For much-needed clarity in thought I would like to thank Jeroen Franse, Yiannis Kanellopoulos, and John Suit for their technical expertise and influence, Noël Baker and Bethanney Standerfer for their ability to categorize some very sporadic ideas, Dave Barnes for a necessary reality check on the very first of the rough drafts, and Tara Nesser for keeping me sane throughout it all.

In addition to the cultivation and encouragement of my thinking, I must also give thanks to the many that nurtured my spirit throughout this process. For the support that had me laughing on the good days and buoying me on the hard ones, I would like to thank Domizia Di Maggio, Bettina Hernberg, Ciara Cray, and Clara Grillet for being the best hype-women I could ask for, Saskia for making sure I left the house, and Peter Paychev for his blind faith in everything that I am.

This book, let alone my work in Responsible AI and Ethics, would not have been possible without the many who have built, championed, and believed in Ethical Intelligence over the years. To all those I have crossed paths with in the wild journey this company has been, thank you for seeing the value that has always been there even when I struggled to do so myself.

And finally, thank you to Popotes Cafe in Brussels where the majority of this book was unknowingly dreamed up between cups of late afternoon coffee.

PART ONE

01

Defining Ethics in AI

And How Values Will Shape the Face of Success

I want to start with the story of the two carpenters. These aspiring carpenters were both new to the job, having just decided to take up the profession of carpentry. In order to learn the profession, they started apprenticeships with two different well-known and respected carpentry teachers. Both teachers started the lessons from the basics, beginning with the simple task of hammering a nail into a block of wood.

The first aspiring carpenter was taught the exact action of how to hammer in the nail. The teacher took the hammer, showed the student the rounded end, and then took the nail and pointed out the flat top. The teacher then showed how to use the rounded end of the hammer to hit the flat top of the nail so that the pointed end of the nail would sink into the block of wood, taking special care to demonstrate the exact arm motions in detail. Once the first aspiring carpenter had memorized the specific action of hammering a nail into a block of wood, the teacher ended the lesson for the day.

Meanwhile, the second aspiring carpenter was taught about the hammer as a tool. Instead of showing the student how to hammer the nail, the second teacher spent the day explaining what makes a hammer a hammer. Going into excruciating detail, the teacher showed the student how the hammer is a tool designed to help a person use the laws of force to achieve different results. Never even picking up the nail or block of wood, the second teacher ended the lesson once they were satisfied that the second aspiring carpenter understood the whole entire hammer in full.

The next day the two aspiring carpenters returned for their next lessons. Deciding to test the students on what they had learned the day before, both teachers gave their students a hammer, a nail and a block of wood, and asked the students to hammer the nail into the wood. The first aspiring carpenter quickly picked up the hammer and, remembering the instructions from the day before, followed the exact actions necessary to hammer in the nail. The first teacher stood back and smiled with pride at how perfectly the student had followed instructions. The second aspiring carpenter was then given a hammer, nail and block of wood, and asked to complete the same task. Taking a moment to observe the hammer, the student recognized that they could use the rounded end of the hammer to apply force to the flat end of the nail and so sink it into the block of wood. The second teacher smiled as the student easily completed the task, having applied their knowledge of the hammer as a tool into action.

The second teacher then decided to issue a challenge, and asked both students to take their block of wood and now remove the nail that had been hammered into it. The first teacher watched in dismay as their student struggled to comprehend the task, flipping the block of wood over and trying to hit the nail out from the other side. Meanwhile the second student took a moment to look at the hammer, flipped it over in their hand, and easily popped the nail out of the block of the wood by using the forked end of the hammer as a tool to apply force to the nail in the opposite direction. The second teacher nodded in approval as the first teacher stood back, mouth agape with surprise.

Having only been taught the motion of hammering a nail into the wood, the first aspiring carpenter didn't understand that the hammer had other potential uses. They had been taught one specific action, and although they had mastered that action, they did not know how to expand that knowledge into new domains. On the other hand, the second aspiring carpenter had not been taught a specific action, but instead had been taught all about the tool. With a deep understanding of the hammer in hand, the second carpenter was equipped to handle whatever task they were given with ease, as their knowledge of the hammer was not confined to only one action.

In this book, I am not going to teach you how to hammer a nail. Instead, I am going to show you everything you need to know about the hammer so that you are well equipped to handle whatever comes your way.

How to Use a Hammer in the World of AI

Obviously, the carpenter story is only a metaphor for this book, as I am not really going to teach you about hammering nails. This book is about how to use Responsible AI and Ethics as a tool to enable you, as a business leader, to capture the full potential of AI by driving innovation responsibly forward to a future of both high value and human-centric values. Think of the block of wood as your AI systems, the nail as your ethical values, and the hammer as your Responsible AI strategy that will enable you to hammer your values into your AI systems, although hopefully with more finesse than this imagery suggests.

In this chapter I am going to introduce you to your hammer, showing exactly what purpose Responsible AI and Ethics serve in the world of emerging technology. We will dive into what is ethics in the context of AI, how our values affect our decision making, and why Responsible AI is the future of artificial intelligence. Setting the stage for the conversations and lessons to follow, I will wrap up with a breakdown of what to expect for the remainder of the book, giving you an overview of everything to come. By the end of this chapter you will be able to define the goal of embedding ethics into AI practices, what it means to be a Responsible AI-enabled organization, and how this book will empower you to achieve both.

The Silent Killer of AI

The route to successful AI seems deceptively clear. All that is needed is quality data and a strong algorithm developed for either productization in a defined market or deployment in a compelling internal use case. As long as your technology is sound and your business case is thoroughly developed, the major blockers seem to have been addressed and you would expect to see a high rate of success.

However, this is unfortunately far from the reality of AI in practice. For all the praises sung of AI and its ability to multiple opportunities for enterprises, only 20 percent of AI projects will actually reach deployment in some form or another. In other words, while you are hoping that the development of that new AI tool will bring you exponential success, there is an 80 percent chance that your AI project will end in total failure (Bojinov, 2023). And even if you manage to be one of the 20 percent making it to deployment, this is not an indicator of whether or not you will make a return on your investment into AI. For something that can cost upwards of $500k for an initial solution, excluding maintenance and updates, that seems like a rather high failure rate to risk.

So what's happening here? Why is there such a gap between carrying an AI project safely from conception all the way to profitable deployment?

There are of course a multitude of factors that this gap can be attributed to such as poor project management, ill-defined business problem, lack of necessary talent, difficulty in obtaining high-quality data—the list goes on (Fayyad, 2023). However, in current AI practices, there is a silent killer that often goes unaddressed, let alone recognized, by even the strongest of AI business leaders. While most are distracted with busily trying to identify and solve technical challenges as the root of potential AI failure, the true source sits far deeper than the lines of code and sets of data. In fact, this silent killer is not even technical at all; instead, it is something as human as the intelligence that we are striving to translate into our machines.

As any true leader in AI will know, the success of an AI project depends at its core on the foundational values and responsible practices it has been built on. In other words, you can't have sustainable AI success if you do not have Responsible AI and Ethics.

Hopefully this does not come as a complete surprise. With each new AI development, such as onset of general purpose LLMs and image generators in 2023, AI Ethics comes further out from behind the scenes and into the spotlight of core AI conversations. Cloaked in a variety of names such as Responsible AI, AI Risk and Safety, AI Governance, and so on, the application of ethics in artificial intelligence aims at aligning technology to human values in order to create a better future for all. However, in the case that this is in fact news to you, or you are not entirely convinced that ethics really has such an important role to play in modern technology, let's take a moment to look at why this is.

Getting What You Intended Out of Your AI Investment

When it comes to developing AI for business purposes, you must always start with an intended use case for your solution in mind. As any seasoned executive will know, the intended use case for your AI solution and the actual resulting solution are often divided by a wide dissonant gap. In other words, you set out to create an AI solution with one intended use case, and instead experience a very different result. With the amount of time and resources being invested into any given AI solution, all you really want is to be able to know that you are going to get the results that you expect.

Responsible AI strategies, as you will come to learn in this book, are the practical tools needed to lessen this infuriating gap, and bring your resulting AI solution into alignment with its original intended use case. This is because Responsible AI enables you to gain a new depth of understanding into what is the exact intended use case for your AI systems by requiring you to define the purpose and values that you need to see reflected in the final AI system in order to determine the success of the project. A Responsible AI strategy then is essentially the action plan for how you will ensure that throughout the development life cycle of your AI project, the critical decisions being taken to build your AI system remain in alignment with the original intended purpose and values for your project.

Allow me to elaborate with an example here. Imagine you begin your AI journey with the intention of building a solution that will help small businesses better expand their reach beyond their immediate communities. You collect quality data on user profiles within select communities, draw insights into where these communities are located online, and create a model that will target a small business's posts toward the relevant user profiles. Simple, straightforward, your intended use case seems to be easily within reach. However, after deploying the model, it is only a matter of weeks before you realize that instead of expanding a small business's reach into new communities, your AI solution has amplified the already existing divides between local communities. You begin receiving complaints from your small business customers that their posts are receiving even less visibility than before the model was deployed, and worse, that the AI solution seems to be targeting select user profiles based on race. Now, instead of helping expand small businesses' reach, you have instead segregated and restricted their reach. Clearly, not what you expected, nor wanted, to achieve.

If you had instead begun the project with a clear Responsible AI strategy, you would have been able to identify early on that the value of fairness would be essential to the success of this AI solution since you would be dealing with demographic data. Once identified, you would have been able to build the strategy that would outline the necessary steps to clean unwanted bias from your datasets and implement a variety of safeguards to ensure that racial targeting would not occur. This would have then eliminated the undesired restriction on the small business's audience, opening again the potential for the small business to expand its reach. Simply put, if you had utilized ethics as a practical tool in the design and development of this AI solution, your results would have more closely matched your original intended use case.

Reducing the Risk of Unintended Consequences in AI

When an AI system causes harm or behaves in an unexpected manner, we often will call this an unintended consequence of the project. These unintended consequences are significant contributors to the high failure rates of AI projects, potentially disastrous deviations from your originally intended use case for your AI systems. Responsible AI practices work to significantly reduce the probability of unintended consequences by actively embedding ethics into the entirety of your AI projects.

Let's put it this way, if you do not have a guiding strategy in place that ensures alignment between intended use case and results for your AI solution, it can be quite easy to lose direction of the project and arrive at the end with a completely different outcome than you had expected. You could have the highest quality data and most brilliantly designed system in the world, but without the foundational ethical values or Responsible AI practices, you risk losing the time and resources invested to an actualized unintended consequence that could have easily been prevented.

As a business leader, your primary concern when embarking on a new AI project will be to reduce the high risk of failure as much as possible. One of the best places to start eliminating this risk is in closing the gap between intended use case and actual results, something that can only be achieved through building on robust and practical Responsible AI foundations. If you want to increase your chances of exponential commercial success in AI, you must first start with the very human practice of ethics.

What Is Ethics Anyway?

By now you have probably noticed that I am using the terms ethics and Responsible AI fairly interchangeably. This is not because they are the same thing, but rather because Responsible AI cannot exist without ethics. Working on the ethics of an AI system means that we are using our values as critical decision-making factors in the build of our AI systems, while Responsible AI looks at how to operationalize ethics as one of the core strategic tools to align AI systems with our human-centric values. Think of it this way, ethics focuses on decision making, and Responsible AI focuses on the operational structure through which that decision making takes place. To help you gain a deeper understanding of this distinction and what it means for the content of this book, let's start with a dive into the practice of ethics.

If I asked you to define ethics for me, would you be able to? And if you are able to settle on a definition, would you have the confidence to stand on stage and present that definition as the truth?

It's OK if your answer to both of these questions was no. You'll be happy to learn that you are not alone, as my years of being an ethicist has taught me that although people theoretically understand what ethics is, it is rare that someone has the depth of knowledge on the subject that they would be willing to stake their reputation on their definition. Often when I begin a discussion about ethics, whether it is on a global stage, in executive work-shops, or simply in a one-on-one conversation, I ask my audience for their definition of what ethics is. Inevitably, someone will answer sooner or later that ethics is the law of nature that tells the self-driving car to run over Hitler and save the baby. Although not technically wrong, this definition is slightly too limited in scope to be of use when applied to the entire field of artificial intelligence and to any other human than Hitler and a baby.

One insight that I have gained from these answers, beyond the fact that we seem to have a general obsession with theoretically running people over with self-driving cars, is that although everyone will recognize the terms ethics, it is very rare that the average person will have a strong definition of what ethics really is. More often than not, my question is met with a slightly confused silence, as it slowly dawns on listeners that no one has ever actu-ally asked them to define something that they have taken for granted throughout their life.

The Shortest Possible History of Ethics

Ethics is not a new or shallow concept. In fact it has been a focus of critical thought and debate among philosophers for many a millennia. Humans have been grappling with the concepts of good and bad before attempts to understand intelligence ever even began. Within this rich field of study, a few branches have developed, each with its own purpose and subsequent uses. Starting at the very theoretical top, you will find Meta-Ethics, the branch devoted to understanding what it means to be good or bad in existence (Sayre-McCord, 2023). Diving deeper in, you have Normative Ethics, which takes those definitions of good and bad from Meta-Ethics and begins to apply them to actions in order to understand what constitutes a right or a wrong act. This is where you will find different ethical frameworks such as Virtue Ethics, Utilitarianism, Deontological Ethics, and Care Ethics, which are essentially different mental frameworks on how to prioritize your values in your decision making (Gustafson, 2020). Finally, there is Applied Ethics, the practical branch of the lot, devoted to understanding what is a right or wrong action within a specific situation (Dittmer, 2023). In other words, Applied Ethics is where the decision making and action happens, and so also the branch that is home to the practice of AI Ethics.

I briefly touch on the various branches not to offer a history lesson of moral philosophy, but instead to highlight the extensive depth of knowledge there exists to gain in the field of ethics. From abstract guiding values to precise detailed decisions, ethics can be applied at every level to better understand and direct the decisions at hand. Ethics, at its core, is the practice of delineating right from wrong. By nature, it is something that requires both thought *and* action. You can understand conceptually what is good, but if you do not act in accordance to this good, then you have only engaged in the preliminary steps of ethics and will never see the full benefit of the practice.

If you are indeed a human reading this book, then you will be happy to know that you are not a stranger to the practice of ethics. In fact, ethics is something so innately human by nature, that we often do not even realize we are engaging in critical ethical thinking throughout our day-to-day lives.

Ethics in the Business of AI

But what does this all mean for AI, let alone your business? Fascinating and fruitful as discussions on right and wrong can be, there first needs to be a reason for why this matters to the development and eventual commercialization of your AI solution. Essentially, you need to understand what ethics is in relation to your AI-driven business.

Translating our philosophical definition into one applicable to industry, the definition I use in practice with my clients is that ethics is a decision-analysis tool used to evaluate for value alignment in AI systems. Essentially, ethics strategically reduces AI-related risk by enabling you to critically assess key technical and business decisions for alignment to fundamental values and intended use cases. When it comes to engaging ethics in your AI and business practices, all you are doing is surfacing a thought process that is already naturally occurring so that you are better able to fine-tune decisions and get the intended results out of your AI solution.

Let's put it this way—you would never embark on a robotics project without first understanding the laws of physics, so why would you embark on an AI project without first understanding the laws of intelligence, of which ethics is essential?

Ethics as a Decision-Analysis Tool

As you begin to understand why ethics has such an important role to play in the success of an AI solution, the next question to address will of course be how. How exactly does ethics function as this decision-analysis tool?

A helpful way to conceptualize ethics is to think of it as a compass. The sole purpose of a compass is to keep you on the path to your intended destination by pointing you, literally, in the right direction. You have your end destination and the directions needed to get there, the compass is simply the tool that supports your ability to follow the directions to your destination.

On a human level, ethics works much the same. Its purpose is to keep you on the path to your intended destination in life by guiding you in the right direction. The end destination in this case, however, is not a geographical location on a map, but instead a fulfilling life of purpose, and the directions are not cardinal points but instead values that work to align you to your purpose. For example, if you find fulfillment in connecting with others, you will most likely believe in the value of spending quality time with loved ones. By using ethics in your daily decision making, you will naturally make decisions that enable you to spend more time with loved ones instead of taking you away from them. Essentially, ethics is the active tool you are using in this scenario to guide your decisions into alignment with your values and ultimately arrive at your purpose.

Now what does this have to do with AI and your business? Artificial intelligence is fundamentally a reflection of humanity, which means that ethics works in exactly the same way on a technical level as it does on a human level. Just as you use ethics in your daily life to guide your decisions in accordance with your values, so too can you utilize ethics in AI to guide the design and development of your solution in accordance to your foundational values. As a business leader, it is your responsibility to set your company objectives and then direct your teams on how to achieve them. When it comes to ethics in AI, you are aligning current and adding additional objectives for your company based on your values, and then directing your teams using ethics to guide the decision making supporting the build of your AI systems. And, as we discussed before, these foundational values in AI are essential to achieving the intended use case of your solution. In aligning your technology to your values, you are setting yourself up to successfully reach your intended end results for your AI solution.

What Is Responsible AI and Why Do You Need a Strategy for It?

With your mind wrapped around the concept of ethics and how it works, we can now move on to discussing what this has to do with Responsible AI. As I mentioned previously, if ethics is focused on decision making, then Responsible AI is focused on providing the operational structure necessary for that decision making to happen. Without structure, even the best decisions will go unused and misplaced, as knowing when, where, and how to use a decision is just as important, if not more so, when it comes to affecting any kind of outcomes for both your organization and your AI.

The ultimate objective of Responsible AI is to reflect human-centric values in AI systems. By providing the operational structure for ethical decision-making, Responsible AI operationalizes our human-centric values in the build and use of AI solutions. A Responsible AI enabled organization is an organization that has invested into the strategy and resources necessary to building the structure for operationalizing ethical values at scale.

The purpose of this book is to guide you through the process of developing that exact Responsible AI strategy and unlock the opportunity of ethically aligned AI for your organization.

Structure Not Substance

Expanding further on the purpose of Responsible AI and this book, I must stress that I am not here to provide you with an encyclopedia of ethics solutions. If you are looking for a list of answers to every possible ethical question you may encounter when developing AI, you should drop this book immediately or risk immense disappointment. The purpose of this book is to show you the Responsible AI structure needed to utilize ethics and guide your team to successful execution of an AI project, not provide a database of pre-selected solutions. Ethics is a compass, not a GPS system.

In such a fast-paced world, it can really be tempting to try and skip to the end, immediately demanding the nicely simplified answers, yet forgetting the thought necessary to arrive at such answers. My years as an ethicist have taught me that people prefer to ask "what are the top three risks associated with AI" rather than "how can I identify and prevent the risks in my specific AI solution." Although it would make my job a whole lot easier, I simply cannot provide you with this kind of cheat sheet to implementing ethics into your AI.

Why? Ethics flat out just doesn't work like that. In the AI world of binary black and white, ethics is a masterpiece of gray. You will very rarely ever find a yes or no situation in ethics, which is why vague questions like "what are the top three risks in AI" can only truly be infuriatingly answered with "it depends." Ethics is a highly contextualized practice, without the input of context variables, it is impossible to have the clarity required to make definitive decisions. (Keep in mind, though, that variability does not mean a lack of validity, just because ethics depends on context does not mean that the answers it offers are not legitimate.) Even if I were to offer you a list of ethics answers, I would only be able to provide surface level insights to generic scenarios that would quickly become irrelevant with the next phase of AI advancement. At that point, the most use you could get out of these pages would be to use them for fire starters.

If you take a step back from the technical and look at the overall organizational level of AI development, you will quickly come to realize that it is far easier to embed ethics into AI practices than it is into lines of code. Or, in other words, to establish a robust Responsible AI strategy that creates the operational structure that enables ethical decision making at scale. Every dysfunctional family is dysfunctional in its own way, while every healthy family is healthy is a similar way. When it comes to embedding ethics, every company and AI solution can go horribly wrong in its own way, while every successful company and AI solution follows a similar strategy of best practices in Responsible AI. As a business leader, your quickest path to the highest ROI for your AI solution is to utilize this strategy to implement ethical practices, unlocking the true value of ethics and thus realizing the full potential of your AI.

Immediate Not Existential

Another important distinction to make when it comes to the purpose of Responsible AI, and more specifically the content of this book, is the need to address the real immediate risks over potential future existential risks. Although this may sound counter intuitive as ethics is focused on long-term success and consequences, the purpose of developing a Responsible AI strategy is not to address the theoretical question of artificial general intelligence (AGI) impact on the humanity. Yes, it is crucial to look into the future to try and predict the changes AI is bringing to society, and yes it is imperative that we devote time and resources to understanding these existential questions of AI. However, grappling with these questions is not a replacement for Responsible AI practices, and having a company stance on AGI is not the same as building AI systems that are ethically aligned.

Philosophers, of all people, are the most intimately familiar with existential questioning. As a philosopher by background, I completely understand the burning need to dig into the growing existential questions that AI is forcing humanity to ask, it's one of the reasons that first drew me to the field of AI Ethics and still holds me captivated to this day. There is a time and place for these questions of what it means to be human in the world of AI, what constitutes consciousness, and whether or not we can create a higher intelligence. However, Responsible AI is neither the time nor the place. The purpose of Responsible AI is to address the very real gaps and risks that organizations are currently facing in AI development, not the theoretical harms of a system yet to be created. Do not be distracted by the red herring of AGI when the immediate risks of narrow AI are threatening the failure of your organization and detrimental consequences for society.

The Purpose of This Book

With the rapid changes happening in artificial intelligence, it is essential that you as a business leader are able to strategically adapt to these advancements. A list of generic answers and existential debates will not cut it. What you need is evergreen knowledge that empowers you to critically assess your technology and business plan for ethical risks and opportunities.

Ethics is a compass, if you learn how to read and use this compass to guide your teams to success, then the terrain you encounter along the way is trivial. The answers to ethics challenges may be variable and depend highly on the context, but the technique for how you arrive at these answers is consistent with clear standards that are easily learned. That technique, or in other terms strategy, is what we call Responsible AI.

So I ask you, as you embark on this book, to resist the urge to scour the internet for the latest blog post claiming to know how to prevent the top five risks in AI, and instead invest your time into learning how to create and implement your own ethics strategy for long-term AI success. Learn to read the compass, and you'll never be stranded without a GPS system again. Learn how to use a hammer, and you'll never be stuck with a solution that doesn't fit the problem.

How This Book Works

Over the next however many pages, I will be walking you through my approach to operationalizing ethics and how you can become a Responsible

AI-enabled organization. This book is a product of my years of experience leading Responsible AI projects for companies of all sizes, my research into ethics-by-design in the context of AI, my entrepreneurial success in building and running one of the first ever AI Ethics advisory firms, Ethical Intelligence, and the thousands of hours I've spent in conversation with business leaders grappling with how to bring Responsible AI to life for their organization.

Responsible AI and Ethics is a newly blossoming field, and I am very familiar with the fact that it can be incredibly difficult to find resources that will translate to practical action in this space. Everyone wants to discuss ethics, but finding someone who knows how to get ethics into action for your specific use case can feel like hunting for a needle in the haystack. Although I am only one of many active Responsible AI practitioners, which I am honored to call my peers, I recognize that the expertise I hold is unique even within my field. My fascination has always been with the people and process behind the scenes of AI development, which has led me down the path of specializing in the strategy and operations of Responsible AI. Understanding how to strategically operationalize Responsible AI has now become a top priority for companies looking to lead the future of AI, while the lack of knowledge on how to do so has simultaneously become the biggest blocker to achieving ethically aligned AI. Saving you the time of hunting needles in haystacks, I have consolidated my expertise into this book in the hopes that it will serve as the key to begin unlocking Responsible AI for your organization, and the catalyst for future ethicists to contribute work far more brilliant than mine to this space.

This book is written for modern AI business leaders in search of strategic solutions to reduce risk and increase ROI on AI-driven projects and solutions. However, anyone with an interest in understanding the operational mechanisms needed to responsibly develop AI will find value within these pages. It is important to note that technical knowledge of AI is not required for this book. Instead, we will be focusing on how AI is operationally designed and built, hence some prior knowledge in management and strategic thinking would be beneficial.

The book is broken down into three parts. Part One will focus on understanding ethics for modern organizational decision making. In these chapters I will discuss the concept of ethics as a decision-analysis tool, empowering you as a reader to fully grasp what ethics looks like in action and how to engage in ethical thinking in your everyday practices. We will be tackling common misconceptions and objectives to ethics, such as the seeming subjectively of values and the stifling of technical innovation, and will go through the process of selecting foundational ethics values sets for your organization. Additionally we will look into the duality of ethics use cases, breaking down the difference between a risk- and innovation-based approach to ethics and how to determine which approach is best suited to your Responsible AI needs. Overall, you can think of Part One as an introduction to understanding your values and how to work with them in your decision making.

Once you have a strong understanding of ethics and your values, you will then need to know how to use them. Part Two will address how to construct a Responsible AI strategy for any AI project by introducing the three key pillars that will enable you to embed your foundational values into the final AI system. To help aid in the design of your strategy, I will be introducing and then walking you through the Values Canvas, the conceptual matrix for building successful Responsible AI strategies. Keep in mind that Part Two will focus on how to embed ethics on a project level, looking at the different categories of solutions and intervention points necessary to creating AI systems that are reflective of your foundational values. By the end of this section, you will have the knowledge and tools necessary to go from conception to actualization of a fully developed Responsible AI strategy for any AI project.

Finally, in Part Three, we will take a step back from the granular details of project-level strategy, and transition into a higher-level discussion looking at developing an organization-level strategy for becoming Responsible AI enabled. In this section we will cover the different phases of Responsible AI adoption, and how to determine where your company is currently at in this journey. With this framing in mind, we will then look at how to prioritize your ethics initiatives to enhance your company's development in Responsible AI, including highlighting the differences in approaches needed depending on the size of your organization. We will then round out this section by discussing who within your organization will be responsible for executing your new Responsible AI strategy, and what the role of Responsible AI professionals and AI Ethicists should be in this execution. By the end of Part Three you will have the knowledge base and conceptual structure necessary for designing, building, and implementing your Responsible AI strategy on the organizational level at scale.

Although we all wish that people would be intrinsically motivated to embed ethics into their AI practices, at the end of the day a business exists for economic reasons and therefore must make money. What this means for Responsible and Ethical AI is that the business case for exactly why and how ethics can drive better return on investment is absolute essential to understand. Throughout these chapters you will find a variety of use cases, benefits, and examples of real-life success in Responsible AI, all of which are dedicated specifically to help you make the business case for ethics within your organization. By the end of this book you will be able to knowledgeably present a strong business case for ethics in order to drive greater ROI on your AI, design and execute a robust Responsible AI strategy for your organization, and once and for all be able to confidently embrace advances in artificial intelligence without the fear that you haven't catastrophically missed something crucial.

Getting Started

There are many ways to approach AI development, some better than others. At the end of the day, the whole purpose of embarking on the journey of investing in AI is to drive revenue and impact for your business, which means that you want to take the approach to AI that promises the biggest return on your investment. As you will come to discover throughout this book, an ethical approach to AI is not a novel solution out in left field, but is instead simply just good business and AI practice. If one day I were to receive a critique of this book saying that it had nothing to do with ethics and was just another business book on AI best practices, I would consider that as one of the biggest compliments I could receive.

Implementing an ethical approach to AI is simply good business, and having a Responsible AI strategy is what is going to get you there.

02

Know Your Values

How to Find and Define Your Values for Responsible AI

When used to its full extent, ethics is the compass that helps you as a business leader guide an AI project from promising start to successful finish. However, if you are going to use this compass as the tool to reach your desired destination, you must first understand the directions you need to follow. In the case of ethics, these directions are otherwise known as values.

Values form the critical foundation for any ethics practice, and Responsible AI is built on the strength of your ethics practices. Without values, it would be impossible to engage in ethics, as the whole purpose of applying ethics is to fine-tune decisions based on the determining factors detailed by selected ethical values. Essentially, ethics is the summary of a complexity of values in action, the code by which you execute sets of principles.

This means that unless you know the values you want to implement, a Responsible AI strategy without values will simply be a fruitless framework without purpose or direction. We like to joke as Responsible AI practitioners, one cannot simply order "five ethics in blue, please."

As values are the foundation for ethics, logically your first step as a business leader in creating a Responsible AI strategy is to start by understanding the specific foundational values off which you are going to build your practice. You need to establish your directions before you will be able to learn how to read your compass.

The purpose of this chapter is twofold. First, to teach you how successfully establish your foundational values for your AI Ethics strategy. And second, to prepare you to best tackle the initial conceptual blockers.

To do such, we will begin by addressing the first concern that ethics is too subjective to be useful by diving into objective universal values and where to find them. Next, we will move on to the second blocker and discuss whose ethics we will be using anyway, as well as presenting a simple framework to guide your own selection process of foundational values. Once we have cleared the conceptual blockers, we will move to covering two of the most common pitfalls in value selection: hyper fixation and under definition. Finally, we will end with a discussion on when and how to incorporate feedback in the value selection process so as to efficiently secure buy-in. As you will learn in throughout this chapter, the process of value selection is straightforward and logical, as long as you know where to look.

Breaking Down the Conceptual Blockers to AI Ethics

I am sure that as soon as I began the discussion on ethical values, one of the first thoughts that immediately came to your mind was where in the world do these values come from? This simple question, although valid and well-founded, is the source of the two biggest conceptual blockers you will face when first beginning your Responsible AI and Ethics journey. Of course you need to know where the ethical values that you will build your entire Responsible AI strategy on top of are coming from, but my goal with this chapter is to ensure that you do not get stuck in the never-ending cycle of defining and redefining your values without ever moving into action.

When first introducing the concept of ethics to your colleagues, you will inevitably have someone raise the concern that ethics is too subjective to be useful, followed closely by the demand to know whose ethics you will be using anyway. Both of these objections are rooted in the same uncertainty of where the values are coming from. This uncertainty, when left unchecked, can quickly kill any ethics initiative and so is paramount to address from the start.

Is Ethics Really Subjective?

"Ethics is subjective" is a common objection you will encounter to the viability of ethics as a reliable tool in AI practices. By highlighting the contrasting nature of subjective versus objective factors, what this objection is attempting to do is undermine the validity of decisions based on ethical reasoning.

A common belief that has only been reinforced with the rise of modern technology is that something is true if and only if it is based on objective facts. In saying that ethics is subjective, what a person is claiming is that ethical values are only truly relative to the individual, thus making it impossible to apply the values to a technology that reaches a few million users daily. We are naturally opposed to the idea of forcing our own ideals and moral codes on others, rightly so, and it is this natural opposition that the objection of subjective ethics taps into.

As a business leader, it is your responsibility to immediately address this objection head on. If you leave it open for debate, you risk undermining the very underpinnings of your entire initiative.

You will need to work closely with your technical departments when it comes to implementing your Responsible AI strategy, and technical-minded individuals work strictly within what they consider to be objective facts of technology. So, if you allow the misconception that ethics is purely subjective seep into your efforts around Responsible AI and Ethics, then you will never stand a chance of incentivizing adoption of Responsible AI practices within your technical teams and beyond.

The good news, however, is that there are two very effective ways in which to tackle this objection.

Understanding Universal Values in the Context of Responsible AI

First is that ethics is not a solely subjective discipline. Allow me to explain. Subjectivity is a spectrum, not a yes or no characteristic. A field can have both subjective and objective values in it, it does not have to exist in either a fully subjective or fully objective extreme. What this means in the discipline of ethics is that the ethical values we rely on to guide decision making have both subjective and objective characteristics. Because there is a wide range variety of possible ethical values, and each individual value can be applied in a multitude of different ways, there is a common false conclusion drawn that ethics as a whole must be completely subjective. However, the variety of values does not directly imply complete subjectivity, nor does it negate the existence of objective universal values.

What is a universal value? It is simply a value that is objectively true for everyone (Lang, 2020). For a well-known example, we can look to Plato, according to whom there are four universal values that apply equally across all people, these being wisdom, courage, moderation, and justice (Frede and Lee, 2023). Each value, at its core, has the same worth that it brings to every individual, and is something that every individual should strive for. It is in this concept of universal values that we can find the objective truth needed to support any practice in ethics.

I am not claiming that Plato's four cardinal virtues should be the basis of our modern moral code, nor am I leading us down a philosophical rabbit hole of virtuous debate. Instead, I want to raise in your mind the potential for the existence of universal values in AI Ethics. If they really do exist, then what that means for your Responsible AI strategy is that you will be building on an objective foundation of universal values, instead of the shifting sands of subjectivity.

Some of you reading this will naturally resonate with the idea of universal values, and so will need no further explanation in order to convince you of their existence. However, I know that we live in society skeptical of anything that cannot be proven by fact, so allow me to present you with the current global state of AI policies.

As of 2023, there are over 1,000 AI policy initiatives from 69 different countries (OECD, 2023). Every country with a policy lists, to some extent or another, the need for AI governance, and the majority reference the intention of making AI ethical and trustworthy. Some of the most commonly listed ethical values are fairness, privacy, transparency, and accountability, appearing on policies from all over the world. In fact, we even see countries coming together to sign guiding policies on AI principles, such as the 42 countries that signed the OECD's AI principles that were backed by the European Commission and endorsed by the G-20 (OECD, 2019). Although these ethical values may hold different purposes and definitions depending on what international policy you are reading, there is a clear pattern emerging on what is expected from our AI systems. If ethical values truly were completely subjective, then we would expect to see little to no commonality across these international policies on AI. Instead, we find there is significant overlap in values and even across cultures that are typically assumed to be at odds.

What this all goes to show is that there are in fact universal values emerging in the context of Responsible AI. It is only in the interpretation of these objectively held values that we see the spectrum of subjectivity, not in the values themselves. These internationally accepted values will consistently apply to any AI solution, and so form the objective foundation upon which you can begin to build a robust Responsible AI strategy.

Why Ethics Is Just as Subjective as Data Science

Now, if you arrive at this point and are still doubting the underlying objectivity of ethics, or if you have presented the above argument to your colleagues and are still struggling to convince them, there is a second argument you can utilize to tackle the skepticism that ethics is too subjective to be useful in AI.

Simply put, ethics is just as subjective as data science. And if we accept the validity of data science despite its elements of subjectivity, then why should we not do the same for ethics?

Although it may seem counter intuitive at first, data science does in fact have elements of subjective reasoning that are comparable to those in ethics. Data science is based on objective data points, however it is in the evaluation metrics that we find the elements of subjectivity. When it comes to evaluating for success in data science, there are three primary metrics to choose from: accuracy, precision, and recall.

Among these three there are natural trade-offs, for example precision and recall can often have conflicting results where according to one metric you are highly successful and the other not at all (Google, 2022b). Who, though, gets to decide which metric to use? Two equally qualified and skilled data scientists can make a credible argument for opposing evaluation metrics, which means that the selection metrics is, at the end of the day, a matter of personal preference of the data scientist and thus a subjective decision. Now of course the data scientist is not just selecting a metric at random, they will have critically evaluated the scenario in order to understand which metric they believe to be most effective. But it still remains that the best fit evaluation metric depends on the context of the situation, the intentions of the model, and the data scientist's subjective preference.

The ethicist works in much the same way when evaluating a scenario against ethical values. Just as the data scientist uses critical reasoning to arrive at the logical conclusion for which metric to use in evaluation, so does the ethicist critically reason within the context of the technology to understand which values should be prioritized and how. Thus, data science is just as subjective as the practice of ethics.

So, whether you decide to accept the existence of universal values, or prefer to accept that there is a layer of subjective reasoning in every field, including data science and artificial intelligence, you will still arrive at the same conclusion. The objection that ethics is too subjective for AI is invalid, and there are in fact objective decision factors on which you can build a successfully operating Responsible AI strategy.

Whose Values Are They Anyway?

Your values will form the foundation of your Responsible AI strategy. As you strive to ethically align your technology, you will need to have a set of values clearly selected and defined to align to in the first place. But where do these values come from?

We are surrounded by values—from your own moral code to the company values written on the wall in the break room, you are no stranger to the depth and nuance of the possible values you can choose from. As you begin outlining your foundational value set, you could go about cherry picking values from various sources, highlighting ones you particularly resonate with and ignoring the ones that feel unnecessarily tedious. After all, there is no great overseer of values that will frown down upon your selection.

As you may have guessed, though, this is both an erroneous and simply inefficient approach to value selection. First, if you base your value set only on your own personal preference, you have already introduced personal bias risks into your strategy before you've even begun to implement it. However balanced and thorough you believe yourself to be, you will always want a second opinion in value selection, because even the best of us are still blind to our own innate biases. For example, I may select the value of patience, but not consider that if I am working for a health tech company, the last thing a doctor will want out of software is to have to patiently wait for an analysis while her patient is quickly dying before her eyes. So, you must collaboratively include different opinions during the value selection process, preferably from people who come from a very different background and demographic than yourself, in order to counter balance any personal bias that may occur.

Second, it is inefficient because you will inevitably lose an important value to confusion. As we discussed previously in this chapter, there are global foundational values, as well as cross-industry best practices values, that you will either be required to meet by regulation or expected to meet by market pressure. If you do not have a methodical approach to locating these values, followed by a deliberation to understand which are applicable to your specific context, then you are destined to lose at least one critical value to the confusion and sheer mass of Responsible AI policies in existence.

Thankfully, there is a straightforward and simple framework you can utilize to aid in your value selection. It is called the Foundational Value Finder, and its purpose is to guide you in selecting the most effective value set for your organization. Conceptually, this framework functions like a

GPS system, helping you triangulate between a variety of value sets inputs to understand where exactly your organization needs to stand. It also helps in providing insight into where your organization should focus time and resources in implementation through three different layers of prioritization of the selected values.

The Foundational Value Finder Framework

The Foundational Value Finder framework is composed of five columns. Moving from left to right, the columns are labeled "Value," "Government," "Industry," "Organization," and "Alignment" as shown in Table 2.1.

The core of the Framework rests on three different value set inputs from the government, industry, and organizational level. Value set simply means a set list of specific values, usually accompanied by a definition of each individual value. For example, the list of values detailed by the European High Level Expert Group in the AI White Paper would be considered one value set. The first column is where you will list the values from these different value sets, whereas the following three columns will track which value set that specific value can be found, and the final column is used to illuminate points of alignment between value sets.

Government Value Set

Your first value set will come from government level, and can typically be found either in regulation or policy. To find this value set, look to see if your country (or countries) of operation have any policies or regulations on AI. Typically, any national AI policy will include to some extent a list of ethical values. You can also look on an international level, for example the European Union's overarching EU AI Act incorporates a core value set. Wherever you

TABLE 2.1 The Foundational Value Finder Framework

Value	Government	Industry	Organization	Alignment

draw this value set from, it is important to remember that the purpose of this value set is to have input on any regulated values that may exist and require you to follow. Additionally, if you are looking on a national level, you will also be incorporating values based on the culture of that specific country.

I suggest starting with only one value set on the government level; however, you may want to include additional sets depending on the size and scope of your operating markets. If your country does not have any AI regulations or policies containing a value set, I would suggest using the EU AI Act value set as a default for this first input, as this is the farthest reaching regulation to date. Once you have selected your first value set input, enter it into the first column of your framework, spreading one value per row. You will then want to mark an "X" in the second column titled "Government" in the row for each corresponding value you find on your government value set.

For example, let's say you are a Belgian company operating in the European Union market, which means you will want to draw your government value set from High Level Expert Group guidelines and EU AI Act and input them into the framework, as in Table 2.2.

Industry Value Set

Next, for your second value set input, you will be drawing from industry. Oftentimes industries will have their own respective value sets specific to the context of that industry. In some cases these are known as codes of conduct, in others they are best practices or industry standards. For example, if you are operating in health tech, you will want to draw on the four pillars of

TABLE 2.2 The Foundational Value Finder Framework: Government Value Set

Value	Government	Industry	Organization	Alignment
Privacy	X			
Transparency	X			
Fairness	X			
Well-being	X			
Autonomy	X			
Accountability	X			
Safety	X			

medical ethics found in the Hippocratic oath. These four values have become the standard of operations in the field of medicine, and as health tech is an industry operating within medicine, these values will provide practical insight into what will eventually become your foundational values.

The point, though, is to be able to draw on what is expected behavior in your given industry to form this second value set for your framework. Once you have selected your second value set from industry, look back over the first column on your framework and add any additional values from your industry value set that were not previously listed. Then, working your way down the values, mark an "X" in the third column titled "Industry" in the row for each corresponding value you find on your industry value set.

Continuing on with our Belgian company example, let's say your Belgian company is indeed operating in health tech. You will want to then take the values of justice, autonomy, non-maleficence, and beneficence from the Hippocratic oath and input them into the framework, as in Table 2.3.

Organization Value Set

Finally, for your third value set input, you will be looking at your own organization. This value set is unique to your organization, and seeks to tangibly capture the mission of your company. To find this value set, there are many places you can look. From your company's code of ethics or conduct, to the

TABLE 2.3 The Foundational Value Finder Framework: Industry Value Set

Value	Government	Industry	Organization	Alignment
Privacy	X			
Transparency	X			
Fairness	X			
Well-being	X			
Autonomy	X	X		
Accountability	X			
Safety	X			
Non-maleficence		X		
Beneficence		X		
Justice		X		

company values written on the break room wall, to the unspoken cultural values, each of these are valid sources to draw on for this value set. You can even list some values that your organization may not necessarily currently exhibit, but that you are striving to strategically embed. The main purpose of this third value set is to provide the contextual perspective to your foundational values that is relative to your distinct organization. Once you have selected your third value set input, look back over the first column on your framework and add any additional values from your organization value set that were not previously listed. Then, working your way down the values, mark an "X" in the fourth column titled "Organization" in the row for each corresponding value you find on your organization value set.

To round out our Belgian health tech company example, let's say your company has a strong code of ethics already in place that focuses on the values of fairness, autonomy, well-being, privacy, safety, and humility. You would take that code of ethics and enter it into the framework, as in Table 2.4.

Alignment of Values

You will have noticed two things about the framework so far. First, I have only entered in the values, and not the definitions. This is not to say the definitions are not important, on the contrary they are vital to the success of

TABLE 2.4 The Foundational Value Finder Framework: Organization Value Set

Value	Government	Industry	Organization	Alignment
Privacy	X		X	
Transparency	X			
Fairness	X		X	
Well-being	X		X	
Autonomy	X	X	X	
Accountability	X			
Safety	X		X	
Non-maleficence		X		
Beneficence		X		
Justice		X		
Humility			X	

your strategy as you will see later in this chapter. Instead, the definitions are not currently listed so as to keep the framework clear and concise. The purpose is to locate your foundational values, then once this step is complete, you will be able to bring the definitions back into the discussion.

The second thing you may have noticed is that in some cases there is different wording being used to describe the same value. In the cases where there is different wording for the same value, or in other words, synonyms, you can either adjust by selecting a standard word choice, or listing the variations next to each other. For example, responsibility and accountability are similar enough that both can be condensed to simply responsibility. You can debate which term is most accurate for your organization later on when you are defining your values, the important point is that you recognize both terms point at the same value of taking ownership over one's actions and consequences. Think of this cleaning process as synonymous with cleaning your data. For instance, in the case of our Belgian company, we can choose to condense fairness and justice, as well as well-being and beneficence.

With your values list now cleaned, you are ready to move on to the fifth and final column, "Alignment." As you move row by row, read how many times a single value is found on each of the three different value sets. If the value is listed in all three columns, enter "1" in the fifth column. If the value is listed in two out of the three columns, enter "2" in the fifth column. If the value only appears one in the row, enter "3" in the corresponding fourth column. To help visualization, you can also color code the cells: green signaling the value is on all three value sets, yellow for the value found on two value sets, and red for the value only found on one value set.

If you were filling out the framework for our example Belgian company, your framework would look like Table 2.5.

Locating Your Foundational Values

Now you have completed your framework, the next step is to use it to locate your foundational values. As you look down column five, the alignment column, any cell marked with "1" or colored green indicates that the corresponding value is a foundational value. Otherwise known as your primary values, these should form the core of your Responsible AI strategy. We will cover how to strategically implement values in Parts Two and Three, but for now simply keep this value set close at hand.

TABLE 2.5 The Foundational Value Finder Complete Framework

Value	Government	Industry	Organization	Alignment
Privacy	X		X	2
Transparency	X			3
Fairness / Justice	X	X	X	1
Well-being / Beneficence	X	X	X	1
Autonomy	X	X	X	1
Accountability	X			3
Safety	X		X	2
Non-maleficence		X		3
Humility			X	3

After you have identified your foundational values, you can then go back to column five again, this time selecting the "2" or yellow values from the list. These are known as your secondary values, and they will have a specific function in the execution of your Responsible AI strategy. As you begin to put your primary ethical values into practice, you will notice that you will occasionally be faced with an instance in which two of your primary values are in conflict. You will need to find the right trade-off to make between the two primary values. It is at this point that you can fall back on your secondary values to help guide your trade-off decision, drawing on the practical insight they can provide. It is important to note as well that in some cases you will want to make a secondary value into a primary value. That is a perfectly valid strategic decision if it aligns with your overall Responsible AI objectives. To be clear, these are secondary values because although you may not build your strategy directly around them, they can still be critical to decision making and so you need to clearly select and define them. For instance, you can imagine finding yourself in a scenario in which you must make a trade-off decision between your primary values privacy and transparency. To help make this trade-off, you look to your secondary values and find that the value of well-being is better supported by privacy over transparency in this scenario, and so make the trade-off in favor of privacy.

Finally, you will be left with the values marked as "3" or in red. Think of these values as extracurricular—if you want to engage with them that is OK but not necessarily mandatory. As you go through these remaining values, critically assess whether or not any of these values could provide necessary support to your primary and secondary values, or if any could provide you with a strategic competitive edge if properly implemented. If not, feel free to leave these values to the side for now. You can always return to them later down the line once you've successfully implemented your first two layers of values. However, be sure that you first address whether or not any of these values have any legal requirements attached to them, as you must still be compliant with the law even if it is not a primary value.

In summary, your primary values should have top priority in implementation and will form the foundation of your Responsible AI strategy. Your secondary values will support decision making in the execution of your strategy, while your tertiary values are your nice-to-haves once your strategy is successfully implemented. You should now have a value set complete with prioritization of each value and balanced between input from three critical sources of ethical values.

The Pitfall of Hyperfocused Value

As you select your foundational values, it is important to keep in mind that these values must all work in balance together. A common pitfall that new Responsible AI teams will fall into when first engaging with ethical values is to forget that a successful strategy must enable each of the foundational values, your primary values from the Foundational Value Finder framework, without neglecting the other foundational values. This is not to say that each value must be engaged equally, there will be times when you find it necessary to emphasize one value over the other. However, the important point is that this emphasis of one value does not come at the cost of the others. If a team pursues one out of, say, seven foundational values, and forgets to balance among the entire set of foundational values, then the organization is taking on significant risk of Responsible AI failure as well as wider market criticism.

Think of it this way, if a company claims that it pursues the values of privacy, fairness, and trust, but only engages privacy in practice, it doesn't mean that the risks associated with neglecting fairness and trust have disappeared. Instead, the risks associated with neglecting fairness and trust have now become even far greater, as the team's attention is distracted by engaging with privacy and they will risk failing to recognize a fairness or trust problem until it is too late. This common pitfall of either forgetting or simply ignoring the necessity of balancing engagement across the entirety of your foundational values is otherwise known as the Hyperfocus Value Challenge. It is called such because of the temptation when first establishing a Responsible AI strategy to hyper focus on only one (or maximum two) of your foundational values in order to seemingly gain quick initial wins, when instead in reality opening your strategy and teams up to unforeseen risks.

A good example of the Hyperfocus Value Challenge is with Meta's Responsible AI team. Back when Meta was still known as Facebook, Karen Hao published a story in March 2021 with *MIT Technology Review* titled "How Facebook Got Addicted to Spreading Misinformation." In the article she focuses on the story of Joaquin Quiñonero Candela, a director of AI at Meta, and his efforts as the leader of Meta's Responsible AI team. Although the article was written during the time that Meta was facing accusations of mass misinformation and spreading of hate speech thanks to Cambridge Analytica, Hao struggled to get Quiñonero to engage on any of these topics. Instead, he only wanted to speak on how his Responsible AI team was planning to tackle AI bias. It soon became clear that even though Meta was causing quantifiable harm through misinformation, it had pigeonholed its own Responsible AI team into engaging on the sole value of fairness.

Even though fairness is a very important value and essential to tackling AI bias, it is not necessarily useful in addressing the larger and more significant problem of misinformation. As Meta's Responsible AI was busy plugging away at how to make algorithms more fair, the problem of misinformation continued to grow, exposing the company to further and further risk, until eventually leading to the storming of the US Capitol in January 2021. Suddenly, it didn't matter how much progress the team had made in terms of fairness. The hyperfocus on fairness, without regard to the larger context of challenges being faced by Meta, came at a far greater cost to the company than any progress made by the Responsible AI team's efforts.

The Blindspot of Undefined Values

Before you can begin to balance engagement across your foundational values, you must first remember to create clear definitions for each of the values. As mentioned earlier in this chapter, it is of the utmost importance that you clearly define each of these values, because if you do not, you again open your teams up to risk of misinterpretation and confusion. There is a tendency to assume that everyone shares the same understanding of a value, taking for granted, for example, that each individual on a single data science team all share the same practical definition of fairness. This, however, is far from the case, as each person can have a different way of interpreting the same value. If everyone is interpreting the same value in a different way, then there is no chance for consistency, growth, or improvement on that value. It is perfectly OK for people to have different interpretations of the same value in their day-to-day, but when it comes to successful executing on that value across teams and departments within an organization, you must ensure that everyone is operating on the same definition. The assumption that people will naturally share the same definition can lead to the common pitfall of leaving your foundational values undefined, exposing your Responsible AI strategy to what is otherwise known as the Undefined Value Risk.

The Undefined Value Risk was a challenge that the Royal Bank of Scotland, recently acquired by NatWest Group, was facing at scale across their three separate data science teams. The Board of Directors, in light of avid customer feedback and new financial regulations, had issued the directive to implement fairness, along with other values inherent to AI Ethics, across their data science teams. A fairness campaign was quickly created and set into motion, encouraging the data scientists to test their systems for bias and to look for creative ways to solve bias-related problems. However, the lead for all three data science teams, along with the head of digital innovation, were struggling to get the data science teams to adopt fairness practices and were frustrated by the lack of progress being made. Everyone knew fairness was important, everyone knew technically how to check for different biases, and yet there didn't see to be any tangible progress made in making the models more fair.

To help address the growing frustration, NatWest brought in ethicists to try and uncover what was going wrong. Within just a few weeks of meeting with the various data science teams, as well as additional interconnected departments such as risk and compliance, it was quickly made clear that no one was operating on the same definition of fairness. The data scientists were engaged, saw the value in eliminating unwanted bias, and desperately wanted to be able to collaborate with colleagues on creative ways to tackle bias. However, every time they tried to do so, they were faced with the problem of having no central definition for fairness, and so could not determine what biases to check for, nor how to correct them once located.

The lack of shared definition was leading to confusion across the teams, causing them to either push fairness efforts to the side or waste time and resources trying to find a solution that could not consistently be applied to solve the problem. Without clear definitions, the Undefined Value Risk opened NatWest up to the risk of wasted time and resources, as well as the original risks associated with biases. Eventually, NatWest did create a multi-layered living definition of fairness, which it deployed across its teams, successfully bringing the much-needed progress in implementation.

When it comes to the Undefined Value Risk, the simplest and most effective solution is to ensure you have clearly defined, as detailed and practical as possible, your foundational values before you begin implementing them. It is good practice to think of these definitions as living, establishing a routine check-up of the definitions to see if any new developments in Responsible AI have led to necessary updates in your definitions. In order to write these definitions, you can draw on the definitions listed in the government, industry, and organizational value sets, or you can start from scratch. The important thing is that you make the definitions clear, concise, and actionable. In some cases, you may want to create a multilayered definition, with one layer focusing on the high-level abstract nature of the value, while the subsequent layers focus on either department or products concrete levels. This multilayered approach is helpful if you notice your team struggling to adopt a certain value due to lack of clarity.

Securing Buy-In for Your Values

Finally, when it comes to establishing your foundational values for your Responsible AI strategy, it is important to seek a certain level of collaboration during the process. As mentioned earlier in this chapter, it feels innately wrong to force your values onto someone else. If you do not enable some form of feedback or collaboration in the value selection and then definition process, you risk having your colleagues push back due to the feeling that these values are being forced onto them. This will hinder adoption and create internal blockers to your Responsible AI strategy. We will address the different types of stakeholders you will need to incorporate in to the execution of your Responsible AI strategy in Part Three of the book, but for now all you need to know is that if you make the value selection process collaborative, your colleagues will feel they have invested into the larger mission of your strategy, and so be more motivated to successful implement the values.

However, there is such a thing as too much collaboration at this stage. When it comes to selecting and defining values, it can be easy to get stuck in the granular details. If you wanted to, you could sit and debate word choices and values for months on end. When inviting feedback and collaboration at this stage, you need to understand when and where to seek it. As you embark on this value selection process, do not be afraid to create strict deadlines and guides for feedback. I would highly suggest to give yourself, at maximum, a timeline of three months to create your foundational value set and accompanying definitions. It is OK if the first round is a rough draft, you will always be able to readdress your values and definitions later on down the line if something is not working. However, you will never know if a certain definition is not working in practice if you never get past the definition stage.

Two of the most effective points to seek collaborative input is after you have completed the Foundational Value Finder framework to arrive at your initial list of foundational values, and again after you have your rough draft of definitions for each of the values. These are both efficient and effective points for collaboration as it allows necessary feedback, checks on personal biases, and outside opinions to be collected at the time that this information can be processed and potentially incorporated. Setting a time constraint on when feedback is being accepted is also helpful, as it creates the necessary pressure to encourage people to engage, and it prevents you from getting sucked into a never-ending cycle of edits. At this stage, you must create clear firm deadlines and restraints, otherwise you run the risk of stalling out before you even begin designing your strategy.

Bringing Direction to Your Responsible AI Strategy

You can't have Responsible AI without knowing what direction you want to take your AI practices in the first place. To achieve Responsible AI, you must first understand what values to build your AI on.

In this chapter, we laid the foundations necessary to building any Responsible AI strategy by covering exactly where and how to locate the values you need to align your AI to. Starting with a discussion on the subjectivity of ethics, we looked into how set standards of values can be found globally in AI Ethics, and what this means for objective application in Responsible AI. Next, we learned how to use the Foundational Values Finder framework to gain insight from government, industry, and organization value sets in order to create a prioritized set of foundational values for your own Responsible AI strategy. Following the framework, we addressed the two major pitfalls of Hyperfocus and Undefined Value Risk, what they look like and how to mitigate them. Finally, we finished with insight into when and where to seek feedback during this initial stage of value selection and definition.

Continuing with our moral compass analogy, we now know the directions (foundational values) that we want to follow. Now, let's take a look at how to read the compass (ethics) in order to follow these directions.

03

The Duality of Ethics

Managing Risk and Innovation in AI

So far, you've come to understand how the practice of applying ethics is a targeted decision-making process involving focused analysis and reflection. You have also uncovered in the previous chapter your foundational values, specific to your organization, which will provide the perspective lens by which you will be analyzing your AI. Now it's time to dig into how to align your use of ethics with your organization's high-level objectives, creating a Responsible AI strategy that will drive real business impact.

Although the aim of your Responsible AI strategy is to align technology to values, your Responsible AI strategy itself must be aligned with your organization's wider objectives to be successful. Think of it like you are calibrating your compass to true north. There are two primary approaches to accomplishing this. The first takes a risk-forward approach to implementing ethics, while the second focuses on emphasizing innovation.

With this in mind, this chapter is devoted to helping you understand how to bring your Responsible AI strategy into alignment with your organization's objectives in order to drive positive impact. We will start by discussing what causes this duality in ethics and what it means for the eventual design of your strategy. Next, we'll dive in to unpack the risk-based approach, looking at how to utilize ethics as a mitigator to proactively prevent worst case scenarios for your technology. Following this, we'll switch over to the innovation approach, and dig into how ethics can be used to create a competitive edge in the market. By the end of this chapter, you will understand theoretically how ethics can further your organizations objectives through either a risk mitigation or innovation emphasis to your Responsible AI strategy.

The Dual Purposes of Ethics

Life exists on a spectrum. On one end, you have the worst possible scenario where everything that could have gone wrong has, leaving you miserably trying to manage problem after problem without any progress. On the opposite end, you have the best case scenario where everything that could have gone right has, bringing you one success after another and leaving you with a deep sense of fulfillment. Your actual life sits somewhere between these two extremes, a mixture of both the good and the bad. It is dynamic by nature, as your life is in constant change, so will be your position on this spectrum depending on your circumstances on any given day. It is up to you to make informed and critical decisions that help move you towards the positive end of this spectrum and avoid the negative side.

When it comes to making these decisions, ethics functions as the analyst tool that enables you to examine the potential outcomes of any given action and to determine if that action will bring you closer or further away from your best life. How does this work? Thinking back to the compass metaphor, your end destination that you are striving to reach is that best case scenario. It's a life in which you have fulfilled your purpose, while at the other end of spectrum sits the life gone horribly off course. You use your values as your directions along the way to assess your actions and make decisions that will either lead you closer or further from that best case scenario end of the spectrum. Essentially, you use ethics to align yourself in the direction of your best case scenario life.

The Dumpster Fire on Cloud Nine

All AI-driven solutions or products also exist on this same spectrum. There is the worst case scenario, when everything has gone wrong and the AI is causing both widespread societal harm as well as significantly costing your organization. This end of the spectrum is lovingly known in the startup world as the dumpster fire, when things have gone so bad that even the dumpster of trash has gone up in flames. Meanwhile, on the other end of the spectrum is an AI solution that has gone even better than originally imagined, bringing immense benefit to users and turning a profit that continues to increase quarter over quarter. This end of the spectrum is what we would call cloud nine, when it's almost unbelievable how perfectly everything has panned out. What we want to do is protect your organization from making headlines for a dumpster fire, and instead be top news for a cloud nine solution.

Ethics works in the same capacity when it comes to artificial intelligence as it does in your everyday life. When used correctly, ethics becomes a powerful tool utilized to assess key decisions against your foundational values to understand whether or not these decisions are getting you closer or further away from cloud nine. It is on this spectrum that we are able to see the duality of ethics brought to the surface and put to work. On one end, ethics is used to prevent the dumpster fire, while on the other end it is used to promote cloud nine. Although ethics is used in the same decision-analysis capacity on both ends, the approach on how this capacity is carried out will vary depending on which end of the spectrum you are working with.

The Dual Impact on Your Responsible AI Strategy

This spectrum, and the dual approach to working with ethics, will heavily influence the overarching objectives of your Responsible AI strategy and the techniques you will use to carry it out. This is because when it comes to preventing the dumpster fireside of the spectrum, ethics becomes a risk mitigator, while on the other end when pursing cloud nine, ethics becomes an innovation stimulator. Ethics is equally impactful in both roles, but it is up to you to decide what combination impact is needed most in your organization.

It is also necessary to highlight here that simply preventing the risks associated with the worst case scenario is not the same as pursuing the benefits of the best case scenario. In preventing risks, you are only working towards ensuring nothing goes wrong, but not necessarily towards reaching full potential of benefits. For example, let's take the value of privacy. If properly implemented in a risk capacity, privacy will prevent data breaches and GDPR violations, but it will not ensure that your AI solution is privacy-preserving in such a way that it provides you a competitive edge. That benefit is only achieved if privacy is engaged in an innovation capacity by deploying privacy-by-design techniques to create a solution that customers can trust will respect their data. Risk and innovation are two sides of the same ethics coin, but do require different techniques to achieve and thus a thorough understanding of what is needed in your organization.

Now that you are able to visualize this duality of ethics, let's take a deep dive into the two approaches, starting with the risk-mitigation end of the spectrum.

Ethics as a Tool for Risk Mitigation

Risk in business is not a new concept. By now, you are probably familiar with how risk management works in some capacity or another. Whether it be operational, financial, legal risks, and so on, you will have at some point encountered an internal strategy designed to mitigate such risks and associated consequences. Perhaps you have been the one to design and implement a risk management strategy yourself, or you play an active role in the execution of one, or you are simply aware of a risk process being run in another department. Whatever your experience with risk management may be, you should be familiar with the fact that the key to its success is to make it a part of daily operations to enable real-time mitigation (Silva Rampini, Takia, and Berssaneti, 2019).

When it comes to using ethics as a risk mitigator, the approach is much the same. Your goal is to create a cyclical process by which new and ongoing risks are continually identified, assessed, managed, and monitored. The difference, though, between risk management in ethics versus other risk strategies that you have come across before, is that in this case you are addressing ethical risk in the context of your AI. This is otherwise known as ethical risk management (Francis, 2016), and it is used in Responsible AI strategies to prevent the ethical risks associated with the development and use of artificial intelligence.

What Is Ethical Risk Management?

Ethical risk refers to when there is a lack of ethical consideration or value implementation, resulting in costs to reputation, operational efficiency, and product quality (Guan, Dong, and Zhao, 2022). This can occur as an overall lack of ethics, as is exhibited when an organization has asked the question if it *can* build a specific AI solution but fails to ask if it *should* in the first place. Or it can occur on an individual value level, when a specific value has been neglected in implementation. For example, a lack of fairness implementation in a dataset can result in unwanted and potentially harmful bias. In either case, an organization will acquire ethical risk when it fails to consider the wider societal impacts of its AI solutions.

There are two different types of ethical risk you are likely to encounter when you begin digging into the potential dangers of AI. First, and the more click-bait worthy of the two, is the existential ethical risk of artificial intelligence. It is existential because it refers to any long-term risk associated with the idea that we will one day develop an AI that we will either lose direct control over the system, or lose control of the consequences of the system. This risk is often centered around the growing fear of the seemingly inevitable development of artificial general intelligence (AGI). AGI, and the subsequent singularity problem (Boden, 2018), focus on the idea that one day we will create an AI that can be applied to any scenario and still produce intelligent results (hence the general). This will then lead to an AI system creating another AI system even more intelligent, repeating the process over and over creating an intelligence boom until eventually reaching super intelligence. Although there is validity to these long-term risks, such as job displacement and a significant decrease in societal well-being, these are not necessarily risks you will be able to directly address. Due to the magnitude and scale of such risks, no one company will ever be able to mitigate them for an entire population. Additionally, the likelihood of such risks occurring is not as high as media and PR stunts would lead you to believe.

Although the existential risks do make for interesting intellectual debates, they can often overshadow the much more tangible and urgent ethical risks an organization will encounter on a daily basis when developing or using AI. This second classification of ethical risks are the true dangers to an organization, as they are not segregated to the long-term future of AI but instead are hidden within poor operational processes, lack of standard AI practices, and uninformed or analyzed decisions, resulting in far more significant costs in time, resources, and people when gone unaddressed. Common tangible risks include reputational damage caused by the discovery of unethical behavior, financial costs of having to retrospectively fix ethical challenges after an AI solution has been deployed, legal fines issued from regulation violations, operational costs due to having to pull faulty models from production, and societal harm caused by manipulative or poorly executed technology, to name a few (Stahl, 2021).

An easy way to differentiate an existential risk from a tangible risk is the ability to relate the risk directly to one of your foundational ethical values. Existential risks have less focus on individual values, and instead focus more on a vague general lack of ethics in AI. On the other hand, tangible risks can be related directly back to the lack of a specific ethical value, and are best uncovered by assessing your AI per each of your foundational ethical values.

Though the tangible risks are numerous and ever evolving, the good news is that it is these tangible ethical risks that an organization can easily address and mitigate with the proper strategy in place. The realization that there are concrete and immediate ethical risks to your organization and its AI should not be daunting or cause for alarm. Instead, it should be empowering as it places control directly back into your hands, as opposed to the hopelessness that is often felt when up against the larger existential risks.

To the Source: Ethical Debt and Drift in AI

How do these immediate ethical risks come about in the first place? We have already covered that ethical risk comes from a lack of ethical values in AI development and use, but how does an organization accumulate such risk? There are two main ways you need to know in which ethical risk is amassed: through ethical drift or through ethical debt.

Let's look at ethical drift first. If you have ever held a product manager or similar position, you will be familiar with the concept of scope creep. Scope creep happens when the scope of a specific project or product was not fully defined from the start, resulting in continuous changes and growth of the original scope, and eventually leading to a gradual drifting away from what was originally intended (Komal et al., 2020). Ethical drift works in much the same way. If the ethical values of a project or product are not clearly defined from the start, then as the project develops, it will inevitably drift further and further away from the original intended purpose (Blanchard and Taddeo, 2023). For example, if a company sets out to develop a fitness tracker app but fails to properly define the value of user privacy before beginning, the app can drift from its intended purpose of helping users take control over their health and instead result in the company selling user data to health insurance companies. While this seems like a drastic difference between intended and actual outcome, and so unlikely to occur, ethical drift happens little by little in everyday decisions. Although the company will probably not go from one extreme to the other with its fitness app, this drift can and does happen over many months, if not years, of development. The important thing to realize here is that strongly defined ethical values, and a process by which to continuously assess a project or product for these values, is essential when it comes to preventing ethical drift and the resulting risk accumulation.

Ethical drift happens when an organization has identified its values, but fails to remain aligned to them. But what happens if the organization is not even aware of its ethical values in the first place? The result is the second source of ethical risk and is known as ethical debt. If you come from a technical background, you will already be familiar with the term technical debt.

Essentially, technical debt describes the business costs of future reworking necessary to fix any easy but limited technical solution that was used in place of a better, but more time-demanding, approach. It is the definition of taking the easy way out, but having to pay for it later. The longer an organization goes without addressing tech debt, the more it will build, exponentially growing in scale and costs to fix overtime (Sculley et al., n.d.). Ethical debt is synonymous to tech debt, but instead of being caused by poor technical decisions, it is caused by poor ethical decisions (Petrozzino, 2021). When an organization has failed to identify the relevant ethical values to its AI, it becomes incredibly difficult to recognize when an ethical decision is being made, let alone make a well-informed and analyzed decision based on foundational ethical values. The longer an organization goes without addressing the necessary values, the more ethical debt is accumulated, the higher the cost it will be to fix the eventual ethical problems.

Going back to our fitness app company example, imagine that instead of starting with the value of user privacy, the company started the project without any regard to privacy at all. The company then starts making critical decisions around data collection and management, but because of the lack of privacy considerations is continuously making questionable decisions in regards to user privacy. Eventually, the company discovers during an audit that its fitness app is in violation of critical privacy regulations, and so is now faced with having to rework its entire data management processes, at great cost. The accumulation of ethical debt due to poor ethical decisions, or even uninformed decisions, is a common source of ethical risk in AI use and development. When taking a risk-based approach to implementing ethics, a strong strategy will address both ethical drift and debt.

Points of Ethical Risk Mitigation Interventions

Now that we understand what ethical risk is and where it can be found, let's bring it back into the context of traditional risk management. When mitigating risk you are working to proactively prevent certain consequences, whether foreseen or unpredicted, from happening. There are four main components to any traditional risk management strategy: identification, assessment, management, and monitoring.

In the identification stage, you will be looking for instances of ethical drift or debt, seeking out any potential points in your decision making relevant to the development or use of AI in your organization that do not align with your foundational ethical values. Remember, you are looking for tangible current risks, such as reputational or legal risks, as opposed to the long-term existential risks associated with AI. The challenge specific to ethical risk in AI is that AI is ever evolving, so you will need to have a strategy in place for both identifying known risks, as well as identifying potentially newly surfaced risks brought about by technological advancements.

After identification comes assessment, during which you will be assessing the likelihood of each of your identified ethical risks occurring, and then prioritizing the order and resources allocated by which you will address such risks. To support this assessment, refer back to your foundational value set and the original three-tier prioritization you established among the values.

Finally, the management and monitoring of ethical risk will rely heavily on internal governance processes spanning all design, development, and deployment phases of your AI solution. With the right risk management strategy in place, preventing such consequences becomes second nature, which in return brings about its own set of benefits. When taking a risk-based approach to ethics, emphasizing risk mitigation in your Responsible AI strategy, you are using a combination of training on ethical risk, fine-tuned AI governance, and continuous assessment of your technology to proactively prevent harmful unintended consequences from occurring.

Ethics as a Tool for Innovation

Flipping over the coin, let's take a look now at how an innovation-based approach to ethics works.

Risk management, especially when risks are easily foreseeable, is fairly straightforward to handle. The same method should work, more or less, for the vast majority of organizations operating within the same sector or developing similar AI solutions. Innovation, on the other hand, is a trickier beast to tackle and does not always come with guaranteed results. Perhaps this is why ethical innovation is often overlooked by organizations looking to execute a successful Responsible AI strategy. Or maybe it's because we are used to hearing ethics used in terms of a constraint, telling us what we should not do, instead of used in a creative capacity to tell us what could possibly be capable of. Whatever the reason is, ethics is often cast into a risk and compliance role, and although this is an incredibly important side to ethics, not creating space to use ethics for innovation purposes is a huge missed opportunity.

Just as the risk-based approach focused on transitioning traditional risk management strategies into addressing ethical risk, so too the innovation-based approach focuses on transitioning traditional innovation strategies into creating ethical innovation. However, if you have ever been involved in an innovation initiative, in whatever capacity, then you are already well aware that innovation is notoriously tricky to execute successfully. Not only do you need to have the right idea that promises to drive new value for your organization, you must also have the right strategy in place to take that idea from creation all the way to implementation. On top of all this, strong innovation looks different for every company. You can't take the methods of a competitor and expect to have the same results. Instead, you need to be highly sensitive to the context of your own organization in order to design an innovation strategy that will work for your business, market, and customer base.

If there are so many variables full of potential pitfalls, why bother with innovation in the first place? Simply put, innovation is the only way in which a company can create and maintain a competitive edge among its competitors. You could have the world's best product, but if you do not continue to innovate in order to stay ahead of the advancements in the market, your top-quality product, and potentially even organization, will soon become a relic of the past.

Take for example Skype, once the leading provider for video calling. The company has long been surpassed by Zoom, a video-calling company that developed later, because Skype failed to respond to changes in demand and innovate fast enough to capture the market for work video conferencing (Stokel-Walker, 2020). This just goes to show that the primary purpose of innovating is to build and maintain a competitive company and offering. Without innovation, it is only a matter of time before an organization is obsolete—and these days with the pace of AI, that timeline has been seriously shrunk.

What Is Ethical Innovation?

If the purpose of innovating is to create a competitive edge, how does this translate to ethics in AI? Simply put, ethics in innovation, otherwise known as ethical innovation, is when the focus on human-centric values is used to gain and sustain a competitive edge. As with any innovation, there is some factor or another that is used as a differentiator and therefore the driver of the competitive edge. In the case of ethical innovation, that differentiator is specifically the ethical values embedded into the organization and its technology.

Take Apple, for example. Starting all the way back in 2014 with an open-letter from CEO Tim Cook, Apple made the strategic decision to be a privacy-sensitive big technology company (Colt, n.d.). Privacy is one of the most common ethical values in technology, as it focuses on respecting the autonomy over personal data. Ever since this shift towards being a privacy-first company, Apple has turned this ethical value into a business advantage through innovative advancements in user security and data tracking management. In turn, these advancements have created a strong differentiator in a global market that is becoming ever more concerned with individual data privacy, winning Apple major market gains among the more privacy-informed and younger generations. Apple took the ethical value of privacy, brought it to the forefront of its innovation strategies, and is now benefiting from the clear competitive edge this ethical innovation approach has created for the company.

Ethics-by-Design

This technique of designing specifically for a selected ethical value is also known as ethics-by-design. Essentially, this technique centers around making either a set of ethical values or a single ethical value a critical KPI for your technology. In order to accomplish this, you must start from the very beginning stages of ideation, laying out exactly which value you will design for and how you will track the success of implementation. This is then carried on throughout the enter design, development, and deployment phases of your AI, as each critical design decision along the way is strategically aligned to support and embody the selected ethical value. It is called ethics-*by-design* to show that the ethical values have not been tacked on at the end, but instead have intentionally been front and center from the very beginning.

Beyond centering innovation around a single ethical value, ethics can also be used to guide decision making into alignment with the organization's overall mission and foundational values. The key to good sustainable innovation is the ability to strategically map out an organization's resources, initiatives, and operations to align to its mission and value proposition. As previously discussed, ethics is a decision-analysis tool best utilized for value alignment. Naturally, as you look to align your AI to your organization's mission, and that mission is based on core foundational values, ethics logically becomes a practical tool in the execution of this alignment. The better aligned, the smoother processes will run, the stronger the creativity becomes, and the more impactful the innovation is all around. So, in addition to value-driven design, innovation strategies can also benefit by using ethics as this essential alignment tool. The important thing to remember is that either way, ethical innovation is when the values of a company and its technology are utilized to create a competitive edge in the market.

Tackling the Misconceptions Holding Ethics Back

When the conversation of ethics in AI first started to reach industry, there was an immediate pushback, especially from technology startups, out of fear that ethics would stifle innovation. Ethics was seen as yet another blocker to successful AI deployment, creating the misconception that we would never be able to reach the full potential of AI if we were hindering it through constraints. The bottom-line question behind AI advancement was whether or not you could do it, leaving little to no room to ask the even more important question of whether or not you should. Although we have come a long way from this initial pushback and ethics has been granted a seat at the table, there are still two misconceptions that continue to cast ethics in the light of an innovation blocker instead of stimulator. Let's take a moment to address them both head on.

First, there is the misconception that values don't matter. As long as the technology works and the customer is willing to pay for it, then what else can ethics add? Essentially, if values, or lack thereof, do not impact the bottom line, then there is no possibility for these values to create a competitive edge for an organization. However, this is a short-sighted misbelief. Values do matter, now more than ever. In a world of ever expanding choice and options, customers need a way to filter their buying decisions through specific factors that matter to them. And it just so happens that one of the major decision factors rests on the values of the company.

Studies have shown that 55 percent of consumers would purchase more products if a company's AI is perceived to be ethical, 34 percent of consumers would completely cut any interactions with a company if its AI resulted in ethical issues, and 97 percent of consumers expect technology companies to behave ethically (McKendrick, n.d.). Whether we acknowledge it or not, humans do not always make decisions based on logic, and instead rely heavily on emotions and values to guide us. Thinking that values do not drive customer buying behavior is essentially actively choosing to ignore one of the most basic laws of human nature, and would be very remiss of the potential to align with these laws to innovate a leading competitive edge.

Second, you can believe that values matter but still misconceive that any form of constraint will always be a blocker to innovation. Ethics is a decision-analysis tool, it provides the layer of perspective that guides our thinking in one direction or another. This can often be interpreted as constraining our thinking, as ethics will filter creativity through the lens of our values. In the world of technology, fueled by the entrepreneurial motto of moving fast and breaking things, we falsely correlated blue-sky thinking with the ability to successfully innovate in AI. Which now creates an overall misconception that the only way to truly achieve great innovative success in AI is to remove all constraints, including the value filter of ethics.

However, as anyone who has ever contributed to an innovation initiative will immediately understand, good innovation always starts with finding the right constraints (Murray and Johnson, 2021). Whether those constraints are financial, human capital, regulatory, or, yes, ethical, creativity is spurred and sparked by the implementation of these controls (Acar, Tarakci, and Knippenberg, 2019). Think of it this way—if you give your team $100k to build an application, they will build it using that entire budget. However, if you cut the budget in half to $50k, they will have to get creative and find different, more cost-effective solutions to building the app that would not have considered otherwise had the constraint not been there in the first place.

Of course, too many constraints will in fact stifle innovation, so it is important to understand when and where these controls are needed. But, when the right balance is struck, constraints bring clarity to the problem at hand, efficiency through prioritization of tasks, and effectiveness to the solution being developed. If you or your team really do see ethics as a constraint, something that enforces a filter to your creativity, then look at making the critical shift in perspective to seeing constraints as something good, even necessary, to successful innovation.

Points of Ethical Innovation Interventions

The purpose of innovation is to create a competitive edge, and the purpose of ethical innovation is to use ethical values to achieve that edge. Where, though, within an organization should this innovation be taking place?

Of course the simple answer to this is that it depends on the organization. However, there are three different places within your organization that you can assess for the potential of implementing ethical innovation. The first, and the most obvious, of the three is implementation on the product level. This means you are looking for opportunities to innovate on your AI solution with the end goal of better aligning your technology to your foundational values. When innovating on the product level, there are many instances in which you can look to implement ethical innovation. Some of these include adding a new value-centered feature, redesigning your metrics of product success with your foundational values, or even starting from scratch to create an entirely new product based on promoting a specific ethical value. The possibilities are endless, but the main point is that this type of ethical innovation happens on the specific technical capacities of your AI solution.

The next point of innovation rests in your AI development processes and is akin to standard process innovation. Process innovation looks at creative ways to make a process either more efficient, effective, or both. When adding ethical innovation into the equation, you are looking to improve your AI development processes by streamlining value alignment and establishing best practices across your entire organization. Although not necessarily glamorous, this process of ethical innovation will be essential to the success of your Responsible AI strategy, as you will come to discover in Chapter 8.

Finally, the third point of innovation, and often the least obvious for ethical innovation, is on the business model itself. Oftentimes it is easy to forget that the business model, and therefore subsequent revenue driver, is one of the biggest influences on the direction of your AI. If your business model does not allow for the necessary value-aligning adjustments to your technology, then any work done to implement ethics in your AI will never be pushed into production.

For example, think of Meta's ad-based revenue model. The more eyes on an advertisement, the more money Meta makes. This leads to a tricky situation with the platform, as it incentivizes the company to find ways to maximize the screen time any single user spends on the platform. This results in manipulative algorithms that play into human behavior and attention spans in order to keep a person attached to their screen and viewing more ads. Now, if someone at Meta wanted to realign these algorithms with the value of facilitating human connection, this would go counter to the needs of the business model as it would pull users away from extended screen time (Lauer, 2020). What this all means is that in order for ethical innovation to take place on a technological level, you must first ensure that the business model is value-aligned and allows for the necessary technical innovation instead of hindering it.

All three—product, process, and business model—provide points of opportunity to implement ethical innovation in your organization. However, it is up to you to identify and pursue which of the three will provide the biggest and most beneficial impact to your company. One way to look at this is through the four different types of innovation: routine, disruptive, radical, and architectural. Routine innovation builds on an organization's current technology and business model, adding incremental improvements on a continuous basis. Disruptive innovation looks at creating a new business model but not necessarily technology, while conversely radical innovation focuses on new technology but not necessarily new business model. Finally, architectural innovation is the most aggressive of the four, as it requires both a new business model and a technology (Satell, 2017).

A mistake that business leaders often make in AI is to go directly for radical innovation, focusing only on how to create a new technological advancement. This can be very difficult to do, and is not necessarily what your company needs. Instead, the best place to start when first working with ethical innovation is on the routine level. Look to improve your existing technology and business model first, before reinventing the wheel. Once you have this under your belt, then you can begin to assess if a change needs to happen on the business model or product level. If the routine ethical advancements of your AI have plateaued, consider looking at innovating on your business model through disruptive innovation. Or conversely, if your business model is effective but your customers are complaining about a lack of an ethical value such as privacy or fairness, then you may want to consider radical innovation of your technology. As with any innovation initiative, you need to listen to your customer and understand their true needs in order to assess what kind of ethical innovation is best suited for your organization.

Finding the Right Direction for Your Strategy

At this point, ethics should be feeling more like a tool you are excited to learn how to harness. In fact, you should be able to start imagining potential use cases for ethics within your organization, or at the very least be able to think of a key decision or two that could benefit from a value-aligning analysis.

A strategy designed to align technology to values is, in theory, something worth doing for its own sake. In practice, however, if such a strategy has been designed without regards to the larger purpose it must serve for the organization, it will only ever remain a pleasant theory in passing. In other words, you may have your compass ready in one hand, and your directions in the other, but do you have any idea what your destination is? You can perfect your ability to use the compass to follow directions, but without a clear destination in mind, you risk simply wandering aimlessly through an ever deepening forest.

Now that you understand the duality of ethics and the opportunity this tool holds for both risk mitigation and innovation, it is time to determine which approach is best suited to the needs of your organization.

04

Calibrating the Compass

Aligning Responsible AI to Your Organization's Objectives

Does it really matter what kind of approach you take to your Responsible AI strategy? At the end of the day, the goal of your strategy is to reflect your foundational values in your AI systems, so taking a risk versus an innovation approach shouldn't matter as long as you reach this goal. Or at least that's how it seems. Let's take a look at the example of WhatsApp and Signal, two popular international messaging apps, to explore this assumption further.

From a feature standpoint, WhatsApp and Signal function in much the same way. You connect your phone number to the app, and then are able to message international numbers, enabling your grandmother in another country to send you unlimited GIFs as a new form of love language. However similar the basic functionality is, the two messaging apps took very different approaches to the value of privacy. On the one hand, WhatsApp took a risk-based approach, focusing on compliance with data privacy laws such as General Data Protection Regulation (GDPR) and the California Consumer Privacy Act (CCPA). Depending on where in the world you are, you will have a different privacy policy that you agreed to in the Terms and Conditions when you downloaded the app. On the other hand, Signal took an innovation-based approach, incorporating privacy-by-design to the app through end-to-end encryption, ensuring that privacy was not an optionality but rather simply how the app fundamentally works.

Both WhatsApp and Signal embedded the value of privacy into their solutions, WhatsApp protecting for privacy while Signal aligning with privacy. In both cases you could say that each organization was successful in reflecting privacy in the messaging app, which was the primary intended purpose, and so should theoretically have the same outcome. However, in January 2021 when WhatsApp updated its privacy policy users panicked that their personal information could be shared with WhatsApp's parent company, Meta. Although this was not the case—the update primarily affected business accounts, and was compliant with data privacy regulations—the damage had been done. In just four days following the privacy update, Signal experienced 7.5 million downloads, the biggest surge in app downloads to date (Hamilton, n.d.). The market had spoken, in the case of personal private messaging, Signal's innovation approach was better aligned to the values and expectations of messaging app users.

Although both a risk and innovation approach to ethics will help you achieve your Responsible AI goals, how you go about reaching those goals will influence the impact your Responsible AI strategy will have on your organization and your ability to achieve your objectives. Which is why in this chapter we are going to take the theory of risk versus innovation approaches in ethics from the previous chapter and practically assess which approach will better serve your organization's needs. We will be covering two tools you can use for this assessment, moral imagination and the Ethics Risk and Innovation framework, as well as walking through an example case of how this assessment works in action. By the end of this chapter, you will be able to take these tools and apply them to your own organization to gain clarity on what kind of approach to ethics will best align your Responsible AI strategy with your organization's mission and objectives.

To Protect or to Promote?

At this point, you may start to already find yourself inclining towards either the risk- or innovation-based approach. This inclination will come either from your personal preference or is influenced by the culture of your company. People with a higher risk tolerance will naturally incline towards the innovation-based approach, while an organizational culture that emphasizes the importance of compliance will naturally influence an inclination towards the risk-based approach.

Whatever your first instinct is when reading the two different approaches, take note of it, as this is your baseline bias that you will need to be aware of. To be clear, this baseline bias is not bad, nor is it good per se. It is simply your preference, and it is perfectly valid to hold. The important thing is that you are able to identify your preference, that way as you move to select one of the two approaches, or a combination, for your organization, you are able to objectively analyze what the best approach is for your company, separate from your own preference.

Aligning With Your Organizational Objectives

The purpose of selecting an approach is to calibrate your compass, or in other words align your Responsible AI strategy with your organization's mission. We will discuss in detail the different risk versus innovation techniques and methods in Part Two, but for now your objective is to understand which approach to emphasize and when for your strategy. A good question to be asking yourself now is which approach will get you closer to achieving your organization's objectives and mission? For example, companies that operate in a highly regulated industry such as finance, or an industry such as healthcare that deals directly with human life, usually tend to lean more towards a risk-based approach. This is because the costs of getting it wrong are so high that no justification would suffice for taking on unnecessary risk. Imagine a healthcare AI that when it works can detect skin rashes on different skin tones, but when it doesn't work costs people their lives due to skin cancer going undetected. The return is a correctly identified rash, but the risk is the cost of a life. Clearly, the focus here should be placed on ensuring that risk is never realized.

Meanwhile, companies that provide consumer goods in highly competitive markets will tend towards an innovation-based approach in search of the elusive competitive edge. For example, think of the market for personal laptops and the consumer trying to make the decision between a Mac or PC. There is the potential that the increased privacy measures could sway privacy-sensitive consumers in the direction of the Mac. This results in the potential for high return, whereas the lack of additional privacy measures does not create an extreme risk. When the return outweighs the risk, it is worthwhile considering the innovation-based approach to try and capture that potential high return.

If you are taking a risk-based approach, your Responsible AI strategy will focus on providing the solutions necessary to protecting for your foundational values. On the other hand, if you are taking an innovation-based approach, your Responsible AI strategy will focus instead on establishing the resources necessary to promote value alignment.

Striking a Balance

This all being said, it is important to stress that selecting an approach to your Responsible AI strategy does not have to be an all or nothing decision. Although ethics has the ability to be a dual purpose tool, it does not imply that this duality is a dichotomy. You can have a combination of the risk and innovation approach within the same strategy; in fact it is encouraged.

The decision to emphasize one or the other approach is also not a final, hard-set decision. Keep in mind that when it comes to implementing ethics in AI, you need to remain flexible. AI changes at such a rapid pace, you need to be able to adapt to the advancements and adjust your strategic approach when necessary. Typically, a company will begin with a heavier risk-based approach to ensure they are both legally compliant and ethically safeguarded, essentially making sure that they haven't missed something that could cause significant harm. As a company matures in its Responsible AI strategy, the emphasis will naturally shift more in the direction of innovation. This is because once an organization is able to sustainably monitor and address all major risks, it will be able to free up both time and resources to look at how it can stretch beyond the risks and start to reach some of the bigger rewards. So whatever combination of risk and innovation you decide works best for your organization, keep in mind that this can change overtime.

It should be clear now what each approach entails, and how each could be used to support your organization's objectives. Which leads us now to the question of how to assess which approach, or combination of approaches, is best suited to your organization's needs. You may have an idea already clearly formed in your mind, or you may be completely in the dark without even an inclination of where to begin. Either way, your next step is to map out exactly what approach you will start with for each of your foundational values. A great way to visualize this is to fill out an Ethics Risk and Innovation framework. This framework helps you break down your potential risks and competitive edges per foundational value, enabling you to gain a clear understanding of how to best calibrate your compass in order to align your Responsible AI strategy with your organization's mission.

Before we dive into the Ethics Risk and Innovation framework, though, you must first understand the concept of moral imagination and how you will need to use it.

Moral Imagination in AI

Moral imagination is a term that comes straight out of moral philosophy, and in the context of artificial intelligence and business may feel a bit misplaced. However, moral imagination is a natural part of your personal ethical decision-making process, and so all we are doing here is surfacing this part of the process for you to utilize on a strategic level for your organization. Philosophers have never been known for their creative terms, so moral imagination is fairly self-explanatory just by name alone. Essentially, moral imagination is the process of imagining different outcomes of an ethical decision, analyzing the imagined outcomes to understand which is most desirable, and then making a decision based on which outcome you most want (Narvaez and Mrkva, 2014).

For example, you have to choose whether or not to tell your best friend that their spouse is cheating on them. In this instance, you can imagine how distraught your friend will be if you tell them, while on the other hand you can imagine how destroyed your friend would be if they found out you knew and didn't tell them. Having imagined these possible outcomes and many more, you are able to assess which decision is most likely to result in the best outcome, and so you choose to tell your friend. The reason it is called moral imagination is twofold. First, the moral comes from the fact that it is being used in a morally laden scenario, or in other words, to help aid you in making an ethical decision. Second, the imagination comes from the fact that you are not entirely sure what decision will lead to what outcome, but based on your previous experiences, and perhaps some advice and research, you can imagine what action will lead to which effect. So although imagination may seem like it has no place in the world of AI, it is in fact a very important tool when it comes to making informed ethical decisions.

What does this have to do with the Ethics Risk and Innovation framework and calibrating the approach of your Responsible AI strategy? In order to fully utilize the Ethics Risk and Innovation framework, you are going to need to engage with your moral imagination. As we walk through the framework, you are going to be tempted to do a quick Google search for risks and benefits of various ethical values in AI, and populate your framework using only search-engine results. I highly advise that you challenge yourself to stretch beyond the obvious in this exercise, and push your moral imagination past common generic answers and towards contextually sensitive reflections. The more relevant to your organization you can make your answers, the stronger your strategy will become. With this in mind, let's get started.

The Ethics Risk and Innovation Framework

The Ethics Risk and Innovation framework is a conceptual tool designed to help you examine not only what approach to ethics is best fit to your organization's needs, but also to explore the potential pitfalls and opportunities of

TABLE 4.1 The Ethics Risk and Innovation Framework

VALUE	WORST CASE	BEST CASE	FOCUS
Fairness			
Privacy			
Autonomy			

your foundational values. By working your way through the framework, you will be able to confidently determine how to shape your Responsible AI strategy so that it aligns with your organization's objectives.

To begin, make four columns and label them as follows: Value, Worst Case, Best Case, and Focus. Next, take your foundational value set from Chapter 2 and add one value per row in the first column. For this example, we are going to take a simplified foundational value set of Fairness, Privacy, and Autonomy. When done, you should have the start to your framework that looks similar to Table 4.1.

Worst Case Scenario: Imagining Doomsday

Now it's time to start using your moral imagination as you go to fill out the "Worst Case" column. This column is your dumpster fire, capturing everything that could possibly go wrong, no matter how outrageous or likely it seems. Going value by value, ask yourself what the consequences would be if you experience a lack of each individual value in your AI or even organization. If you're stuck, you can start with some simple research into common risks for each of your foundational values. It can also be helpful to create a working group to go through each of the values, as it is important to ensure you are gathering multiple perspectives on worst case scenarios. For example, a lack of fairness always results in some kind of unwanted and harmful bias, but what you want to do in this framework is think of what kind of specific biases there could possibly be in the context of your AI and company. As you make your way through your doomsday scenarios, be sure to bullet point them in the Worst Case column.

It is normal to feel a sense of dread or worry when filling out the Worst Case column. It can be overwhelming to list out all the possible terrible things that could go wrong. However, remember that in this case, ignorance is not bliss. It is better to be fully aware of all the potential consequences and harms rather than to remain in the dark. You cannot work to prevent a harm if you are not aware of its existence in the first place.

Let's say that the simplified value set from Table 4.1 belongs to an American mid-sized company called HireAI which provides HR hiring software and operates out of the state of New York. Specifically, the company provides a platform for customers to conduct both recorded and live video interviews, using speech-to-text systems to transcribe the interviews. Once the once interviews have been transcribed, an algorithm is used to evaluate the quality of the interview candidate for the interviewing customer. HireAI is also in the process of piloting some emotion AI systems on the platform that would analyze the video for tone of voice, energy, and facial expressions, using the information to assess the interviewee for different personality traits. Putting our moral imagination to the test, the Worst Case column should start to look something like Table 4.2.

TABLE 4.2 The Ethics Risk and Innovation Framework: Worst Case Scenario

VALUE	WORST CASE	BEST CASE	FOCUS
Fairness	• Non-native English speakers continuously receive low scores on intelligence metrics • Women are tagged as having a lack of ambition due to vocabulary choice • System has difficulty registering faces of people with darker skin tones		
Privacy	• Personal sensitive information from interviews is leaked • Interview evaluations are accessible to anyone in the company, so internal employees interviewing the job can read evaluations and get an unfair advantage • Interviewee is unable to ask for the removal of their personal information from the system from the interview process is complete		
Autonomy	• The system suggests interviewees for positions even if the interviewee has stated they do not want that job • Interviewee cannot object to interview questions that may be sensitive or offensive • Emotion AI does not allow for significant differences in self-expression		

Best Case Scenario: Imagining Blue Skies

Now that you are thoroughly concerned about the scope of risks that go hand in hand with your AI, let's flip the coin and put your moral imagination to a positive use and fill out the "Best Case" column. This column is your cloud nine, capturing all your best case scenarios. Again, going value by value, make your way down the column filling out all the ways through which the selected value could positively impact your AI or organization. Ask yourself what the benefits could be if each value was fully embedded into your AI solution, and be sure to think in all terms from product quality, to social impact, even to financial benefit. Again, it is helpful to create a working group for this exercise so as to ensure multiple perspectives. Taking fairness for example again, the presence and successful embedding of fairness leads to better representation of different demographics in your data and eventual algorithm, which in turn leads to a better product for a wider range of users. This results in a larger and more satisfied customer base. As you work your way through the Best Case scenarios, don't be afraid to include financial and business gains in your bullet points. It may feel strange at first to be thinking of ethical values in terms of profit, but good ethics makes for better business, so it is only natural to include.

Continuing with our example of HireAI and its interviewing platform, the Best Case column should look something like Table 4.3.

Focus: Understanding Your Approach

Hopefully flexing your moral imagination to cover best case scenarios has translated some of those risks concerns into encouraging hope over what is possible. Having completed both the worst and best case scenario columns, you are now looking at the ethical spectrum that your AI and organization is sitting on. From here, we can start to analyze what focused approach your Responsible AI strategy will need in order to move you further from the worst case and towards the best case scenarios.

You will need to keep your organization's mission and objectives in mind as you go to fill out the final column titled "Focus." Your goal will be to determine whether a risk- or innovation-emphasized approach is needed per value. If it is risk-based, then fill in "risk" into the final column, and if it innovation-based, then fill in "innovation."

You may already be able to fill out the Focus column without further analysis, having had a clear need surface during the moral imagination

TABLE 4.3 The Ethics Risk and Innovation Framework: Best Case Scenario

VALUE	WORST CASE	BEST CASE	FOCUS
Fairness	• Non-native English speakers continuously receive low scores on intelligence metrics • Women are tagged as having a lack of ambition due to vocabulary choice • System has difficulty registering faces of people with darker skin tones	• Platform helps customers locate and mitigate their own biases during the interview process • Helps customers expand their talent pool to include new hiring characteristics that had been previously ignored • Emotion AI is built using robust datasets on different cultures, enabling different forms of expression from interviewees	
Privacy	• Personal sensitive information from interviews is leaked • Interview evaluations are accessible to anyone in the company, so internal employees interviewing the job can read evaluations and get an unfair advantage • Interviewee is unable to ask for the removal of their personal information from the system from the interview process is complete	• Data on interviewees is only shared with the relevant interviewer • Interviewee can opt-out of sensitive data collection that does not impact hiring decisions • Interviewee doesn't feel like they are being tracked or monitored unnecessarily during the interview process	
Autonomy	• The system suggests interviewees for positions even if the interviewee has stated they do not want that job • Interviewee cannot object to interview questions that may be sensitive or offensive • Emotion AI does not allow for significant differences in self-expression	• Interviewee has the ability to apply for multiple relevant positions as they choose • Interviewer can set preferences on characteristics or experience needed for a specific role • Interviewee or interviewer can object to an analysis from the platform that they feel is misrepresentative	

exercise. It could be the case that one of your values has such an extreme potential risks, or such an exciting innovation opportunity, associated with it that your decision is made clear. However, this may not always be the case, as the risks and opportunities seem to be equally important at first glance. If this is the case, we can further break down your Ethics Risk and Innovation framework to help guide a deeper analysis of your options.

To do so, we are going to break out the values into separate tables. You will have two sets of tables, one for Worst Case and one for Best Case, and each will be used to evaluate the scenarios associated with each of your values. Starting with Worst Case, you will list your values in the first column, the worst case scenarios in the second column. For each scenario you will be assigning two numbers. The first number will rank likelihood of that risk occurring on a scale of 1–3, with 1 being highly likely and 3 being very unlikely. The second number will rank the harm that will be caused if that risk were to occur, on a scale of 1–3, with 1 being extremely harmful and 3 being little to no harm. Be sure to rank each bullet point on both scales for all values.

To help visualize this scale, you can break out the Worst Case column into its own table. Using HireAI as an example, your Worst Case table will look something like Table 4.4.

Now you will need to repeat the same ranking for the Best Case column. Just as with the Worst Case, you will rank each scenario twice on a scale of 1–3. Your first number will be for the likelihood of the scenario occurring, again with 1 being highly likely to achieve while 3 is unlikely. The second number will be for the benefit you stand to gain, with 1 being highly beneficial if the scenario were to occur, and 3 being only slightly beneficial, if at all.

TABLE 4.4 The Ethics Risk and Innovation Framework: Focus

VALUE	WORST CASE	LIKELIHOOD	HARM
Fairness	Non-native English speakers continuously receive low scores on intelligence metrics	2	2
	Women are tagged as having a lack of ambition due to vocabulary choice	3	2
	System has difficulty registering faces of people with darker skin tones	2	1
Total		7	5

TABLE 4.5 The Ethics Risk and Innovation Framework: The Best Case

VALUE	BEST CASE	LIKELIHOOD	BENEFIT
Fairness	Platform helps customers locate and mitigate their own biases during the interview process	2	3
	Helps customers expand their talent pool to include new hiring characteristics that had been previously ignored	3	2
	Emotion AI is built using robust datasets on different cultures, enabling different forms of expression from interviewees	3	2
Total		8	7

Breaking the Best Case column out into its own table to visualize rankings and using our HireAI example, you should end up with something like Table 4.5.

As you see from the example tables, after totaling the numbers of each ranked columns, the Worst Case scored lower on both scales than the Best Case rankings. What this means is that the Worst Case scenario is more likely to occur, and stands to risk greater harms if any of the scenarios do occur. In other words, the risks outweigh the potential gains for fairness in this case. What that means is that for fairness, you will want to start with a risk-based approach as that is where the greater impact will be had.

Repeat the ranking process for each of your values, filling out the Focus column as you go with the results of your rankings. Keep an watchful eye as you fill out the rankings for any scenarios that rank 1 in likelihood to happen, as well as 1 in level of impact, be that positive or negative. If you have a 1-1 scenario in your Worst Cases, this is a hot spot that you will need to immediately address. If it is a 1-1 scenario in your Best Case, though, this is a golden opportunity that should be likewise immediately addressed. You should end up with a complete framework looking something like Table 4.6.

Congratulations, you have now calibrated your compass. You should now be able to clearly see which approach, or combination of approaches, is needed per your foundational values in your Focus column. Depending on your organization and its needs, you may have a heavier inclination towards

TABLE 4.6   The Ethics Risk and Innovation Complete Framework

VALUE	WORST CASE	BEST CASE	FOCUS
Fairness	• Non-native English speakers continuously receive low scores on intelligence metrics • Women are tagged as having a lack of ambition due to vocabulary choice • System has difficulty registering faces of people with darker skin tones	• Platform helps customers locate and mitigate their own biases during the interview process • Helps customers expand their talent pool to include new hiring characteristics that had been previously ignored • Emotion AI is built using robust datasets on different cultures, enabling different forms of expression from interviewees	RISK
Privacy	• Personal sensitive information from interviews is leaked • Interview evaluations are accessible to anyone in the company, so internal employees interviewing for the job can read evaluations and gain an unfair advantage • Interviewees are unable to ask for the removal of their personal information from the system after the interview process is complete	• Data on interviewees is only shared with the relevant interviewer • Interviewees can opt-out of sensitive data collection that does not impact hiring decisions • Interviewees don't feel like they are being tracked or monitored unnecessarily during the interview process	RISK
Autonomy	• The system suggests interviewees for positions even if the interviewee has stated they do not want that job • Interviewees cannot object to interview questions that may be sensitive or offensive • Emotion AI does not allow for significant differences in self-expression	• Interviewees have the ability to apply for multiple relevant positions as they choose • Interviewers can set preferences on characteristics or experience needed for a specific role • Interviewees or interviewers can object to an analysis from the platform that they feel is misrepresentative	INNOVATION

risk or innovation. That is perfectly fine for the start, but eventually it will be your goal to have a balance of risk and innovation among your values.

It is good practice at this point, though, to gut check your results by asking yourself whether protecting your organization from the risks associated with any given value will better support your organization's mission, or if promoting the benefits associated with the same value will provide better support to the mission? Ideally, your gut check will align with what is already listed in the Focus column. However, if it does differ, then it is best to seek a second opinion.

Where to Next?

By now, you are well on your way to understanding what is needed out of your Responsible AI strategy. In Chapter 1 we covered what ethics is, why it matters for Responsible AI, and how to conceptualize it as the decision-analysis tool you need to achieve full success of your AI solutions. In other words, you learned how the compass works. In Chapter 2 we built on your understanding of ethics and uncovered the foundational value set, your directions to be followed, that will sit at the core of your Responsible AI strategy. And finally, after having established your compass and your directions, we dove into what that final destination is that you are aiming for. By calibrating your compass, we were able to understand whether you need a risk, innovation, or combination approach to each of your foundational values in order to align your Responsible AI strategy with your organization's mission and objectives.

With all this in mind, it's now time to start building your actual strategy.

05

Five Reasons Why You Shouldn't Invest in Responsible AI

And One Reason Why You Should

At this point, your interest should be at least peaked in the prospect of unlocking ethics as a decision-analysis tool for your organization. But if you're anything like me, there still remains a nagging question to this whole ethics thing: why are we doing it in the first place? In theory ethics sounds like an interesting exercise that comes with some vague benefits attached. But in a fast-paced competitive world driven by an AI revolution, you need more than just the promise of future benefits to make the business case for ethics tempting enough, let alone the whole transformational change that is Responsible AI.

I remember back in the early days of Ethical Intelligence, when I was testing different Responsible AI services through trial and error, I was often taken aback by the responses I would get to both my company and services. It was always a mixed bag in terms of reaction, some were interested, others skeptical, and still others generally supportive. But across this variety of responses, there was always a common underlying theme—people were always excited to hear that a company, and even profession of AI Ethicist, like mine, existed. Seems a bit odd to have someone tell you that they are so glad to hear that the job you do is out there in this world, right? When was the last time you told your bank teller, your hairdresser, or the data scientist down the hall that you were glad their profession existed? And not only were people excited to hear my profession existed, but they had a genuine interest in whether I had a growing number of clients for my business.

In the world of startups it is common to ask how your numbers are growing, but the questions I had about Ethical Intelligence were different in nature. It felt almost as though the inquirer was hungry for reassurance, almost begging to hear that there were AI-driven companies out there that cared enough to invest time and resources into something like ethics. Intrinsically, we all seem to share, for the most part, this underlying desire for the industry of Responsible AI and Ethics to not only exist, but to be a vibrant and growing one. Not because of the business opportunity it holds, but because of the larger promise to society it implies. We are afraid of the technology we are creating, or at the very least concerned with the risks, and so we crave the reassurance that the companies out there pushing the cutting edge of artificial intelligence forward are doing so in a way that puts the well-being of humanity at large in the center of the conversation.

The tricky part, however, is that even though we may all share this desire to see our human values reflected into the technology we are creating, this deeply held desire does not always translate into the high priority business case we need to drive change. Although some of you will whole heartedly agree, others will feel a vague neutrality, and still others of you will down right disagree with me, I can guarantee that no matter your opinion, you will all agree that we need more than the argument "because it's the right thing to do" in order to stimulate any degree of adoption for Responsible AI at the scale necessary to enact significant change in our technology practices today.

Simply put, we don't just need a why for Responsible AI, we need a why rooted in real business and technological impact.

So now the question is, what is this why and where do we find it? I could spend this entire chapter outlining for you all the reasons why Responsible AI creates positive business impact, improved AI product quality, reduces fines and development costs, increases top-talent retention, and more. But a quick Google search will do the trick just as well, bringing you a steady stream of content on the reasons why you should invest in Responsible AI for your organization. I also know that a laundry list of "should dos" never results in creating the desired feeling of "must do," and that in the world of business there is a large gap between should and must when it comes to actual execution. So, instead of a list of reasons why you should invest in Responsible AI for your organization, I am going to try something a little different, something that will hopefully push you over the "should do" to "must do" edge.

I'm going to tell you all the reasons why you shouldn't invest in Responsible AI.

The Five Reasons Why Not to Invest

Seems a bit strange, right? I, of all people, should be trying to convince you that Responsible AI is a worthwhile investment, not giving you the reasons for why you shouldn't bother with it. It's easy enough to find information on why Responsible AI matters, what's harder to find are reasons why Responsible AI doesn't matter for business, even though most companies can give plenty of excuses for not investing into Responsible AI when asked. Over the years, though, I've heard plenty of reasons, some more valid than others, for why not to embark on Responsible AI. And now, after much time and deliberation, I have managed to boil the why nots down into five simple reasons, all of which I am going to share with you now in the hopes of finally giving you the full picture of what it means to implement Responsible AI.

Number One: Responsible AI is a Long-term Strategy in a Short-term Market

There is no denying it: the world of artificial intelligence moves at such break neck speeds that even those working on the cutting edge of the technology are continuously suffering from whiplash. With new technological advances becoming what feels like almost daily occurrences, the market is continuously in flux, and businesses must learn how to adapt or quickly become obsolete. No one is safe from the impact of AI. Startups that were thriving one day are shutting down the next, while even industry giants fear that if they don't keep pace with new solutions, they will soon be left behind.

This creates the pressure to view technology and the market as a cycle of short-term problems to solve. How can you possibly look to plan five years in advance when you can't even predict what the market, let alone the AI developments, will look like in the next five months? While the AI development cycle continues to shrink, and the ever-mounting pressure to deliver new products or get left behind grows, it becomes more and more difficult to look beyond the short-term problems to fix and opportunities to grab.

However important it may be to plan for the long run, it can be difficult to devote time and attention towards long-term benefits when it can be so easy to go for the short-term gains. This is where the first reason not to invest in Responsible AI lies. According to research done by MIT and BCG, it takes around three years for an organization to see the business impact of any Responsible AI initiative (Stackpole, 2023). So although Responsible AI promises to bring with it improved AI product quality, more sustainable business, and an increase in original innovation, all of which are very real and very valid measures of significant business impact, it is a long-term strategy. If you are looking for immediate short-term business impact for your organization when it comes to AI, then investing in Responsible AI may not be the best fit.

But before you make your decision on whether or not you can afford to implement a strategy that may take up to three years before you see significant impact, let's consider three important points of contextualization to that number. First, the average amount of time it takes to reach ROI for any given AI investment is 1.2–1.6 years. Although this is half the time of a Responsible AI investment, the average ROI for AI is only 1.3 percent. Imagine, though, what that ROI could look like if the failure rate for AI was reduced by 28 percent which is the average failure reduction rate for organizations with Responsible AI practices (Renieris, Kiron, and Mills, 2022). Second, Responsible AI is still a new practice, with novel solutions and routes to increased efficiently being released almost monthly. It may take up to three years to realize business impact from Responsible AI at this point in time, but three years is not a definitive number, it is only a starting point for a young and vibrant field. And third, it very well may take you three years to realize any kind of business impact, but if 52 percent and counting of AI-driven companies have started investing into some level of Responsible AI in 2023, you are going to be far behind more than half of the industry by 2026. One way or another the time will pass. It just depends if the time passing is getting you closer to realizing new business impacts, or if you are instead letting it slip through your fingers. Regardless of what you do, Responsible AI is coming and you need to make a decision.

Number Two: Ethics Requires You to Slow Down

Artificial intelligence itself is already a highly complex technology to develop or even simply use. With hundreds of different factors going into a single critical decision, the thought of adding one more thing to your lengthy list of to-dos can feel overwhelming, unnecessary, and a demand on time that you don't necessarily have. The problem here is that in order to use ethics as a decision-analysis tool, you do in fact need to add yet one more consideration to your list of decision factors for your AI. This of course will add time to that critical decision-making process, as you will need to slow down enough to consider whether you are protecting or aligning for your foundational values. On top of this, implementing a Responsible AI strategy complete with action plans, initiatives, and changes to the AI development life cycle, requires, you guessed it, time. Responsible AI is not something you set up to run automatically in the background, it is a foreground conversation and practice. So, when it comes to utilizing ethics and implementing Responsible AI, it can really feel like you are having to slow down your AI development life cycles in order to account for the additional steps and discussions.

Instead of throwing spaghetti at the wall to see what sticks during the AI life cycle, you not only have to take the time to analyze why the individual noodles of spaghetti are sticking to the wall, but also to consider if you should even be throwing the spaghetti in the first place. Sounds exhausting, right? If you already feel strapped for time in the context of the rapidly changing environment of AI, and can't possibly imagine having to slow down to find the additional effort needed to execute on ethics, then perhaps Responsible AI is not for you.

Before you make your decision, though, let's contextualize this fact again. The effort required to successfully utilize ethics as a decision-analysis tool can sound draining, but do you know what is also exhausting? Getting to the end of an AI project life cycle, going to deploy your model, watching it fail, pulling it out of production, and having to start all the way at the beginning of the cycle due to a simple mistake that should have been caught along the way. Let's recall that, on average, Responsible AI reduces AI failure rates by 28 percent. This is no fluke in the system, the reason Responsible AI reduces failure rates is exactly because of the time and consideration for values and risks it embeds into the AI life cycle. One way or another you will eventually have to face the potential risks, the regulatory compliance, and the value alignment considerations for your AI solutions. It is only a matter of when in the life cycle you will have to take these factors into consideration. Is it at the start of the life cycle as you utilize Responsible AI frameworks to predict and proactively design for these considerations, or is it when you are having to pull yet another model from production and having to retrospectively fix problems that could have been prevented in the first place? When you look at it this way, you start to question whether slowing down for ethics is really a matter of slowing down at all, or is instead a matter of strategically managing your AI risk portfolio.

There is an old contrarian adage a good friend of mine Dave Barnes likes to quote from his time in the US Military that goes you must slow down to speed up. Essentially, when you slow down enough at the start to truly understand what you are doing and fully clarify the direction you need to go in, then you end up speeding past those who started with speed and ended up having to slow down to try to figure out what keeps breaking. Clarity is the true friend of speed, and nothing brings clarity like Responsible AI and ethics.

Number Three: Responsible AI Costs Financial and Human Capital

Artificial Intelligence takes a significant amount of investment, costing anywhere between $10,000 to well over $500,000 for a single AI project, not to mention the amount of human capital and specialized professionals you will need for execution. With the costs of AI significantly high, it can be hard to justify another budget line item to add to the mix. Unfortunately, it should come as no surprise that Responsible AI is an additional cost to AI enablement and that in order to implement any ethics-based initiative, you will need to invest time, people, and money. How much exactly depends on the depth of your commitment to Responsible AI, the complexity of your AI systems and the size of your organization.

There are of course ways to cut corners in terms of cost. Thanks to the vibrancy of the AI Ethics field, there is a plethora of resources available open-access online. From free educational material to open-access toolkits and frameworks, you can find the basics of a Responsible AI practice for free online. However, keep in mind that these shortcuts will still cost you one way or another. There may be a quantity of resources available, but the quality and applicability to your exact needs will vary. For example, there's plenty to sort through when it comes to finding the right educational material. High-quality knowledge and training in ethics is essential, but with thousands of blogs, online courses, and podcasts available, it can be next to impossible to discern quality education from the noise of mass content. The same goes for the open-access frameworks and toolkits.

Although there are many high-quality Responsible AI frameworks and toolkits produced by reputable organizations available for free online, the problem you may face with these is the applicability to your organization and challenges. The problem with these free frameworks is not that they are not well researched and developed, it's that they are, by nature, for general purpose. And, as we have learned from the first few chapters of this book, the devil is in the details of Responsible AI. General purpose frameworks just won't cut it. They are a great starting point but when put to the test you will quickly reach the outer limits of viability as soon as you begin to ask contextualized questions. For success in Responsible AI, you need quality and customized solutions, both of which cost capital. This capital can come from paying external suppliers for Responsible AI solutions, it can come from investing internal personnel, or it can even come from combination of both. So, if you are not ready to invest both the finical and human capital necessary to execute on Responsible AI, then perhaps you should consider an alternative direction.

Again allow me to contextualize the costs of Responsible AI within the wider picture of basic AI. Recall that one AI project alone can cost upwards of $500,000. At such a high investment cost, you would logically want to do everything in your power to ensure a return on that investment, yet somehow the failure rate of AI projects is between 83–92 percent. Now imagine that there was a solution that could reduce that failure rate down to the range of 55–64 percent. The costs saved from the 28 percent reduction in AI failures would far outweigh whatever the costs of the solution would be, right? For the sake of the argument, let's say you are investing into 100 AI projects at $250,000 a piece, totaling a $25 million investment in AI. If you are operating with the standard failure rate of 83–92 percent for those 100 projects, then you risk losing $20.8–$23 million in failed AI projects. However, if you were to implement the solution that reduces the failure rates to 55–64 percent, then you are cutting failure costs down to $13.8-$16 million, saving you 28 percent of your initial AI investment thanks to the reduction in AI project failure rate. Of course, this is all hypothetical in terms of costs savings, but the 28 percent reduction in AI failure rate is a very real outcome of Responsible AI. So, although Responsible AI does cost finical and human capital, be sure you do not get lost in the weeds of budget lines and instead take the step back to view Responsible AI in the wider picture of AI investment.

Number Four: There are No Straight Answers in Ethics*

[*Exceptions may apply]

If you have ever had the chance to ask an ethicist the open-ended question about how to apply ethics to AI, you are very familiar with the frustration you feel when the ethicist tells you simply "it depends." Sometimes I think we ethicists run the risk of being written off as broken records caught on loop of "it depends." I have to say it frustrates us as much as it does you. However, we are not frustrated because that the answer to general questions "depends" on further context, but because we are expected to supply blanket solutions to very complex problems that really, truly do depend on context. Ethical challenges and solutions have been, and always will be, contextual by nature, which means there is no universal playbook that tells you all the definitive answers to every possible ethics problem you could face in AI. If there were, then every single answer would have a little asterisk next to it with a footnote following to say "exceptions may apply."

In the world of AI, this hint of relativity when it comes to ethical solutions can be infuriating when you are trying to code for definitive answers. In AI, you are striving for clarity and certainty in your outputs, so operating in the abstract and uncertainty of ethics can feel like too far of a leap. We want to be able to definitively say "this is right" or "this is wrong" about our AI solutions, especially when there is so much risk on the line thanks to the scale and scope of AI. The gray zone of ethics also makes the ethical challenges annoyingly open-ended, as there is no "one-stop" or "one-size-fits-all" solution. Ethical challenges are ongoing, the progression of identifying, solving, managing, and monitoring ethics problems is a cyclical process, not an end destination. Essentially, if you are looking for one-off clear-cut solutions to achieve making AI ethical, then I am sorry to tell you that you have set off on an impossible task, and perhaps Responsible AI is not the right solution for you.

However, I want to draw an important distinction here. Although I am confirming that ethics is an "it depends" kind of solution, I have not said the same for Responsible AI. As I have been stressing throughout these initial chapters of this book, there are definitive solutions when it comes to enabling Responsible AI practices within your organization. There are countless ways in which AI can go wrong, but the times that AI goes right all have similar attributes rooted in Responsible AI best practices. So although ethics may be tricky to pull general answers out of, there are universally applicable solutions when it comes to implementing Responsible AI in your organization. And it is once you have these Responsible AI practices in place, that the contextualization and variability of ethics is no longer a blocker, but instead becomes an advantage.

How? Well although there are no overarching one-size-fits-all answers to ethics in AI, there are very clear universal guidelines that ethical values provide. These guidelines, based on the values we hold as individuals and as a society, act as creative constraints on what we are and are not willing to accept from each other, as well as our AI systems. It is through these guiding values that we are able to gain clarity and direction for our innovation practices. You already have your technical and business specifications, both of which require creative thinking. Think of ethics as an additional specs layer forcing better and stronger creativity within your teams. Now, the fact that ethics has no straight answers, only guidelines in need of context, works in your favor as those guidelines become the creative constraints needed to stimulate innovative problem solving, instead of relying on a one-size-fits all answer. In fact, companies leading in Responsible AI implementation have reported not only an increase in product quality thanks to this creative stimulus, but also up to 43 percent increase in innovation speed (Mills et al., 2022). Sometimes a little bit of constrained uncertainty is all you need to create remarkable solutions.

Number Five: External Communications about Responsible AI Can Be Risky to Navigate

Sometimes speaking publicly about Responsible AI initiatives can feel like a lose-lose situation. On the one hand, you are risking something called ethics-washing. Much like green-washing, ethics-washing occurs when a company is making claims for being ethical in its practices, when in actuality there is no substance backing up the statements (van Maanen, 2022). A classic example of ethics-washing is when an AI-driven organization markets itself as being an ethical company, but the extent of its ethics initiatives is a list of Responsible AI values on its website and a few blog posts about the importance of values. There is the promise of action, but in reality it is merely a promise with no action to fulfill it, and values are nothing if not backed by actions. Although it may seem harmless to advertise being an ethical company without any significant backing to the statement, the truth of the matter is that it is only a matter of time before some decision reveals the lack of Responsible AI in your organization to the market. And these slip-ups cost. Just ask Volkswagen, a company that claimed sustainability yet hid its true emissions rates from the public, resulting in a $33.3 billion cost to the company when revealed (BBC News, 2022).

It feels like there is an easy solution to mitigate this risk, just don't claim things that you aren't doing when it comes to ethics. Seems easy enough, expect that is only half of the risk associated with Responsible AI external communications. On the other hand, your actions could match your statements, and you can still risk backlash. Ethics can be a highly sensitive subject, and amid what has been termed "cancel culture" there is a significant risk to being "canceled" even when you are acting in accordance to your values that you should be aware of. Cancel culture can be a fickle creature to try and navigate, as different values or opinions that were trending the week before are now taboo just a week later. Making any kind of definitive statement about anything, let alone about values, can become a potential hotbed for PR backlash in this complicated environment. So, when it comes to external communications around Responsible AI, you can risk ethics-washing or you can risk cancel culture, creating what can often feel like a lose-lose dichotomy. Meanwhile, Responsible AI is quickly becoming an expected standard, requiring companies to speak about their efforts to some extent. If your organization is not prepared to navigate the delicate intricacies of external communications on Responsible AI, then perhaps this is not the solution for you.

However, there are two contextual points that need to be added to this dilemma. First, the risk of ethics-washing or cancel culture is really only significantly present when your communications teams are disconnected from your Responsible AI initiatives. Marketing and PR teams are not often seen as having a significant role to play in the execution of Responsible AI, when in fact they play a pivotal role in mitigating this exact challenge. As we will discuss in depth in Chapter 13, any team responsible for external communications within an organization needs to be included in your Responsible AI initiatives. They are the best resource to understanding how different actions will be perceived on the market, helping predict and mitigate the risk of reputational damage. They are the ones responsible for accurately communicating what your organization is and is not doing internally in terms of Responsible AI, and so can mitigate the risks of ethics-washing. The second point of context is that of the companies actively implementing Responsible AI and effectively communicating their efforts, 48 percent of those companies experience significant enhanced brand differentiation in their industry (Renieris, Kiron, and Mills, 2022). The potential for positive brand differentiation using Responsible AI breaks this false lose-lose dichotomy, showing that it is possible to avoid the double edged risk of ethics-washing and cancel culture, if and only if external communications are handled responsibly.

Why You Shouldn't Invest

From investment costs, to long-term timescales, to lack of black and white answers, these five reasons to not invest in Responsible AI encapsulate and summarize all the potential rational reasons why it might not be the right solution for you. Responsible AI and Ethics costs money, it takes time, and it comes with its own unique set of risks. Pick any of the five, and you will have a valid reason for why not to embark on this journey.

However, as you work your way through the reasons, there are a few things to keep in mind. Responsible AI requires financial investment, but so does AI. Responsible AI requires time and specialized professionals, but so does AI. Responsible AI comes with a unique set of risks, but so does AI. When you take a step back and look at the five reasons why not to invest in Responsible AI, you begin to see that these reasons are very similar to the reasons why you wouldn't invest in basic AI. It costs money, it takes time, and there are risks to investing in AI. And yet we still do. Some $91.2 billion in 2022 worth of investment proving that we do (Stanford University, 2023). We do so simply because the benefits of investing in AI far outweigh the costs. And if the benefits outweigh the costs of investment in AI, who is to say that the same is not true for Responsible AI?

We are at a point and time in history where you risk more by not investing in artificial intelligence then you do by investing in it. When done well, AI generates significant business advantages, and you better believe your competitors are either in the process of taking advantage of the potential competitive edge of AI. In a competitive and capitalistic market such as this, you simply can't afford not to invest in AI. When you look at it this way, all the reasons for why you shouldn't invest in AI are no longer blockers, but instead become problems to solve and challenges to overcome.

And I am here to tell you that Responsible AI is on the same trajectory path as AI. There are significant business advantages to investing in Responsible AI, benefits that far outweigh any of the costs or risks, and you better believe your competitors have already started taking advantage of them. It is quickly becoming the case that not investing in Responsible AI will be a far higher cost to an organization than investing in it. So, although there are five good and valid reasons not to invest in Responsible AI at this moment, when you finally come to the realization that Responsible AI is inevitably becoming the standard of AI practice, all those reasons are suddenly no longer blockers but instead simply problems to solve and challenges to overcome.

Which leads me now to turn the question back to you. Can you tell me why you shouldn't invest in Responsible AI?

The One Reason Why You Should

Of course, I can't in good conscience leave you with only a handful of reasons not to do Responsible AI when there are so many reasons for why you should. From technical enhancements, to improved product quality, to stronger company culture, to regulation readiness, the list goes on, as you will find peppered throughout this book. As I sat down to write this specific chapter, though, I considered the possibility of illuminating all of these potential benefits to Responsible AI for you in detail. But as I started to do so I realized that although the technical and business benefits are numerous, for me personally there is really only one reason for investing in Responsible AI, all the rest are just bonus benefits.

When it comes down to it, the "why" driving Responsible AI and Ethics, in my opinion, is simply the opportunity to truly understand what you are building in such intricate depth that it is impossible to not to build something you can be proud of. There are many layers to AI. You have the technical layer, the business layer, the operational layer, and so on. But the layer that often goes forgotten in AI is the ethical layer, the very one that determines whether you are bringing something into this world that you can be proud of or will want to hide in shame from.

This is not just some theoretical ideal, to be clear. Over my years as an ethicist, I have had the pleasure of working with a wide range of clients. Regardless of the organizational size, industry, product, business model, or technology, it is safe to say I have had the opportunity to apply my work in many a different context. Each instance brings with it its own new challenges, limitations, and potential, creating a client project that is beautifully unique in its own intricate way. Although every client is different in its own way, one of the guaranteed outcomes I can expect every time is the client's comment that thanks to the work done in implementing Responsible AI and utilizing ethics as a decision-analysis tool, they now have a level of holistic understanding for the AI they are building (or using) at a depth they never imagined before was possible. In the words of Alfred Malmros, cofounder of Anyone Technologies, engaging in ethics work made him "fall in love again with what he was building."

So why Responsible AI? In a world driven by business impact and technological advancement, I will give you one very simple, very human reason why. Responsible AI and Ethics is worth the investment because it is the only way to, without fail, build something you can be truly proud of.

PART TWO

06

The Responsible AI Blindspot
You Didn't Know You Had

And the Tool to Fix It

Imagine you work for a startup that is developing AI solutions for the HR industry. Lately, your company has been finding business success in its suite of interviewing tools, one of which is a recommendation system. This system analyzes a job candidate and then recommends who within a specific team would be a good fit to sit on an interview panel for said candidate. The idea is that this recommendation system will not only be able to find the best matches for the interview process, but also be able to ensure that there is a diversity among the interviewers on the panel. However, you've been receiving some complaints from your customers in the past few months saying that this recommendation system tends to only suggest male interviewers for the panel. Clearly you have a growing case of gender bias in your system, and one that if you don't fix it soon could turn into a catastrophe for your company.

Thankfully, you are an informed business leader, and recognize that gender biased outputs of a system are indicative of gender biased inputs. In other words, you understand that the gender bias must be coming from the data that the system has been trained on. So, you go directly to your data scientists and select three of the best to work on developing a set of three fairness metrics to help measure your data inputs for gender bias. After a month of research and development, followed by another month of testing validation, your dream team comes back to your with your set of fairness metrics nicely wrapped and tied with a bow. The set is beautifully designed, and when they show you a test case, it is quickly able to identify what is causing the biased outputs through pinpointing the issue in the input datasets. Great, you think, this will surely solve your growing gender bias problem. You release the metric to the entire team of 40 data scientists and check the gender bias problem off your to-do list.

Three months go by, and you get a call from one of your star customers. They sound upset as they explain to you over the phone that for the past month, the recommendation system hadn't suggested a single woman to sit on a hiring interview panel. Embarrassed and confused, you launch into an explanation of the state-of-the-art fairness metrics your team had designed and been using to help fix that problem. You manage to placate your customer for the moment with promises of doubling down your efforts to fix the gender bias problem, but they sound skeptical at whether or not they want to continue using your recommendation system.

Once off the phone, you immediately turn to your data science team to try and get to the root of things. There was a clear fix to the issue, the team had a well-designed technical solution, so why had the system still continued to develop a gender bias in its outputs?

The Techno-Value Blindspot

This is a textbook example of something I like to call the techno-value blindspot, a blindspot I have seen many a well-intended Responsible AI solution fall victim to time and again. The techno-value blindspot occurs when you treat an ethics problem like a technical problem and only focus on developing a technical solution to fix things. When you are experiencing an ethics problem with your AI, logically you will be tempted to focus your attention on the AI system and develop a technical solution in the hopes of fixing the ethics problem. However, these technical problems are only the symptoms of the deeper ethics problems you face.

We did not discover ethical values through technological invention. Values have existed far before the term artificial intelligence was ever coined, and far beyond the limits of interactions with a technological system. Although we experience ethical values in AI systems, we also experience the manifestation of those same values in the behaviors, beliefs, and actions of the people around us. Our ethical values exist independent of our technology, which makes trying to fix an ethical problem in an AI system with solely a technical answer a short-sighted solution at best. This tendency to want to solve the ethics problems exhibited in an AI system as solely technical problems creates the techno-value blindspot. In other words it is when solutions are made to tackle the technical issues but fail to address the ethical problem in its entirety.

When you are a Responsible AI-enabled organization, you are aware of this techno-value blindspot and have the proper strategy in place to ensure you are implementing solutions that address the whole of your ethics problems. Remember, Responsible AI solutions empower the ethical decision making required to reflect our values in our technology. Ethics functions as a tool for decision-analysis, and the decisions that affect the outcomes of our AI systems are more than simply technical decisions.

In Part One of this book, we unpacked and redefined ethics in a modern-day business setting, illuminating its practicality and potential for driving positive impact for your organization and AI. From learning how to identify your organization's foundational values, to understanding how to use those values to assess critical decisions for ethical risk, to experimenting with the possibility of unlocking innovation through values-by-design thinking, you should have a clear grasp on how to use ethics to fine-tune your decision making in AI.

But conceptually knowing how to use ethics to analyze your AI decisions for alignment with your foundational values versus practically using it to develop Responsible AI solutions that address the entirety of ethics problem occurring in your AI systems are two very different things. You can have a full set of foundational values along with the motivation to tackle the ethics problems, and still fall victim to the techno-value blindspot by limiting the scope of your Responsible AI solutions to solely the technical layer. And that's assuming you've been able to identify and solve for the technical layer of your ethics problem in the first place.

What you need now is a structured process for assessing all the layers of an ethics problem, aligning the right Responsible AI solutions, and acting on those solutions at scale in order to enable foundational values-based decision making for your AI projects. In other words, what you need is a Responsible AI strategy.

In this chapter we are going to lay the foundations of your Responsible AI strategy. We will start by going over the three different layers of ethics problems, and the corresponding pillars to your Responsible AI strategy that you will need to solve for if you want your AI systems to fully reflect your foundational values. Then I'll introduce you to something called the Values Canvas, your go-to Responsible AI enablement tool for mapping out the solutions and strategy needed to embed ethical values into your AI systems. Finally, we'll round things out with a closer look into the primary use case for the Values Canvas. By the end of this chapter you will understand from a 1,000-ft view what layers are needed to form a holistic Responsible AI strategy that enables ethical decision making and avoids the pitfalls of a techno-value blindspot.

The Three Pillars of Responsible AI

As you've probably picked up on by now, I've been dropping not-so-subtle hints that there is more to Responsible AI than what meets the AI. This may be a terrible play on the word "eye," but there is an important truth to my feeble attempt at an AI pun here. In fact, it is quite possibly the single most important takeaway from this book. In fact, this simple realization is one of the most crucial keys to success in becoming a leader in enabling Responsible AI for your organization (Stackpole, 2023). So to be sure there is no confusion on the point, I will state it, in as plain of language as possible:

Responsible AI is not primarily a technical problem to solve.

When you are looking to become a Responsible AI-enabled organization and to utilize ethical decision making to align your AI with your foundational values, you must first look beyond your technology (Mills et al., 2022). Yes, AI in general is riddled with ethical problems, and yes these problems are the ones that will make headlines, but they are only the tip of a rather large iceberg. At the top sits the ethical problems you are witnessing in your AI, but as you dive beneath the surface you will quickly find that these problems are most often rooted in poor people management and operational processes, not in technical execution. Essentially, that means that in addition to the technical layer of Responsible AI, you also have a people and a process layer.

To help illustrate these different layers, let's return back to the story of our imaginary HR startup struggling to mitigate a growing gender bias problem. We left off with you questioning why after having developed a technical solution for monitoring and mitigating gender bias in the data, you were still experiencing biased outputs from your recommendation system. You decide to investigate the issue further by talking to your team of data scientists to figure out what was going wrong with the fairness metrics. Much to your despair, you quickly discover that even though there was a technical solution available, the fairness metrics were going largely unused by your data scientists. What happened?

First, it is brought to your attention that the culture of your data science team did not support the adoption of the fairness metrics. Over the years, your data science team had developed an underlying mantra that "the data doesn't lie" which in practice translated to the idea that if there was an inequality in the data, then it was just a reflection of reality that couldn't be fixed. This proved to be a problem when it came to adopting the fairness metrics because the team viewed the gender bias occurring in the recommendation system as something that could not be prevented. If the data said there was a disproportionate amount of men better suited to sit on interviewing panels than there were women, then that was just how things worked and couldn't be changed. This, you realize, is not a technical problem, but a people one. The culture of your data science team was preventing the use of your technical solution for mitigating the gender bias. It dawns on you that you don't need better fairness metrics, you need a solution to help fix the team culture blockers to using the fairness metrics you already had. This, you discover, is the people layer to your ethics problem.

But it doesn't stop there. As you start tackling the team culture issues, you notice that the adoption of the fairness metrics is still not happening at the scale you had hoped for, nor is it bringing the desired impact on mitigating the gender bias in your recommendation system. Although you have managed to train your data scientists on the importance of fairness in mitigating bias and have motivated them to use the specifically designed fairness metrics, it still seems like no one is using the technical solution. This is when you realize that the problem now was that your data scientists didn't know at what point in their workflow they needed to be using the fairness metrics, and even if they did run a fairness check, they had no idea what to do with the results. Your data scientists could now tell when there was a fairness problem in the data, but they didn't have any process in place for making tangible changes to mitigate the identified bias. Again, you realize that this wasn't a problem with the fairness metrics themselves, but instead a problem with lack of procedure for your data scientists to be able to effectively and practically using the metrics. This, you discover, is the process layer to your ethics problem.

Both of these blockers have nothing to do with the technology, and everything to do with people and process. Without the right team culture or procedure for change in place, your fairness metrics, no matter how good of a technical solution it is, will never reach the adoption or achieve the impact you had intended. Essentially, it does not matter how good the decisions around your technology are if you do not have people that are trained to implement those decisions, or a process for carrying through and scaling the decisions. If you make the mistake and jump immediately to applying your technical solutions layer without first examining the people and process layers, at best you will see a few instances of positive impact on your AI, but at worst you will see your time and resources go to waste in an initiative that never produces any of its desired results. In order to reap the benefits of Responsible AI, you need to address all three layers in your ethics solutions.

The purpose of having a robust Responsible AI strategy is to ensure that you are tackling not only the symptoms of an ethics problem, but that you are also getting all the way down to the root causes. In order for your AI to be reflective of your organization's foundational values, your values must be reflected throughout all three layers. Which is why, when it comes to enabling Responsible AI, there are three pillars to a holistic and sustainable strategy. As you may have already guessed, the Responsible AI pillars align with the three layers of ethical solutions: People, Process, and Technology.

People

Starting with the first of the three, we have the People Pillar to your Responsible AI strategy. With each pillar comes an overarching question that guides the thinking and solutions for that pillar. For your first pillar, we are asking the question "who is building your AI?"

As the name implies, this pillar focuses directly on the people behind the technology. It may seem counterintuitive at first, considering your goal is to embed ethics into the technology, not the person. But you can't have AI without people, and so if you don't have your foundational values reflected within your teams, you certainly won't have your values reflected in your AI systems. This means that you need to ensure the people that are building your AI systems, or that are using AI tooling in their daily workflow, are trained in how to implement the relevant foundational values, have incentives aligned to furthering the goals of your Responsible AI strategy, and know how to identify ethical challenges in their work. Above all else though, the People Pillar relies on building an open company culture that is not only receptive, but supportive of Responsible AI.

Process

Moving a layer up, we have the Process Pillar. In this pillar we are seeking solutions to the question "how is the AI being built?"

Now that you understand who is building your AI, you need to understand how that AI is being built. Again, it may seem strange at first to be looking at operational processes when you are concerned about the technical outcome. But good AI practices lead to good AI, so having processes that support the value alignment of your AI is essential. This is where AI governance takes center stage, as you will need to ensure your ethically trained teams have the right workflows, policies, and checkpoints in place that encourage and facilitate values-based decision making. You will be looking for opportunities to fine-tune your AI practices to enable natural points in your teams' workflows to identify ethical challenges, make value-aligned decisions, and carry out those decisions at scale. Think of this pillar as the one that builds protocol and structure for ethics, ensuring that the critical decisions influencing the ultimate outcomes of your AI systems is reflective of your foundation values.

Technology

To complete the trifecta we have the Technology Pillar. Having answered the who and how in the first two pillars, it is in this third pillar that we ask the question "what AI are you building?"

It is not until this final pillar that we turn our attention to the technology your organization is actually building, and the reason to have started the Responsible AI in the first place. It is incredibly important here to understand that it does not matter whether your organization is building an AI system to be sold on the market, procuring AI solutions to support internal operations, or customizing your own internal AI systems, your Responsible AI strategy must hold any and all AI associated with your organization to the same ethical standards. Another company can be responsible for building the AI systems your teams utilize, but it is your organization that will be held accountable at the end of the day for the consequences of poorly designed technology. This all means that when it comes to implementing ethics, you need to have the right metrics of success to measure your AI and data practices that align with your foundational values, keep up to date on developments in Responsible AI techniques such as bias-mitigation practices or privacy enhancing methods, and have the right tooling in place that supports responsible AI development. Your People Pillar built the skillsets for Responsible AI, your Process Pillar built the mechanisms for carrying out Responsible AI, and now your Technology Pillar will build the actual AI responsibly.

There you have it, the three pillars of a Responsible AI strategy. Remember, every successful strategy will incorporate elements from People, Process, and Technology without preference to one over another. Each of the three pillars builds on the others to create an interdependent and intricately simple system which, when executed with intention and care, results in holistic Responsible AI solutions addressing ethical problems at every layer.

The Values Canvas

Three pillars are a nice way to neatly conceptualize and organize your Responsible AI strategy, but how does this translate to actual practice? There is a wide gap between the understanding that ethics problems exist on multiple layers and the ability to implement a holistic strategy addressing all three. You want to embed your foundational values into your technology, to move beyond discussion and into action, but where do you even begin to plug an abstract concept into concrete code? What you need now is a tool specifically designed to help guide your strategy development, assign resources to the right initiatives, and ensure you are addressing all of the critical points to success in Responsible AI.

The Tool

Allow me to introduce you to the Values Canvas, the strategic management tool used to embed ethical values into an organization and its technology. The end goal of Responsible AI is to create AI systems that reflect our values, and as we have been discussing in this chapter, that must be built on three different pillars in order to be successful. The Values Canvas enables you to visualize all three pillars to your Responsible AI strategy simultaneously, providing a high-level comprehensive view over the details necessary to execute ethical decision making at scale and align your technology with your values.

The canvas is made up of four specific sections: Value, People, Process, and Technology. The first section deals with the value itself you are trying to reflect in your AI systems by prompting you to select the value, and its definition you need to embed. The process of value selection, definition, and approach have all been covered in Part One of this book, in case you need to flip back a few pages for a refresher. The following three sections of the canvas each encompass one of the three pillars to your Responsible AI strategy. Each pillar has its own three elements you will need to activate or address in order to bring your selected value to life. Don't worry, we will be covering People, Process, and Technology, and their subsequent elements, in depth over the next three chapters. All you need to know for now is that there are four sections to the Values Canvas, and each covers a pivotal aspect to the overall success of your Responsible AI strategy. Putting it all together now, you will find your own blank Values Canvas at www.koganpage.com/responsible-ai. Figure 6.1 shows an overview of the canvas.

I had the good fortune to work with a group of bright Design MBA students from the California College of the Arts to fine-tune the design and

FIGURE 6.1 The Values Canvas

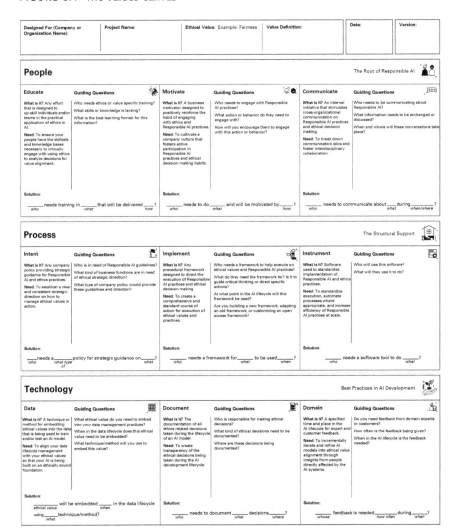

usability of this tool into the Values Canvas you see today. During the process, one of the students likened the canvas to the map of Middle-earth you find at the start to *The Hobbit*. As you make your way through *The Hobbit*, you find yourself oftentimes referring back to the map to orientate yourself in the Middle-earth universe. The Values Canvas, in its own way, is much like the Middle-earth map. As you embark on the journey of AI development, it can be easy to turn yourself around and forget where you are in terms of implementing your values into your technology. The Values Canvas enables you to look back and reorient yourself whenever you need, keeping the bigger picture and objective in mind as you work through the details. As relevant that you may or may not find this metaphor to our discussion of AI, I enjoyed the imagery far too much not to share.

How to Use It

Before we dive into the details of the Values Canvas sections, I want to first take a step back to make a note on how to use this tool. It's great to have the ability to visualize and develop your strategy for Responsible AI, but when exactly does that need to be done? In other words, let's talk about the use case for the Values Canvas.

When I talk about Responsible AI strategy, there are two levels to the conversation here. First, you have the overall strategy for the organization. This strategy is high level and focuses on transforming your organization into being Responsible AI enabled. The second level is more granular, as it refers to the strategy you are deploying on an AI project-by-project basis. When you are at this level of strategy, you are looking at specific solutions for embedding your foundational values into your AI project and eventual system. The Values Canvas can be used on either level to help guide the development of your Responsible AI strategy. For now, in Part Two, we are going to look at how to use the Values Canvas on the granular project basis, while Part Three will take a step back and look at how to utilize this same template to help design your organizational strategy for Responsible AI.

Looking at the project-level use case, the Values Canvas becomes a powerful tool in mapping out what resources, solutions, and efforts will be needed to translate your foundational values into your AI project. To be filled out at the start to an AI project, the Values Canvas will enable, but is not limited to, product and project managers in developing the necessary Responsible AI strategy for the specific AI project, or even product, in question. If completed at the start, the Values Canvas will allow for the individuals working on the AI project to be able to understand firstly what Responsible AI solutions and values related resources are available to them on this project, and secondly what they should be doing in order to embed the selected values into the AI system.

Remember, the goal of Responsible AI is to create AI technology that reflects your foundational values. To do so, you must start any given AI project with a reflection on what values from your foundational value set are relevant to this project. Once selected, you will want to complete a Values Canvas per selected value. It may be tempting to complete only one single Values Canvas for all of the values you want to embed into any given AI project. However, each ethical value will have different impacts and required solutions depending on the project, and so needs to be considered as a separate entity. For example, you will not have the same solutions for the value of Transparency as you will for the value of Privacy. There may be overlap in certain sections on how you will address your values, but in order to ensure you are not adding unnecessary blindspots to your value implementation, it is best to treat values as separate entities and fill out a Values Canvas per each value at the start to an AI project.

Learning Your Hammer

Over the remainder of Part Two I am going to walk you step by step through how the Value Canvas works. You have in fact already completed the first step in Part One of this book, value identification and definition. That leaves us with the steps of People, Process, and Technology to now tackle. Along the way I will cover in depth what elements are needed to be addressed in each of your Responsible AI strategy pillars and provide some real-life examples of the elements in action. To help illustrate the use case of the Values Canvas, I will be walking you through a fictional AI project with you as the project manager to see, in real time, how you would go about using the tool. In this imaginary scenario, you are a project manager at a well-respected Fortune 500 bank called R&AI Bank. You've been assigned to lead a project developing an AI system to help detect credit card fraud in real time. One of the primary values you need to ensure is reflected in this system is the value of fairness, which in your company is defined as "equal quality of service" for all customers. By the end of Part Two, you have a comprehensive understanding and experience on how to utilize the Values Canvas to develop a Responsible AI strategy on a project-, or product-, level basis.

I started this book with the story of two carpenters. One was taught an action, the other was taught a tool. The end goal was to hammer in a nail, whereas in your case your end goal is to reflect your foundational values in your organization and its technology. The Values Canvas is your hammer, the tool that will you will use to accomplish your goal. I am not going to teach you sets of specific actions needed to fulfill each section of the canvas. I am going to teach you over the next four chapters instead how to use the tool to its full extent so that you can take and apply it to any AI-related scenario you encounter in your work.

07

Who Is Building Your AI?

The People Driving Your Responsible AI Success

A priest and a medium apply to join a social networking app. Believe it or not, what sounds like it should be the start to an off-beat joke is in fact the start to a call I once had with a client.

The company was working on a new social networking app that focused on the power of creating serendipitous connects through exchanging advice. Although they weren't using AI yet, they were building the foundations to take full advantage of the insight generating capabilities of AI and wanted to make sure that critical ethical values were present from the start. Busy working out the kinks inherent to building a new product, the team designing the app had just starting letting beta users join the platform. To do so, a prospective user would have to apply to join and list what kind of advice they wanted to give. It was a straightforward process until one day the team had both a priest and a medium apply to join the app and offer spiritual advice. What should have been a simple conversation among colleagues quickly blew up into a heated debate on spirituality, religion, and the supernatural, bringing the team to a complete standstill. The founder quickly identified this debate as an ethical one, and called me up to seek advice on how to resolve the current, and future, debates.

Clearly, this team was facing an ethical challenge. And it was just as, if not more so, clear that this challenge had nothing to do with the technology. It didn't matter if the company automated the application process for users, or used recommendation and filter systems to help users customize who they could connect and seek advice from, this was not a problem with a technical solution. This was a people problem.

To be clear, when I say people problem, I don't mean there were things wrong with the individuals on the team. What I mean is that the people building the application were not equipped to handle the situation at hand and needed a solution. When it comes to building AI, or any technology solution for that matter, we are tempted to jump to the conclusion that any problem can be solved with a technical solution. However, as my client in this story so colorfully discovered, not every problem comes with a technical solution.

The Root of Responsible AI: *People*

Imagine trying to build an AI system with a team that has little to no experience in coding, let alone artificial intelligence. Seems ludicrous to even pretend such a scenario could exist, right? Now imagine trying to build an AI system that is reflective of your foundational values with a team that has little to no experience in Responsible AI practices. Responsible AI is no different fro AI in this scenario, you can't build something that you have no skill or knowledge in.

This is why building Responsible AI will always start with empowering your people to engage in ethical decision making and Responsible AI practices first. If you are going to become a Responsible AI-enabled organization, you need to ensure your people are equipped to do so. You simply can't have Responsible AI if you don't have your people ready and trained in how to develop or use it.

Although our end goal is to enable you to build and use AI responsibly, which theoretically is a technical outcome, in reality we need to start at the root of Responsible AI, which is and always has been a people problem. So, it is in this first layer of your strategy, we will be focusing on the true root of success in Responsible AI by building out your approach to the *People Pillar*.

In this chapter we will cover the three elements necessary to forming a successful *People Pillar*, going into depth on what the elements entail, the purpose of each element, and the considerations needed when designing your strategic solution for each element. Once you have an understanding of what goes into each element, we take a step back and look at the bigger picture of the *People Pillar* to understand how the three should be interwoven for an overall strategy, as well as how a risk versus innovation approach will influence this strategy. Finally, we will close the chapter with a look at what indicators determine if your *People Pillar* strategy is being adopted, and what impact dictates if it is a successful strategy.

The Elements of the People Pillar

When it comes to developing the *People Pillar*, think of it as an endeavor focused on further developing your current company culture to embrace and support the application of ethics in your AI and data practices. You do not necessarily have to start from scratch to build an entirely new culture, instead what you are looking for are initiatives that are already working well for your teams and then explore how to further emphasize these positive points of impact. The three elements, and therefore points of impact, to a successful *People Pillar* are *Educate*, *Motivate*, and *Communicate*.

Each element serves its own purpose and has a variety of ways by which you can meet the needs of that purpose. We will go into detail for each of the elements in the following sections, but for now all you need to know is that *Educate* is about training and up-skilling your workforce, *Motivate* looks at incentive structures and positive peer support, and *Communicate* focuses on fostering open discussions and shared language. When looking for exponential points of impact in building out your *People Pillar*, you will want to design your strategic solutions to meet the needs of each of the three elements. This will create a balanced approach to the *People Pillar*, and ensure you are creating a foundation for your Responsible AI strategy that is built to last.

As you work your way through the three elements to your *People Pillar*, you will find guiding questions on your Values Canvas. These questions are designed to help direct your thinking towards innovative and robust solutions for each element. When using the Values Canvas to embed ethical values into your AI project, walk through the *People Pillar* with your team using the space under the guiding questions to brainstorm solutions for each of your elements. The deeper you go in ideation, the stronger your final *People Pillar* will be. Eventually, you will want to convert those ideas into the solution statements at the bottom of each element's section, arriving at your end goal of three cohesive solutions to round out the strategy for your *People Pillar*.

Educate: Do your people know how to use ethics?

What Is an Educate Solution?

Any effort that is designed to up-skill individuals and/or teams in the practical application of ethics in AI.

This element essentially focuses on the education of your workforce, ensuring they are properly equipped to identify, address, and manage ethical challenges as they relate to your foundational values. The most common form of *Educate* solutions is corporate training; however, you do not necessarily need formalized workshops and education modules to fulfill this element. There are many ways to configure a strong solution to this element, as informal exercises such as book clubs or employee-led informational sessions can also meet the requirements of an *Educate* solution. As long as whatever configuration you decide on focuses on up-skilling your workforce in ethical decision making and the application of your foundational values, what that education looks like can be customized to best fit with how your organization already trains employees.

The Purpose of Educate

> To ensure your people have the skillsets and knowledge bases necessary to critically engage with using ethics to analyze decisions for value alignment.

Although ethics may be something we are used to engaging with on a daily basis at a human level, it is not a process we are generally accustomed to in the context of AI and business. Ethical problems arise in AI when key technical and business decisions are misaligned with your foundational values. The ability to identify these cases of misalignment, analyze the situation for relevant ethical decision factors, and apply the best solution is skillset new to the context of AI and one that your workforce most likely has not been specifically trained on before. In fact, 53 percent of companies cite a lack of training or knowledge among staff members as the biggest blocker to Responsible AI and Ethics in their organization (Stackpole, 2023). The challenge *Educate* addresses head on is the gap in skillset and knowledge of ethics that holds companies back from enabling Responsible AI practices within its workforce.

Designing Your Educate Solution

We know the purpose of this element is to bridge knowledge gaps, but now we need to determine exactly what gap is being bridged and how. If you will recall, we are currently walking through how to use the Values Canvas on a project level. This means that you should already have a set project and set of ethical values in mind, and so are now looking into what kind of knowledge gaps may exist given the specifics of the context. Identifying the gaps, along with the best ways to bridge them, will lead you to your *Educate* solution.

In order to understand what additional training and education is needed in order for your team to execute on embedding your foundational values into your specific AI project, there are a few key factors to consider when designing your *Educate* solution. First, you need to assess for who exactly needs the education. To answer this question, look at who will be working on the project to understand what teams and individuals will be involved. This will give you an idea of the specific organizational roles with the potential to influence the outcome of the project, and the most likely to need training on your ethical values. As you determine what teams or departments will be involved in your project, don't forget to also consider levels of positions, as leadership roles typically require different training from executers and so on.

Once you know who needs additional education, you will need to consider what exactly they need to be educated on. You've identified a gap in knowledge between what someone needs to know in order to embed the ethical values into the specific AI project and what they currently know, but what content exactly is going to bridge that gap? Perhaps you need basic education on what your organization's ethical values are, or maybe you need training on new technical techniques for measuring and tracking the ethical values, or maybe even still you need a briefing on incoming regulation requirements. As with any skillset, in addition to the content of the education there are also different levels of understanding and comprehension to consider. From basic awareness building all the way to advanced practice and expertise enhancement, what you need to determine is what level your workforce is at when it comes to practicing your foundational values in the context of your AI project.

Having identified who is in need of education and what knowledge they are in need of, you finally will want to consider how they are going to learn this information. In other words, what's the format? Nowadays there is a wide variety of learning mediums and methodologies available for you to choose from. The important thing here is that you select the format that is easiest for your intended audience to engage with. For example, the busy engineer may prefer a virtual class that they can take over a period of a few weeks, while an executive might prefer an onsite two-hour workshop. It can be helpful here to consult with your HR department, or whoever heads your corporate training practices, to understand what kind of formats, and at what frequency, work best in which scenarios.

Summarizing all of the above considerations, here are the three questions you can use to guide ideation and determine what kind of *Educate* solution is needed for your AI project:

- Who needs ethics or value-specific training?
- What skills or knowledge is lacking?
- What is the best learning format for this information?

As you ideate on different solutions for *Educate*, keep in mind that you will eventually need to narrow down the ideas into a solution for your element. Your goal is to be able to answer the following solution statement in your Values Canvas:

[who] needs training in [what] that will be delivered [how]?

Educate in Action

To help illustrate what the *Educate* element looks like in action, let's take a look at our example of the R&AI Bank and its AI project for credit card fraud detection that was introduced in the previous chapter. Sitting down as project lead with your team, you begin ideating solutions for training on fairness. Looking at who needs education, your team recalls that R&AI Bank already requires all employees to complete yearly training on company values, spending significant time addressing what fairness means for the bank and its ability to serve its customers. The business analysts and customer service representatives on your project agree that this is sufficient fairness training for their needs on this project; however, the data scientists raise concern that they feel they are not up to date on the latest bias-mitigation techniques for underserved communities. Although the data scientists have a good base knowledge in how to monitor for fairness, they express the desire for a refresher on the latest techniques since the demographics you will be servicing can be difficult to account for. As you discuss the different needs for further education with your team, you add the ideas to your Values Canvas in the *Educate* section, leaving the solution statement blank to return to after you've had the chance to fill in the rest of the *People Pillar* elements as shown in Figure 7.1.

FIGURE 7.1 People Element

People

The Root of Responsible AI

Educate

What is it? Any effort that is designed to up-skill individuals and/or teams in the practical application of ethics in AI.

Need: To ensure your people have the skillsets and knowledge bases necessary to critically engage with using ethics to analyze decisions for value alignment.

Guiding Questions

Who needs ethics or value-specific training?
What skills or knowledge is lacking?
What is the best learning format for this information?

- Data scientists need training, but full team could also benefit from further education
- Data scientists need a refresher on new techniques in bias mitigation
- Format could be a one-off workshop
- Bank already requires all employees to have basic training on company values

Solution:

_____ needs training in_____ that will be delivered _____ ?
   who   *what*   *how*

Motivate: Are your people motivated to engage with your values?

What Is a Motivate Solution?

A business motivator designed to positively reinforce the habit of engaging with ethics and Responsible AI practices.

Responsible AI and Ethics will require behavioral and workflow changes from your people, and in order for these to be successful, your people will need to be motivated to adopt the changes. This element looks for solutions that will motivate your people to embrace the use of your foundational values in critical decision making, as well as utilizing the new skillsets being taught through your *Educate* solutions. There are many ways by which you can motivate an individual or team to engage with ethics, the key here is to understand what exact habits or actions you need to support and how you plan to do so. As discussed in Chapter 1, using our values to help guide critical decisions is something that we as humans naturally do. However, this ethics decision-making process is something we are not always aware of, which means that when it comes to applying the same reasoning capacities to our decision making around technology, we need additional reinforcement to bring that process to the conscious surface. The more tangible you can make the positive reinforcement, through say incentives or shout-outs, the better, as it helps turns ethics, something often thought of in the abstract, into a concrete practice.

The Purpose of Motivate

To cultivate a company culture that fosters active participation in Responsible AI practices and ethical decision-making habits.

As with any new behavior or habit, there is a certain amount of motivation needed to encourage engagement. For instance you can easily learn a new skillset, but without the right motivating factors supporting it, it is likely that the new skillset will go generally unused. Responsible AI and Ethics requires people to form new reasoning behaviors and workflow habits, both of which are incredibly difficult to adopt if engagement is not a priority or encouraged. In fact, 43 percent of companies list limited prioritization and attention by senior leadership as a major blocker to becoming a Responsible AI-enabled organization (Stackpole, 2023). The challenge *Motivate* addresses head on is the need to create a company culture that is motivated to prioritizing and engaging in Responsible AI initiatives.

Designing Your Motivate Solution

Knowing that the purpose of *Motivate* is to encourage usage of Responsible AI practices, we now need to dive into exactly what is needed in order to design an effective business motivator. Remember, we are currently working through the Values Canvas on a project level, which means we want to determine what motivators will be needed to engage your people in habits and activities specific to the project at hand.

Just as with *Educate*, there are a few factors to consider in the design of your *Motivate* solution. The first of which is again who, as in who among your people, are you needing to motivate. Luckily, this should be an easy answer to find, as who you are motivating should be reflective of who you are educating. Your *Educate* solution is ensuring your people have the necessary training and education in order to execute on foundational values for a specific AI project, which means your *Motivate* solution should be looking to motivate those same people to use that training and education in action.

After identifying who needs to be motivated, we can then turn our attention to considering what specific Responsible AI practice or ethical decision-making habit needs to be encouraged. In other words, we need to ask ourselves what specific action do you want to reinforce in your people so that it transitions from being a conscious action, to a natural behavior and eventually to becoming a second-nature habit. As you consider what action to take to motivate your people, keep in mind it should be something definitive and repeatable. Instead of trying to motivate your people to use foundational values in general, you need to pinpoint a specific value-enabling habit relevant to your AI project to reinforce.

Once you know who of your people and which of their actions needs encouragement, the final consideration for your *Motivate* solution will be focused on understanding the tangible mechanism you will use to positively reinforce the specific behavior. Essentially, you are asking yourself how you will motivate your people to engage with the Responsible AI practices relevant to your AI project. In the case of *Motivate*, we are looking for something tangible such as an incentive, KPI, or even performance review. The key here is that whatever reinforcement mechanism you select, it is something the receiver can easily identify and will want to receive. A pat on the back may be a nice gesture, but it is difficult to ensure a pat on the back is given every time the specified action is executed, and may not be something everyone would want to receive. Instead, including the desired behavior on performance reviews creates a clear and tangible reinforcement that someone will be encouraged to strive for, as a strong performance review usually leads to further benefits.

As you work your way through these different considerations, be sure that you critically ask yourself whether or not the business motivator you are establishing will have high enough significance and power that it will indeed motivate someone to carry out the desired action. Remember, this is your point of enforcement, and while we want it to be a positive one so as to encourage a healthy company culture around ethics, it does need to have teeth. With this in mind, we can summarize the above considerations into three guiding questions you can use to design your *Motivate* solution:

- Who needs to engage with Responsible AI practices?
- What action or behavior do they need to engage with?
- How will you encourage them to engage with this action or behavior?

As you work through your Motivate element on the Values Canvas, your goal will be to eventually use your ideas to fill out the following solution statement:

[who] needs to do [what] and will be motivated to by [how]?

Motivate in Action

As the lead for R&AI Bank's credit card fraud detection project, you know that motivating your team to engage with fairness will be vital to the success of the project. Filling out the Values Canvas with your team, your data scientists state that it will be their responsibility to measure for specific types of unwanted bias that could be exhibited in the system. However, your business analysts and customer service representatives point out that although the data scientists will be in charge of monitoring for fairness, the analysts and representatives have better insight into what kind of metrics would be indicative of a fair system for the bank's customers. Overall, your team agrees that having fairness regular checks throughout the build of the credit card fraud detection system should be a priority and indicator of success for the project. You continue adding the ideas to the *Motivate* section on your Values Canvas, again leaving the solution statement blank to return to once you've finished ideating for all three *People Pillar* elements as shown in Figure 7.2.

FIGURE 7.2 Motivate Element

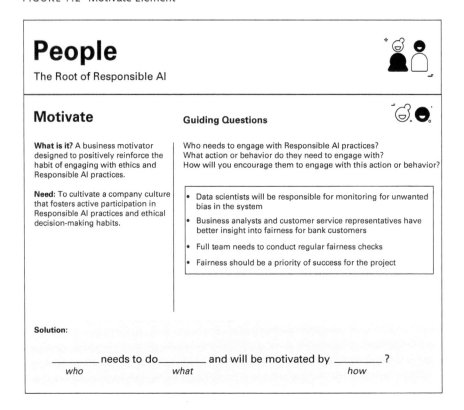

People

The Root of Responsible AI

Motivate

Guiding Questions

What is it? A business motivator designed to positively reinforce the habit of engaging with ethics and Responsible AI practices.

Need: To cultivate a company culture that fosters active participation in Responsible AI practices and ethical decision-making habits.

Who needs to engage with Responsible AI practices?
What action or behavior do they need to engage with?
How will you encourage them to engage with this action or behavior?

- Data scientists will be responsible for monitoring for unwanted bias in the system
- Business analysts and customer service representatives have better insight into fairness for bank customers
- Full team needs to conduct regular fairness checks
- Fairness should be a priority of success for the project

Solution:

_____ needs to do_____ and will be motivated by _____ ?
    who   *what*   *how*

Communicate: Are your people talking about your values?

What Is a Communicate Solution?

An internal initiative that stimulates cross-organizational communication on Responsible AI practices and ethical decision making.

As the final element to complete the *People Pillar* trifecta, *Communicate* focuses on ensuring that your people are all operating on the same page when it comes to Responsible AI practices. Although external communications about your Responsible AI efforts are important for marketing and PR purposes, your *Communicate* solution should be turned inwards to focus on equipping your own people instead. Depending on the complexity of the AI project and value at hand, there can be many moving pieces to the successful embedding of your selected value, so it is essential that the right people have access to the right information at the right time. It is common for people to conceptualize and use foundational values differently if not given a frame of reference for execution on the values. It is important to note here that this does not mean everyone must agree on definitions or uses, in fact fostering differing perspectives and opinions is actually a strength in this element. Rather, it means everyone is functioning with the same North Star conceptualization that serves as the base reference point for discussion and implementation.

The Purpose of Communicate

To break down communication silos and foster interdisciplinary collaboration.

Ethics and values are subjects that naturally make their way into conversations, typically at inconsistent frequencies and depth. In the context of AI, we must surface these subjects in our discussions by stimulating proactive discussions on Responsible AI practices, especially when it comes to embedding a selected value into a specific AI project. Instead of mentioning values from time to time, there needs to a clear time, space, and medium of discussion, raising the collective consciousness of your people to a new awareness of when and how they are intentionally engaging with ethics. Additionally, a common problem organizations face is information silos between departments and even within teams. This is something that can be especially damaging in Responsible AI as ethics practices require consistency and multidisciplinary collaboration to be successful. Lack of synergy and awareness is cited by 42 percent of companies as a major blocker to Responsible AI, causing inefficiencies in execution and miscommunication of objectives (Stackpole, 2023). *Communicate* solutions are designed to address the need to break down information silos in order to foster collaboration, intention, and awareness of the ethical decision making in progress.

Designing Your Communicate Solution

With an understanding of what constitutes a *Communicate* solution and why you need one, let's turn our attention to what is needed in order to design an effective solution. As a reminder, we are walking through the Values Canvas project level use case, which means we will want to look at how to design a solution that enables your people on a specific AI project to communicate on your foundational values.

The first of the factors to consider when designing your *Communicate* solution is again the question of who is communicating. However, this time you are asking yourself not only who is communicating, but who are they communicating with exactly. Perhaps it is all within the same team, but you are looking to stimulate communication between the different levels. Or maybe it's the same level, such as management, but spread across a variety of teams. It can even be the same team and level, the important thing here is that communication must always involve at least two parties, both of which you need to identify.

The next factor to consider will be the substance of the communication, essentially asking yourself what information needs to be exchanged in accordance to your selected value. The purpose of *Communicate* is to stimulate constructive collaboration and debate on a focused topic, such as a specified use case of your selected value in the context of the AI project. It is important to ensure that the information being exchanged and conversation topics being discussed are both practical and consequential for your *People Pillar* overall. Although it may be an interesting intellectual pursuit to debate existential implications of new emerging technology, if this topic does relate to your current AI project nor lead to any concrete actions, your time and efforts will be better spent on a topic with more substance. Three of the most common topics a team will need to discuss in relation to an ethical value is the definition, the challenges they are facing relevant to that value, and what solutions or actions they are taking to implement that value.

Now having considered who and what needs to be communicated, we can turn to the final factor and look at how that communication will take place. It can be tempting to assume that conversations about values and Responsible AI implementation will naturally make their way into the work day; however, relying on a casual water-cooler conversation simply will not cut it when it comes to practice. Although you want to encourage a company culture in which employees are comfortable and interested in engaging in ethics chit-chat, your *Communicate* solution must be focused more on effective and efficient sharing of information relevant to your values and project. By designating a time and place for conversation on your selected value for your specific AI project, you increase the efficiency of adoption as well as ensure that the high-level value is not being lost in the granular details of the day-to-day. *Communicate* can come in the form of specified meeting discussion points, weekly stand-ups, or even a designated slack channel, the important thing is that you can point to a time and place that your team and relevant stakeholders are communicating on your selected value.

With the factors to considered in mind, we can summarize the necessary considerations for designing your *Communicate* solution into three guiding questions:

- Who needs to be communicating about Responsible AI?
- What information needs to be exchanged or discussed?
- When and where will these conversations take place?

As you add your ideas to your Values Canvas for *Communicate*, keep in mind that your goal is to arrive at a final solution for your project. To help determine what that should be, use the following solution statement:

> [who] needs to communicate about [what] during [when/where]?

Communicate in Action

You've reached the final element in your *People Pillar* and are feeling confident in your team's ideas so far for solutions to embedding fairness into the people working on the credit card fraud project for R&AI Bank. Looking at your final element, your team starts to discuss possible solutions for *Communicate*. Everyone has agreed so far that fairness is going to be a difficult ethical value to embed into a credit card fraud detection system, especially knowing that R&AI Bank services a significant amount of under-represented demographics. Your data scientists, business analysts, and customer service representatives all agree that they will have different insights to bring to the table about whether or not the fairness interventions are working, and so start ideating on ways to share those insights. Someone suggests a monthly all-hands focused only on discussing fairness, while another person suggests an internal communication channel to enable asynchronous updates to be shared across the team. Excited by everyone enthusiasm, you keep track of the ideas being shared on the Values Canvas, once again leaving the solution statement blank until you have the chance to look at the *People Pillar* as a whole as shown in Figure 7.3.

FIGURE 7.3 Communicate Element

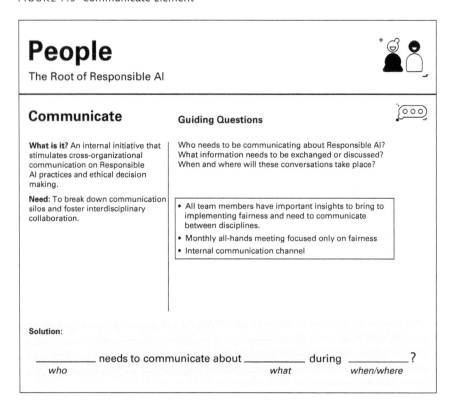

Bringing It All Together: Finalizing Your *People Pillar*

We started this chapter out by talking about the importance of the human in the equation, and how people are at the root of not only your Responsible AI strategy, but also simply at the heart of your AI practices. Although our end goal is to have your organization's foundational values reflected in the final outcome of an AI project, it is the people within your organization that will be building the AI and so are the source of critical decisions that will highly impact that final goal. We have now spent this chapter diving into the details of what is needed for your *People Pillar*, the first of the three pillars to a holistic Responsible AI strategy.

As we have seen, there are three elements to the *People Pillar*: *Educate*, *Motivate*, and *Communicate* as shown in Figure 7.4. Each element addresses an important challenge to embedding foundational values into your company culture and workforce, and will result in enabling your people to build AI that is reflective of your values.

When using the Values Canvas to embed a selected value into a specific AI project, you will have at this point gone through all three elements writing out your ideas for potential solutions to *Educate*, *Motivate*, and *Communicate*. In *Educate* you will have ideas listed for how to train your people on skillsets relevant to your foundational values. In *Motivate* you will have ideas listed for how to encourage and reinforce your people in the use of these skillsets and use of your foundational values in critical decision making. In *Communicate* you will have ideas listed for how your people will share information and collaborate on your foundational values. As you look over your lists of ideas, you should be encouraged about the different possibilities for viable solutions to embedding your selected value. The key now, though, is not to get stuck in the ideation phase and instead select which solutions you will plan to move forward with for your specific AI project.

Synchronizing Your People Pillar

As you work through your *People Pillar*, you should think of the solutions in *Educate*, *Motivate*, and *Communicate* as elements to a larger cohesive story. It is not necessarily the case that you will need three separate solutions, one for each of the three elements. Instead, think of it as designing one solution for your *People Pillar* that has three different purposes it needs to serve. As you select which ideas from each of your elements you will put into action, keep an eye out for possible synergies between initiatives, as well as

FIGURE 7.4 People Pillar. For the full figure, please see www.koganpage.com/responsible-ai

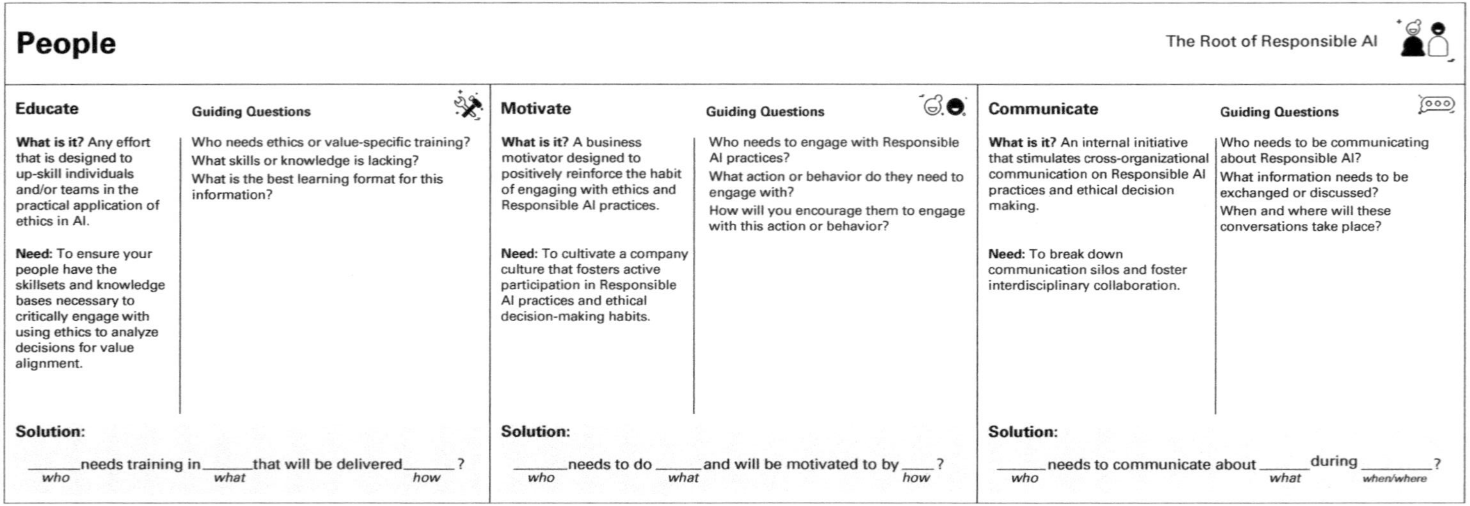

People

The Root of Responsible AI

Educate

Guiding Questions

Who needs ethics or value-specific training?
What skills or knowledge is lacking?
What is the best learning format for this information?

What is it? Any effort that is designed to up-skill individuals and/or teams in the practical application of ethics in AI.

Need: To ensure your people have the skillsets and knowledge bases necessary to critically engage with using ethics to analyze decisions for value alignment.

Solution:

_____ needs training in _____ that will be delivered _____?
who _ _ what _ _ _ how

Motivate

Guiding Questions

Who needs to engage with Responsible AI practices?
What action or behavior do they need to engage with?
How will you encourage them to engage with this action or behavior?

What is it? A business motivator designed to positively reinforce the habit of engaging with ethics and Responsible AI practices.

Need: To cultivate a company culture that fosters active participation in Responsible AI practices and ethical decision-making habits.

Solution:

_____ needs to do _____ and will be motivated to by _____?
who _ _ what _ _ _ how

Communicate

Guiding Questions

Who needs to be communicating about Responsible AI?
What information needs to be exchanged or discussed?
When and where will these conversations take place?

What is it? An internal initiative that stimulates cross-organizational communication on Responsible AI practices and ethical decision making.

Need: To break down communication silos and foster interdisciplinary collaboration.

Solution:

_____ needs to communicate about _____ during _____?
who _ _ what _ _ _ when/where

opportunities to multiply your efforts across the elements. As you answered the guiding questions for each of the elements, you should have seen natural alignments occurring in your responses. These could be an alignment across the people you are looking to educate, motivate, and communicate solutions for embedding your selected value into the specific AI project. Or perhaps you notice an alignment in the content of each element, so that you educate your people on one skillset, motivate them to use that skillset, and ensure they are communicating on that skillset. Identifying these natural alignments between your potential solutions to *Educate*, *Motivate*, and *Communicate* indicates points of high impact where you can multiple your efforts in an efficient and effective way.

If instead you find discrepancies or misalignment in your answers, go back through your guiding questions and critically assess why your responses are not aligning. *Educate*, *Motivate*, and *Communicate* are designed to build off each other, supporting and combing efforts across the entirety of your *People Pillar*. Although the three elements all serve different purposes, if they are treated as siloed challenges to solve through one-off solutions, you risk both duplication in efforts being made for other elements as well as counterproductive or even contradictory solutions across your *People Pillar*. As you begin selecting the solutions for each of your elements, be sure they tell a cohesive story. Keep an eye out for inconsistencies or marked differences in your elections as these are potential points of friction in your *People Pillar* and will shine a spotlight on areas where your efforts will experience inefficiency or become ineffective.

People Pillar in Action

Returning back to the R&AI Bank and its credit card fraud detection AI project, we can now look at completing the *People Pillar*. As the project lead, you have taken the time with your team to ideate using the guiding questions on the Values Canvas different possible solutions for each of the three *People* elements. Now it is your responsibility to review the ideas and select the solutions you will use for the credit card fraud project.

Starting with the *Educate* element, you recognize that the missing skillset in your team is with your data scientists and their ability to utilize the latest techniques in bias mitigation. Your team is relying on your data scientists to be able to mitigate bias once it is detected in the project, and so without this knowledge of the latest bias-mitigation techniques you risk crippling your teams overall fairness efforts. Pulling on the suggestions in the *Educate* section, you arrive at the following solution statement:

> [data scientists] need training in [the latest bias-mitigation techniques] that will be delivered [in a half-day workshop].

Next you move on to the *Motivate* element where you identify that although it is the data scientists who will be executing on the techniques needed to mitigate bias for a fair system, your business analysts and customer service representatives need to be involved in setting the metrics of success in fairness as they have direct insight into how customers on the market are experiencing the system. You decide that the best path forward is to have the business analysts and customer service representatives design the metrics that will direct bias-mitigation efforts for the project. As this will be a full-team effort, you decide to set those metrics as critical OKRs for the overall project. Summarizing your decisions into a solution statement for *Motivate*, you arrive at:

> [data scientists, business analysts, and customer service representatives] need to do [engage in consistent bias-mitigation efforts] and will be motivated to by [setting fairness metrics of success as critical OKRs for the overall project].

Finally you notice as you work your way through the ideas on the remaining element of *Communicate* that enabling communication on fairness across the different work functions will be essential as everyone will have a different role to play. Since fairness is a sensitive topic, and you are not entirely sure what the best methods for embedding fairness into your credit card fraud project are just yet, you decide that you need your team to be able to communicate with each other on different techniques they are trying to mitigate bias and discuss whether or not it is having the desired impact on your fairness metrics. To ensure open conversations, you settle on establishing an all-hands meeting once every three weeks to address fairness, resulting in the following solution statement for *Communicate*:

> [data scientists, business analysts, and customer service representatives] need to communicate about [bias-mitigation efforts and the impact on fairness metrics] during [an all-hands meeting hosted every three weeks].

With all your ideas and solution statements in place, your completed *People Pillar* on your Values Canvas should look like Figure 7.5.

FIGURE 7.5 Example of a Completed People Pillar

People

Educate

Guiding Questions

What is it? Any effort that is designed to up-skill individuals and/or teams in the practical application of ethics in AI.

Need: To ensure your people have the skillsets and knowledge bases necessary to critically engage with using ethics to analyze decisions for value alignment.

Who needs ethics or value-specific training?
What skills or knowledge is lacking?
What is the best learning format for this information?

Data scientists will be responsible for monitoring for unwanted bias in the system
Business analysts and customer service representatives have better insight into fairness for bank customers
Full team needs to conduct regular fairness checks
Fairness should be a priority of success for the project

[Data scientists] need training in [the latest bias-mitigation techniques] that will be delivered [in a half-day workshop].

Motivate

Guiding Questions

What is it? A business motivator designed to positively reinforce the habit of engaging with ethics and Responsible AI practices.

Need: To cultivate a company culture that fosters active participation in Responsible AI practices and ethical decision-making habits.

Who needs to engage with Responsible AI practices?
What action or behavior do they need to engage with?
How will you encourage them to engage with this action or behavior?

Data scientists will be responsible for monitoring for unwanted bias in the system
Business analysts and customer service representatives have better insight into fairness for bank customers
Full team needs to conduct regular fairness checks
Fairness should be a priority of success for the project

[Data scientists, business analysts, and customer service representatives] need to do [engage in consistent bias-mitigation efforts] and will be motivated to by [setting fairness metrics of success as critical OKRs for the overall project].

Communicate

Guiding Questions

What is it? An internal initiative that stimulates cross-organizational communication on Responsible AI practices and ethical decision making.

Need: To break down communication silos and foster interdisciplinary collaboration.

Who needs to be communicating about Responsible AI?
What information needs to be exchanged or discussed?
When and where will these conversations take place?

All team members have important insights to bring to implementing fairness and need to communicate between disciplines
Monthly all-hands meeting focused only on fairness
Internal communication channel

[Data scientists, business analysts, and customer service representatives] need to communicate about [bias-mitigation efforts and the impact on fairness metrics] during [an all-hands meeting hosted every three weeks].

The Root of Responsible AI

Risk versus Innovation Approach in Your *People Pillar*

In addition to synchronizing your *People Pillar*, you will also need to fine-tune your solutions to reflect either a risk-based or innovation-based approach to value implementation. As you will recall from Chapter 3, there is a nuanced yet highly influential difference between a risk versus an innovation approach, and from Chapter 4 that there is a method for determining which approach your organization needs in accordance to each of your foundational values. As you work through the elements of your *People Pillar*, you now have your first opportunity to design your solutions to either reflect the risk or innovation approach you had determined necessary for your selected value. To help guide your thinking, let's take a moment here to consider what the key differences would be in your *People Pillar* for either approach.

Working through the risk approach first, when it comes to developing your *People Pillar* your main objective will be to ensure your people know how to protect the specific AI project against the risks of failing to account for your selected value. In other words, if you are looking to implement fairness, you will be designing your strategy so that your people are taught to protect against a failure in fairness, otherwise known as unwanted bias. Because the risk approach is focused on mitigation and protection, your *People Pillar* will need to address your people's ability to identify, safeguard, and retrospectively rectify significant challenges and consequences as they relate to your selected value in the context of your AI project. This means for your different elements that *Educate* will need to emphasize compliance and regulation factors, *Motivate* will need to reinforce the habit of double checking work for ethical blindspots, and *Communicate* will need create space to discuss either new developments in AI safety or best mitigation practices. Overall, if you are taking a risk-based approach, you are looking at answering the question "how can I best equip my people with the ability to efficiently identify and effectively address potential disasters in my AI?"

On the other hand, if you are taking an innovation-based approach, the main objective of your *People Pillar* will be to ensure your people have a critical understanding of how your selected value works as well as how to use this value to achieve the desired outcomes for your AI project. Essentially, instead of *protecting* against the lack of your selected value, an innovation approach will look to *promote* the optimized use of that value and to *align* the outcomes of your AI project with that value. Although the difference between protecting versus promoting an ethical value may seem small in text, in practice it creates a completely different mindset and approach to problem solving among your people. With the risk approach you are safeguarding an ethical value, but with the innovation approach, your *People Pillar* will instead address your people's ability to identify, design, and proactively build for ethics opportunities in your AI project. This means for your elements that *Educate* will need to cover ethics-by-design principles, *Motivate* will need to reinforce the behavior of questioning whether or not a solution can be further aligned with your selected value, and *Communicate* will need to look at sharing success stories and fostering open conversation on creative ethics problem solving. Overall, if you are taking the innovation-based approach, you are asking yourself how you can best equip your people with the knowledge, space, and resources needed to push beyond compliance and achieve value alignment.

How Will You Know Your *People Pillar* Is Working?

With your *People Pillar* well under way, it's important to take a moment and ask yourself, how will you know it's working? It's all well and good to theorize about a strategy and to plan out details of execution, but when it comes to the rubber hitting the road, you need to know how to tell whether or not your efforts are working. Otherwise, you won't be able to tell if adjustments in your strategy are needed, or maybe even a change of course is required.

Remember, at this point in time we are working through the Values Canvas on a project or product level, not an organizational level. We will cover expected impacts for your *People Pillar* on the organizational level in Chapter 10, but for now we are going to take a look at expected impacts on a more granular level. In the current context, you have selected one of your foundational values and have been designing *Educate*, *Motivate*, and *Communicate* solutions for a specified AI project. At this level, there are two indicators you will be looking for to see if your *People* strategy is being effectively adopted. The first is that your selected value is tangibly present in critical decisions through references to the value during decision making and open conversations about how to better improve the AI project to reflect your selected value. The second is that your people are actively and concretely using the new skillset they have been taught to help implement your selected value in their workflow. If both indicators are present, then you have successfully adopted your *People* strategy for your selected value into your AI project.

Of course, adopting a strategy is important, but ensuring that it is the right strategy that will lead you to success is even more so. In this case, a successful *People Pillar* will drive two different types of impact for your AI project. First, if your *People* strategy is working, you will see an increase in your team's ability to identify and problem solve challenges in the AI project associated with your selected value. For example, if you have selected fairness, you will see an increase in speed of bias detection and quality in problem solving for that bias in your people. This is due to the fact that problem solving for specific ethical values requires new skillsets and knowledge bases in order to effectively perform, all of which is enabled through an effective *People Pillar*. In addition to impact on your people's ability to problem solve for your selected value, you will also see an increase in enthusiasm and even pride among your people in the AI project. People get excited and have pride in a project that has a purpose, or in other words that they believe provides substantial benefit to those who use it. The embedding of ethical values into a project brings further purpose to people's work, and results in an end product that they can feel good about building.

The Human in Your AI Equation

As we finish out the first of the three pillars to a holistic Responsible AI strategy for your AI project, it is a good time to re-emphasize the importance of starting with the *People Pillar*. It may be tempting to skip ahead to the *Technology Pillar*, or try to kick-start your initiative with a new AI policy. However, if you are looking for long-term success both for your Responsible AI strategy and also for the AI project itself, then it is essential to start with addressing your people. At the end of the day, AI won't exist if there is no one there to build it, and AI will not generate results if there is no one there to use it. The impact of artificial intelligence still, and always will, exists in relation to the people that build and use it. So, before you go diving in head first to this cutting-edge technology, be sure to first start at the root of it all, the humans.

08

How Is Your AI Being Built?

The Process Making the Responsible AI Engine Run

As an ethicist, my job is not to come in and tell you that you've been doing everything wrong, far from it. My job is to come and listen, seeking to understand the current landscape and get a sense for where we will need to dig deeper. I often find that companies already hold the answers to their own ethics problems, all it takes is a trained philosopher to probe with the right questions in order to unlock the potential that is already there.

This was the exact case for one of my clients, a Fortune 100 bank struggling to implement a strategy for fairness across all three teams of data scientists (this was an actual case and is separate from the example we have been using to walk through the Values Canvas with). My client had just finished a year-long initiative to build out solutions for fairness implementation, but was frustrated when they did not see any results for their efforts. To get to the bottom of this conundrum, I brought together a mixed focus group of data scientists, middle managers, and leadership, and along with a select group of Responsible AI specialists from Ethical Intelligence, we spent two weeks simply asking questions, probing, and, above all else, listening. By the end of the two weeks, we knew exactly where the problem was stemming from and what was needed to solve it.

During the discussions, we started to notice a common theme. Whenever we spoke with the data scientists, they expressed a frustration of being responsible for bias mitigation, but not being in the position to make it a priority nor to make any substantial decisions that would lead to any significant change. Not only that, but they didn't have any standard fairness metric or bias-mitigation technique to use across the teams, and so didn't have the possibility to exchange insights or best practice tips with each other. On the other hand, whenever we spoke with middle management and the leadership of the data science teams, we heard a different frustration that they were the ones being held responsible for the lack of adoption of the fairness initiatives, but they had no access, and sometimes not even visibility, into the daily operations where the bias-mitigation techniques were supposed to be in use. The middle management and leadership didn't even know where to begin when it came to tasking or holding their teams accountable for adopting the fairness initiatives.

So, what was the root of the problem? The people on the data science teams had been trained and were motivated to engage, and the technical solutions had been developed and were ready to use, but still nothing was happening. Although the people and technical solutions were in place, my client had a gaping hole right in the middle of their strategy; they were missing the operational processes needed to translate the fairness initiatives into action. Without clarity on execution, chain of command, or visibility into efforts, the data scientists were left without direction and the middle managers and leadership were stranded without visibility. What they needed was a process to unite the two and bring the company's fairness initiatives to life. This was a process problem.

The Structural Support of Responsible AI: *Process*

Imagine handing a group of perfectly capable people all the parts to an IKEA desk, but not the instructions for how to put it together. It won't matter how smart or skilled the people are, or the fact that they have everything they need to build the final product right there in front of them, without the instructions someone is bound to lose an eye and the desk will never get built. Although even with the instructions, building IKEA furniture can be quite the adventure, the point is that it would be next to impossible to do without any insight into the process needed to build the desk. The same goes for Responsible AI. You can have very capable people ready to build, and all the technical ethics solutions at the ready, but if they do not have the instructions on how to use those technical ethics solutions in action, then someone is losing the other eye and your AI is not going to reflect your foundational values.

If people are the roots to your Responsible AI strategy, then process is the structural sportive trunk. In the previous chapter we looked at how to holistically create a strategy to enable the people building your AI systems. Now we will move on in this chapter to dissect what is needed for the next layer of your Responsible AI stagey, the *Process Pillar*. Think of it this way, the *People Pillar* enables a new specific ethics skillset or Responsible AI technique, now the *Process Pillar* must empower the operational use of that skillset or technique.

This chapter will look similar to the prior, as we dive into the three elements necessary to your *Process Pillar*, the purpose that the elements serve, how to go about fulfilling the needs of these elements, and examples of the elements in action. Once we've gone through the elements and you have an understanding of what makes them up, we'll take a step back and look at your *Process Pillar* as a whole and for opportunities to interconnect the elements. Following this we will discuss what the difference between a risk versus an innovation approach to the *Process Pillar* would look like, and then close the chapter with a look at the types of results you can expect to see with a successful *Process* strategy.

The Elements of the Process Pillar

When it comes to developing the *Process Pillar*, think of it as an initiative to revise or adopt your AI development life cycle in such a way that it reflects and enables a clear path to execution on your foundational ethics values. In some cases you will need to adopt new process management systems; however, in others you can simply revise what is already there. For the sake of simplicity and adoption, always seek first to build off what is currently in place before completely reinventing the wheel. The points of impact that you are looking to build off of in the *Process Pillar* can be categorized into the following three elements: *Intent*, *Implement*, and *Instrument*.

These three elements form the essential core of your *Process Pillar*, with each serving a specific and crucial role in its success. We will go into detail on the definition, purpose, functionality, and what each element looks like in action in the following sections. For now though, you just need to know that *Intent* is about setting intentions for embedding foundational values into your AI through company policies, *Implement* focuses on execution of ethical decision making and governance frameworks, and finally *Instrument* looks at how best to equip your people with the software and artifacts necessary for execution. When it comes to designing your strategy for the *Process Pillar*, you will want to capture all three elements, as each builds on the other to create a robust and holistic solution.

As you make your way through the *Process Pillar* and its three elements, you will again find the guiding questions on your Values Canvas to help direct your thinking towards well-rounded and effective solutions for each element. Use the open space under the guiding questions on your Values Canvas to brainstorm solutions with your team, hashing out different ideas that would bridge the gap between ideals to action for your organization in Responsible AI. Ultimately you will look to convert those ideas into the solution statements you will find at the bottom of each element's section to create a cohesive strategy for your *Process Pillar*.

Intent: Responsible AI policies

What Is an Intent Solution?

> **Any company policy providing strategic guidance for Responsible AI and ethics practices.**

The first of the three elements begins with a focus on the underlying intention for what you are trying to accomplish in the *Process Pillar*. It is important to emphasize here that we are not talking about implementation of the guidelines in this element, that comes next. Before you can even begin to dissect what actions or decisions are needed to execute on your ethical values, you must first understand the purpose beneath it all. In other words, you are looking at establishing company policies for specific scenarios that will guide your people towards achieving a standard intended result. These guidelines must be clear, concise, and easily accessible.

The Purpose of Intent

> **To establish a clear and consistent strategic direction on how to manage ethical values in action.**

The core purpose of *Intent* is, quite literally, to define the purpose of your *Process Pillar*. We have already touched on the fact that the *Process Pillar* is designed to establish the structure needed to execute on embedding your foundational values into action in your specific AI project. However, as we move into the details on *Process*, your intention for this pillar cannot just be to use ethical values when the inspiration strikes. It is at this point in time that we begin to specify exactly how we will be using your foundational values in practice for your AI project by establishing the strategic guidelines for its use. With the right policy in place, you will bring the necessary organization, productivity, and harmony to your Responsible AI strategy for success (Expert Panel®, 2021).

Designing Your Intent Solution

The purpose of *Intent* is to establish direction for the use of your foundational values, typically through company and department policies. With this in mind, we must now dissect what needs to be covered by specific Responsible AI policies in order to create this direction. As we are currently working through the Values Canvas on a project level, this means we are exploring what direction or policies on your foundational values will be most useful to the given AI project at hand. Identifying the guidance needed, and how best to formulate that guidance, will lead you to your *Intent* solution.

To start, you will again need to consider who is in need of strategic direction, effectively identifying who the target profiles are for the policy. Looking at who will be involved in your specific AI project, consider if you need a project policy, a team policy, or perhaps even a policy for different select roles. Identify who within the project team is in need of guidelines to support them in actively using your select value for its intended purpose. It is possible to assess retrospectively, once the project is underway, if the scope of intended audience can or needs to be expanded. For example, perhaps you start with your data scientists as the "who" but realize once the policy is in place that your engineers would also benefit from the same policy. Either way, begin with a targeted "who" in mind to help ensure that the strategic direction you are establishing is applicable to the necessary parties.

The next factor you need to consider when designing your *Intent* solution is what type of policy is needed. Generic Responsible AI policies can be helpful in communicating to external stakeholders what internal efforts are being made to embed values, or even give an idea for how your company interprets different values. However, generic policies will not help guide critical decision making during your AI project. Your *Intent* solution is meant to set the guiding North Star for embedding your foundational values into your AI project, but you need to decide if this is happening on an operational, product, technical, or personnel level. Remember that policies are designed to set strategic direction, but you need to understand what level this direction is taking place on.

Finally, the third factor to consider is what exactly the policy needs to cover. You already know that the policy needs to provide strategic direction for using your foundational values in action, but how exactly will that value be used? This factor can cover a wide range of possibilities, as you can essentially have a different policy for every single kind of decision who are looking to make during the life cycle of your AI project. Of course, this is not feasible, so instead of looking to specifically cover every type of decision possible, consider the types of scenarios you may run into during the project life cycle that would particularly need alignment with your foundational values. Think about specific scenarios that you will need to make decisions based on your selected value for, do you know how to navigate these decisions? Or instead are you unclear about what would be the best direction forward in accordance with your company and foundational values? Identifying these types of decision scenarios will help you consider what needs to be covered in your policies.

If your company is a Responsible AI-enabled organization, then you will have plenty of Responsible AI and value-specific policies to choose from when selecting your *Intent* solution. However, if your company is still early on in Responsible AI adoption, you may encounter the need to develop a new policy. Either way, you can use the following guiding questions to help you either identify the relevant company policies already in place, or build a new policy to fit your needs:

- Who is in need of Responsible AI guidelines?
- What kind of business functions are in need of ethical strategic direction?
- What type of company policy would provide these guidelines and direction?

As you fill out the *Intent* section of your Values Canvas, you are working towards the answering the following solution statement:

> [who] needs a [what type of] policy for strategic guidance on [what]?

Intent in Action

To help illustrate what the elements of your *Process Pillar* should look like, let's continue with the example of R&AI Bank and its AI project on credit card fraud detection. As the project lead, you've just finished filing out the *People Pillar* of your Values Canvas and have your solutions for *Educate*, *Motivate*, and *Communicate* laid out. Now that you know your people on the project will be well equipped to handle the value of fairness, you now must move to ensuring that your people know the process for how to execute on fairness for your AI project. As you sit down with your team again to begin with the first element of *Process*, *Intent*, you realize that in assessing R&AI Bank's current company policies there is a significant gap when it comes to AI and fairness. Although the bank has policies on credit fraud and treating customers fairly, the company does not have any policies on what a responsible use of AI is when it comes to servicing customers. On top of this, you discover that even though R&AI Bank has defined fairness as "equal quality of service" there is no guidance on what that should mean when it comes to detecting credit card fraud. Taking stock of the gaps, you fill out the *Intent* section in your Values Canvas, leaving the solution statement blank until you've completed the guiding questions for all three *Process* elements as shown in Figure 8.1.

FIGURE 8.1 Intent Element

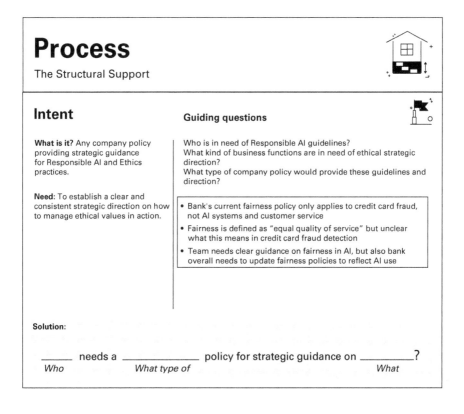

Implement: Governance and operational frameworks

What Is an Implement Solution?

> Any procedural framework designed to direct the execution of Responsible AI practices and ethical decision making.

In this second element of the *Process Pillar* we will build off the foundations set in the first element, *Intent*. In *Intent* we created the guidelines for how your organization will ideally use its foundation values, and now in *Implement* we are looking at how to execute on those guidelines. In other words, we are diving into the details, determining precisely where key decisions need to be made and what distinct actions are needed to implement our Responsible AI policies. Think of this as the framework element that is focused on establishing operational structures that enable practical execution of your foundational values.

The Purpose of Implement

> To create a comprehensive and standard course of action for execution of ethical values and practices.

Just as the core of *Intent* was to define the purpose of your *Process Pillar*, the core of *Implement* is to execute on that purpose. A common blocker to ethics implementation and the overall success of a Responsible AI strategy is that a company will establish a strong Responsible AI policy, but then fail to create the supporting framework that will ensure execution of the policy (Chowdhury et al., 2020). Having a statement of intent saying that you will mitigate unwanted bias in your models is very different from having a framework that details exactly how to carry out that mitigation for your employees. In this element, we are focused on making the details as practical as possible, while still striking the right balance of oversight to ensure that the established framework is effective in implementing values without becoming restrictive or cumbersome.

Designing Your Implement Solution

In this second element of the *Process Pillar*, the *Implement* solution is in the details. Governance and operational frameworks are designed to integrate policy intentions into action, which means in this case we are diving into what kind of framework is needed to embed your foundational values into key decisions and actions taken during the life cycle of your AI project. Thinking through *Implement* on a project level using your Values Canvas, you will want to consider what kind of specific actions you need your people to take in order for your foundational values to be reflected in your project and how the process of those actions should take place.

As always, the first consideration we begin with is who will need to use this framework. Simply put, we need to identify whose job it will be to execute on your foundational values. Another perspective can also be to consider whose Responsible AI functions on your project can be made easier by having a standard procedure of operation to help guide decision making. The goal of your *Implement* solution should not be to create more work, but instead make your team's ethics responsibilities easier to execute. By identifying who needs the support of a framework, and who will be accountable that the framework is used, you can understand the direct use case of your *Implement* solution.

With the understanding of who will be engaging with the framework, you must now consider at what point in the project life cycle they will be engaged in using it. You may have the world's most beautifully designed framework, but if your people do not know when exactly to use it, the likelihood of the framework actually being used significantly decreases to bare minimal amounts. Looking at your project life cycle, is this a framework for the design, develop, or deploy phase of your AI? Perhaps instead of a framework for a specific phase of the life cycle, what you need instead is an operational framework that complements your teams workflow already in place. Or maybe you even need a framework that is used to support a predetermined set of decisions that will need to be taken throughout the project development cycle. Whatever your answer is, you want to be able to clearly state when exactly someone should use the framework in order to maximize the return on impact of its use.

The right framework can make significant impact by reducing risk of failure for your AI, but the wrong framework can threaten to derail your entire project. The key factor you need to consider in order to ensure you end up with the first option is what kind of framework it is that you need. On the one hand, you can have thinking frameworks that are designed to guide your thought process through specific checks and considerations in order to arrive at an ethically aligned decision. On the other hand, you can have action frameworks that are designed to instruct a precise set of actions that will lead to your foundational values being reflected in your AI. If you try to use a thinking framework when an action framework is better suited, you expose your project to unnecessary risks by leaving certain actions open-ended that should instead be back and white. While if in the reverse you use an action framework when a thinking framework is better suited, you risk stifling innovative thinking and opportunity for improvement by locking your teams into a plan of action that may not be ideal for their context. The best way to tell if you need a thinking or action framework is to ask yourself whether or not you can say with confidence that you know the right actions needed in order to achieve your desired outcome of value implementation. If you already know what needs to be done, a prescriptive action framework is the best fit for your needs. However, if you are unsure of what kind of actions are needed and instead have a better understanding of generally what factors should or shouldn't be guiding decision making in your project, then the flexible advice of a thinking framework is best.

The final consideration to make when developing your *Implement* solution is to think about where you will get the framework from. In other words, are you creating a new framework from scratch, revising a current framework in use, or even adopting a general open-access framework and customizing it to your needs? The important aspect to consider here is the path of least resistance. If you have the time and resources to create a new framework from scratch, that is a significant advantage in terms of applicability to your specific organization. However, if that is too time-and resource-intensive, or if you do not want to add yet another procedural framework onto the workload of your people, then you can look at revising current frameworks in use to reflect specific ethics checks. Additionally, there are hundreds of Responsible AI frameworks already available online that you can access and customize to your own needs.

Just as in *Intent*, if your company is a Responsible AI-enabled organization you will have plenty of frameworks to choose from when selecting your *Implement* solution. However, this may not always be the case, which means you may encounter the need to develop a new framework. Whichever direction you find yourself in, you can use the following guiding questions to help you decide on what framework is best suited to support your teams in embedding your foundational values into your AI project:

- Who needs a framework to help execute on ethical values and Responsible AI practices?
- What do they need the framework for? Is it to guide critical thinking or direct specific actions?
- At what point in the AI life cycle will this framework be used?
- Are you building a new framework, adapting an old framework, or customizing an open-access framework?

As you add your ideas to the *Implement* section of your Values Canvas, keep in mind that you are ultimately working towards the answering the final solution statement:

[who] needs a framework for [what] to be used [when]?

Implement in Action

Returning back to R&AI Bank and the credit card fraud project, you begin to consider what kind of framework is needed to execute on fairness. You already know that your data scientists will be the ones implementing bias-mitigation techniques, but you're not sure when and where that should happen. Since you have certain fairness metrics you will need to meet, and will already know what kind of bias-mitigation techniques your data scientists will be using, it seems as though a framework to direct specific actions would best fit your needs. You consider that all R&AI Bank data scientists use the same workflow when it comes to developing systems, and that there are natural checks already built into the weekly reviewal process on project progress and model performance. You take these ideas and add them to your Values Canvas, working through each of the guiding questions but leaving the solution statement blank until you are ready to look at the *Process Pillar* as a whole.

FIGURE 8.2 Implement Element

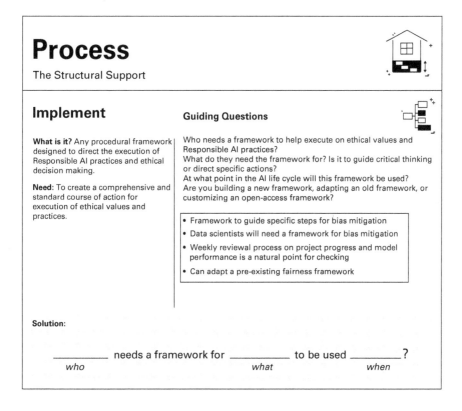

Process

The Structural Support

Implement

What is it? Any procedural framework designed to direct the execution of Responsible AI practices and ethical decision making.

Need: To create a comprehensive and standard course of action for execution of ethical values and practices.

Guiding Questions

Who needs a framework to help execute on ethical values and Responsible AI practices?
What do they need the framework for? Is it to guide critical thinking or direct specific actions?
At what point in the AI life cycle will this framework be used?
Are you building a new framework, adapting an old framework, or customizing an open-access framework?

- Framework to guide specific steps for bias mitigation
- Data scientists will need a framework for bias mitigation
- Weekly reviewal process on project progress and model performance is a natural point for checking
- Can adapt a pre-existing fairness framework

Solution:

_____ needs a framework for _____ to be used _____?
who   what   when

Instrument/**Tools**

What Is an Instrument Solution?

Software used to standardize implementation of Responsible AI and Ethics practices.

The final of the three *Process Pillar* elements once again builds on top of the foundations laid in the first two elements as shown in Figure 8.2. *Intent* gave us the guidelines, *Implement* brought us the actions to execute on those guidelines, and now *Instrument* brings both the guidelines and actions to life in your organization. This element is focused on understanding what kinds of artifacts are necessary to support the standardized execution of your policies and frameworks. Typically, *Instrument* solutions come in the form of software platforms designed to help automate repetitive tasks, track progress across objectives, and most importantly scale your Responsible AI practices.

The Purpose of Instrument

To standardize execution, automate processes where appropriate, and increase the efficiency of Responsible AI practices at scale.

Establishing policies and frameworks are essential to Responsible AI success; however, it is incredibly important to ensure that these practices are supported by the proper tools. Although a presentation deck detailing the intricacies of your new Responsible AI framework may work for board meeting presentations, it is doomed to quickly be forgotten in desk bottom drawers if not given a place to live. Simply put, you are looking at what kind of artifact or digital tool is needed to reinforce your Responsible AI practices. In doing so, you are establishing the path to effective implementation, and ideally one that has the capacity to scale throughout your organization (Vartak, 2022).

Designing Your Instrument Solution

In the final element of the *Process Pillar*, we are looking at what kind of software is needed to enable effective implementation of your Responsible AI policies and frameworks. The key to *Instrument* is that you must establish an actual tool for your teams to engage with. Be it a digital worksheet all the way to a software platform, you need a place for the frameworks guiding your Responsible AI practice to live. Emphasizing usability, your *Instrument* solution is the supportive software that will help your *Process Pillar* run smoothly.

Diving into our first consideration for *Instrument*, we must first ask who will be using the software. Thankfully this is fairly straightforward if you have already worked your way through *Implement*, as the people using your Responsible AI frameworks are most likely the ones that will also need a supportive software tool to execute. There is also an opportunity, though, with *Instrument* to consider if other profiles would benefit from access to the software by gaining insights into Responsible AI processes and progress.

Once you know who will be using the tool, you can consider what software functionality is needed. Using software for the sake of having software is counterproductive at best, and extremely costly in time and resources at worst. That is why it is essential to understand what exactly you need the tool for in the first place, prior to shopping on the market or investing in the development of one. Take a moment and list out all of the possible software functions you would ideally want, keeping in mind the goal is a tool that supports efficiency in your Responsible AI practices. Ultimately you will want a software that can scale and automate where appropriate your Responsible AI processes, so be sure to examine what kind of functionality will be needed to support your efforts in the long run. If you're still not sure what kind of functionality is needed, seek input from those who will ideally be using it.

In some cases, you will find that a third-party governance software designed specifically for Responsible AI is the best solution, in other cases you may find that a current project management software better fits your needs, and in some rare cases you may consider building your own software solution altogether. To help you consider what *Instrument* solution is best suited to your needs, here are a couple of guiding questions:

- Who will use this software?
- What will they use it to do?

As you go through your *Instrument* element answering you guiding questions, your end goal will be to complete the following solution statement:

[who] needs a software tool to do [what]?

Instrument in Action

Looking to finish out the *Process Pillar* elements for the R&AI Bank and its credit card fraud detection project, you as the project lead, along with your team, begin to consider what kind of software tool could help aid in the implementation of fairness. By now you have come to realize that the data scientists will be responsible for the execution of bias mitigation, but it is the whole team that will be responsible for ensuring a fair system in the end. Because of this, you consider if there is a software that your data scientists could use to monitor the data being used the train and test the AI system, but also still be readable by the rest of your team. Filling out the final element section to your *Process Pillar* but leaving the solution statement blank, you add your ideas to the *Instrument* section as shown in Figure 8.3.

FIGURE 8.3 Instrument Element

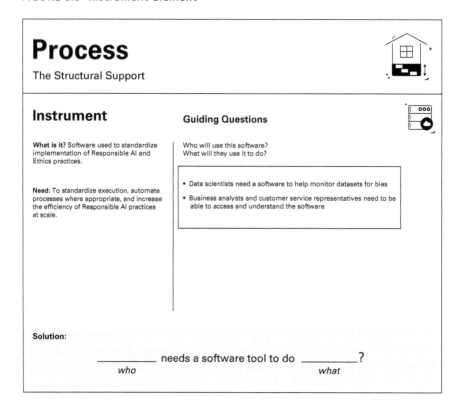

Bringing It All Together: Finalizing Your *Process Pillar*

We began our dive into your Responsible AI strategy with *People* and a look into who is building your AI. That led us next to *Process*, where we are currently exploring how your people are building your AI. As was stressed at the start, you can have a top-talent team with the best training on ethical decision making, but if the team has no clear operational structure for how to execute that ethical decision making, then the team loses the ability to effectively embed ethics into your AI project. As with any business function, if there is no supporting process then there are no results.

As we have covered in this chapter, there are three elements to the *Process Pillar*: *Intent*, *Implement*, and *Instrument* as shown in Figure 8.4. The three elements each cover an important component of the business operations needed to execute on Responsible AI practices, essentially building the processes that translate your foundational values into decisions and actions.

Using your Values Canvas to visualize how to embed your foundational values into the processes behind your AI project, you should have ideas written out for solutions to your *Intent*, *Implement*, and *Instrument* elements. For *Intent* you've been identifying the high-level guidance your teams need and what kinds of policies will provide it. In *Implement* you've been brainstorming what kind of frameworks could bring your Responsible AI practices to life and ensure the execution of your ethics objectives. For *Instrument* you've been looking at different types of software that will support efficiency in your Responsible AI practices at scale. As you look over the ideas, you should start to see how your three elements will come together and be excited by the potential it creates. The key now, though, is to not get stuck at the ideation phase and move forward to planning out the exact solutions you will need.

Synchronizing Your Process Pillar

With your three elements in hand, it's time to take a step back and consider your *Process Pillar* as a whole story. As you did with your *People Pillar*, you are looking for synergy between the elements in *Process*, actively searching for how *Intent*, *Implement*, and *Instrument* can interconnect and support each other. Unlike the *People Pillar* though, you do need to design a different solution for each of your *Process* elements instead of having the possibility to design one solution to fit all three elements' purposes as you did in *People*. A complete *Process Pillar* should read like a plan of action for embedding

FIGURE 8.4 Process Pillar. For the full figure, please see www.koganpage.com/responsible-ai

Process

The Structural Support

Intent

Guiding Questions

What is it? Any company policy providing strategic guidance for Responsible AI and Ethics practices.

Need: To establish a clear and consistent strategic decision on how to manage ethical values in action.

Who is in need of Responsible AI guidelines? What kind of business functions are in need of ethical strategic direction? What type of company policy would provide these guidelines and direction?

Solution:

_____ needs a _____ policy for strategic guidance on _____ ?
who   what type of   what

Implement

Guiding Questions

What is it? Any procedural framework designed to direct the execution of Responsible AI practices and Ethical decision making.

Need: To create a comprehensive and standard course of action for execution of ethical values and practices.

Who needs a framework to help execute on ethical values and Responsible AI practices? What do they need the framework for? Is it to guide critical thinking or direct specific actions? At what point in the AI life cycle will this framework be used? Are you building a new framework, adapting an old framework, or customizing an open-access framework?

Solution:

_____ needs a framework for _____ to be used _____ ?
who   what   when

Instrument

Guiding Questions

What is it? Software used to standardize implementation of Responsible AI and Ethics practices.

Need: To standardize execution, automate processes where appropriate, and increase the efficiency of Responsible AI practices at scale.

Who will use this software? What will they use it to do?

Solution:

_____ needs a software tool to do _____ ?
who   what

foundational values into your project, as you start with the abstract objectives in *Intent*, move into what needs to be done to reach those objectives in *Implement*, and end with how it all will be put into action in *Instrument*. Another way to think about the elements of *Process* is that *Intent* creates the why, *Implement* the what, and *Instrument* the how for the Responsible AI organizational operations needed to achieve reflecting your foundational values in your AI project.

As you read through your answers, look for discrepancies or misalignment across the three elements. If you find any, go back to critically assess your original answers and examine the thinking behind the answers that led to the misalignment. Just as the elements in the *People Pillar* are designed to support each other, so are the elements of the *Process Pillar*. Attempting to execute on a single solution from *Intent*, *Implement*, or *Instrument* without supporting efforts from the other two elements will inevitably lead to inefficiencies and eventual ineffectiveness of your overall strategy. Think of the three elements of the *Process Pillar* as three legs of a stool, you need all three legs in order to effectively place any weight on the stool, just as you need all three elements in order to place any time, resource, or projected impact on *Process*.

Process Pillar in Action

Looking back to our case study of the R&AI Bank and its credit card fraud detection AI project, we can look to complete the *Process Pillar*. As the project lead, it is your responsibility to take the ideas you brainstormed with your team for the three elements and distill down the possibilities into the solutions you will ultimately use for *Process*.

Starting with the first element *Intent*, you realize thanks to the work you did looking into the current policies of R&AI Bank and comparing them to the needs of your team, that there is a gap in guidance when it comes to applying fairness in AI projects that will ultimately service customers. Because you are looking embed fairness into what will eventually be a customer-facing system, you recognize that your team needs a policy that guides product quality for customer-facing AI systems. Bringing your ideas together, you summarize your team's need into the following solution statement:

> [data scientists, business analysts, and customer service representatives] need a [product quality] policy for strategic guidance on [fairness in customer-facing AI systems].

From *Intent* you move on to *Implement*, thinking about how to translate your policy on fairness in customer-facing AI systems into practical action for your team. You consider the fact that the execution of fairness will rely on the data scientists, and so decide a framework on specific actions to be taken during the data scientists' workflow will best complement the policy your team will be following. Noting that the data scientists already have a weekly review process in place for the project, you decide that building a framework for bias mitigation and checks on top of the existing workflow would make it easy for your team to adopt the framework and efficient in executing on fairness. Taking your decisions in mind, you complete the following solution statement:

> [data scientists] need a framework for [bias mitigation and checks] to be used [during the team's weekly review process].

Finally you move to the last of the *Process* elements, looking into the needs of your team for *Instrument*. You see that your data scientists will be executing the bias-mitigation techniques that will help embed fairness, while your business analysts and customer service representatives will be providing insights as to whether or not the techniques are actually resulting in equal quality of service for R&AI Bank's customers. Because of this, you realize that if you have a data dashboard that will track the fairness metrics you created in *Motivate*, then your data scientists will be able to track their progress on bias mitigation, and your business analysts and customer service representatives can help monitor whether or not the metrics are translating to actual impact on R&AI Bank customers.

> [data scientists, business analysts, and customer services representatives] need a software tool to [create a data dashboard that will monitor fairness metrics].

Bringing all three elements and their solution statements into one cohesive strategy, your completed *Process Pillar* for the credit card fraud detection project should look something like Figure 8.5.

FIGURE 8.5 Example of a Completed Process Pillar

Process

The Structural Support

Intent

Guiding Questions

What is it? Any company policy providing strategic guidance for Responsible AI and Ethics practices.

Need: To establish a clear and consistent strategic direction on how to manage ethical values in action.

Who is in need of Responsible AI guidelines?

What kind of business functions are in need of ethical strategic direction?

What type of company policy would provide these guidelines and direction?

> Bank's current fairness policy only applies to credit fraud, not AI systems and customer service
>
> Fairness is defined as 'equal quality of service' but unclear of what this means in credit fraud detection
>
> Team needs clear guidance on fairness in AI, but also bank overall needs to update fairness policies to reflect AI use

[Data scientists, business analysts and customer service representatives] need a [product quality] policy for strategic guidance on [fairness in customer-facing AI systems].

Implement

Guiding Questions

What is it? Any procedural framework designed to direct the execution of Responsible AI practices and Ethical decision making.

Need: To create a comprehensive and standard course of action for execution of ethical values and practices.

Who needs a framework to help execute on ethical values and Responsible AI practices?

What do they need the framework for? Is it to guide critical thinking or direct specific actions?

At what point in the AI life cycle will this framework be used?

Are you building a new framework, adapting an old framework, or customizing an open-access framework?

> Framework to guide specific steps for bias mitigation
>
> Data scientists will need a framework for bias mitigation
>
> Weekly reviewal process on project progress and model performance is a natural point for checking
>
> Can adapt a pre-existing fairness framework

[Data scientists] need a framework for [bias mitigation and checks] to be used [during the team's weekly reviewal process].

Instrument

Guiding Questions

What is it? Software used to standardize implementation of Responsible AI and Ethics practices.

Need: To standardize execution, automate processes where appropriate, and increase the efficiency of Responsible AI practices at scale.

Who will use this software?

What will they use it to do?

> Data scientists need a software to help monitor datasets for bias
>
> Business analysts and customer service representatives need to be able to access and understand the software

[Data scientists, business analysts and customer services representatives] need a software tool to [create a data dashboard that will monitor fairness metrics].

Risk versus Innovation Approach in Your *Process Pillar*

As you begin to synchronize your *Process Pillar*, you again have the opportunity to design your solutions with either a risk or innovation approach. Depending on your organization's needs, you can emphasize protective measures for a risk-based approach, or you can emphasize alignment design thinking for an innovation-based approach, or you can strike a balance of both. Remember, you are not restricted to only taking one or the other approach to Responsible AI solutions, you can have a mixture of risk- and innovation-based resources, shifting between the two as demand dictates. With this in mind, let's take a brief look at what the difference between a risk versus innovation approach would look like for your *Process Pillar*.

Starting with the risk-based approach, when it comes to developing your *Process Pillar* your main objective will be to ensure the right checks and safeguards are in place to protect against the risks and ethical blindspots that occur naturally during the entire AI life cycle. Risks can be predicted, but they are only taken account of in retrospect, meaning that your people will need a process that instructs them to go over their work and check for any risks or even for realized problems that have been uncovered. There is some ability to proactively predict potential risks, but the true bulk of the work happens as a retrospective check once there is something in fact to check, such as when the AI has been deployed and your people must react to how it performs in the wild. These checks will need to be closely documented as well, providing evidence of risk tracking for your AI project. This means that your elements will need to heavily emphasis compliance and safeguarding throughout your *Process Pillar*. *Intent* will need to establish clear and hard lines that should not be crossed in accordance to both regulation and foundational ethics values. *Implement* will be focused on creating the points in time for the checks to happen, and *Instrument* must be a tool that enables close documentation of your development process so as to facilitate auditing. Overall, if you are taking the risk-based approach, you are asking yourself how can you best enable your people to execute on the required risk and safeguard checks throughout the AI life cycle?

Coming from the opposite direction, if you are taking an innovation-based approach the main objective of your *Process Pillar* will be to ensure that your people are given the time, space, and direction necessary to engage in ethics-by-design creative thinking. Unlike the risk approach that focuses on checking back on completed work, the innovation approach primarily happens at the start to the AI life cycle. Essentially, you must create time to innovate at the start of a project, otherwise the likelihood of innovation occurring or being integrated significantly decreases if done at the end of a project. In other words, the innovation approach must be a proactive, not a retroactive, process. While the risk approach looks at safeguarding, the innovation approach looks at creating a safe environment in which your people can experiment and test ideas. As the innovation approach rests heavily on design thinking, you are looking for opportunities in which a process can help support this design emphasis. What this means for your different elements is that *Intent* will promote value-centric design principles, *Implement* will create the time and space necessary to explore new solutions, and *Instrument* will look to support the safe testing of new ideas. It is important to note what I hope is a blatantly obvious fact here that it if you do chose an innovation-based approach, you are still legally liable to comply with regulations relevant to your technology, which in many cases will require documentation and auditing of AI systems. Overall, if you are taking the innovation-based approach for your *Process Pillar*, you are asking yourself how can you create the time and place through standard processes in your people's workflows to proactively explore new ways of designing for your foundational ethics values.

How Will You Know Your *Process Pillar* Is Working?

With your *Process Pillar* now coming together, it's important to take a moment to reflect on how you will be able to tell if your efforts are working or not. The purpose of the *Process Pillar* is to understand how your AI is being built, but also to build off your *People Pillar* in a way that creates a clear path to success for your people in executing on your foundational ethics values. In the case of the *Process*, there is a fine line between a successful policy or framework, and a cumbersome policy or framework that becomes counterproductive to your AI development. In order to ensure you are walking on the right side of the line, you need to establish clear indicators of success for your *Process* efforts, that way you can catch a suboptimal process before it becomes too ingrained.

Looking specifically at what kind of tangible impacts you should be looking for as indicators of a successful *Process Pillar* for your AI project, we turn to measuring performance and tracking progress. On one hand, you will be looking at the performance of your people and expecting to see an increase in efficiency thanks to the direction and streamlining of actions you've established with the Responsible AI the policies, frameworks, and tools. On the other hand, you will be looking at your AI models' performance and expecting to see a reduction in the percentage of models needing to be pulled post-production due to unforeseen risks or misbehavior, as these will be caught earlier on in the AI life cycle thanks to your Responsible AI processes. Overall, across the organization you should see a measurable increase in regulation readiness, as current and incoming digital regulations all have process and documentation requirements that are perfectly complemented by a strong *Process Pillar* strategy. In fact, 51 percent of Responsible AI-enabled organizations feel ready to meet incoming AI regulations even before these regulations are in effect (Stackpole, 2023).

Beyond the type of impact that can be measured and tracked, a successful *Process Pillar* will also lead to the more intangible increases in clarity and creativity. Thanks to your newly established processes, you should have created a sense of clarity that previously was lacking in regards to execution on Responsible AI, but also even within your AI development life cycle in general. If done properly, your *Process Pillar* will enable a sense of clarity in direction and thinking for your people, as they transition from a place of vague assumptions to a solid foundation of concrete and comprehensive guidelines. Additionally, this newfound clarity will also lead to an increase in creativity within your teams, as you remove any confusion or doubt in your AI development processes and replace it with the mental space and capacity for creative problem solving and thinking. Overall, with the combined effects of intangible impacts of clarity and creativity, you will experience an increase in your AI quality thanks to a successful *Process Pillar*.

From *Process* to *Technology*

We started with your people and looking into how to equip your workforce with the skillset necessary to execute on Responsible AI and your foundational values. With your people addressed, we moved on to your process and in this chapter went into depth on exactly how your people will operationally be executing Responsible AI practices and foundational values. It may be tempting to jump immediately from your people to your technology, thinking that as long as your people understand your foundational values, they should be able to implement them into your AI project without any hiccups or bumps in the road. However, as we have seen throughout this chapter, your people will not be able to execute on anything if your operations are not supportive of Responsible AI practices. So before you jump straight into embedding foundational values into your AI, look first at how to create a clear and supported operational path to success through organizational processes. You can build the most sophisticated technological ethics solutions possible for your AI, but if your people do not know how to execute on those solutions, you will never see the adoption or impact you had hoped for.

09

What Are You Building into Your AI?

The Technical Interventions of Responsible AI

A while back I was leading a project with Ethical Intelligence that was auditing a client's AI system. Keeping all sensitive information anonymous, the client operated in a highly sensitive and regulated market, but was in need of an audit in order to build trust in their system. They were achieving amazing results from their AI system, almost too good to believe, and so decided that having an AI Ethics firm audit their AI system would bring the layer of transparency necessary to building trust but without compromising the security of the system.

On the project, I was leading a small team of ethics, model, and industry experts through the process of auditing the client's AI system. One of the claims that the client was making about their system was that they had removed all demographic biases, but were still struggling to convince customers to trust that they had. Upon digging deeper into the client's biasmitigation techniques, we discovered that the client did not collect any data on ethnicity so that it could not be included in the data used to train or test the AI systems. The idea was that since there were no data points on ethnicity being used, then it was not possible for racial bias to exist within the AI systems. Thanks to the interdisciplinary mix of expertise, my team quickly picked up on this as an ethical challenge that the client had unknowingly exposed themselves to, and that was causing some of the mistrust issues.

The client had removed all data points on ethnicity with the best intentions of creating a fair system. However, the client did not realize that in doing so, they had exposed an ethical blindspot in the build of their AI systems. Although removing data points on ethnicity in training and testing datasets can help mitigate racial bias, it does not account for proxy data on ethnicity. What this means is that within the datasets the client was using to train and test models, there could be data points that would serve as a proxy for ethnicity due to underlying patterns in different ethnicities' behaviors. Where the client had unknowingly exposed themselves to risk was that in not collecting the data on ethnicity, they had no baseline dataset to compare the results of the models to. Even though data on ethnicity had been removed from the training data, the client had no way to confirm whether or not the model outputs had discovered an underlying proxy point for race. This blindspot had nothing to do with the organizational processes; clearly the client had done their due diligence in establishing governance frameworks for monitoring bias in their model outputs. Nor did it have to do with the people, as the client had a highly educated and advanced team working on the models, as well as a company culture that prioritized ethics. What the client had was a technology problem.

Best Practices in AI Development: *Technology*

There is the saying that goes "I'm building the plane while I'm flying it," which people will use when they have taken a leap into a new project without necessarily knowing exactly how they will pull it off. Maybe it's my personal opinion, but I were flying a plane while I was building it, the first thing I would start with would be the wings. Structurally essentially to the planes ability to fly, building a plane without wings is a nonstarter. Embarking on new AI projects can often be a similar process. You have a general understanding of what is needed to build a successful AI system, but aren't entirely sure what obstacles you will encounter along the way. This means you will want to start by building the essentials first, otherwise you may find yourself hurtling through the air in a metal tube. The *Technology Pillar* to your Responsible AI strategy is like the wings of your plane; you need to ensure the key components to success are in place before you can continue forward.

If people are the roots to your Responsible AI strategy, and process is the structural sportive trunk, then the technology itself is the fruits of your labor sitting atop a strong and healthy tree. In the previous two chapters we looked at how to create holistic solutions for the people and processes behind the scenes. Now it is time to transition our thinking and focus specifically on what is being built into the AI itself in the final layer of your Responsible AI strategy, the *Technology Pillar*.

This chapter will mirror the previous two, as we take a deep dive into the three elements necessary to your *Technology Pillar*. We will discuss the definition and purpose of each element, as well as covering what is in included in each element to fulfill its purpose and an example of that element in action. Once we have gone through all three elements, we will take a look at the differences between a risk versus innovation based approach to this pillar, and then close the chapter with the different impacts you can hope to see with a successful *Technology Pillar* strategy.

The Elements of the Technology Pillar

As you embark on your *Technology Pillar*, think of it as an initiative to build the points of intervention into your AI life cycle for either protecting or aligning your AI solution with your foundational ethics values. In other words, we are looking at what needs to be built into your AI systems in order to reflect your foundational values in your technology. There are an infinite number of ways in which an AI solution can inherent ethical challenges, which means there is the potential for an infinite number of narrow point solutions you can create for ethical challenges found in your AI. The goal in this *Technology Pillar* is not to spin a web of point ethics solutions, instead it is to establish the technological structures that enable those point ethics solutions to be implemented, as well as create the foundations upon which your organization can effectively identify ethics challenges and efficiently deploy solutions. These structural points of impact not only lead to a successful Responsible AI strategy, but are also simply best practices in AI development. The points of impact you will be looking to build for your *Technology Pillar* can be categorized into three elements: *Data*, *Document*, and *Domain*.

Each of the three elements serves its own purpose for your *Technology Pillar*, on which we will go into greater detail throughout the remainder of this chapter. For now though, what you need to know is that *Data* looks at adding data ethics practices to your already existing data management process, *Document* focuses on the documentation of ethical decision making throughout the life cycle of your models, and *Domain* brings in the human oversight and feedback needed to refine your AI systems. Although we are again looking at processes in this pillar, *Technology* is different from *Process* as *Technology* focuses specifically on technical processes and solutions, while *Process* is focused on operations. When it comes to designing your strategy for your *Technology Pillar*, a holistic and robust solution will capture all three elements.

It is important to note two points here unique to the *Technology Pillar*. First, if you do not come from a traditional technical background, it is good practice to collaborate with someone who does when designing this pillar. And second, if you do not already have data management, documentation or feedback processes already in place, you are missing key technical components of any AI system build that you must fill before you can begin to consider how to align them to your foundational ethics values.

As you work your way through this final pillar of your Responsible AI strategy for your AI projects, you will find again a list of guiding questions in each element on the Values Canvas that will help support your conceptualization of solutions for your elements. As you have been doing in the prior two pillars, use the open space below the guiding questions to brainstorm solutions with your team, especially the ones from traditional technical backgrounds, to create the structural points of ethics interventions in your AI systems. Ultimately you will take those ideas and convert them into the solution statements you find at the bottom of each element's section to create a cohesive strategy for your *Technology Pillar*.

Data

What Is a Data Solution?

> **A technique or method for embedding ethical values into the data that is being used to train and/or test an AI model.**

To kick off the *Technology Pillar*, we go straight to the source of your AI by diving into your organization's data practices. You cannot have AI if you do not have data, and you cannot have Responsible AI if you do not have data ethics. From data labeling, to data sourcing, to data security and beyond, data is socially constructed (Broussard, 2019) which means there are multiple entry points for ethical risk throughout the data life cycle, which means there's just as many, if not more, opportunities to align your data practices with your foundational ethical values. When it comes to the *Data* element of your *Technology Pillar*, we are not necessarily looking at your general data practices, but more specifically looking for data ethics techniques or methods you can harness to embed your foundational ethics values.

The Purpose of Data

To align your data life cycle management with your ethical values so that your AI is being built on an ethically sound foundation.

To truly solve a problem, you must go to the source of it, which in the case of AI is the data. The purpose of the *Data* element in your *Technology Pillar* is just that, to get down to the source of technical ethics challenges in AI systems. From data privacy to data bias, there are countless ways in which your data can either reflect or contradict your organization's foundational ethics values (Nassar and Kamal, 2021). The goal of this element is to understand what is needed in order to ensure the alignment of ethical values, because if your data reflects your ethical values, then your ethical values will be embedded into your AI systems. There is an old adage about data that goes "garbage in, garbage out," but what would it look like if we changed it to "ethics in, ethics out"?

Designing Your Data Solution

As we dive into the design of your *Data* solution, two things need to be clarified. First, the *Data* element in this context of Responsible AI is not referring to data management in general, but instead specifically on data *ethics*. I will not be covering what goes into good general data management, at this point your organization should already have a team dedicated to that. Second, I will not be giving you specific data ethics solutions in this section, as that is a subject for another book as I can't possible fit an entire professional expertise into a few short paragraphs. Instead, I will be giving you the strategic perimeters that will enable you to conceptualize what kind of data ethics technique or method it is you need. With this in mind, if you do not come from a background in data yourself, I strongly urge you to collaborate with a data professional on this element.

To start, the first consideration you will need to make is exactly which ethical value it is you want to embed. Unlike the elements from previous pillars where you could create a solution that fit multiple ethical values, *Data* behaves a bit differently. When it comes to embedding ethical values into your data practices, there are different methods and solutions for each ethical value, as well as different points within the data life cycle that these methods will need to be deployed. For example, the same technique you use to eliminate bias in data cannot be used to build consent options for privacy.

With ethical value in mind, the next thing to consider is when in the data life cycle would be the highest point of impact for this ethical value. Walking through the stages of the data life cycle, critically assess the potential for an ethics intervention at each stage for both feasibility and positive impact. For example, let's say you are focusing on fairness, an ethical value that is embedded in data through bias-mitigation techniques. As you go through the stages of the data life cycle, you see that there are points during this cycle in which bias mitigation naturally fits. Upon reflection, you determine that the greatest point of impact would be to implement fairness during the data-processing stage while the data is being cleaned. It is important to emphasize here that you can embed an ethical value at multiple stages of the data life cycle, but what you are looking for is the most effective point of entry, which may require some trial testing to fully uncover.

When it comes to responsible data, there is a rich field of research, techniques, and methods widely available as potential solutions to embedding your ethical values into the data life cycle. The final consideration for your *Data* solution is to figure out which one is going to work for your organization. A good way to do this is to consult with your data science teams, or at least a lead data scientist, in order to understand what kind of methods your organization is already accustomed to using, and to see if they have any insights into what would work well for a specific ethical value in the data life cycle. The key in the end to a successful *Data* solution will be consistency, which the frameworks from the *Process Pillar* should be an effective support in achieving.

There are hundreds of potential data ethics solutions available, which is why it is important to stress here that this selection process itself is a cynical journey. You will need to monitor progress and adjust your methods over time if you are not seeing the results you had intended. With this in mind, here are the guiding questions to help you work through what kind of *Data* solution you need to embed your ethical values into your training and testing data:

- What ethical value do you need to embed into your data management practices?
- When in the data life cycle does this ethical value need to be embedded?
- What technique/method will you use to embed this value?

Working through the *Data* section of your Values Canvas, keep in mind that you will eventually want to distill your ideas down into the following solution statement:

[ethical value] will be embedded [when] in the data life cycle using [what] technique/method?

Data in Action

As the project lead on a credit card fraud detection AI project for the R&AI Bank, you've now made your way through the *People* and *Process* pillars of your Responsible AI strategy for this project, leaving you with the last remaining layer of *Technology*. Starting with your *Data* element, you sit down with the lead data scientist on your team and start to hash out some ideas for how to embed fairness directly into the data the team is using to train and test the AI system. You already know that in order to embed fairness, you will need to rely on bias-mitigation techniques, but now the question is what techniques will best fit your specific project needs. Your lead data scientist brings some options to the Values Canvas, such as sampling during pre-processing or input correction during post-processing (Fernandez, 2023). Taking notes on the different techniques, you begin to fill out your options on the Values Canvas, leaving the solution statement blank until you have the chance to look at the *Technology Pillar* as a whole as shown in Figure 9.1.

FIGURE 9.1 Data Element

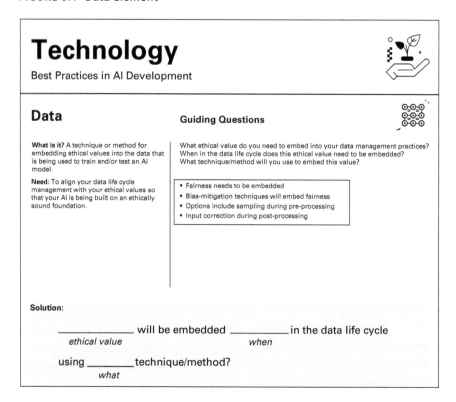

Document

What Is a Document Solution?

The documentation of all ethics-related decisions taken during the life cycle of an AI model.

When it comes to developing AI solutions, hundreds of decisions will go into the production of even a single model. One type of decision being made during this process is ethical, or decisions taken based on ethical values. In the context of Responsible AI, your *Document* solution is defined as the recording of all ethical decisions, as well as iterations of those decisions, taken during the life cycle of an AI model, system, or product. It is important to note as well that the documentation must be organized in a way that is easily accessible and interpretable for all your people.

The Purpose of Document

To create transparency of the ethical decisions being taken during the AI development life cycle.

In life, things rarely ever turn out how you expected. The same is true for AI, you are never certain of the outcome until you see it. This means that when it comes to embedding ethical values into your AI systems, it may take some refining of your models before you are able to fully reflect your foundational ethics values in the AI systems. To do so, you need to have the ability to retrace the ethical decisions made taken during production in order to identify the cause of misaligned results (Micheli et al., 2023).

Designing Your Document Solution

As we begin to design your *Document* solution, I want to take a moment to differentiate *Document* in Responsible AI from standard documentation in AI development. Just as *Data* referred to specifically data ethics, *Document* refers specifically to ethics documentation. Standard documentation of data, algorithms, models, and experiments that go into a single AI project is essential to the success of that project, as without the documentation you are crippling your ability to iterate and refine your AI systems. However, this is again a topic for perhaps even a series of books. In this section I will not be covering standard documentation, I will instead be providing you with the conceptual structure you need to determine what kind of ethical decision documentation is right for your organization.

With this clarification in mind, we can turn to the first consideration of *Document*. By now you should be accustomed to starting with who, as in who is going to be using your *Document* solution. A simple way of determining this is to ask yourself who will be making the ethical decisions during the life cycle of your AI system, as this will be the same who that will need to document those decisions.

Once you know who will be documenting decisions, you will then need to consider what decisions they will be documenting. We already know that *Document* is focused on ethical decisions, but ethical decisions can take on many shapes and forms. It is one thing to tell a team to document any vaguely ethics-related decision they take, it is another to identify what specific ethical decisions will need to be made for your AI project and spotlight it so your team is aware that they are even making an ethical decision in the first place. For example, asking a team to document all fairness decisions is too abstract a request, but asking that same team to document the bias-mitigation techniques they used to make the AI system fair is a concrete and useful requirement. If you are having trouble understanding what ethical decisions will need to be documented, you can look back to the *Process Pillar* at the frameworks in *Implement*, as these frameworks will be guiding ethical decision making for your teams.

The final consideration for your *Document* solution will be where this documentation is going to live. Think of this documentation practice like you are building an ethical decisions database, one that you can look back on to either refine current decisions, or as reference points for future decisions to see what worked and what didn't in previous projects. All of this decision documentation of course needs a place to live, one that is secure yet accessible to the necessary individuals and well organized in such a way that it is easy to locate critical foundational decisions that have been taken along the way.

With proper ethics documentation you enable the ability to audit your systems and adjust for value alignment throughout the AI life cycle. In order to create this necessary transparency, here are some guiding questions for your *Document* solution:

- Who is responsible for making ethical decisions?
- What kind of ethical decisions need to be documented?
- Where are these decisions being documented?

As you add your ideas to the *Document* section of your Values Canvas, you are working towards the answering the following solution statement:

[who] needs to document [what] decisions [where]?

Document In Action

Returning to our example of R&AI Bank and credit card fraud detection, you as the project lead begin to consider how you will document efforts in fairness for the project. As you being to think through your options, you consider how although it will be the data scientists working on bias mitigation, the whole team, including the business analysts and customer service representatives, will be making critical decisions based on the performance of the AI system in terms of fairness. The business analysts will be assessing whether or not the system is accurately detecting credit card fraud in real time and monitoring if there is an increase in fraud cases for different demographics, while the customer service representatives will have direct insights into the quality of service a diverse range of customers is experiencing. With this in mind, you realize that your documentation of fairness will need to extend beyond just the tracking happening on the data dashboard you selected for your *Instrument* solution, and so consider if you could add additional fairness considerations to the model cards you team has already planned to use. You add your ideas for *Document* to the Values Canvas, leaving the solution statement blank until you've finished all three *Technology* elements as shown in Figure 9.2.

FIGURE 9.2 Document Element

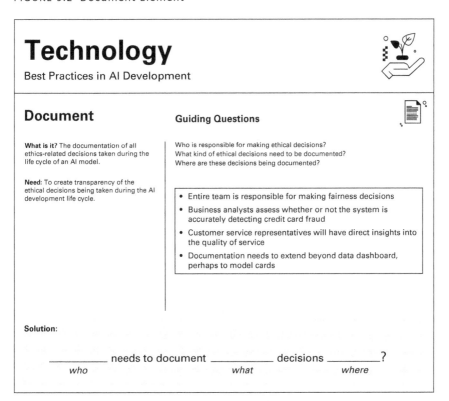

Domain

What Is a Domain Solution?

A specified time and place in the AI life cycle for expert and customer feedback.

You have the data practices in place, you have the proper documentation in order, now in this third and final element of the *Technology Pillar* we look to bring in the component of human oversight into AI development. Essentially, *Domain* looks at the process by which human intelligence is leveraged within the training, testing, and monitoring stages of the AI life cycle through feedback loops. This feedback will come from either domain experts of the industry or market you are developing for, or from the customer domain of your AI solution. The key factor is that you are gathering relevant and timely feedback from the people who understand the domain your AI system is operating in, whether that be from an expert point of view or from a direct user perspective.

The Purpose of Domain

To incrementally iterate and refine AI models into ethical value alignment through insights from people directly affected by the AI systems.

Even in the *Technology Pillar*, humans still play a vital role in Responsible AI execution. Life is full of nuances, which means the markets and industries an AI system will service are also full of nuances difficult to distinguish unless you are coming from firsthand knowledge. A mistake so often made in AI development is to create a solution without having any direct expertise in the market or experience from intended user base. It is only in this first-hand knowledge that you are able to truly understand if your AI models are behaving in alignment with your foundational ethics values. The only way to validate this alignment effectively for your AI systems is to bring in strategic human feedback loops. This element of human oversight enables critical analysis of the outcomes from an AI system (Omar, 2023), combining both machine and human intelligence to leverage the speed and scale of the machine, while simultaneously balancing this with the refinement and critical analysis of the human.

Designing Your Domain Solution

In your final *Technology Pillar* element, you should not be surprised to hear that establishing feedback loops with experts and customers is an AI good practice even before it is a Responsible AI practice. In the connect of *Domain* for Responsible AI though, we are looking for expert and customer feedback as it pertains to your foundational ethics values. It is not possible to have an AI system monitor its own alignment to your foundational values; this requires critical thought, reflection, and the ability to assess what are often novel scenarios. You need to be able to draw on the strength of human critical thinking in order to properly assess the development and evolution of an AI solution in accordance to your foundational ethics values.

As you go to design your *Domain* solution, the first consideration that you will need to address is who will be involved in this feedback loop. Looking at who will be giving the feedback, you are asking yourself if either a domain expert or a customer would have better insight into whether or not your foundational ethics value is being reflected in the AI system. Say for example you are developing an AI system for healthcare, but none of your team comes from the healthcare profession. You may develop a high functioning system, but it doesn't matter how well that system works if it does not reflect your foundational ethics values within the healthcare context. This is an ethical blindspot that a domain expert would be able to identify. On the other hand a customer feedback loop would better serve your needs if you were producing a B2C healthcare app and needed to understand if the customer experience was reflective of your foundational ethics values. Either way, the crucial point here is that you are seeking feedback on the value alignment of your AI system externally to the team that built the system. You can't check your own homework, just as you can't always catch misalignment and ethics blindspots in your own AI system.

Feedback can be a tricky thing to navigate, too much of it and the receiver is overwhelmed with input, too little and it begins to lose effectiveness, which is why the next consideration for your *Domain* solution is the cadence at which the feedback is given. It is important to strike a balance and rhythm that works for your teams, so look to complement the flow of the development methodology already in place. For example, if your teams are accustomed to the Agile methodology, there is a natural point of feedback already built in at the three-week mark. If the AI is high risk, or perhaps deployed in a volatile environment, a higher cadence of feedback may be necessary. On the other hand, a lower-risk model deployed in a stable environment will experience change at a slower rate, and so a lower cadence of feedback would be something to consider. You can also look to start with a high frequency of feedback in testing phases to validate the model is performing as desired, and then decrease the frequency of feedback when transitioning into the monitoring phases of the AI to ensure against model drift.

The final conservation of your *Domain* element is focused on when exactly during the AI life cycle this feedback is happening. In other words, do you need to target the human element during design, development, deployment, or a combination of all three? During the design phase, there is the potential to create a feedback loop that provides alignment to the foundations of an AI system by ensuring values are reflected in both feature and data design. In the development phase there is potential for a feedback loop to support in iterating the AI solution, refining the build to create alignment with foundation ethics values. And finally, in deployment there is ample opportunity for a feedback loop to create the necessary monitoring of a live model to catch model drift or adverse effects before they become too large and likely catastrophic.

Monitoring model behavior is a critical function of the teams developing the AI system. In the context of *Domain* we are looking at additional monitoring, this time focusing not on the technical performance of a system but on the impacts of the system as they relate to your foundational ethics values. By seeking expert and customer feedback at critical points in the AI life cycle, you are gathering the necessary insights that will lead to value alignment in your AI systems. To help conceptualize what this should look like for your AI project, here are some guiding questions:

- Do you need feedback from domain experts or customers?
- How often is the feedback being given?
- When in the AI life cycle is the feedback needed?

As you work your way through the guiding questions for *Domain*, keep in mind that you are working towards answering the following solution statement:

[whose] feedback is needed [how often] during [when]?

Domain in Action

Reaching the final element of your Values Canvas, we return to the R&AI Bank and its credit card fraud detection system. In order to understand if the system is aligned with your value of fairness, you begin to consider what kind of feedback would help achieve this goal. On one hand, direct feedback from customers once the system has been deployed will help bring you insight into the quality of service different customer basis are experiencing. On the other hand, bringing in credit card fraud specialists during design phases to help your team understand the specific indicators of fraudulent behavior would provide domain expert feedback into how to build a system that fairly assessed your customers. As fairness is a sensitive topic, you consider that a higher frequency of feedback would be better in terms of catching any model drift before it becomes critical. Pulling your thoughts together, you add the ideas to your Values Canvas in the *Domain* element, leaving the solution statement blank so you can go back and assess all three elements together as shown as Figure 9.3.

FIGURE 9.3 Domain Element

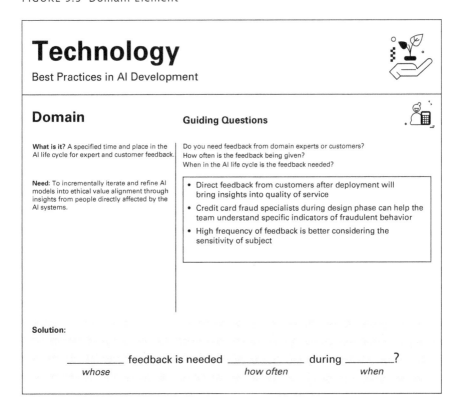

Technology
Best Practices in AI Development

Domain

Guiding Questions

What is it? A specified time and place in the AI life cycle for expert and customer feedback.

Need: To incrementally iterate and refine AI models into ethical value alignment through insights from people directly affected by the AI systems.

Do you need feedback from domain experts or customers?
How often is the feedback being given?
When in the AI life cycle is the feedback needed?

- Direct feedback from customers after deployment will bring insights into quality of service
- Credit card fraud specialists during design phase can help the team understand specific indicators of fraudulent behavior
- High frequency of feedback is better considering the sensitivity of subject

Solution:

_____ feedback is needed _____ during _____?
whose   how often   when

Bringing It All Together: Finalizing Your *Technology Pillar*

Having worked our way up through *People* and *Process*, we are now rounding out your Responsible AI strategy with the final pillar of *Technology*. In this chapter we finally addressed the question of what you are building, in the sense that we focused specifically on what is going into your AI systems. As I stressed at the start, this is not a chapter meant to give you narrow ethics solutions for specific problems you may be experiencing in your AI systems. Instead, the purpose of this chapter has been to lay out the key technical processes that must be present in your AI project and how these components should be utilized to reflect your foundational ethics values.

The three elements of your *Technology Pillar* are *Data*, *Document*, and *Domain*. Each element covers an essential technical process within your Responsible AI strategy, looking directly at the AI systems being built. In the *Process Pillar* we looked at business operations and processes; in the *Technology Pillar* we looked specifically at components of your AI project. Bringing all three elements together now, we can take a step back and look at your *Technology Pillar* as a whole, in Figure 9.4.

Looking over your Values Canvas, you should be able to now start to conceptualize what this pillar will be through the solutions ideas you have written out for *Data*, *Document*, and *Domain*. In *Data* you've been looking into specific data ethics methods and how to use them to embed your organizations own foundational ethics values. For *Document* you've been exploring what ethical decisions taken during the AI life cycle need to be documented and how that could look. In *Domain* you've been considering what kinds of feedback loops are needed and from whom during your development stages. With all three elements laid out, it's time to move beyond the excitement of ideation and move into a plan of action for your AI project.

Synchronizing Your Technology Pillar

You will see that each of the three *Technology* elements have the ability to stand alone from the others, a unique aspect to the *Technology Pillar*. Data can function without *Document*, *Document* can function without *Domain*, and so on. Although there is not as strong an interdependence between elements in *Technology* as in the *People* or *Process*, there is still some potential for overlap in who is responsible for carrying out each of the elements. Additionally, *Document* can be used to support both *Data* and *Domain*, as you will need to document your data ethics practices, as well as document

FIGURE 9.4 Technology Pillar. For the full figure, please see www.koganpage.com/responsible-ai

Technology

Best Practices in AI Development

Data

Guiding Questions

What is it? A technique or method for embedding ethical values into the data that is being used to train and/or test an AI model.

Need: To align your data life cycle management with your ethical values so that your AI is being built on an ethically sound foundation.

What ethical value do you need to embed into your data management practices?

When in the data life cycle does this ethical value need to be embedded?

What technique/method will you use to embed this value?

Solution:

ethical value will be embedded _when_ in the data life cycle
using _what_ technique/method?

Document

Guiding Questions

What is it? The documentation of all ethics-related decisions taken during the life cycle of an AI model.

Need: To create transparency of the ethical decisions being taken during the AI development life cycle.

Who is responsible for making ethical decisions?

What kind of ethical decisions need to be documented?

Where are these decisions being documented?

Solution:

who needs to document _what_ decisions _where_?

Domain

Guiding Questions

What is it? A specified time and place in the AI life cycle for expert and customer feedback.

Need: To incrementally iterate and refine AI models into ethical value alignment through insights from people directly affected by the AI systems.

Do you need feedback from domain experts or customers?

How often is the feedback being given?

When in the AI life cycle is the feedback needed?

Solution:

whose feedback is needed _how often_ during _when_?

the decisions and feedback given from your feedback loops. Overall, the primary common factor between the three elements is the need for the solutions to be systemic and consistent, as it is in this standard consistency that successful scaling, ability to draw insights from comparable efforts, and capacity to catch blindspots will be found.

Technology Pillar in Action

As we work towards closing out the Values Canvas with the final pillar of *Technology*, let's return back to our case study of the R&AI Bank and the credit card fraud detection AI Project one last time to round out the Responsible AI strategy for the project. Having made your way through all three elements, it is your responsibility now as the project lead to take those brainstorming sessions and extract the solutions you plan to use for *Technology*.

Beginning with *Data*, after having sat down with your lead data scientist on the project to discuss the different options for bias mitigation, you now need to review which of the techniques will best fit the requirements of fairness for your project. You recall that your *Educate* solution for this project is to give your data scientist further training in bias mitigation, and so decide to capitalize on the skillsets your data scientists will already be learning. You are informed that the training will include a deep dive into Synthetic Minority Over-Sampling Technique (SMOTE) (Chawla et al., 2002), and after discussing it with your lead data scientist, agree that your team will start the project using this technique. In filling out your solution statement for *Data*, you now have a record of what the primary technique to start will be, enabling your team to go back and revise the strategy if indicators show this technique as ineffective for your project. With this in mind, you fill out your *Data* solution:

> [fairness] will be embedded [during the pre-processing of the algorithms] in the data life cycle using [the SMOTE] technique/method.

From *Data* you move on to *Document*, considering how your team will keep track of the different decisions being made around fairness throughout the project. Although your fairness metrics will be tracked and housed in the dashboard from your *Instrument* solution, you know that the dashboard will not be able to also document the fairness decisions being taken by your business analysts and customer service representatives, and so decide to document all fairness decisions on the model cards you will already be using for the project. With this in mind, you go to complete your *Document* solution statement:

> [data scientists, business analysts, and customer services representatives] need to document [all fairness] decisions [on the project model cards].

Moving on to the last of the *Technology* elements, you look back at the ideas you have listed for *Domain*, which include thoughts about feedback from customers as well as experts in credit card fraud. You know that customer feedback will be important to ensure that equal quality of service is being experienced across your customer base; however, you also have customer service representatives on your team who are already in charge of monitoring customer satisfaction and relaying that back into the project. You then consider how sensitive credit card fraud can be, especially when it comes to minority groups with different spending habits than the majority customer base. Because of this, you decide that if you bring in credit card fraud specialists during the design phase of your project, you will be able to preemptively catch problem areas for discrimination. As your team will be working on the project through agile sprints, you decide that feedback from these experts at the start of each sprint will help give the insight needed to your team, and so complete your *Domain* solution statement as follows:

> [credit card fraud specialists'] feedback is needed [at the start of every three-week sprint] during [the design phase].

Bringing all three elements and their solution statements into one cohesive strategy, your completed *Technology Pillar* for the credit fraud detection project will look something like Figure 9.5.

Risk versus Innovation Approach in Your *Technology Pillar*

As you begin to design the solutions for your *Technology Pillar*, keep in mind that this is, once again, an opportunity to emphasize either a risk- or innovation-based approach to your Responsible AI strategy. If you are not sure which approach you want to take, refer back to the thinking you did in Chapters 3 and 4 when we discussed the difference between the two approaches, as well as the framework for helping determine what kind of approach your organization currently needs. With these needs in mind, let's take a look at what a risk- versus innovation-based approach would look like for your *Technology Pillar*.

FIGURE 9.5 Example of a Completed Technology Pillar

Technology

Best Practices in AI Development

Data

Guiding Questions

What is it? A technique or method for embedding ethical values into the data that is being used to train and/or test an AI model.

Need: To align your data life cycle management with your ethical values so that your AI is being built on an ethically sound foundation.

What ethical value do you need to embed into your data management practices?

When in the data life cycle does this ethical value need to be embedded?

What technique/method will you use to embed this value?

Fairness needs to be embedded

Bias-mitigation techniques will embed fairness

Options include sampling during pre-processing

Input correction during post-processing

Document

Guiding Questions

What is it? The documentation of all ethics-related decisions taken during the life cycle of an AI model.

Need: To create transparency of the ethical decisions being taken during the AI development life cycle.

Who is responsible for making ethical decisions?

What kind of ethical decisions need to be documented?

Where are these decisions being documented?

Entire team is responsible for making fairness decisions

Business analysts assess whether or not the system is accurately detecting credit card fraud

Customer service representatives will have direct insights into the quality of service

Documentation needs to extend beyond data dashboard, perhaps to model cards

Domain

Guiding Questions

What is it? A specified time and place in the AI life cycle for expert and customer feedback.

Need: To incrementally iterate and refine AI models into ethical value alignment through insights from people directly affected by the AI systems.

Do you need feedback from domain experts or customers?

How often is the feedback being given?

When in the AI life cycle is the feedback needed?

Direct feedback from customers after deployment will bring insights into quality of service

Credit card fraud specialists during design phase can help the team understand specific indicators of fraudulent behavior

High frequency of feedback is better considering sensitivity of subject

---

[fairness] will be embedded [during the pre-processing of the algorithms] in the data life cycle using [the SMOTE] technique/method.

[data scientists, business analysts, and customer services representatives] need to document [all fairness] decisions [on the project model cards].

[credit fraud specialists'] feedback is needed [at the start of every three-week sprint] during [the design phase].

Let's start with the risk-based approach. When it comes to the *Technology Pillar*, the main objective of a risk-based approach will be compliance, assessments for risks relevant to your foundational ethics values, and anticipatory mitigation. Unlike the previous two pillars, there are significant regulations, both in effect and in the process of, that will govern what kind of solutions you will need in each of your elements. Starting with the *Data* element, you will be looking towards regulations such as the GDPR (Intersoft Consulting, 2013) or CCPA (State of California Department of Justice, 2023), the two leading regulations in data privacy, to govern your data life cycle. Both regulations have strict rules for how data can be sourced, processed, and utilized, and have become the standard for data privacy practices cross-industry. It is important to note here, though, that the GDPR and CCPA are data privacy acts, not data ethics acts. Privacy is only one of the many foundational values you will be looking to embed into your data. However, the laws themselves do cover a variety of other ethical values such as autonomy and agency over personal data, and there are industry-specific regulations designed for data bias. Essentially, when it comes to the *Data* element, your risk-based approach will need to prioritize compliance with the GDPR or CCPA, as well as take into account any industry-specific or foundational ethical value-specific regulation as it relates to the data life cycle. Looking next at your *Document* element, the essential regulation you will need to comply with in this element is the EU AI Act (European Commission, 2023). Depending on the risk level of your AI system, you will be legally required to document the decisions taken during the development life cycle. Additionally, you will be required to perform regular audits on your systems, which of course require proper documentation to be able to run smoothly and without too significant of cost to your organization. Finally, your *Domain* element will also be reinforced by a variety of regulations, most notably again being the GPDR and EU AI Act, and requirement in some cases to human oversight in the design and development of AI systems. Specifically, Article 14 of the EU AI Act requires that a human must be able to "disregard, override, or reverse the output of the high-risk AI system," while Article 22 of the GDPR states that data subjects have the right not to be subjected to "a decision based solely on automated processing," both of which can be classified as human oversight requirements.

Essentially, compliance is a major component of the risk-based approach to the three elements of your *Technology Pillar*, it would be to say there are currently ample regulations guiding how you should be acting on each of the three elements, and there are only more regulations to come. However, remember that compliance is only ever the minimum of what you can do in Responsible AI. In each of your *Technology* elements consider how you can use the technical processes to better protect your foundational ethics values through anticipatory mitigation techniques.

[*It is important to note here that although the GDPR and EU AI Act are European regulations, they apply to any company using European Union citizen data or operating in the European market. There are other national regulations besides those coming from the EU; however, the EU has taken the forefront in regulating both AI and the digital markets, and so is setting the standards that other countries follow with their own regulations. With this in mind, it is best to default to the EU regulations, unless your country of operation has specific laws for data, documentation, or human oversight.]

Let's now turn our attention to the innovation-based approach. Before going into detail on how this approach can look in action, it is essential to emphasize here that the *Technology Pillar* is unique in the fact that it is the most strictly regulated of the three pillars. What this means is that even if you are taking an innovation-based approach to your *Technology Pillar*, you must still ensure that you are compliant with the various regulations governing data management, AI development, and the digital markets. With that in mind, we can look more closely at the nuances of an innovation-based *Technology Pillar*. The main objective here is create ample opportunity for secure experimentation within your three elements. What this means is that essentially you will want to encourage your teams to ideate on new solutions to embedding foundational ethics values into your AI systems through data management, documentation, and feedback loops. The crucial part to keep in mind, though, will be that these experiments and innovation sprints must be done in a secure and safe environment, one that is completely detached from live models, and will not reach production unless proven to be beneficial. Looking at the specific elements, an innovation approach to *Data* would invest into new and innovative methods to managing ethical values such as data privacy, data bias, user autonomy, and so on. Your *Document* element will need to focus on the ability to review previous ethical decisions, and then iterate based on results to help refine value alignment. Finally, your *Domain* element will need to focus on bringing expert guidance into the design phases of your AI life cycle. Overall, an innovation approach to *Technology* is to push current Responsible AI research further and experiment with new techniques for embedding ethical values into technical processes.

How Will You Know Your *Technology Pillar* Is Working?

By now you should have an overall view of the elements needed to fulfill the third pillar of your Responsible AI strategy for your AI projects. The purpose of a holistic *Technology Pillar* is to understand the ethics interventions possible on a technical level, looking directly at mechanisms that will allow you to further align your AI system with your foundational values. This is meant to build off your *People* and *Process* pillars in a way that your people are able to execute on your foundational values in a very tangible and practical context beyond the organizational operations.

As with any strategy, it is important to take a step back and consider how you will know if your efforts are working or not, or in other words, set your metrics of success. When it comes to the *Technology Pillar*, all three elements are essential to simply building a functional AI solution, but there is a difference between building AI and building Responsible AI. In order to ensure you are not only practicing good AI development standards, but are also developing Responsible AI through the embedding of foundational ethics values, you need to establish clear indicators of success for your *Technology* efforts. Just as was the case with both the *People* and *Process* pillars, there are two different classifications of results you can look for in *Technology*.

First are the tangible results, the kind that you can easily measure and track progress on. When this comes to the *Technology Pillar*, the tangible results you are looking for are increases in model accuracy and data quality, reduction of models being pulled post-production, and cost savings in both regulatory fines and auditing. To start, the efforts in the *Technology Pillar* that go towards data governance and model documentation will lead to the increase in data quality and overall accuracy due to the fact that you will be closely monitoring the data coming into your systems. The better you are able to manage the sourcing and cleaning of your data, the higher your data quality becomes, which in turn leads to stronger model accuracy as the high-quality data being used to train the model is a better representation of what is really happening in a specific context. This will also contribute, along with your domain feedback loops, to a reduction in models needing to be pulled post-production. An important function of the domain feedback is to be able to monitor AI solutions post-production, providing feedback for iterative refinement. In other words, the human in the loop can catch model drift or an adverse change in impact earlier on before it becomes too much of a problem that the model needs to be pulled. Finally, the combination of all three elements leads to reduction in risk of fines for regulatory violations, as well as costs savings when it comes to mandatory auditing of systems as the documentation needed for the audit has proactively been generated.

Second are intangible results, the kind that you can't necessarily measure but can definitely feel a significant difference. In the *Technology Pillar* there are two primary intangible results you will be looking for: consistency and adaptability. As we have already pointed out, consistent application of data governance factors, documentation of models, and human feedback has been key to the success of each of the three elements. The common thread has been the need for consistency, which translates into the intangible results of an increase in consistency across your development teams. If you have established solutions for all three of your elements in the *Technology Pillar* and have successfully gotten your teams to adopt the solutions, you will see a noticeable increase of consistency not only across your development teams in terms of execution, but also across projects and models, as you will have essentially worked to establish a baseline standard practice. In addition to consistency, the baseline standard practices will also contribute to the intangible benefit of an increase in adaptability of your teams. It is much easier to adapt to changing circumstances when you know exactly where to look within your data, documentation, or feedback loops in order to either identify a problem or enact a change. The feedback loops enable insight, and sometimes even foresight, into a change in circumstances and the needs to adapt, which can then be quickly executed on thanks to the documentation and data efforts already in place. Overall, a sense of consistency and adaptability, along with increases in data quality and model accuracy, reduced numbers of models needing to be pulled post-production, and a decrease in regularity fines and auditing costs are all beneficial impacts you can look for as indicators of a successful *Technology Pillar*.

From *Technology* to Beyond

In the *People Pillar* we worked on who is building your AI systems, in the *Process Pillar* we worked on how they would be building your AI systems, and in the *Technology Pillar* we finally reached the question of what is being built into your AI systems exactly. As mentioned in the previous pillar chapters, it can be tempting to jump immediately to the *Technology Pillar*. If the goal is to embed your organization's foundational values into your AI systems, why wouldn't you start with the technology itself then? However, as we have seen, you must first enable your teams to be able to engage in utilizing ethics as a decision-analysis tool, and then create the standard processes for them to do such, before you are able to enact any kind of meaningful change within your AI systems. This is not to say that the *Technology Pillar* is the least important, but instead to emphasize that the problems in Responsible AI typically run deeper than the datasets and lines of code. With this in mind, it is important to note that the majority of research and literature available on Responsible AI does focus on technical solutions, as Responsible AI has been primary thought of as a technical problem. So, as you embark on your *Technology Pillar*, remember that this chapter and its elements are the structural pieces you will need in place if you are to execute on Responsible AI, not necessarily the narrow ethics solutions you will deploy.

PART THREE

10

The Different Phases of Responsible AI Adoption

And How to Understand Where You Are Currently

Back when I was first starting my career in AI Ethics, I, along with a group of friends, ran a weekly meet-up that brought together philosophers and data scientists to discuss trending topics in AI development. Heated yet friendly, these conversations were always a source of inspiration for new directions to explore and knowledge to gain. One discussion in particular still remains vividly stuck in my memory as one of my favorite paradigm shifts in the context of data and AI to date.

The question was simple: where does data find its worth? Is the single data subject valuable on their own, or is the dataset, a collection of individual data subjects, the only part that is valuable? To my surprise, the room was strictly divided on the topic. The philosophers all argued that the value of data began with the individual data subject, while the data scientists were adamant that the value of data was only created once the individual data subject was added to a dataset. For hours the philosophers and data scientists went round and round in debate, each side defending their position with sound logical reasoning and practical examples. As I sat listening to the discussion, I came to my own conclusion. Both sides, in their own way, were right. Their error was not in their reasoning for one side or the other, their error was in their inability to recognize the validity of the opposing perspective and accept that both could exist simultaneously. Ironically, the philosophers were getting lost in the details of data, while the data scientists were blinded by the bigger picture of datasets. You can't have datasets without individual data subjects, and you can't pull insights from individual data subjects without larger datasets. Both have value.

But what does this have to do with Responsible AI strategies? In Part Two we went over how to strategically embed a selected ethical value into an AI project. Using the Values Canvas as a guiding tool to help you visualize the different elements of Responsible AI and conceptualize the solutions necessary to creating a holistic strategy, we learned how to work with Responsible AI and your foundational values on a project level. This is an incredibly important step to operationalizing Responsible AI, as embedding values on a project level generates concrete and practical ethics solutions. However, there is a large gap between embedding ethical values on a project level and enabling Responsible AI throughout your organization.

On the one hand, it may be tempting to treat Responsible AI as something that happens on a project-by-project basis, only using ethics when it seems immediately relevant to the case. On the other hand, it is also possible to approach Responsible AI from solely a high-level perspective, treating it as an abstract organizational commitment to ethical values. If you only take the project-level approach, you run the risk of getting lost in the details and missing out on the insights you can gain from a scaled collective strategy, just as the philosophers lost the utility of datasets in the individual data subjects. If you instead only take an organizational-level approach, you run the risk of missing the practical execution that exists in the details, just as the data scientists lost the utility of the individual data subjects in the wider datasets. Both project- and organizational-level Responsible AI strategies are essential to the success of your AI and business. And since we have already gone over in depth how to create a project-level strategy for embedding values into AI, now it's time to switch perspectives and look at how to build a Responsible AI strategy for your entire organization.

In this chapter we are going to take a few steps back and look at how to develop a Responsible AI strategy at an organizational level. We will start by looking at what it means to become a Responsible AI-enabled company and how to use the Values Canvas to guide your high-level strategy development. Next, we will look into the three stages of Responsible AI adoption and how to identify where your organization currently sits. For each stage we will define what it means to be at this stage and cover the priorities you will have for Responsible AI depending on where you are in the journey of adoption. By the end of this chapter, you will know what it means to be a Responsible AI-enabled organization, where you are in your current Responsible AI adoption journey, and how to use the Values Canvas to understand what you need to do next.

What It Means to Become a Responsible
AI-Enabled Organization

As you made your way through the pillars of Responsible AI and their various elements on the Values Canvas, it may have crossed your mind that building a solution for all the elements every single time you start a new AI project is a whole lot of work. You would not be wrong. Starting from scratch on Responsible AI with every new AI project or foundational value is indeed a long process and a lot of work. In this respect, ethics can slow project development down if you need to do a hefty amount of preliminary work every time you go to embed a foundational value into your AI. Imagine having to procure or build a new training session every time you start a new project, or design governance framework from scratch. All of these Responsible AI solutions take time and effort, and although they are well worth the investment, it can be a deterrent if you have to start from the basics with every new AI project.

This, however, is not how Responsible AI has to be. Yes, you need to ensure that you are addressing all the elements when it comes to embedding foundational values into an AI project, but you do not necessarily have to start from scratch with each new project. The solutions you brainstormed and eventually selected for your pillars and their elements are first and foremost solutions for your specific project. At the same time, they can also be extended to apply to other similar AI projects or foundational values. Essentially, instead of building one-off Responsible AI solutions for individual projects, you can instead build template or universal solutions for your foundational values that can be applied across a variety of projects.

For example, imagine you are working on a project to release text generation on your platform using a foundational large language model. You identify that your marketers will need to be trained in how to build customer trust in the new feature, and so design a workshop to help teach the new skillset. Although this workshop applies directly to the project at hand, it can also be designed in a such a way that makes it applicable to any marketing team within your company that is managing the release of any new feature in need of customer trust. If you design a workshop only with the specific project in mind, then you have a one-off *Educate* solution. However, if you design the workshop with the overall organization in mind, you now have a Responsible AI resource that can be reused throughout your company as a template for *Educate* solutions.

Becoming a Responsible AI-enabled organization means that you not only incorporate ethical values into different AI projects, but that you also have a portfolio of value-based resources that any AI initiative within your company can access and is encouraged to use. Hence the term "enabled," as you are enabling your company to engage in ethical decision making and Responsible AI practices at scale in a manner that is both cohesive and strategically aligned with your organization's objectives. In other words, you are down in the details of execution on value embedding into projects, while also still guiding the high-level objectives into alignment with those same values.

The Other Side of the Hammer

Now that we understand what it means to become a Responsible AI-enabled organization, the next question is of course how? In theory, you can see how having different ethical resources available for use throughout your organization would be important, but how do you tell what kind of resources are needed at scale? Lucky for you, you already have just the tool for the job. I first started this book with the story of two carpenters, and how one carpenter was taught the action of hammering in nail while the other carpenter was taught about the hammer. When it came time to remove the nail from the block of wood, the second carpenter immediately knew to turn the hammer around and use the other side to pry the nail out. Well, now it's time to turn your hammer around and learn how to use the other side.

To be clear, by hammer, I mean the Values Canvas, and by the other side, I mean using it to help conceptualize an organizational level strategy for Responsible AI.

Although the Values Canvas is a powerful tool for embedding selected foundational values into specific AI projects, you can also take a step back and use it to help visualize your overall Responsible AI strategy. Think of it this way, if all your AI projects will be required to fill out the Canvas to ensure they are addressing the same three pillars and their elements, then wouldn't it make the most sense to align your template Responsible AI and Ethics solutions with these same categories?

Ideally, when a project lead goes to fill out a Values Canvas at the start of a new AI project, they can move quickly through the exercise as they can draw on a portfolio of already refined resources that is aligned with the elements they need to find solutions to. Instead of building new solutions at the start of every project, they are simply looking through a database of options to find the one best suited to the project and foundational value at hand. Not only does this increase efficiency in Responsible AI at the project level, it is also the perfect opportunity to establish standards in practice and values across your entire organization.

With this in mind, we now can see that the Values Canvas, when used at the organizational level, can be used as a heat map to understand where your company's strengths, weakness, and areas of improvement exist in Responsible AI. Looking at the pillars and their elements, you can track which elements have a rich portfolio of resources readily available, versus which elements have little to no resources and are in need of attention. In order to become a fully Responsible AI-enabled organization, you will need resources and template ethical solutions for all three pillars and their elements, including specific solutions for each of your foundational values.

The Difference Between AI and RAI Adoption

Before we go into detail on how to use the Values Canvas to help you visualize where your organization is currently at in the Responsible AI adoption journey, we must clarify the difference between AI and Responsible AI adoption.

When referring to AI adoption, it is a matter of whether or not your organization is currently procuring or building custom AI systems to be used for internal processes or in external customer-facing products and services. If you do not utilize any AI in any of your internal operations nor in any of your external product or service solutions, then your organization has yet to even embark on the journey of adopting basic AI. Responsible AI adoption, on the other hand, refers to the adoption of Responsible AI practices and ethics solutions within your organization. If you are just beginning to consider the potential for Responsible AI within your organization, then you are early on in the adoption journey. However if you have multiple Responsible AI initiatives deployed and are meeting the needs of the majority of your Responsible AI elements, then you are advanced in the adoption journey (Ribeiro, 2022).

It is important to note that although AI and Responsible AI adoption are two different things, it is best to adopt both simultaneously, as Responsible AI will naturally result in a stronger foundation for your AI practices and therefore higher success rates in AI. You do not necessarily have to wait until your organization is fully AI-enabled before starting on your Responsible AI journey, in fact if you are just starting to adopt AI then you are in an advantageous position of being able to complement your AI adoption with Responsible AI practices from the very start.

The Journey of Responsible AI Adoption

As with the introduction of any new initiative into a business, there are of course phases to the adoption journey. As much as we would all love to go from 0 to 100 in Responsible AI enablement, this is not an overnight process (PwC, n.d.). For some of you reading this book, this has all been new information and you are excited to finally understand the concrete path to operationalizing Responsible AI. For others, you've already started experimenting with a few test ethics initiatives and are using this book to help understand what your next steps should be. Still others of you have spent your time reading this book nodding along in agreement and are content to see that your company is well on your way to Responsible AI success. Whatever your experience in reading so far has been, I am sure you are now thinking to yourself, where am I exactly? When it comes to the Responsible AI adoption journey, where is my organization currently and what does this mean for my next steps?

Before we can start categorizing your own organization, let's first take a look at the three phases of Responsible AI adoption and some supporting examples. As you read through the following phases, pay close attention to whether a certain phase resonates with your understanding of your company's current endeavors in Responsible AI, as this will help you identify where you currently stand.

Phase One: Exploration

The first phase of adoption, *Exploration*, is when you are beginning to explore the potential and necessity of Responsible AI for your organization's AI direction and are taking steps towards concrete ethics initiatives.

If you would describe your current focus for Responsible AI as at the point of "exploring our options" then this is your phase. Generally speaking, in this first phase of adoption your organization has just begun exploring the possibility of implementing Responsible AI initiatives, and most likely would struggle with finding any concrete resources to list on the Values Canvas. There are a few key indicators to look for in this stage:

- First, the conversations around Responsible AI and Ethics will tend towards abstract ideas and high-level objectives, rather than concrete initiatives and practical execution. Although ethics has a place in your discussions on AI, you are still working on understanding exactly how it will work into your organization's overall approach to AI.

- Second, Responsible AI has made it on to your list of priorities for either the current or upcoming year. Due to pressure from the market or the board, direction setting from the C-suite, or your own motivation, incorporating ethics into your organization and AI has become a specified top priority.

- Third, you may have already started to deploy an initiative that aligns with one of the Values Canvas elements. It can be tempting to evaluate your organization as being further down the path of adoption if you have already started some form of Responsible AI initiative. However, a single initiative on a small and siloed scale is still indicative of the *Exploration* stage.

For example, let's say there is a large enterprise media company with a vibrant social media platform. We'll call the company ConnectAI, and it runs the third largest global social media platform where users connect through digital avatars. Executives at ConnectAI have lately been hearing about fellow social media platforms struggling with Responsible AI scandals, and have noticed that their users are demanding the company to take a stance on ethics. To meet market pressure, ConnectAI released a public general Responsible AI policy earlier in the year, and has added the abstract point to "look into AI Ethics" onto the list of company objectives in the upcoming year. If an executive from ConnectAI were to sit down and use the Values Canvas to map out the different Responsible AI resources and initiatives in the company, their canvas would look like Figure 10.1.

FIGURE 10.1 Example of ConnectAI in the Exploration Phase

People		The Root of Responsible AI
Educate	Motivate	Communicate

Process		The Structural Support
Intent	Implement	Instrument
• General Responsible AI policy for entire org		

Technology		Best Practices in AI Development
Data	Document	Domain

As you can see, they currently only have one resource listed in *Intent*, the general Responsible AI policy. Even though ConnectAI has now made a public commitment to building AI responsibly, and its executives have indicated it is a top priority for the coming year, they have not built or deployed any other Responsible AI resource, and so are still in the *Exploration* stage. A company-wide policy is a good first step, but it does not show commitment beyond the willingness to further explore Responsible AI.

If you were to fill out the Values Canvas with your own company's Responsible AI solutions and it looked similar to ConnectAI's canvas, or if you particularly resonated with the *Exploration* indicators listed above, then your organization is in the first phase of Responsible AI adoption.

Phase Two: Evaluation

The second phase of Responsible AI adoption, *Evaluation*, is when you begin to evaluate different ethics solutions on their potential to create real business and AI impact, as well as their effectiveness for your specific organization.

In simple terms, your organization is at the *Evaluation* phase when you have an active initiative deployed across each of your Responsible AI pillars, *People*, *Process*, and *Technology*, and are in the process of evaluating if that specific solution is working as intended, requires adjustments, or is ready to scale throughout the organization.

Having devoted time and effort in the previous stage to exploring your different options for Responsible AI solutions, in *Evaluation* you have moved beyond exploring to actually building, deploying, and testing. Here are the key indicators to look for in this phase:

- First, your Responsible AI initiatives are most likely siloed into specific teams or departments instead of stretching cross-department or even discipline.

- Second, your main objective is to find what works best for your needs and organization on a smaller scale, and evaluate whether or not it is a solution that you can then scale throughout the rest of the organization. This is a necessary step in the process of expanding your Responsible AI adoption to permeate throughout your organization.

- Third, and an important one to emphasize, is that you are only at this stage of *Evaluation* if you have started initiatives in all three pillars. As has been stressed throughout Part Two, each pillar builds on the other to form a core essential to a holistic and robust Responsible AI strategy.

Let's return to our example of ConnectAI. A year has passed since the company released its Responsible AI policy and executives made AI Ethics a top organizational priority. Over the past year, ConnectAI has followed the Responsible AI policy up with an AI governance framework designed for middle management to use to ensure their departments and projects are in alignment with the values ConnectAI committed to in its Responsible AI policy. In addition to the framework, ConnectAI is testing a new system for documentation with two select AI teams, have hired a Head of Data Governance who is working on standardizing data practices within the data science teams, and are trialing an external advisory board of psychologists and social media experts with one of their design teams. Overall, ConnectAI has made substantial progress in terms of Responsible AI, deploying multiple test solutions within different departments and beginning to identify what kind of solutions will work best for the company as a whole. If an executive were to fill out the Values Canvas for ConnectAI now, it would look like Figure 10.2.

FIGURE 10.2 Example of ConnectAI in the Evaluation Phase

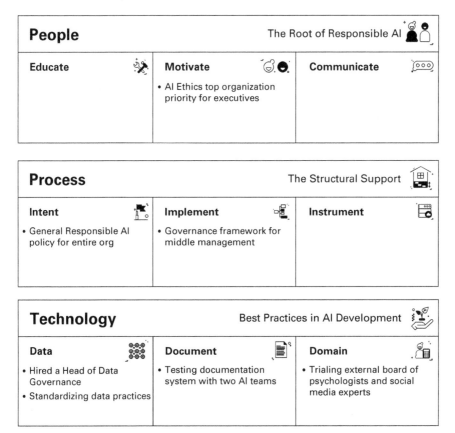

As you can see, ConnectAI now has solutions for both *Intent* and *Implement* in the Process Pillar, as well as solutions for all three elements in the Technology Pillar. The number of Responsible AI resources is still limited, though, as the ones listed are still primarily in testing phases and siloed to specific departments. Additionally, ConnectAI is only just beginning to address the People Pillar with a single *Motivate* solution, leaving the company out of balance in the overall strategy and at risk of failure in the adoption of Responsible AI. It may be tempting to classify ConnectAI as further along in the adoption phases because of the efforts being made across the Technology Pillar, you may think they are all set. However, if ConnectAI does not start building a solution for the People Pillar to test, then it will remain stuck at the *Evaluation* phase, no matter how advanced their Technology Pillar becomes.

Filling out your own organization's Values Canvas, if you find it looks similar to ConnectAI's canvas at this phase, or if you particularly resonated with the *Evaluation* indicators listed above, then your organization is in the second phase of Responsible AI adoption.

Phase Three: Expansion

The third phase of Responsible AI adoption is called *Expansion* and is when you begin expanding your ethics solutions to be across your organization. At this stage, you can say you are a fully Responsible AI-enabled organization and are well on your way to becoming a leader in the Responsible AI space.

Simply put, your organization is at the *Expansion* stage when you have established a solution for the majority of your Responsible AI elements and are in the process of expanding those solutions past the testing and into standard operations throughout your entire organization. Previously in the *Evaluation* stage you were testing different solutions for your Responsible AI elements to evaluate whether or not it was the right solutions for your organization's needs. Now, in *Expansion*, you have moved passed initial testing, validated that the solutions are the right ones to bring the desired impact to your business and AI, and are now in the process of expanding those solutions past their limited testing scopes. Here are the key indicators of what to look for at this phase:

- First, you are moving beyond testing solutions to standardizing solutions. During testing, your initiatives will remain siloed within either specific teams or projects, and won't necessarily bridge multiple disciplines or departments to start. However, once you have validated the solutions, it is time to break down those silos and expand the solutions to reach cross-functional, departmental, and even organizational.

- Second, you have a balance between your Responsible AI pillars. As was stressed in the previous stage, you must work to strike a balance between your different Responsible AI pillars, as too much focus on one at the cost to the other two results in signification blindspots and risks. What this means is that in *Expansion* your organization will have solutions either testing or scaling for the majority of the Responsible AI elements, and that these efforts will be balanced between the three pillars so as to achieve a holistic implementation.

- Third, if you had begun with only a risk- or innovation-based approach, you are now exploring the opportunities the opposite approach may hold to complement your current endeavors, effectively expanding your angles of approach for embedding ethics.

Returning to our example of ConnectAI, we see that the company has once again made significant progress in terms of Responsible AI. Recognizing that their approach was unbalanced, ConnectAI deployed an organization-wide initiative designed to enable its people in ethical decision making. Through company events and a specified company newsletter, ConnectAI brought in experts in the field of Responsible AI and Ethics once a month to speak on current topics to educate its people, and would give shout-outs in the newsletter to teams that had done especially well on their new Responsible AI objectives. In addition to the People initiatives, ConnectAI was expanding its test solutions into standards for the organization, and was adding more Responsible AI resources to its portfolio almost monthly thanks to employee-driven initiatives. ConnectAI even had plans to create a task force specifically for exploring how to use ethics-by-design principles to guide development on new features for the platform. Now, if an executive from ConnectAI were to fill out the Values Canvas, it would look like Figure 10.3.

FIGURE 10.3 Example of ConnectAI in the Expansion Phase

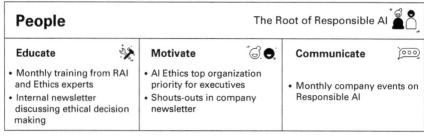

People		The Root of Responsible AI
Educate	**Motivate**	**Communicate**
• Monthly training from RAI and Ethics experts • Internal newsletter discussing ethical decision making	• AI Ethics top organization priority for executives • Shouts-outs in company newsletter	• Monthly company events on Responsible AI

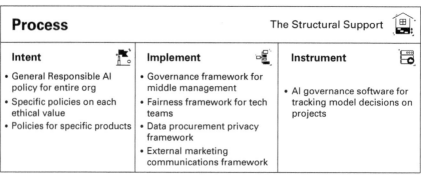

Process		The Structural Support
Intent	**Implement**	**Instrument**
• General Responsible AI policy for entire org • Specific policies on each ethical value • Policies for specific products	• Governance framework for middle management • Fairness framework for tech teams • Data procurement privacy framework • External marketing communications framework	• AI governance software for tracking model decisions on projects

Technology		Best Practices in AI Development
Data	**Document**	**Domain**
• Hired a Head of Data Governance • Established standard data practices	• Established documentation system across all AI teams	• Trialing external board of psychologists and social media experts • Task force on ethics-by-design

As you can see, ConnectAI not only has a solution for every Responsible AI element, in some cases there are multiple resources listed to choose from. At this point, ConnectAI now has the opportunity to become a leader within the Responsible AI space. As the company expands its Responsible AI initiatives throughout the organization, it has the possibility to either showcase how the organization has successfully gone about deploying a Responsible AI strategy at scale and the impact it has brought to the business and AI, or the company has the possibility to begin testing novel ethics solutions on the cutting edge of Responsible AI development. In both cases, ConnectAI is now able to contribute to setting the standard of best practice for not only the Responsible AI industry, but simply the AI industry as well.

As you fill out the Values Canvas for your own organization, if you find that it looks similar to ConnectAI's canvas at this phase, or if you particularly resonated with the *Expansion* indicators listed above, then congratulations, your organization is in the third phase of Responsible AI adoption.

What Happens Next: Advancing Through the Phases

Tying our earlier discussion about the difference between project and organization levels back into the conversation, it goes without saying that if you are only deploying Responsible AI solutions on a project-by-project basis, then your company is still in the *Exploration* phase of adoption. When it comes to being a Responsible AI-enabled organization, we are not looking at what your company is doing in the details of the project level, we are instead looking at the overall picture of what your entire organization is doing in terms of resource and objective building. Your goal, and the purpose of this entire book, is to enable Responsible AI not only on the project level, but on the organizational level as well.

At this point, you should understand what it looks like to be at the different phases of adoption, but how to advance between the phases may still be unclear. In other words, you can see where you are trying to get to, but how to get there may still remain a question. Let's take a moment now to walk back through the three phases and discuss what your priorities should be at each phase in order to help you advance to the next.

Creating Clarity, Direction, and Support through Exploration

As your organization begins its Responsible AI adoption journey, you are focused on exploring what Responsible AI means and what it can do for you. In this phase of *Exploration*, conversations will remind high level and abstract about potential actions to take and objectives to set. In order to advance to the next phase of adoption, your priority should be to transition into concrete planning and execution details on your first trial cases for Responsible AI solutions.

This can be accomplished through a number of ways, the first being to create clarity in terms of your foundational values and objectives. In this first phase of adoption, you may still be exploring which foundational values are right for your organization. By prioritizing the establishment of these foundational values and defining what they mean for your company, you create the clarity needed to transition from vague conversations around "ethics" to concrete ideas of what values you want to see reflected in your technology. In addition to clarity in values, you also need to clearly define what success looks like for your Responsible AI strategy at this point in time. As you explore the potential for using ethics as a decision-analysis tool for your organization and its AI, that exploration must end in a clear picture of what success will look like in order to both motivate your organization as well as provide guiding objectives.

Another way to accomplish the transition to concrete planning and execution is to create direction for your Responsible AI strategy. One form of direction can come from settling on a risk, innovation, or mixed approach to using ethics. Another form of direction can come from determining what Responsible AI pillar, or pillars, you want to start with, keeping in mind you will eventually need to address all three. Use the Values Canvas to help you pinpoint where your current weaknesses are, and direct your attention to filling the gaps first. There are many ways to create direction for your organization's Responsible AI strategy; the important thing is you need to set something otherwise you will never move beyond high-level conversations and theoretical solutions.

The final way you can accomplish the shift from abstract to details you need to transition to the next phase of Responsible AI adoption is through creating support for your Responsible AI strategy. Specifically, support should come in the form of leadership buy-in, company culture, and budget. In other words, support means more than a handful of people sitting around a table all agreeing ethics would be a good idea. It means resources, time, capital, and people are being allocated to work on executing the Responsible AI strategy. This doesn't necessary mean going from 0 to 100 in terms of resource allocation, it can happen in phases. The important point is that in *Exploration* plans for allocation are clarified and solidified.

Testing and Connecting through Evaluation

After making the transition from abstract conversations to concrete execution, you have successfully moved into the *Evaluation* phase. At this point, you have already explored the potential of Responsible AI for your organization, as well as possible ethics solutions, and are now at the point of evaluating what are the right solutions for your given context of organization and AI. In order to move through this phase and onto the next, you will need to transition from pilot programs and evaluating solutions to solidifying practices and scaling solutions beyond sample test cases.

One way to accomplish this transition is to prioritize testing different Responsible AI solutions by selecting specific use cases and deploying pilot programs in order to evaluate these solutions in terms of success in impact and feasibility in adoption. Although you may be designing solutions with your entire organization, or at least department, in mind, it is not necessarily best practice to deploy the solution at grand scale before testing to ensure it is in fact the right one. You don't need to reinvent the wheel when it comes to Responsible AI solutions. Instead, to help with adoption, it is best to look into what your organization already has in place, determine how your Responsible AI solutions can complement this, and build a solution on top of what is already there in order to solidify your ethics practices at scale.

Another way you can achieve the transition from piloting programs to scaling solutions is to look for opportunities to connect initiatives across your organization. It may be tempting to develop Responsible AI solutions independent of one another, keeping them confined to the specific teams or projects they are currently being tested and applied to. However, Responsible AI is not confined to being the responsibility of a single department, instead every department, team, and position will have a role to play in the execution of your Responsible AI strategy. With this in mind, as you set up your various tests and initiatives, be sure to think two steps ahead and consider how any single solution will connect into the wider ecosystem of your Responsible AI strategy, and how it can possible cut through silos to connect different lines of work within your organization.

Standardizing and Scaling through Expansion

You've successfully made the transition from pilot programs to solidifying company standard practices, bringing you to the *Expansion* phase of adoption. At this point in the adoption journey you have already explored the potential for Responsible AI as well as evaluated different solutions for feasibility and impact within the context of your organization, and are now expanding the scope of your ethics solutions. In order to move through this phase and embrace the opportunity to become a true leader in Responsible AI, you need to transition your internal initiatives and standards into external case studies and thought leadership pieces, championing Responsible AI and cutting-edge developments in the field.

The first way you can accomplish this transition is by standardizing Responsible AI practices, resources, and solutions across your entire organization. In *Evaluation* you tested whether or not specific solutions would align with your organization's needs, and now in *Expansion* you will want to focus on making the validated solutions standard practice when it comes to AI in your organization. The important aspect here is transitioning the Responsible AI solutions from something additional to your AI practices into something that is an integral standard for how you develop and use AI. In addition to updating the standard AI practices of your organization, you will also want to standardize the process by which you identify the need for ethics, design a solution, develop that solution, and then deploy that ethics solution throughout your origination.

The second way you can accomplish this transition is through scaling your Responsible AI solutions to reach all necessary parts of your organization and AI practices. In the *Evaluation* phase your Responsible AI solutions were confined in scope and reach. Now in the *Expansion* phase, your goal will be to go beyond this single test cases and scale your solutions to a cross-functional, departmental, and even organizational reach. In order to be able to scale your solutions, you will need to focus your efforts in the *Expansion* stage on what kind of tooling, high-level objectives, and direction is needed within your organization in order to enable your solution to scale both to fit the size of your AI endeavors, but also alongside your AI development as your AI solutions continue to scale in terms of size and impact.

Responsible AI Is a Journey, Not a Destination

As we come to the end of our adoption phases, I must stress again that Responsible AI is not a destination, rather a journey that continues to grow alongside your organization and AI. This means that the ethics solutions you develop today will either need to be updated alongside your AI developments, or you will need to create new solutions if the AI developments occur in a direction that is not currently covered by your solution. In order to support this growth and to efficiently adapt the rapid changing pace of AI, creating a standard for how you update your Responsible AI strategy and practices becomes indispensable to staying on top of, and even ahead of, AI developments.

You are not striving to arrive at a single point in the future that marks you have completed your Responsible AI duties. Instead, you are working to establish the scaffolding of best practices necessary to enable ethical decision making in a manner that scales and adapts with the changing challenges of AI. So although there are three phases of Responsible AI adoption, reaching phase three does not mean you are finished with Responsible AI. It just means you have reached the point at which you have best practices in place and are able to keep pace with the rapid develop of AI.

11

Becoming a Responsible AI Enabled-Organization

How to Build a Strategy for Success

Imagine you're standing at the top of a peak looking out over a stunning view of an impressive mountain range. Looking down to the path in front of you, you find the trail options seem to endlessly multiply, splitting and fanning out in all directions around you. Some point in the direction of other spectacular peaks, while others turn into the lush valleys in between, and still others meander along the sides of the mountains. Although you brought a map, you did not come with a plan, and are now facing the burden of choice. Every trail option looks to hold its own challenges and rewards, and even though you know you can't physically take them all, you are tempted to try as much as you can just to see the opportunity each holds.

You have no idea where to start. Instead of diving in on the first trail and figuring it out from there, or taking the time to consult your map and make a plan of action, you stand frozen at the peak, debating with yourself what direction to go in first. Time slips by, the sun begins to set, and you realize that in your indecision you have wasted the day without even trying one trail.

For my fellow hikers, you can closely relate with this feeling of overwhelm when faced with too many directions and too little planning to choose from. For those of you that would rather leave the outdoors to the creatures, I've always found the mountains to be a beautiful source of visual metaphors, and so hope that although you have never experienced the burden of too many choices while out on the trail, the sentiment of confusion and inertia still carried through. No matter who you are, when you are faced with too many opportunities but no way to shift through the options, it is all too easy to slip into the tendency of paralysis.

Which is exactly the critical point that we find ourselves now.

The Burden of Choice: Overcoming Responsible AI Inertia

We have covered many essential topics in how to operationalize Responsible AI so far, including the major action points of finding your foundational values and embedding those values on a project level. But now we have taken a step back to look at your organization as whole, asking the question what is needed in order to become Responsible AI enabled. At this point we are looking beyond one-off ethics projects and into developing your organizational level strategy.

If you haven't done so already, take the simplified version of the Values Canvas below and list out all of your Responsible AI resources, active initiatives, and ethics projects into each of the elements. The more thorough you can be, the better, so don't be afraid to ask around with your colleagues to see if they know of any Responsible AI projects you may have been unaware of. Remember though, only list things your company has already completed, currently active projects, or plans that are about to be put into action. At this point in time do not list ideas or vague future plans.

FIGURE 11.1 Simplified Values Canvas

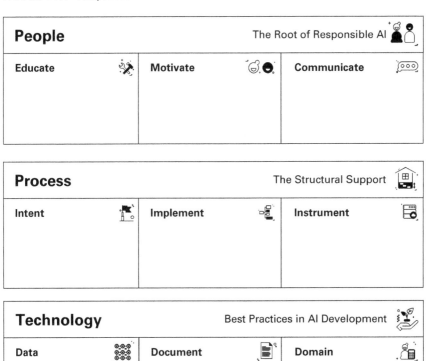

Looking at your canvas, you now have a heat map of Responsible AI for your organization. Some elements will have multiple resources listed under them, while others will have little to nothing. You are able to identify the gaps in your current AI practices, you can conceptualize where your strengths and weakness lie and you can visualize the points of improvement. These are powerful insights for your organization, having gone from little to no visibility on Responsible AI to now having a holistic in-depth view of where you are now and where you ultimately want to be. There is so much opportunity for advancement in AI sitting right in front of your eyes, there are so many directions you can take your Responsible AI strategy in, but in reality you still just have a matrix of Responsible AI elements all in need of solutions.

Just like the hiker left frozen in decision paralysis at the top of the mountain, you may also be experiencing the same paralysis when it comes to deciding exactly where to start your Responsible AI strategy. Whether you are at the very start to your journey, or are coming to this book from a more advanced adoption phase, it can be quite daunting to work through the entire Values Canvas only to arrive on the other end with three pillars and nine elements all equally calling for attention. You know you need a comprehensive plan of action, a holistic strategy that supports your organization in becoming Responsible AI enabled, and you know you need to allocate time, resources, and budget in order to successfully execute it. But where do you even begin?

If this sense of confusion is resonating with you, then know you are not alone. I have lost count of the number of conversations I've had with companies all stuck at this exact point, knowing they want to engage with Responsible AI but have no idea where to even begin.

Because of this confusion, and at times even a sense of overwhelm at the thought of everything that needs to be done, there is the risk of falling into a state of inertia, clinging to the false sense of comfort that doing nothing can bring. But it doesn't have to be like this.

The entire purpose of this chapter is to get you through this inertia, removing the final blockers to starting your Responsible AI strategy and getting your ball rolling down the path to success. Keep in mind, we are moving beyond embedding values on the project level, and are now looking at how to build a strategy that will enable Responsible AI throughout your entire organization.

Do Not Pass Go

It should go without saying that Responsible AI will always start and end with your values, no matter what. The entire objective of becoming a Responsible AI-enabled organization is to have your foundational values reflected in your AI solutions. So, if you are stuck at the peak of starting your organization-wide strategy and are unsure of where to start, be sure that first and foremost you have gone through the process of selecting your set of foundational values, have strong living definitions of this values, and understand what success should look like in having these values reflected into your technology. If you have not done any of the above, do not pass go until you have your foundational values firmly in hand.

Once you have your foundational values in hand, it is time to dive into your Responsible AI strategy. As we discussed before, the Values Canvas turns your current Responsible AI solutions and resources into a matrix to help you conceptualize where the work is needed. It does not, however, necessarily help you prioritize where to start this work.

It's time now to bring the method to your madness and explore the three stages of implementing a Responsible AI strategy. In the following sections I am going to walk you through the foundation laying, structure building, and reinforcement setting of your Responsible AI strategy. As I lay out the three stages of your strategy, we will cover what elements belong to each stage, how to interconnect your efforts between pillars, and what successful adoption for the elements looks like so that you can conceptualize what a Responsible AI strategy should look like. Remember, the ultimate goal is to have multiple Responsible AI resources and ethics solutions available for your teams to use in each of the elements from the Values Canvas, interconnecting strategies for your *People*, *Process*, and *Technology* pillars, and overarching foundational values that guide the direction for your organization's efforts in AI.

A quick note before we dive into the strategy stages—these stages are only suggestions. The purpose of walking you through them is to help you overcome any inertia you may be experiencing in starting with Responsible AI, as well as help you conceptualize how your Responsible AI strategy should interconnect holistically. Although following the three stages is best practice in Responsible AI, you can start your Responsible AI efforts with any of your pillars or elements as suit your particular needs, remembering to balance between the pillars as you go. The one key factor is that you do start.

Laying Your Foundations

As you go to build your plan of action for becoming a Responsible AI-enabled organization, think of it like you are building a house. One that will be home to both your Responsible AI resources and the standards of your AI practices, you want to build a strong house that will last in the long term and weather the maelstrom of AI development. A sturdy home always begins at the foundation. If a house does not have firm foundations built to last, there is no hope for the rest of the structure, no matter how well designed it may be.

Looking at your Responsible AI strategy, you can imagine the three pillars of *People*, *Process*, and *Technology* as the design for your Responsible AI home. We are already familiar with the fact that in order to build a holistic and robust Responsible AI strategy you will need to look for balance between the three pillars, both for your project-level and organizational-level strategies. It may be tempting to start your build by focusing your attention on one pillar at a time, working your way up through each element before moving on to the next pillar. However, this would leave you with a significantly lopsided house for quite some time as you worked your way pillar by pillar, exposing you to the natural elements of risk existing in AI. Instead of going pillar by pillar, think about setting the foundations for each of your pillars to start. Remember, a sturdy home is defined by the strength of its foundations, just as your Responsible AI strategy will be defined by the strength of its pillars' foundations.

To begin constructing your Responsible AI house, start by laying the foundations to each of your three pillars. In ascending order, this means that *People* is built on *Educate*, *Process* is built on *Intent*, and *Technology* is built on *Data*.

By starting with the foundations, you ensure synergy between your three pillars and set yourself up for success in enabling Responsible AI across your organization for the long run. With this in mind, let's take a quick deep dive into the foundational elements.

Foundational Education for Your People

As people are at the root of your Responsible AI endeavors, let's start by looking at the foundation to your *People Pillar*: *Educate*.

Educate sits at the foundation to *People* because it brings the training and knowledge on ethics to life within your organization. Before your people can do anything when it comes to Responsible AI, they first need to know

FIGURE 11.2 Laying Your Foundations

Educate

What is it? Any effort that is designed to up-skill individuals and/or teams in the practical application of ethics in AI.

Need: To ensure your people have the skillsets and knowledge bases necessary to critically engage with using ethics to analyze decisions for value alignment.

Intent

What is it? Any company policy providing strategic guidance for Responsible AI and ethics practices.

Need: To establish a clear and consistent strategic decision on how to manage ethical values in action.

Data

What is it? A technique or method for embedding ethical values into the data that is being used to train and/or test an AI model

Need: To align your data lifecycle management with your ethical values so that your AI is being built on an ethically sound foundation

what your foundational values are and be trained on how to use those values in action. Think of it this way, the next two elements in your *People Pillar* that you will look to build are *Motivate* and *Communicate*. You can't motivate a team to engage in ethical decision making if they don't know what ethics is or how to use your foundational values in the first place, and you can't create channels of communication on Responsible AI factors if no one understands what they are communicating about in the first place. Both *Motivate* and *Communicate* rely on having strong foundations set in *Educate* in order to continue building out your Responsible AI strategy.

Your end goal for your foundation element to *People* is to adopt standard basic Responsible AI and ethics training across your entire organization, in addition to departmental, or even job function, specific education on particularly relevant topics. When done correctly, the education being given to your people will help support the execution of all your Responsible AI elements, proving the details and know-how needed to bring your initiatives to life. Of course this full adoption of *Educate* does not happen overnight, as it will require you to first understand exactly what education is needed for your company in order to support your Responsible AI initiatives, and then to scale that education throughout the organization.

Linux Foundation's Educate Solution

The Linux Foundation is a non-profit organization that has been supporting Linux development and open-source software projects since 2000. It provides tools, training, and events to the open-source community which foster the ability for developers and organizations to code, manage, and scale open-source projects and ecosystems. In partnership with edX, the Linux Foundation surpassed the 1 million mark for people enrolled in courses on edX in 2018, solidifying the organization as a leader in open-source training. With a deep commitment to building the open-source community and supporting developers in democratizing code, the Linux Foundation has become a hub for trusted insights and knowledge. This means that as new best practices emerge, it is the Linux Foundation's duty to capture the necessary information and skillets in their online courses so that their open-source community can stay ahead of the curve.

The Linux Foundation in recent years noticed the growing importance of ethics in technology, as well as a growing gap in resources for open-source development and ethics. In order to fill this gap in knowledge, the Linux Foundation set out to pioneer a course specifically in ethical developing open-source projects. Partnering with Ethical Intelligence in 2022, the course "Ethics for Open Source Development (LFC104)" was created to teach developers how to practically embed ethical values into open source development. Since its release, the course has served the Linux Foundation's community as a foundational resource in ethical critical thinking in the context of open source (Linux Foundation – Training, n.d.).

Setting Intention as a Foundation for Process

Looking to our next pillar, we find that the foundation to *Process* is the element of *Intent*, as it lays down both the direction and purpose necessary to building strong governance processes for your AI. If you were to build and deploy protocols and frameworks without first taking the time to understand why you need them, or what the end goal of the process is meant to achieve, you risk the potential of creating, at best, mounting amounts of busy work, and at worst, counterproductive, tedious, and useless blockers to development. Remember, the following two elements of *Process* are *Implement*, which looks at building process frameworks, and *Instrument*, which focuses on supporting software and tools to help execute on governance frameworks. You can't create a useful framework if you don't first have the guiding policies in place, and you can't find the tools to support execution if you don't know what your end goals are for execution in the first place. Both *Implement* and *Instrument* require the foundational guidance of *Intent* in order to build a strong *Process Pillar* for your Responsible AI strategy.

Ultimately, you will want to arrive at the point at which you have guiding Responsible AI policies for your organization, your departments, relevant operational functions, and perhaps even specific AI use cases. Essentially, the scope of your policies should cover the scope of your AI usage and development. Anywhere AI is in use or is being developed needs to be complemented by a policy outlining the intent of your foundational values within the specific AI use case. Again, this is not something that happens overnight, as you will want to start with broad general policies, and then slowly work your way down into granularity as the needs of your company demand.

> The Marketing AI Institute was first established in 2016 to explore how AI was shaping the marketing industry. Over the years, the Institute has grown into a media, event, and online education company with more than 60,000 subscribers, solidifying the Institute's position as a leading contributor to the future of AI in marketing. Recognizing its position of influence in the market, the Institute saw the opportunity to further the mission of Responsible AI and created the Responsible AI Manifesto for Marketing and Business in January 2023. This manifesto, which is accessible through the Institute's website, can be used under a Creative Commons license and details the primary principles necessary for AI and marketing (Marketing Artificial Intelligence Institute, n.d.).

Data: The Foundation of AI

Finally, moving on to our third pillar of *Technology*, we complete the foundation trifecta with *Data*. Simply put, there is no AI without data, which also means that there is no *Technology Pillar* without *Data*. When looking for the root to ethical challenges in the AI itself, the first place you always look is in the data, as it is one of the most influential components of an AI solution. *Data* so becomes the foundation to *Technology*, as the data governance and ethics practices that go into this element will enable the documentation of foundational values in *Document*, and the starting point for expert feedback in *Domain*.

The overall objective to *Data* is to adopt a standard for data management across the entire data life cycle for all data-related activity in your organization. If you have multiple teams working with data, you should be able to take an individual from one team and place them in a completely different team, project, or even department and they will be able to understand what needs to be done in terms of data management without hiccups. A core component of this data management standard must of course be data ethics practices to ensure that your foundational values are being embedded from the start. But, as discussed in the *Technology Pillar*, *Data* extends beyond just data ethics practices to encompass strong data practices in general, even if they are not directly related to your foundational values, as you can't fix any problems you may find in your AI if your data is not in order first.

Apple's commitment to the value of privacy can be traced all the way back to 2014 when CEO Tim Cook wrote an open letter stating the company's intentions of becoming the most privacy-sensitive of the big tech companies. Since then, Apple has continued to roll out new features such as restrictions to access to personal data on iPhone apps. According to the company's privacy policy, it supports the principle of privacy through methods such as data minimization, on-device processing, user transparency, and control. Each of these methods can be deployed at different points in the data life cycle, so in order to help us distill part of Apple's *Data* strategy, let's zoom in on the method of data minimization. Data minimization is a technique that is deployed during the data collection stage of the data life cycle, and essential limits the amount of data collected on a data subject to the minimum amount required for the technology to work (Apple Newsroom, n.d.).

Designing Your Structure

With the firm foundations laid, you can begin constructing the actual structure to your house. The foundations to a house are essential of course, but if you stop at the foundations you will be left with only the hint of what could have been something great. We may visit ancient ruins to see the foundations of house from another era, but the purpose of building a house in the present day is to create a structure that will eventually be able to home people. Without the structure, there is nothing bringing a the house from an abstract idea into reality.

In the case of your Responsible AI strategy, this means that we are transitioning from foundations to structure. Just as a house is built to be a home for people, we need to establish the structure of your Responsible AI strategy so that it can eventually be able to home your different initiatives and objectives. Essentially, think of this step as building the internal operational systems necessary for smooth implementation of your foundational values and effective adoption of Responsible AI practices. The effectiveness of your Responsible AI strategy is ultimately determined by the pillars' structure. The more refined and thoughtfully built the structure, the more useful, and even beautiful, the house in the end.

Maintaining the balance we so carefully set in the foundations, we can look again to build in each of the three Responsible AI pillars in order to create as stable a structure as possible. This means that *Motivate* will build the structure for *People*, *Implement* the structure for *Process*, and *Document* the structure for *Technology* as shown in Figure 11.3.

Establishing Motivational Structures for Your People

As we work our way up the *People Pillar*, we look to build a structure of *Motivate* on the foundations of *Educate*. *Motivate* is structural to *People* as it focuses on establishing business motivators within day-to-day operations that encourage your people to engage in Responsible AI practices. Objective setting brings structure to your people's tasks, creating hierarchies of priorities and establishing an order of operation to the job at hand. Without the structure of *Motivate*, your people will not know where they should be using their newfound skillsets from *Educate*, nor be able properly prioritize new Responsible AI practices in their daily workflow. Essentially, think of this element as the necessary step in bringing structure to your people's efforts in Responsible AI.

FIGURE 11.3 Designing Your Structure

Motivate

What is it? A business motivator designed to positively reinforce the habit of engaging with ethics and Responsible AI practices.

Need: To cultivate a company culture that supports and fosters the active participation of employees in ethics-based decision analysis behaviors.

Implement

What is it? Any procedural framework designed to direct the execution of Responsible AI practices and ethical decision making.

Need: To create a comprehensive and standard course of action for execution of ethical values and practices.

Document

What is it? The documentation of all ethics related decisions taken during the lifecycle of an AI model.

Need: To create transparency of the ethical decisions being taken during the AI development lifecycle.

Mature adoption of *Motivate* looks like an internal structure for designing and implementing objectives in alignment with your organization's foundational values on a combination of company, department, and individual levels. Trickling high-level values down from the top, the motivational structure should create the guiding intentions in Responsible AI that your people will be held accountable to and encouraged to reach, while simultaneously stimulating bottom-up buy-in and execution. As anyone that has ever held a management position will tell you, selecting the right KPIs for your team is an art form. It takes time to fine-tune the right business motivators, just as it takes time to develop company objectives that bring the right desired results. The important fact is that you provide the structure necessary for your people to understand how to prioritize their tasks and objectives in order to align with your Responsible AI strategy.

Salesforce's Motivate Solution

In September 2022, the World Economic Forum in collaboration with the Markkula Center for Applied Ethics at Santa Clara University published an in-depth case study on Salesforce's responsible use of technology. The report covers Salesforce's journey from first setting out to become a Responsible Tech company all the way to present day practices and standards. From the start, Salesforce knew that the commitment to ethics would require some way of clearly establishing and tracking goals for the new Responsible Tech initiatives. This resulted in the V2MOM, a model for a planning and evaluation form that combined top-level values and strategies with bottom-up ideation and buy-in.

The V2MOM is a strategic tool that enables Salesforce's people, teams, and business as a whole to set goals, track progress against the goals, and be held accountable for the goals thorough living documents visible to everyone in the company. The system is set up to cascade down top-level strategies, as the corporate level V2MOM sets the priorities for the team and individual level V2MOMs. Ethics and inclusion efforts have been consistently included within the number one goal of the highest level V2MOM for the past several years, influencing leaders and product teams with Salesforce to include ethics and inclusion as top priorities on their own teams' V2MOMs. To further support the adoption of ethics goals across the company, the Office of Ethical Humane Use hosts quarterly Ethical Use Advisory Council meetings during which Salesforce's executive leaderships reviews the progress of the company's progress towards the ethics and inclusion efforts encapsulated in the top-level V2MOM (Firth-Butterfield, Heider, and Green, 2022).

Implementing Structure to your Process

In *Intent* we set the foundations for *Process*, now in *Implement* we build off those foundations to create much-needed operational structures. *Implement* is focused on creating frameworks for Responsible AI, which means it essentially provides the structure to your decisions and actions necessary for execution on ethics solutions. Frameworks in general build structure into how a team or company will go about implementing objectives into action. Coming in a variety of forms, frameworks can be built to direction specific actions within a daily workflow, or they can be built to implement necessary compliance checks throughout a project life cycle, still even they can be designed to help guide critical decision making. No matter the form a framework comes in, it establishes the structure for practical and detailed execution of your high-level intents and objectives. In the case of Responsible AI, this means that *Implement* establishes the structure for execution on the foundational ethics values laid out by the policies from *Intent*.

The end goal of *Implement* as a structural element for *Process* is to establish a database of different frameworks covering all of your foundational values and AI use cases that your teams can take off the shelf ready to use, or use as a base to customize for specific initiatives. Whether you are building, customizing, or externally sourcing, any governance framework worth its investment will take time and resources to make it effective for your teams. The key to *Implement* is to create, when you are able to, frameworks that can be applied beyond just the current use case. In order to not slow down your teams in the execution of your Responsible AI strategy, your goal should be to have a portfolio of structural frameworks designed to help guide critical decision making and actions readily available to seamlessly transition into use.

Rolls-Royce is a terrific example of a traditional company that has undergone a successful digital transformation. Embracing the modern age with open arms, Rolls-Royce has actively adopted AI and advanced data analytics to the heart of the business for more than 20 years. Alongside this AI transformation, Rolls-Royce has made a significant and public commitment to Responsible AI. One of the initiatives undertaken by the company was to create the Aletheia Framework (Rolls-Royce, n.d.), a practical toolkit that considers 32 different facets of social impact, governance, trust, and transparency. The framework was created with the intention to guide developers, executives, and boards through ethical considerations both before an AI system is deployed, as well as when the system is in use. It mandates users to provide clear evidence for each of the ethical facets so that approvers, stakeholders, and auditors will be able to easily engage in ethical problem shooting. In December 2021, the Aletheia

Framework was released under creative commons license with an additional module designed specifically to help identify and mitigate bias in training data. The framework has been a success for Rolls-Royce, as its AI developers state that the framework has both sped up certain aspects of their workflow as well as aided in their innovation thinking (Rolls-Royce | It's not what you think, n.d.).

Lee Glazier, Head of Digital Integrity for Rolls-Royce, Civil Aerospace who developed the Aletheia Framework™ says "What was particularly satisfying was the positivity of all those who collaborated in creating the framework, including our Trade Union and Workers Councils, and external bodies. The Aletheia Framework™ methodology has now been extended to take Responsible AI principles into Quality Assurance of Fully Autonomous Safety Critical AI. We have discussed this approach with our Regulators and they are very positive."

Creating Structure to your Technology through Documentation

Again, we round out our structural elements with a look at the *Technology Pillar* and *Document*. While *Data* built the foundations for both your AI and Responsible AI, *Document* continues the process by creating a structured approach to developing your AI. Think of it this way, if you are required to document key decisions made during the AI development life cycle, you should have both the structure in place that reminds you to make those critical ethical decisions, as well as the structure in place that enables you to review and refine decisions to bring your AI into better alignment with your values. By creating an easily navigable structure to the decision making taking place during AI development, you are establishing a powerful layer of transparency to your AI practices and setting yourself up for success when auditing of AI systems is legally required.

Just as the end goal for *Data* is to establish a standard for data management across your entire organization, so is your goal for *Document* to establish a standard for documentation across all of your AI practices and projects. An individual working on one AI project should be able to switch onto a new project and understand what documentation needs to take place, as well as be able to easily locate important documented information, seamlessly. Of course documentation of decisions based on your foundational values is an important aspect of *Document*, but this element also extends beyond ethics to cover all documentation for your AI projects. Without proper documentation, it can be a lengthy, and even impossible, process to retrace decision making to find the source decision leading to unwanted outcomes in your AI.

NVIDIA, a leading manufacturer of high-end graphics processing units (GPUs), first embarked on its journey to AI starting in 2006. One of the company's modern practices in AI development is keeping detailed AI model cards, and it is currently working on advancing these model cards with Model C++. An AI model card is a document detailing how a specific machine learning model works and will include information such as the model's metadata, performance measures it was trained on, model version, and so on. NVIDIA hosts its model cards on the NGC Catalog in order to make the model cards easily accessible, allowing for users to see the model and model card listed side by side. In addition to the technical information being documented on the AI model cards, NVIDIA has also taken steps to include specific ethical considerations. Users have stated that the documentation of these ethical considerations were one of the most important categories of the model cards, just after performance and licensing information. One of the specific considerations that NVIDIA includes in Model C++ are steps taken to mitigate bias, which in other words, is the documentation of fairness in action (Boone et al., 2022).

Reinforcing Your Strategy

You have the foundations and structure to your house built, you can see the whole picture coming together nicely, but you still feel there is something missing. Although the structure is well designed, and the foundations are firmly holding it in place, you fear that one overly enthusiastic wolf could huff and puff all your hard work down. What you need now is reinforcement for your house, guaranteeing it will be built to withstand even the strongest huffing and puffing.

In terms of your Responsible AI strategy, this means that we are moving on to the final three elements of your *People*, *Process*, and *Technology* pillars to reinforce the work we have done in laying foundations and building structure. As was emphasized in the previous chapter, Responsible AI is not a destination, it is a journey, which means you are going to want a strategy that will stand the tests of time, AI advancements, and the occasional tech industry drama. To shape such a strategy, you will need to reinforce the initiatives being made across all Responsible AI elements in a way that strengthens efforts, increases impact, and, most importantly, enables scaling of solutions. If your strategy is going to last, you are going to need to reach a level of scale that your Responsible AI practices and ethics solutions permeate through your entire business.

FIGURE 11.4 Reinforcing Your Strategy

Communicate

What is it? An internal initiative that stimulates cross-organizational communication on Responsible AI practices and ethical decision making.

Need: To break down communication silos and foster interdisciplinary collaboration.

Instrument

What is it? Software used to standardize implementation of Responsible AI and ethics practices.

Need: To standardize execution, automate processes where appropriate, and increase efficiency of Responsible AI practices at scale.

Domain

What is it? A specified time and place in the AI lifecycle for expert and customer feedback.

Need: To incrementally iterate and refine AI models into ethical value alignment through insights from people directly affected by the AI systems.

In order to round out your strategy, we must reinforce *People* with *Communicate*, *Process* with *Instrument*, and *Technology* with *Data*, bringing your pillars once again into symmetry in this final stage.

Reinforcing People through Communication

We started with the foundations of *Educate*, the structure of *Motivate*, and now we reach the final element of *People*, *Communicate*. *Communicate* is the reinforcing element as it centers on fostering the exchange of vital information and collaboration between teams, both of which solidify your Responsible AI practices into your company culture. If people are trained and motivated in using ethics in critical decision making for your AI, the final step you need to take in order to ensure that training is used and that motivation is followed through on is in fact communication. By fostering open communication on ethics solutions, you ingrain Responsible AI into the everyday operations of your organization and transition the concept from being a novel idea into a common place practice. Without the exchange of information, ideas, and collaboration between your people on the topic of Responsible AI, execution becomes a rather more difficult task and the likelihood of your teams keeping up with the new practices quickly dwindles.

Although having dedicated meetings and agenda points on Responsible AI is important, the true marker of mature adoption in *Communicate* is hearing ethics brought up naturally in conversations that it wasn't necessarily listed as a discussion point in. Some companies take the approach of designating ethics champions spread throughout its teams whose responsibility it is to bring ethics into critical discussions and be a resource for peers on the subject. This is a great approach to *Communicate*, but keep in mind there is a difference between actively pushing the subject and having it naturally become a part of your company culture. Either way, if your people are discussing Responsible AI across work silos, then you know *Communicate* is doing its job of reinforcing your *People Pillar*.

Ever since its founding in 1943, IKEA has had a strong company culture centered around the company's values. Even with this foundation, however, IKEA recognized that as they moved into the digital age and sought to keep ethics at the heart of the company, creating clear and open communication on a topic new to the business such as Responsible AI was going to be no simple task. Although IKEA clearly saw the value of values, they also understood that it takes an effort to make Digital and AI Ethics a priority in conversations, as well as connect it to initiatives throughout the business. A key focus for IKEA became to connect the engagement of Digital and AI Ethics to the already vibrant culture and values of IKEA, positioning it as a natural development within the company's future while being firmly anchored to its legacy of values.

In order to do so, IKEA started by communicating a central statement of intent for its Digital and AI Ethics initiatives: "We are taking our IKEA values into the future and what that means in a digital context is what we call Digital Ethics." With the reference point for conversation established, as part of Inter IKEA Group's Digital Ethics team and leading the focus on AI Ethics, Giovanni Leoni went on to meet the people of IKEA where they were already at in terms of their daily business reality, digital maturity, and perception of digital values. To execute on this vision, IKEA would carve out time in department and team meetings, sometimes even as little as 20 minutes, to discuss IKEA's values and what they meant in a digital future. In the allotted time for discussion, teams would spend 50 percent of the time talking about the new Digital Ethics policies along with ongoing work and examples, while the remaining 50 percent would be spent in an open dialogue, giving people the opportunity to share their view, ask questions and building the groups awareness. Overall, the conversations were less focused on presenting Digital Ethics as a topic new to the business, and instead focused on how to contribute to bringing IKEA's long-standing values into the digital future. According to Leoni, the best indicator of success was "when we heard people talking about the topic of Digital Ethics in meetings even when no one from our Digital Ethics team was present, nor had put it on the official agenda. The awareness, understanding and motivation was so high that someone could speak independently about Digital Ethics, that's when we knew communication of our values was working."

The Instrument of Process Reinforcement

You've established *Intent* with Responsible AI policies and created structure to executing these policies through *Implement* frameworks, how do you ensure that these processes are effective, trackable, and scalable? The answer is in *Instrument*, as the final element to your *Process Pillar* reinforces your efforts by providing the software and tools designed to ease governance management and scale usage throughout your teams. Without *Instrument*, your frameworks and policies are confined to traditional business artifacts such as excel sheets, PDFs, and slide decks, making it difficult to encourage usage and complicating tracking. Instead, *Instrument* provides a place for your frameworks and policies to live that is easy to access, can provide new insights through tracking usage, and enables scale of your solutions. Overall, this reinforces the use of your *Intent* and *Implement* solutions, making *Instrument* vital to engraining Responsible AI practices into your organization.

Your objective for *Instrument* will be to adopt the usage of supporting software tools, such as governance software and data dashboards, that bring your Responsible AI frameworks and policies intro practice at scale. When you have the right tools in place, you will be able to automate repetitive tasks in Responsible AI governance, track progress on ethics embedding, and overall increase the quality of your standard AI practices through the reinforced efficient implementation of Responsible AI.

The Ethical AI Database (EAIDB) was created in 2021 to keep record of the expanding number of startups developing Responsible AI software solutions. In 2022 alone, the database went from 100 startups to over 250 different active companies. Each company listed in the database offers a solution designed to support a specific function or set of functions necessary to executing on Responsible AI. For example, Credo AI is an AI governance software designed to track, assess, report, and manage AI projects in accordance to key governance factors. Or there's Fiddler AI, a software platform designed to bring the necessary transparency into development through AI observability. The list goes on, and continues to grow as Responsible AI quickly matures into an industry of its own (Raghunathan, 2022).

Using Domain Expertise to Reinforce Responsible AI

Last but not least, we reach the *Technology Pillar* that has had its foundations laid in *Data* and structure built in *Document*. Now, we look to *Domain* for reinforcement, as this element brings in the domain relevant expertise necessary to refine your AI systems through feedback on impact and effectiveness. *Data* and *Document* both work towards creating strong AI systems, but *Domain* is the final reinforcer of Responsible AI. If you will recall, the entire purpose of your Responsible AI strategy is to have your foundational values reflected in your AI. The only way to truly determine whether you are accomplishing this objective is through active feedback loops from domain experts and customers. It is through the insights of humans that you are able to tell if your foundational values are being reflected in your AI, or understand what needs to be refined in order to better align with this objective.

Your ultimate objective for *Domain* is to establish a standard time and place within the AI life cycle for human feedback loops that will reinforce the ethical decisions being taken throughout your three pillars of Responsible AI. The feedback can come in the form of domain expertise in the relevant field, direct users of your AI system, or customers of your AI solutions. The important factor is that you gather a wide range of interdisciplinary and inclusive perspectives so as to safeguard against blindspots in opinions. Specifically, you will want standard feedback practices in place that continue to periodically monitor the performance of your AI systems once deployed so you can catch potentially harmful model drift as early as possible.

Mednition is an AI-powered decision software designed to support emergency nurses in making better real-time decisions. One of KATE's, Mednition's software solution, specific use cases is in screening triage patients for sepsis (Ivanov et al., 2022). Healthcare is an incredibly sensitive industry for which to develop AI software solutions, which is why Mednition has a special team of registered clinicians on staff collaborating alongside their engineers to ensure accuracy of KATE's sepsis predictions. One specific point that the team of clinicians provide feedback is during the deployment of KATE into new hospitals. Whenever KATE is brought into a new hospital, Mednition first trains KATE's models on that hospital's data in order to refine the system to that exact hospital's needs. However, before the newly trained system is deployed into the use for the hospital, Mednition brings in their team of registered clinicians to test the newly trained model to ensure for accuracy. If the clinicians say the model is not performing per standard, then Mednition engineers go back to training, refining the model until it reaches accuracy standards. The models are then checked at monthly intervals using the same process to ensure against model drift that may occur.

It's All Relative (to Size)

At this point you should understand what a Responsible AI-enabled organization looks like and how to move through the pillars of a holistic strategy to build the foundations, structure, and reinforcements of success in embedding ethics. There is, however, one blocker remaining to your ability to conceptualize what this strategy should look like specifically for you, and that is the variable of organization size. Whether this factor was top of mind or cooling on the back burner, the size of your organization will have an important influence on how your Responsible AI strategy will come together.

Although the Values Canvas is a one-size-fits-all tool designed to help you visualize and plan out the different elements needed for a holistic Responsible AI strategy, what that final strategy will look like depends on what end of the size spectrum you fall towards. To help bring you clarity on what your strategy should look like for your particular organization's size, let's take a look into the key differences in Responsible AI adoption between large and small enterprise.

Deploying Responsible AI at Scale in Large Enterprise

On one end of the size spectrum we have the large enterprises of the world. These are the Fortune insert-number-of-choice-here companies that span multiple time zones, operate in a variety of foreign markets, and have to manage thousands of employees.

In order to imbue the practices of Responsible AI and embed your foundational ethics values throughout the entirety of a large enterprise, you should view your strategy as an ecosystem of initiatives all interconnected and derived from a single source of truth (think similar to single source of truth in data) yet adapted to the needs of your different departments and projects. Seek to have a strong center of objectives and guidelines based on your foundational ethics values, which are then complemented by an ecosystem of solutions that disseminate the strategy throughout your organization. For example, in the element *Implement* your goal here is to establish necessary frameworks to guide specific actions in Responsible AI. In the case of large enterprise, you do not want a handful of central monolithic frameworks, as it is impossible to create frameworks on such a scale and still have them remain practical. It will also encumber teams to have to work around a framework that is not necessarily relevant to their needs. Instead, you will want to have a handful of abstract high-level guidelines complemented with an ecosystem of frameworks designed for specific functions or needs.

Essentially, large enterprise requires a level of complexity in its solutions, which means you should opt for vertical depth rather than horizontal reach for your Responsible AI resources that are all derived from a top-level strategy. To help with the scale of execution required within larger companies, the best practice is to have a designated Responsible AI team. However, it is important to remember that, even though there may be a designated team, it does not mean that Responsible AI is only assigned to that one team. Instead, think of the Responsible AI team as the nexus for initiatives and ethics solutions that are designed to permeate throughout the entire organization.

Getting Bang for Your Buck in Responsible AI for Small Organizations

By now it should come as no surprise when I tell you that Responsible AI is not a "nice to have later down the line," but instead a "need to have now" if you want to find success in AI for your organization. This means that the size of your organization is not a variable in terms of timing for when you need to engage with Responsible AI practices, the answer to the question of timing will always be now, or in some cases even yesterday. Even if you are a newly founded startup, the moment you begin to work on AI is the moment Responsible AI becomes a relevant factor to your success.

With this in mind, let's look to the other end of the size spectrum. While large enterprise must tackle the challenge of scale when it comes to a Responsible AI strategy, small and medium enterprise (SMEs) are instead faced with the challenge of limited time and resources. The smaller an organization is on the size spectrum, the larger the challenge of time and resources becomes for Responsible AI, especially when you get all the way down to early stage startups. While it is much simpler to establish central initiatives that function across the entire organization instead of needing an ecosystem of solutions, SMEs struggle with finding the budget, human capital, and time necessary to dedicate to Responsible AI before even beginning to embark on the journey.

Although these concerns are valid, I would argue that they are only true in the cases when an SME attempts to achieve the same level of governance and complexity in Responsible AI as a large enterprise, instead of adjusting solutions to fit the size of their needs. For example, large enterprises will want to strive for domain and function specific training in AI Ethics, whereas SMEs can scale the needs of *Educate* down to size and instead engage in training around AI Ethics principles that can then be adapted by the individual to their own work. It is important to note, however, that although you can scale back the complexity of your Responsible AI solutions to fit the size and capacities of your organization, the one thing you can't scale back is compliance. Regulations in AI and data will need to be followed, irrespective of your size.

Although SMEs can be limited by resources, a significant of advantage of being smaller sized is the ability to quickly adapt to changes in the market, and in the industry of AI, this can prove to be a massive advantage given the rate at which the technology develops. This means that an SME should be less concerned with setting strict guidelines and standards in Responsible AI, and instead focus on creating a Responsible AI strategy that adapts to the pace of AI development by setting foundational objectives to build off of and regular alignment check-ins. Think of it this way—while large enterprise is focused on achieving vertical depth through an ecosystem of solutions, SMEs should focus instead on achieving horizontal adaptability through a few core yet versatile solutions.

David versus Goliath in the Three Pillars of Responsible AI

Although all three Responsible AI pillars are essential to success in AI no matter the size of your organization, the extent of influence each pillar has over your success will vary slightly depending on the size of your organization.

For both large enterprise and SMEs, getting the right *Technology* elements in place is crucial, as these have less to do with organizational operations and more to do with the technology itself. An AI system is an AI system, no matter the size of organization that is building it. Thus, the *Technology Pillar* only differs in the scale that the solutions will need to reach when it comes to size of organization. However, the *People Pillar* and *Process Pillar* are more heavily influenced by size of organization, as these two pillars are focused on the operations of the company. When it comes to large enterprise, the *Process Pillar* will have greater influence, while for SMEs it is the *People Pillar* that holds the greater influence.

Large enterprise must operate on a massive scale, which results in a small, relative to the size of the company, select group of people taking the key decisions in Responsible AI for a large portion of the company. Responsible AI naturally becomes a top-down practice in large enterprise, so the objective must be to effectively carry out the key ethics decisions at scale throughout the entire organization. This is where a strong *Process Pillar* will really make a difference in success of your Responsible AI strategy. The policies, frameworks, and tooling of your *Process Pillar* are the elements necessary to carry out crucial Responsible AI decisions at scale.

On the other hand, SMEs are not faced with the same challenges of disseminating key decisions from a select group to scale throughout a proportionally much larger body of individuals. Instead, the Responsible AI decision making for SMEs will generally rest more in a bottom-up approach. SMEs need to remain nimble and adaptive to changes in AI in order to stay competitive, and so also require their Responsible AI strategies to remain equally nimble and adaptive. This is hard to achieve if ethical decision making is confined to select groups, causing teams to have to wait for decisions to be made and only then be able to act once the decisions have made their way through protocol. SMEs instead will want to focus on enabling the individuals within the organization to make decisions in accordance with the Responsible AI strategy so that the company can stay agile and adapt quickly to changes. This means that the people need to be equipped with the right knowledge, motivating factors, and communication channels, resulting in SMEs being influenced more by the strength of their *People Pillar*.

The Elephant in the Room

As we round out this chapter on building the Responsible AI strategy for your overall organization, we still have a final elephant hanging out in the corner that needs to be addressed. This entire time that we have been discussing Responsible AI at both project and organization level, we have talking about what to do if you are the one building the AI systems. Which means our elephant in the corner is the question sitting in the back of your mind asking "but what if I'm just using the AI?" In other words, what changes if your organization is not building its own AI, and is instead simply adopting AI solutions to use for either internal or external purposes?

The simple answer: from a high-level perspective, nothing. It does not matter if your organization is building or just using AI, Responsible AI is relevant to your success either way. Let's put it this way, if your company is caught in an AI Ethics scandal, the press, and more importantly your customers, will not care if you built the AI yourself or if you had procured a faulty system, you are still going to be held accountable for the harmful consequences.

The more complex answer is that there is a slight change in how you approach your Responsible AI pillars. In the case that your organization is not building AI but simply using it, the *People* and *Process* pillars both remain relevant, the only change being in the details of the ethics solutions and resources you provide will have a different emphasis in use case. How the AI is being used is often times more influential on the outcomes than the technology itself, so ensuring your people are trained in your foundational values and know how to operationalize through values is still highly important. The *Technology Pillar*, on the other hand, does experience a more notable change. If you are building the AI, then you are developing solutions for each of your *Technology* elements. If you are using another company's AI, then instead of building out the *Technology* resources yourself, you are instead asking your AI provider which of the *Technology* recourses they actively use. Essentially, you want to hold your AI provider to the same standard as you would hold your own AI to.

It's a Matter of Time

A robust and holistic Responsible AI strategy is not born overnight, just as it is not deployed in a day.

The beautiful, yet potentially daunting, fact is that Responsible AI is a complex endeavor full of opportunity to increase your organization's ROI on any AI initiative. Although there are in total nine different elements necessary to enabling Responsible AI and embedding foundational ethics values, this does not mean you need to do all nine at once. Instead, you can make your way through the foundation, structure, and reinforcement stages of your strategy, allowing time for the change to take root, teams to adapt to the new solutions, and your organization to more closely monitor impact.

Ideally, as you embark on deploying your newly designed Responsible AI strategy, you will move through each stage, balancing implementation between your three pillars and allowing your elements to build on each other. Again though, let me emphasize here that this is in no way a mandatory flow of Responsible AI implementation, it is instead a template for you to utilize and adapt. You may find that your organization's needs require a different approach, and it is better to follow the needs of your organization than a template.

Now that you have your newly designed Responsible AI strategy and ready to take your first steps, let's turn our attention to the last big remaining question: who is going to be responsible for all of this?

12

Who's Responsible for Responsible AI?

How to Bring About Responsible AI Change for Your Organization

So far we have discussed a substantive number of ways in which to make AI responsible, but that still leaves us with the question of who is responsible for executing on these necessary initiates. Although our final objective is a technical output, as in we are striving to produce top-quality AI products and systems, the AI is not going to build itself, nor will the AI govern itself in accordance to our human values. It is up to the humans within this AI equation to be able to build and use the systems in a way that accurately reflects our values.

Responsible AI is vital to the success of a modern-day company looking to grow in this technology-driven era, but knowing who within your organization is necessary to the success of your Responsible AI strategy will determine whether or not you ever realize the full potential of AI for your company. It is one thing to say you are committed to implementing ethical values, it is another to thing to break down and assign accountability for implementing those exact values into your AI development life cycles. Without clear and predetermined roles assigned in to the execution of your Responsible AI strategy, you will remain stuck and frustrated in the theoretical.

If you recall from Chapter 7, people have been and always will be the root to either the success or failure of your AI. Your Responsible AI strategy rests on the foundations of your *People Pillar*, a pillar devoted solely to ensuring your people are educated, motivated, and communicating in such a way as to enable Responsible AI. In this chapter, we will return again to the topic of who; however, this time we will be approaching this topic through the lens of implementation. This means that instead of looking at who is building or using your AI, we will be focusing on who is in charge of the design and execution of your Responsible AI strategy. To do so, we will first start with discussing the different functions operational roles must play in a holistic implementation of Responsible AI, and then will move on to looking at the potential strengths and weaknesses of how your organization tends to approach change management. By the end of this chapter, you will be able to identify the different roles of Responsible AI and how to instigate the necessary change within your organization.

The Pitfall of Responsibility in AI

If you are reading this book then it is safe to assume that you, on some level, feel a sense of responsibility to embedding ethics into your AI. However, that does not necessarily mean you are the person, or have the exact answer, for who is responsible within your organization. With the ever-mounting fear of AI gone wrong, the general knowledge in and recognition of the importance of Responsible AI is quickly spreading on a global scale. This means that even the average person is beginning to care, on some level or another, about whether or not our AI reflects our values, independent of whether or not they work in an AI-driven organization. Although there is a lively debate about whether companies can be trusted to self-govern their AI, or if we must rely on a harder hand of international regulations to keep the development of AI in check (Heskett, 2023), at the end of the day you as a business leader are responsible for ensuring your company remains competitive on a market that is demanding Responsible AI to be the standard.

What this translates to is a widespread feeling of responsibility throughout mainstream AI development. On the one hand, it is heartening to see a growing number of people concerned about how AI is built and utilized, while on the other there is a significant difference between caring and action. The transition from caring to action requires someone to be in charge be and accountable for the implementation of Responsible AI practices. Why is this such a dilemma, and even potential blocker, to effective Responsible AI? It is easy to assume that because of the importance of the subject, everyone will want to contribute to a Responsible AI initiative, and that ethics will naturally work its way into the technology. I must stress that if this laissez-faire approach is the one you choose to take, you are setting yourself up for failure. Assuming that Responsible AI will naturally come to be within your organization because you "are ethical people" is the quickest path to failure, not because you are bad or unethical, but because successful Responsible AI is an operational, technical, and business endeavor that must be treated with the gravitas of such.

The Roles of Responsible AI

To help prevent falling into this pitfall, you must not only understand but also assign the different roles of implementing Responsible AI within your team. The responsibility for executing on ethics will not fall to just a single department or team, but instead will encompass a variety of cross-departmental functions. In addition to specific Responsible AI teams, which we will cover in the next chapter, each department in your organization will have something different it can contribute to the execution of your Responsible AI strategy, but it is up to you as a business leader to understand what that something is, and how to best go about unlocking the potential within each. Everyone has their role to play in Responsible AI, which, when done successfully in a strategic and systematic fashion, also has the side benefit of breaking down internal silos between teams and increasing the quality of cross-departmental and cross-functional collaboration.

So, what are these different roles, and who is meant to fill them? There are five basic Responsible AI functions you will need to allocate across your organization:

- strategy building
- designing
- executing
- communicating
- knowledge gathering

Each of these five functions has a natural place within the universal organizational structure, as the needs and purpose of each action will lend themselves inherently towards the objectives already in place for your different departments. Think of your Responsible AI efforts as an organizational puzzle, and what you need to do now is to understand how this puzzle, with all its subsequent roles and responsibilities, fits together to form the bigger picture. To help you do so, let's now dive into the five functions covering what the purpose, roles, and objectives are for each.

Strategy Building

Purpose: To align the various departments, initiatives, intentions, and responsibilities for Responsible AI into one cohesive and holistic strategy.

Roles: This function falls to the leadership and management teams within an organization as it requires both oversight and authority for execution. Typically you will see positions such as CEO, CTO, and Board of Directors fulfill the strategy building of Responsible AI.

Objectives: When it comes to strategy building, the leadership and management teams that this action falls to will be responsible for setting the direction of Responsible AI within your organization. This is truly where the journey to ethics implementation must begin. Without intentional direction, then any effort in ethics, no matter how well designed, will never reach the scale and impact necessary. Strategy building is quite literally in the name, as this action focuses on building the strategy and leadership necessary to implementing ethics. It is up to leadership teams to be able to set the direction and goals for their departments and to ensure that these goals align with the overarching Responsible AI strategy. Additionally, leadership buy-in is essential to success in strategy building in terms of allocation of time and resources within an organization for the execution of a Responsible AI strategy. Simply put, the objective of this action is to set the direction, intentions, and indicators of success for Responsible AI.

Designing

Purpose: To ensure ethical values are embedded into the foundational functions, features, and perimeters of an AI solution or product.

Roles: This function can happen in one of two main divisions: design and business teams. It may seem strange at first to pair these two very different departments under the same function; however, there is one important commonality between the two that lends itself to designing for Responsible AI. Both departments have, to some degree, influence over how the AI solution or product will look, function, and be perceived by the real-world market. With this in mind, the positions typically involved in this action are UX and UI designers, Business Analysts, and Business Developers.

Objectives: Since there are two different departments that this action belongs to, the objectives needed to fulfill the purpose will look slightly different for each department. On the one hand, design teams are in charge of designing not only what an AI solution will look like, but also designing functionality and features of the AI product. This means that design teams have the unique opportunity to embed ethics into the foundational designs of an AI solution, and so will be looking to incorporate various ethical values by design (Verbeek, 2008). On the other hand, business teams are in charge of assessing a market opportunity and determining the right product fit for the needs identified. What this means is that business teams have the ability to design the perimeters in which the AI product must fit and will greatly influence what features are and are not designed. Often times it is easy to forget that the business model will have just as much, if not more, influence over the ethics of the final AI product than even the code itself. There are immensely important ethical factors at play within different business and revenues models, all of which fall under the responsibility of business teams to design, and frankly are deserving of an entire series of books to address (Lauer, 2020). Whether it is the design team or the business team carrying out this action, the objectives of this function is to incorporative innovative ethics-by-design practices to shape the direction of your AI system so that you will not have to back track in your AI development cycles to retrospectively fix preventable and predictable problems.

Executing

Purpose: To implement ethics decisions and solutions during the development of an AI system in a structured manner, and to monitor the impact of these solutions over time.

Roles: As this function focuses on the execution of your Responsible AI strategy in action, you can probably guess that this role goes to your technical teams. Your technical teams are responsible for building the AI itself, so logically it is down to these teams to execute on the ethics decisions and solutions you have designed for the AI system. Typically, technical teams include but are not limited to positions such as data scientists, engineers, AI developers, programmers, and data analysts. Essentially, anyone with visibility and access into the AI systems being built can fall into this category.

Objectives: Although it is important to include your technical teams for feedback at key points during the initial stages of building your Responsible AI strategy, they will not necessarily be the ones building your strategy. Instead, your technical teams' primary objective will be to execute on the Responsible AI solutions, ensuring that the ethical values are embedded during the development of your AI system. Think of it this way, when you go to design your *Process Pillar*, the builders of the frameworks and policies will be a mix of leadership, Responsible AI professionals, and a few select individuals from various technical teams, whereas the users of these frameworks and policies will be primarily your technical teams. It is essential for execution that your technical teams are equipped with the necessary processes in order to streamline and scale your Responsible AI initiatives. In addition to the initial implementation of ethical values, the executing function must also be responsible for monitoring the effectiveness of the ethics solutions in action (Lu et al., 2022).

Communicating

Purpose: To effectively communicate internal initiatives and policies on Responsible AI to an external audience.

Roles: Due to the external-facing nature of this action, the departments responsible for this function are marketing, sales, and customer service. Each of these departments is in charge, in some way or another, for communicating with external parties—specifically, your customer base. Positions you will see active in this function include, but are not limited to, Content Marketers, CMOs, Sales Reps, and Customer Success Managers.

Objectives: When it comes to gaining customer trust and thus achieving the full impact of growth Responsible AI brings, how you are communicating with your customer base and audience is essential. It is very easy to write a blog post or two about a quick Responsible AI policy you have thrown together, and claim that your company has prioritized AI Ethics. However, many companies before yours have already done so, causing a general sense of skepticism in the markets and so causing the phenomenon known as ethics-washing. Also known as blue-washing, ethics-washing occurs much in the same way as environmental green-washing when companies claim to be environmentally friendly in name but in action are far from it. In order to build the necessary customer trust and loyalty for success in AI, you must ensure that you are not ethics-washing. This comes down to your marketing, sales, and customer service teams, as they are the teams with direct contact with your customer base and therefore the highest point of impact in communicating your Responsible AI initiatives. When it comes to implementing ethics in to your AI, your customer base cannot always have a front row view into how exactly you've done it. However, your customer base can find a reliable source of information in the right marketing and sales materials (Goncalves, Pinto, and Rita, 2023).

Knowledge Gathering

Purpose: To adapt to the fast-paced advancements in AI and enable teams to stay on the cutting-edge of Responsible AI solutions.

Roles: There are many sources of information on both AI and ethics, which means there is a variety of departments that this responsibility can fall to. Generally speaking, however, any department that includes some form of research or insight-gathering function can fulfill this function. Typically, policy, legal, and R&D teams are the most likely to be knowledge gatherers; however, marketing and customer service teams can also bring insight directly from customer feedback.

Objectives: Every time you check your social media feeds, there seems to be a new AI development being announced. The speed at which new AI solutions are developed happens at a mind-numbing pace, which means that ethics practice and Responsible AI solutions must also adapt and develop at a similar pace. From new regulations and policies to new approaches and tooling, there is a lot to keep up on when it comes to AI, let alone the ethics of it. Because of this, you need your teams already aligned for information gathering to also incorporate aspects of Responsible AI and ethics into their research. In doing so, you will be able to stay on top of the various developments, as well as stay aligned with the shifting demands of your market. Essentially, when it comes to knowledge gathering, the primary objective is to sort through the noise around AI and ethics for the information that will enable strong decision making and AI development within your organization.

Who Is Responsible for Change?

As you may have come to already realize, Responsible AI requires, to some degree or another, a certain level of change management to occur across the organization. Although I have often stressed the advantages of building off of the structures and initiatives that are already pre-existing in your organizations, at the end of the day your AI practices will need to change in order to adapt to the demands of Responsible AI and reflect your values into your technology.

Earlier I briefly touched on the point that the question of who is responsible for enforcing Responsible AI in general is still very much undecided, torn between whether it needs to be through government regulation or company self-governance. Clearly we are in need of a global change in how AI is exactly advanced, but we still remain unclear on who is responsible for this change. This question can also be paralleled, to some extent, on the organizational level as we ask the question of who, at the end of the day, is going to be responsible for instigating and leading the change for Responsible AI for your organization?

Thankfully, this question is much easier to answer when it comes to your organization than it is on the global scale. Change is something that both naturally and intentionally occurs within any organization, which means your particular organization will already have tendencies for instigating and leading change internally. It is your job to critically assess the pre-existing tendencies and break them down to understand something I like to call your organization's responsibility structure. A responsibility structure is essentially how your organization is currently structured when it comes to determining who is responsible for instigating and leading change management. Composed of two spectrums set on opposing axes, your responsibility structure looks at whether change is instigated from the top-down or bottom-up, and whether change is led by individuals or groups. With insight into how your organization tends to approach change already, you will be able to pinpoint who is naturally positioned to lead the charge for Responsible AI, enabling you to either capitalize on how your organization already functions, or actively pivot key elements to achieve a more favorable responsibility structure for achieving success.

Change Instigator Spectrum: Top-down vs bottom-up

The first is called the Change Instigator Spectrum, which looks at where the instigator of change typically originates from within the hierarchical structure of your organization. On the one end, change is initiated via leadership and management teams implementing new strategies and developing programs to create a shift in some aspect or another of the organization. This is the top-down end of the spectrum, as the onus of change rests with the top of the hierarchical structure. On the other end, change is brought about through a groundswell effort of the masses, as employees come together to create the shift, typically in culture, that they wish to see in the organization. This is the bottom-up end of the spectrum, as the responsibility for change is driven by the base of the hierarchical structure. Your organization will naturally lean towards one of the two ends, either exhibiting top-down or bottom-up tendencies (Lupton, 1991). In the context of ethics, this means that you are looking for whether the push for Responsible AI change will come from leadership (top-down) or take a more grassroots approach through employees (bottom-up).

When it comes to determining which end of spectrum your organization leans towards, you need to ask yourself if change is typically instigated by leadership or by employees. Does your leadership introduce new concepts into the conversation, or is it your teams that naturally organize around topics they find interesting? Are your leaders open and embracing of change, or is it more often your teams shaping company culture around new ideas?

Leadership Spectrum: Single vs shared

The second is called the Leadership Spectrum, which essentially looks at whether change is led by an individual or communal group within your organization. On the one end, leadership can come from a single point, meaning that typically change and strategic direction is led by one or two figureheads. This is the single point of responsibility end of the spectrum, as leadership within the organization falls to the individual rather than a group. On the other end, leadership can come from multiple individuals working together as a whole, creating what is commonly termed community or communal leadership as everyone pitches in to some extent in driving change and strategic direction. This is the shared point of responsibility, as leadership within the organization falls to the group rather than a particular individual. Just as your organization will naturally lean towards top-down or bottom-up ends of the Change Instigator Spectrum, so will your organization exhibit a tendency for either a single or shared point of responsibility (Edelmann et al., 2023). In the context of ethics, this means that you are looking for whether the motivation and ownership for Responsible AI will come from individual leaders (single point) or a group (shared point).

In the case of your own organization, you need to ask yourself if leadership is typically concentrated in a few figureheads or shared across a group. Do you typically see committees formed with the motivation to lead the adoption of a new idea or is it more common to see one single voice stand out to gather support? Are you more inclined to follow group consensus or thought leaders within the company?

Understanding Your Organization's Responsibility Structure

In an ideal world, your organization would have a balance of both spectrums, exhibiting the strengths of top-down and bottom-up change, and harnessing the power of both single and shared responsibility. However, it is more likely that your organization has a tendency to lean towards one end of either spectrum, creating a natural default for change management within your company, which will in turn have implications for how change in Responsible AI will be brought about. Plotting the two spectrums of Change Instigation and Leadership against each other, we end up with four different quadrants: Top-down and Single, Top-down and Shared, Bottom-up and Single, Bottom-up and Shared. These are the four general responsibility structures your organization can lean towards. Each structure has its own benefits and challenges, which if you take the time to understand what your own company's tendencies are, you can either take advantage of or preemptively plan for. Let's take a moment now to walk through each of the structures, highlighting the differences and discussing what the implications may be for enabling Responsible AI change.

Top-Down and Single

This responsibility structure occurs when you have a tendency towards top-down change that is led by one of two individuals. One of the major strengths of this structure is that the person who will be taking the lead on your Responsible AI initiatives is already in a leadership position, meaning that they should already control some budget and resources as well as have some degree of influence on important decision making. In other words, the top-down aspect means there is already some internal power influence supporting Responsible AI, which can be incredibly helpful to your organization, especially at the start. The single aspect means that the power of influence is concentrated in one place, which can be a strength in helping create internal motivation for Responsible AI if that person is a natural leader who people generally are inclined to follow. However, this single point of responsibility is also the biggest weakness to this responsibility structure for two reasons.

First, if the single individual cannot find other people in leadership positions willing to help support their efforts, this person will be met with too many obstacles to execution and so quickly burn-out and leave. Second, there is always the possibility that this person will leave the company, and if so, will leave with your entire Responsible AI strategy, motivation, and spearheading in hand.

For example, let's imagine there is a mid-sized company that builds customized Large Language Models (LLMs) for enterprise clients. The company is called LanguAI, and recently the CTO of LanguAI, Sarah, has started to consider the potential impact Responsible AI could have on the company. Being in a position of significant leadership, Sarah decides to be the instigator of change, and begins planning out a Responsible AI strategy. Since Sarah is the CTO, she is in a good position to plan and prioritize for Responsible AI. However, since she is the only person working on designing the initiatives, LanguAI risks stalling in its Responsible AI development if Sarah leaves the company or cannot get other leadership on board. So although Sarah is able to kick-start the change in LanguAI towards Responsible AI, the change will only become deep-seated if she manages to extend the leadership on the initiatives beyond herself.

Top-Down and Shared

This is the other responsibility style with a top-down tendency, but instead of single leader taking up the mantle of Responsible AI, it is shared among your leadership team. This is by far the strongest of the four responsibility structures. It captures the strength of having people already in positions of influence and power, with the potential of budgets and resources, without the weaknesses of this responsibility being concentrated in one person. When the responsibility is shared among leadership, you do not run the risk of lack of support or of losing your entire strategy if that person leaves. Instead, support is spread throughout different leadership positions, reinforcing the importance of the Responsible AI initiatives, as well as lending stronger influence over key decisions in your overall AI strategies. However, the weakness of this responsibility style is that if your leaders fail to motivate their teams to embrace Responsible AI, essentially failing to gather the bottom-up support for change, adoption of your initiatives will face pushback from employees and ultimately fall short of desired impact.

Looking at our example company again, let's now imagine that Sarah at LanguAI is able to gain support from her C-suite peers, effectively spreading leadership for Responsible AI so that it is shared among many. This now ensures that Responsible AI will be a top priority across the company and ingrained into the overall AI strategy. However, this does not mean necessarily that the rest of LanguAI employees are board, and so now Sarah and her C-suite colleagues must look for ways to motivate their teams into adopting the Responsible AI initiatives.

Bottom-Up and Single

Unlike the first two structures with a top-down tendency, bottom-up focuses on grassroots efforts in Responsible AI. The strength of having a grassroots approach is the capacity of scale of effort, as well as the potential for ease of adoption as the effort is being led by those who will be responsible for execution. However, this strength can be incredibly difficult to capitalize on when there is only a single point of responsibility. The success of a grassroots effort lies in the numbers—if there are enough employees engaged on an initiative, then it will gather interest and eventually the leadership support needed to solidify efforts. These numbers are difficult to achieve, however, when it is just a single employee with minimal internal visibility leading the charge. At best, this responsibility structure will gain enough traction for small group discussions. At worst, the individual taking responsibility for ethics in AI will burn-out, leave, and potentially cause a PR or HR nightmare in their wake. Be forewarned, this is the weakest responsibility structure of the four.

For instance, let's imagine that our fictional generative AI company, LanguAI, did not have Sarah as a CTO. Instead of someone in a leadership position taking interest in Responsible AI, one of the engineers, Jacob, has decided to try and bring change to the company. Jacob spends his free time researching Responsible AI and quickly develops a strong conviction for the field, one that he hopes to bring to LanguAI. He tries to gain interest from his fellow engineers by setting up an internal slack channel to share news and articles on ethics, but after an initial peak in interest, Jacob sees the activity on the slack channel dying out. Frustrated, Jacob tries to propose a Responsible AI project for his team, but without buy-in from leadership, nor support from his fellow peers, Jacob's efforts to enact Responsible AI change continue to fall flat.

Bottom-Up and Shared

The final of the four responsibility structures looks again at bottom-up change, but this time with shared leadership. With this structure, you have the strength of scale and potential for ease of adoption that a grassroots effort promises, while also counterbalancing the challenge of numbers presented by the single point of responsibility from the previous structure. Because there is a shared sense of responsibility on an employee level, you will not risk burning out individuals due to lack of support or peers, and you have a greater chance of establishing the numbers necessary to a successful grassroots initiative. The strength of this structure is again in the numbers, as a shared point of responsibility motivates the masses and the onus of change coming from a bottom-up direction creates the ground swell needed to achieve the necessary culture shift within your organization that will enable smooth adoption of Responsible AI initiatives. On the hand, the bottom-up instigation of change can be the greatest weakness of these responsibility structures if initial efforts are not quickly followed by establishment of some form of management leadership. Essentially, you run the risk of too many cooks in the kitchen having a difficult time trying to organize themselves. The shared point of responsibility means that everyone will have some degree of sense of ownership for Responsible AI, which when coupled with the bottom-up approach means that everyone and anyone will be under the impression that they need to take charge of ethics implementation. Although enthusiasm is a good thing, efforts in Responsible AI must be organized and targeted in order to achieve full impact, something that is difficult to do if everyone and yet no one is in a position of power to lead.

Looking back to our example of LanguAI, lets now imagine that Jacob's initial efforts in spreading the desire and enthusiasm for Responsible AI change did catch hold with his peers. The slack channel Jacob started to discuss Responsible AI news and research takes off, and soon the majority of LanguAI employees are contributing to the conversations. Soon, LanguAI employees begin self-organizing to form working groups on different Responsible AI topics with the end goal of proposing specific projects to the leadership team. Thanks to the newfound shared feeling of responsibility among the LanguAI team, Responsible AI is now an openly discussed topic sitting in the back of everyone's mind. LanguAI has started to experience a cultural shift, but in order for it to be long lasting and for the company to experience the full benefits of Responsible AI, Jacob and his peers need to be sure to secure buy-in from the top-down.

Striking the Right Balance

Having gone through the various types of responsibility structures your organization can exhibit, along with their coinciding strengths and weaknesses, you should now have insight into how your organization tends to lean in terms of instigating and leading change. As you may have noticed, some of the structures are more advantageous compared to others, given the opportunities and risks each brings. However, the most important thing to take away from these insights into your organization's responsibility structure is that balance is the true objective in the end. With each of the two spectrums, you need to seek the right balance between the extremes for your organization in order to achieve success. An organization that has only top-down efforts will miss out on the benefits that come with a bottom-up cultural shift, while a bottom-up focused company will lack the directional power of top-down decision making. Single point of responsibility creates a clear center of leadership, but will miss the support of shared responsibility, while shared point of responsibility will miss out on the targeted capabilities of the single point of responsibility, and so on. Where one end of the spectrum is weak, the other end will counterbalance with its strengths, so finding the right balance for your organization is crucial.

Looking back one last time at our example of LanguAI, we see that Sarah's efforts in top-down change would be complemented by Jacob's efforts in gathering company culture support, just as Jacob's efforts would be complemented by the direction and decision-making capacities of Sarah's efforts. If the two were to combine their efforts, with Sarah assigning Jacob as perhaps an ethics champion, they would be able to combat the weaknesses of their end of the Change Instigator Spectrum and play to each other's strengths. Likewise, if Sarah and Jacob worked together in enacting Responsible AI change, both could become the single points of responsibility—Sarah as the point for operational leadership and Jacob as the point for workplace culture. The single point of responsibility then could be counterbalanced by the two gathering support from their colleagues—Sarah sharing responsibility among the executive team, and Jacob sharing responsibility among other ethics champions across LanguAI's teams. Overall, the point being LanguAI would be best set up for success in achieving Responsible AI change by striking the right balance between the responsibility structures.

Who Is Responsible?

At this point, you should start to see some clarity not only on who is responsible for Responsible AI, but also what their responsibilities should include. Everyone has their role to play when it comes to implementing ethics in AI, but it is important to understand exactly what these roles are. Leaving it open-ended will only result in frustration, duplication of efforts, and overall lack of impact within your organization. When it comes to assigning these roles, you want to understand how to play into the strengths your organization already has in terms of leadership and change management, while also identifying the weaknesses and learning to counterbalance for blindspots. With both your organization's responsibility structure and the breakdown of the different functions necessary for Responsible AI in mind, you are able to holistically and practically address our starting question: who is responsible for all of this anyway?

13

The Responsible AI Professional

*The Roles, Responsibilities, and Structures
of Working in Responsible AI*

Having gone over the various roles and responsibilities of Responsible AI implementation in the previous chapter, you may have found yourself with the growing suspicion that one role in particular was missing from the discussion. You may also have started to wonder how it is possible to keep track of all the moving pieces required for the implementation of Responsible AI, and if it would be useful to have someone in charge of guiding teams through using ethics as a decision-analysis tool, someone who's sole responsibility it is to focus on the success of Responsible AI initiatives within your organization. On both of these accounts you would be right.

Allow me to introduce you to the Responsible AI professional, more specifically the AI Ethicist. By now you have heard of the field of AI Ethics, but you may not be familiar with the practitioner of this field, the AI Ethicist. This role is specifically designed to support the design, build, and growth of Responsible AI within an organization through the application of ethical values. It is also a crucial role to the success of your Responsible AI strategy, as the AI Ethicist is the position you turn to for insight into what is needed for a strong strategy, support in the development of initiatives and frameworks, and accountability during implementation. In other words, the AI Ethicist is the grease in the wheels of your Responsible AI machine.

But what exactly does this role entail, where does it fit into an organization's ecosystem, how do you know if you have the right person for the job, and how is it different from a Responsible AI practitioner? In this chapter we are going to discuss what makes an AI Ethicist versus a Responsible AI professional, how to decide what type of practitioner you need for your organization, and what are the primary responsibilities of the different Responsible AI practitioners. Once you have a good understanding of these roles, we will then look at potential additions to a company structure that have been gaining traction and popularity with leading AI companies in recent years: the Responsible AI team and an AI Ethics Board.

Not every company will have an AI Ethicist or even a Responsible AI team, but every company successfully executing on Responsible AI at scale will. Another reason that you may not be familiar with the term AI Ethicist is that this is not often the title someone in the Responsible AI profession will be found under. But just because you are less likely to find someone employed specifically under the title of "AI Ethicist" does not mean there aren't Responsible AI practitioners spread throughout an organization. And as we have discussed throughout this book, Responsible AI is simply good AI practice and business in action. So with the end of high0impact AI in mind, let's take a deeper look into the up and coming role of the AI Ethicist.

What Does It Mean to Be an AI Ethicist?

Although the ethicist may seem like a new role, it is in fact only the context of AI and technology that it is fairly new. Ethicists have existed in professional fields such as medicine, business, and politics far before artificial intelligence was even a common household term. However, previously the ethicist has never been a high-profile position, instead sticking to behind the scenes of general business operations and decision making. That is, until now.

When I first began my work as an AI Ethicist, I was lucky if someone had heard of ethics in technology, let alone of my professional title. In the early days, my time was spent building awareness for AI Ethics, which meant I spent a significant amount of time simply explaining what an AI Ethicist was and joking that it was my job to make sure that the robots don't take over the world. Thankfully, we have come far from those early days. So although it is still common for me to be the first AI Ethicist a person meets, they are no longer asking me what in the world it is that I do, and instead dive directly into questions about how my profession works in the hopes of learning some new insight to help their own organization.

I have had the unique opportunity to "grow up" in my career in parallel with the growth and maturity of the profession itself. This has given me niche but key insights into what makes both an AI Ethicist and Responsible AI professional, enabling me to now pass along that information so that you will be able to find the best person for such a critical role in your Responsible AI strategy.

When it comes to being an AI Ethicist, there are three main characteristics that make an individual a good fit for this role. First, an AI Ethicist must be a critical thinker. This is absolutely crucial to the role, because even though there is a rich database of research and Responsible AI frameworks openly accessible, the work of an AI Ethicist is often happening in uncharted territory. Think of it this way, keeping up with the developments in AI advancement is hard enough, now imagine having to try and understand the controls necessary to place on this development in order to ensure best outcomes, potentially even before knowing what the technical outcomes may be. That is the job of the ethicist; we must be able to easily adapt to the fast-paced nature of AI innovation by taking established ethical value sets, frameworks, and case studies and apply them to a technology that even the engineers who are building it may not fully understand. This is not an impossible task; however, it does require a high level of adaptive critical thinking. When someone works as an ethicist in AI, they have to assume there will not be a playbook for the scenarios they will be working in. They can assume, though, that their ability to critically assess a new scenario for ethical challenges and then apply the relevant thinking and framework to that scenario will result in a strong ethics solution.

The second key characteristic of an AI Ethicist is their ability to engage in active listening. As an ethicist, it is my goal to spend less than 20 percent of a session I am leading actually speaking. When it comes to practicing ethics, it is more important to be able to listen for indicators of specific ethical risk in someone's description of their project than be able to list off different types of ethical risks to that same person. Oftentimes in ethics there are so many things you can be doing that it can quickly become overwhelming. This is why an AI Ethicist needs to be able to listen to the full picture and then prioritize the ethics solutions needed to get to the root of a problem. This of course requires active listening, shifting the ethicist from a position of enforcement to instead a position of support. Another way to think of this is that an AI Ethicist should come into a project with specific objectives, those objectives being to align the project with the foundational ethical value set, but not necessarily specific frameworks or next steps to force an ethics solution on a team. Instead, this needs to be a collaborative process, emphasizing co-create and co-design, which again requires the ethicist to be a strong active listener in order to guide this process.

The third and final characteristic of an AI Ethicist is bravery. This may seem a bit strange to be listed alongside critical thinker and active listener, but it is nonetheless the common characteristic I have seen shared among all successful AI Ethicists. The work of an AI Ethicist will always involve having to operate in uncertainty, to some degree. No matter how hard we try, we cannot always predict how an AI solution will impact society in accurate detail. This means that an ethicist must first be brave enough to handle the unknown, but then secondly also be brave enough to change course if the original solution is seen to not be achieving the right results. When working with ethical values, you must be humble and recognize that not everyone will share your views, nor will everyone understand each other's decision making. Humility requires bravery, both in action and communication, and bravery is required for a profession in which you must navigate strong emotions, egos, and perspectives in high-stakes situations.

There are of course many more characteristics of a good AI Ethicist, but critical thinker, active listener, and bravery are the three that, to me, will make a top-tier ethicist stand out from the rest (Gambelin, 2020).

The Responsible AI Professional: Variations of the Responsible AI Profession

When it comes to Responsible AI professionals, there are four primary specializations you will find among practitioners. We have already touched on one of the specializations, ethics, which can be found in AI Ethicists, leaving still the technology, business, and policy specializations. Although each of the four specializations have their own objectives, they all share the same purpose of supporting the implementation of a successful Responsible AI strategy.

The specializations are essentially determined by the individual's background and what their objectives are when it comes to implementing Responsible AI. Each will fill a different need within an organization, so it is important to understand what types of Responsible AI practitioners exist so you can choose the best fit for your needs. Let's take a look now at each of these variations to discuss the differentiators as well as the needs each fulfills within an organization.

Ethics

Beginning with the roots, we first have the ethics specialization of Responsible AI. As you may have already guessed, these are your AI Ethicists. An ethics emphasis in Responsible AI essentially means that this specialization is focused on translating ethical principles into practice through various ethical frameworks, decision analysis, and solution development (Hickok, 2020). You can find this role either embedded with technical teams to support ethical decision making, within R&D teams to design cutting-edge ethical solutions, or within leadership teams to ensure strategic alignment to ethical values. The type of person that fills this role typically comes from a philosophy or social science background, bringing the necessary diversity of perspective into technical conversations, and will have a strong understanding of how to utilize ethical frameworks in problem solving. You may want to consider an ethics-specialized role for your organization if you are experiencing difficulties in designing solutions for your *People* and *Process* pillars, or if you are experiencing difficulties imbedding discussions on ethical values in product development.

Technology

Next up is the technology specialization of Responsible AI. There are as many positions that fit under this specialization as there are types of technical expertise; however, generally speaking, these are your Responsible Technologists (Polgar, 2020). The common denominator of this specialization is that it is technical position working to embed ethical decisions and solutions into the technology itself. You can find this role integrated into technical teams, as a part of an internal task force focused on implementing a specific ethics solution, or within R&D teams to develop new and innovative technical solutions to ethical challenges. The type of person that fills this role comes from a technical background, and will most likely specialize in the application of a specific ethical value. For example, you can have a data scientist who works specifically on data privacy or an engineer that is focused on explainability for models, or a programmer versed in bias-mitigation techniques. You may want to consider a technology-specialized role for your organization if you are experiencing challenges with the performance of your AI systems or the quality of your datasets, if you are having trouble developing and implementing solutions for your *Technology Pillar*, or if you have an ethics solution that must be translated directly into the coding of your models. It is important to emphasize here that there is a significant difference between the AI Ethicist and the Responsible Technologist, as the two are often mistakenly interchanged. A technologist is not trained to handle ethical frameworks just as an ethicist is not trained to write code. Think of the AI Ethicist as your designer of ethical solutions, while the Responsible Technologist is the developer and deployer of such solutions.

Business

The third specialization of Responsible AI is business. It is easy to forget that the business models we choose have a significant impact on the outcomes of AI solutions, as each business model will hold different implications for how the AI is put to use. This means that the third specialization of Responsible AI focuses on business analysis and strategy, making these your Responsible Business Developers. A business emphasis in Responsible AI focuses on integrating ethical decisions into business solutions and aligning strategic business decisions with foundational ethical values. You can find this role primarily within business teams looking at the wider societal impact of business model and market decisions, or within leadership teams supporting the alignment of the organization's business strategic with its ethical values. The type of person that fills this role will usually come from an economics or business background, as they look to reconcile ethics objectives with financial and business goals through critical analysis and development of responsible business models. You may want to consider a business-specialized role for your organization if you are experiencing ethical challenges even after auditing and patching your AI systems for ethical risks or if you are operating in a highly sensitive market such as healthcare or finance.

Policy

The fourth and final specialization within Responsible AI is policy. Governance and regulation play an important role in the Responsible AI ecosystem, making this last specialization your AI Governance and Compliance experts. A policy emphasis in Responsible AI means that this type of role focuses on ensuring your AI systems are up to date with the latest developments in AI and digital regulation, as well as monitoring the types of potential risks a system can face in accordance with ethical values and legislation. You can find this role within policy, legal, or risk teams helping to interpret and apply incoming digital regulation, as well as monitoring developments on a global scale as national AI policies continue to evolve. The type of person that fills this role will typically have either a policy or legal background, but can also come from various other social sciences such as philosophy or political science, with a keen eye for detail and ability to interpret multicultural approaches to AI governance. You may want to consider a policy-specialized role for your organization if you are operating in a highly regulated field, or if you are behind in compliance to regulations such as the GDPR or the EU AI Act. Again, it must be emphasized that there is a significant difference between the practices of ethics and law, and that although there is some overlap, they are separate specializations within Responsible AI.

Building Your Responsible AI Dream Team

As you can start to see from the different specializations within the Responsible AI profession, there is a lot of ground to be covered here. That is why the majority of companies serious about harnessing the power of AI for the future of their organization have started to establish and hire full stack Responsible AI teams. These teams combine a mix of the four specializations, depending of course on the organization's needs, and provide the focused human capital necessary for carrying out a holistic Responsible AI strategy. They also provide a home within the organizational structure for your Responsible AI hires, creating the necessary space for collaboration and interdisciplinary problem solving to take place.

Having looked at the different specializations of the Responsible AI professional that is available to your organization, as well as highlighting what kind of role or roles you need to make the most impact on Responsible AI in your organization, it is now time to take a deeper look into where these professionals can live within your organization. Although you do not need to go from 0 to 100 and hire a full team right off the bat, it is important that when first setting up your Responsible AI team (or individual contributors), you are setting them up for success. Let's take a look now at the two main considerations when deciding the best way to incorporate this new team into your existing organizational structure.

Centralized versus Decentralized

The first question you will need to consider is whether you want a centralized or decentralized Responsible AI team. Essentially, this poses the questions of if you plan to hire multiple Responsible AI positions, and if so, will they all sit within the same team, will they be dispersed throughout different departments, or will it be a combination of both? Starting with the prior, the strength of a centralized team is in the clarity and direction it provides. As you can recall from the previous chapter, there can be either single or shared points of responsibility for implementing ethics, and having a centralized Responsible AI team can capture both. On the one hand, having a centralized team creates a single clear point of responsibility within an organization, while on the other allowing for that same responsibility to be shared among members of that single team. This enables stronger alignment of Responsible AI objectives to overarching company goals as a centralized team will be responsible for contributing its own milestones of success in support of the strategic direction of the company.

Additionally, having a specific team dedicated to Responsible AI is beneficial when it comes to operational logistics such as allocating budget and resources for ethics initiatives, as there will be one team owning it. The potential downside of a centralized team, however, is the risk of siloing your Responsible AI efforts if the team is not properly connected directly to avenues for business impact or decision making. What can often happen in larger companies with centralized Responsible AI teams is that these teams are given a specific goal, but that goal is siloed from the other departments and overall objectives of the company. At best, a disconnected centralized team will spin its wheels on interesting hypotheses separate from any real impact to the company, and at worst will result in layoffs of entire ethics teams, publicly damaging the organization's reputation.

Turning our attention to the other end of the spectrum, the strength of a decentralized team is in its potential to scale impact within an organization. One of the challenges of a centralized team is being able to successfully communicate and implement ethics solutions at scale across multiple teams, especially when operating within a large enterprise. This challenge becomes a core point of strength for a decentralized team, as having Responsible AI professionals dispersed and embedded within multiple teams and departments enables the dissemination of necessary information and protocols. Additionally, it has the potential to create clear channels for cross-organizational collaboration, as Responsible AI team members become a connection point between the different department within which they sit. The challenge, however, of decentralized teams is the potential for lack of clarity and systematic application of Responsible AI initiatives if there is no clear driving strategy for the dispersed Responsible AI team members to implement. It can be useful to have Responsible AI professionals placed within specific teams in accordance with their specialization. For example a Responsible Technologist within an engineering team makes sense as they will be able to contribute to the objectives of that specific team. However, if there is no central Responsible AI initiative uniting the various team members spread throughout the organization, then advancing a company-wide Responsible AI strategy will be impossible.

With the details of the centralized versus decentralized teams in mind, it is important to counter balance the weaknesses and emphasize the strengths of whichever structure you choose.

Organizational Structure Placement

The next question to consider when establishing your Responsible AI team is where within your organizational structure the team will go. In other words, what department, if any, will it belong to? This is a very important factor to consider, as it will highly influence the objectives and approach your team will take. What often happens is organizations will establish ethics teams as part of legal or risk and compliance departments. As you can probably already guess by the name, this limits your Responsible AI approach to solely risk-based, cutting off the potential for innovation-based initiatives. Now, this may be what your company needs due to high regulatory demands for your industry, in which case establishing an ethics branch within a risk or legal department would work best for your organization. However, the challenge I often see Responsible AI teams facing when placed in legal and risk departments is the negative perception that it must figure out how to overcome. When under legal and risk, ethics initiatives will be perceived as a set of constraints, creating the potential for a sense of frustration and resentment to build against the Responsible AI team. Instead of being placed in a position of support for aligned and informed decision making, this structure choice places Responsible AI teams, both centralized and decentralized, in the position of arbiters of truth, which isn't always very productive when navigating the intricacies of implementing ethical values. With these potential pitfalls in mind, I urge you to consider placing Responsible AI instead in either innovation or technical departments. This shifts the perception of Responsible AI within an organization for one of controlling overseer to one of supportive collaborator. It also allows for your Responsible AI professionals to pursue both risk and innovative-based ethics initiatives, which overall leads to a better well-rounded implementation of Responsible AI.

How Responsible AI Teams Support Your Pillars

By now you should have an idea both about what kind of specializations you need as well as how to place a team within your existing organizational structure in order to execute on your Responsible AI strategy. With all this in mind, let's take a moment to look at the various ways in which your Responsible AI either individual contributors or full team can advance your Responsible AI strategy by walking through the three pillars.

People

Starting, as always, with the humans in the equation, you can recall the three elements of our *People Pillar*: *Educate*, *Motivate*, and *Communicate*. As discussed in Chapter 7, a key factor of a holistic *People Pillar* is ensuring that your teams, in general, are educated on utilizing ethics as a decision-analysis tool, as well as kept up to date on the latest techniques in Responsible AI. Determining what education is needed, building the necessary training, and ensuring the organization has access to foundational Responsible AI knowledge are all initiatives that would fall under the potential domain of a Responsible AI team. In addition to the educational factors of the *People Pillar*, a Responsible AI team can be particularly equipped to facilitate difficult conversations on ethically sensitive topics, as well as add in communication efforts by hosting internal conversations on relevant topics.

Process

Moving up our pyramid to the *Process Pillar*, you will recall from Chapter 8 that the elements of this pillar included *Intent*, *Implement*, and *Instrument*. Essentially, the purpose of this pillar is to build or adopt the internal mechanisms necessary for facilitating ethical decision making and solution implementation. Having Responsible AI frameworks and policies in place to guide teams is crucial to success, but finding the appropriate frameworks and then customizing them to your organization, or building the framework completely from scratch, is no small feat. Not to mention, someone needs to monitor the use of the frameworks and policies post-deployment to ensure both that teams are using them and that they are effective. These functions can again fall under the domain of a Responsible AI team, and often need to, due to the scope and upkeep cycles some frameworks will need to cover. Having a team directly responsible for ensuring things are running smoothly in ethical value implementation can immensely alleviate strain on the time and resources of technical and operations teams.

Technology

Finally we have the *Technology Pillar* with the elements of *Data*, *Document*, and *Domain*. As we saw in detail in Chapter 9, the strategy behind the *Technology Pillar* is not necessarily looking at the details of execution, but instead at the supporting factors necessary to strong AI execution and ethics implementation. With this in mind, there are a few ways in which a Responsible AI team can help navigate the *Technology Pillar*. First, the *Data* element requires ethical procurement and sourcing of data, as well as assumption testing for quality control on datasets, all of which a Responsible AI team can help support through either vetting the data and its sources or by testing for specific blind spots that would otherwise go unnoticed. When it comes to *Document*, someone needs to ensure that the proper document is occurring at the required intervals and is in alignment with current regulation, all of which, again, can fall under the jurisdiction of a Responsible AI team. And finally, the *Domain* element requires that an actual human is indeed checking deployed models for drift and unintended adverse effects. In this case, the Responsible AI team can either be those humans in the loop, or it can provide support to the humans in the loop through education and alignment checks. Overall, the *Technology Pillar* can be supported by a Responsible AI team in either research, monitoring, or analyzing capacities.

As you can imagine, we are only scratching the surface of all the ways a Responsible AI team and professionals can directly support your Responsible AI strategy in intent, impact, and execution. The important takeaway here is that the Responsible AI team should be taking on the work necessary for ethics implementation that would otherwise divert other teams such as design or tech teams from achieving their objectives.

The AI Ethics Board

Before we can wrap up this chapter on the various Responsible AI specializations and team, there is one more potential addition to the company organizational chart to consider: the AI Ethics Board.

By now, you've probably heard of infamous ethics boards, such as Google's that lasted a total of one week before being promptly disbanded for PR related issues (Statt, 2019). Or, perhaps you've heard of more successful cases, such as IBM's multifaceted board that's been running since 2016 (IBM, n.d.). Whether you've seen the good, the bad, or the ugly, you have most likely seen at the very least some article or another offering an AI Ethics board as the best first step towards Responsible AI (Blackman, 2022). In some cases this is true, while in others a full board can be quite impractical for the needs at hand. Let's take a closer look at the break down of an AI Ethics board and its purpose to understand why.

What exactly is an AI Ethics board in the first place? An AI Ethics board is a formal group of experts coming from a variety of backgrounds as so relate to the organization, its industry, its technology, and, most importantly, its foundational ethics values. These experts do not necessarily have to all be Responsible AI professionals, but having a few practitioners mixed in will strengthen the depth of knowledge on your board. The AI Ethics board will convene at regular predetermined intervals to discuss top-of-mind ethics challenges and offer proposed solutions; however, the board may or may not have direct influence as to whether the proposals are put into action. Typically, a board will sit at director level and focus on higher-level questions rather than minute details. The overarching purpose of having an AI Ethics board is to have a formal body within the organization that is responsible for making difficult decisions in high-ethical-risk scenarios or helping drive value alignment in high-level strategy.

When it comes to AI Ethics boards, there are three main factors contributing to the success of the board. First, you need a diversity of expertise on the board. If all you have are too many people from the same profile, the benefits of a diverse set of expert perspectives on specific challenges is lost. Additionally, diversity on the board lends itself to stronger creative thinking and solutions brought about thanks to the interdisciplinary collaboration. Second, a successful board must have, to some degree, decision-making power, or at the very least the ability to influence. There is nothing more frustrating to individuals on the board than seeing their hard work and thought go to waste, and there is no quicker way to damage general trust in the company than by establishing a board for show but no say. Last but not least, the third quality of a successful AI Ethics board is that the board remains focused on high-level deliberation of difficult, and oftentimes existential, ethics questions and avoids being dragged down into the day-to-day execution. Remember, a board is there to debate the bigger picture questions, but also to aid in the execution of detailed solutions.

With all this being said, the utility of an AI Ethics board comes down to whether or not your organization is consistently faced with high-level ethical risks and challenges. If you commonly find yourself debating the right plan of action in difficult to navigate Responsible AI scenarios, then an AI Ethics board could be the best solution to help you think through your decisions. However, if your needs lie more in the execution of decisions, then perhaps a board is not the best fit for your current needs

Moving Forward

As you have seen throughout this chapter, there is a plethora of options when it comes to Responsible AI professions and team structuring. In laying out the different options, it has been my goal to give you a sense of hope and relief to see that although Responsible AI comes with its fair share of complexities, there are plenty of options when it comes to establishing the necessary human capital support for execution.

14

In Pursuit of Good Tech

Bringing Your Responsible AI Strategy to Life

Our technology is a reflection of our humanity.

Unlike humans, artificial intelligence does not have emotions, opinions, or original ideas, which are often used as a selling point for AI systems. The claim is that AI solutions are only subject to pure objective fact, and as they are removed from the subjective volatility of human nature, AI can be the neutral arbiter of truth. Of course, this is not at all true, and for countless reasons. AI is not neutral, it is subject to the reality of whoever created it, and it can be manipulated to present a narrow perspective of the world as an objective truth. There are numerous books written on this is exact point, from Cathy O'Neil's *Weapons of Math Destruction*, to Kate Crawford's *Atlas of AI*, to Carissa Veliz's *Privacy is Power*, the list of brilliant thinkers combating the misconception that AI is the omniscient creation is endless. However, I will save my own thoughts on this matter for another time, as I bring up this point not to discuss the underlying existential questions of AI, but instead to highlight the fact that artificial intelligence has been presented to the world as something other than human by nature.

Although we humans are the creators, AI is often portrayed as some "other." We like to believe that AI will solve our very human problems, that this technical solution is the answer to even the deepest of existential challenges plaguing our societies for centuries. It's a nice thought, to have invented something so powerful that it can solve for world peace, but it is merely an ideal, not a given. AI, and technology in general, is a reflection of our humanity. Data is information on human behaviors, thoughts, and actions, reflecting the hidden human patterns from the world around us into a digital format (Nast, 2019). Data is not creating new insights into humans, it is surfacing and reflecting back insights that we don't have the ability to see with the naked eye but have always been there. Neural networks, a subset of machine learning and the heart of deep learning algorithms, were inspired by the human brain and the way our neurons signal to each other (IBM, n.d.). Even large language models are built to reflect humanity, showing how we as humans use language to communicate information, and embedding aspects of human judgment into the ranking of response quality (Agrawal, Gans, and Goldfarb, 2023). I could go on and on with these examples, showing how each and every one of our advancements in AI can be tied back to a reflection of our humanity.

What this means for us, as humans, in the age of AI is twofold. First, the ethical and societal challenges we experience in our AI systems is not something new coming out of the technology. It is the technology reflecting back our very real and difficult ethical and societal *human* challenges. Second, if AI can reflect our faults, it can also reflect our strengths, and these strengths are defined by the values that we hold. To be human means to have values in life, and to try, to the best of our ability, to live in accordance with those values. If AI, and our technology in general, is truly to be a reflection of our humanity, then it must reflect everything about what it means to be human, values and all.

Our technology is a neutral mirror, reflecting back both the good and the bad. The purpose of becoming a Responsible AI-enabled organization is to ensure that the mirror you are creating is reflecting back the good.

The Key to Responsible AI

There are many ways we can go about reflecting human values into artificial intelligence, and simply just technology in general. From ethics-by-design techniques to safeguarding methods, there is no one-size-fits all when it comes to ethics solutions. When tackling specific ethics challenges in AI, you will need to develop and use narrow solutions, as ethics is contextually sensitive and must be adjusted on a use case basis. Although there is high variability in what specific ethics solutions will look like, there are general best practices an organization can utilize in order to enable ethical problem solving and decision making at scale. The purpose of this book has been to lay the groundwork for that exact enablement, walking you through step by step what it means to become a Responsible AI-enabled organization to achieve value-aligned AI.

Instead of teaching you specific ethics actions to take during your AI life cycle, I focused on showing you how ethics works as a decision-analysis tool and the organizational strategy needed to support its use. There is a wide variety of Responsible AI and Ethics solutions available on the market today, and the number is rapidly growing. However, many business leaders have been stalled at the point of implementation, understanding the need and options for Responsible AI, but having no idea where to even begin for their own organization. We have spent these many pages together learning exactly how to create a winning Responsible AI strategy to bring the ethics to operational life for your organization.

As any good business leader will know though, strategy is only one piece of the bigger puzzle, especially in the world of AI. By now you will be sick of hearing me say that AI is not just a technical challenge, it encompasses so much more, as does Responsible AI and Ethics. Which means that Responsible AI is a multifaceted practice, one that could not have possibly been covered to its fullest extent in a single book. For instance, even though we covered the operations of a Responsible AI-enabled organization, we did not go into the details of how to build the right frameworks, or design the right policies, or establish a full AI governance system start to finish. We discussed the primary points for ethics interventions in the AI build, but we did not cover how to ensure quality of AI implementation, or how to technically design for specific ethical values, or what value-aligned features should look like in action. And even though we established how to build a company culture that embraces ethics, we did not address how a business model is just as influential as the technology, what it takes to design a responsible use case for AI, or what to do if your company values don't seem to be working. The list goes on, and will hopefully fill an entire library one day of books by brilliant thinkers all addressing different needs and challenges in Responsible AI.

I tell you this not to discourage you or showcase the limitations of this book, but instead to open your eyes to all the possibilities for innovation this space holds. Personally, I find one of the most exciting aspects to being an AI Ethicist is the fact that this field is only at the very beginning. There is so much more left to discover and so many opportunities for us to deepen our knowledge of AI and humanity. So although this book does have limitations to the amount of knowledge I could fit into its pages, the information that did make it is the key to unlocking the vast potential for Responsible AI in your organization. With the much-needed strategic structure to operationalizing Responsible AI in place, you finally have what it takes to enable your organization to become a leader in AI by creating technology solutions that are aligned with our human values.

Providing the Conceptual Structure to Responsible AI

My professional philosophy as an AI Ethicist is to enter a room with only questions, and to leave it with others having found the answers. It doesn't matter how many years of experience I gain or how many books I can fill with my thinking, I will never hold all the answers to applying ethics in AI. The intricacies of ethics are far too vast, the possible scenarios far too extensive, the scale of challenges far too expansive for me to ever have even the slightest glimmer of hope to knowing all there is to know about solving for human values in artificial intelligence. Even if I could possibly hold the answer to every single ethics challenge a company will face in Responsible AI, I would still apply the same philosophy. I have found that readily supplying a predetermined solution is far less effective than working through the problem-solving process with a client. No one wants to be told no based on someone else's personal moral code.

It is because of all this that I have shaped my approach to practicing AI Ethics in the way that I have. I am a firm believer that because ethics is something we naturally engage with as humans in our daily lives, when it comes to applying ethics in the context of business and AI, people already hold the answers that they need. This means that my job is not to bring answers, but to guide others through the critical thought processes required to find the answers for themselves. My skillset lies in my ability to listen and ask questions, to provide the mental structures needed to sort through complex subjects and decision making, and to guide people towards the right answer that fits the needs of both business and society.

This is my personal approach to practicing AI Ethics, and I have applied this same approach to this book. My sole objective in writing this book was never to instruct you on how to solve for specific ethical challenges in your AI, it has instead been to unlock for you the world of Responsible AI by guiding you through the mental structures and critical thought processes you need to arrive at the answers best fit for you. Thinking all the way back to the start of this book and the story of the two carpenters, I did not teach you how to hammer the nail, I showed you how to understand the hammer.

Part One of this book was dedicated to understanding ethics and its values. The ultimate goal of Responsible AI is to reflect human-centric values in AI systems, which means in order for an organization to be Responsible AI enabled it must first know the values it needs to reflect. You can't have Responsible AI without ethics, and you can't have ethics without values. With this in mind, we spent this first part of the book breaking down how ethics works in practice, how to find your organization's foundational ethics values, and how to determine what kind of risk- or innovation-based approach to take. This laid the foundational knowledge necessary for Responsible AI, helping you conceptualize the key decision factors to achieving your end goal of embedding ethics into AI.

In Part Two we moved the discussion from theoretical to practical, exploring specifically how to build a strategy that reflects your foundational ethics values into your AI projects. Understanding your values is one thing, being able to put those values into action during the critical decision-making processes of your AI projects is another. Without the right company culture, operational processes, or technical resources in place, your goal of creating ethically aligned AI will continue to remain just beyond your capabilities. In order to unlock the potential of Responsible AI and all its benefits for your organization, you must establish a holistic and well-balanced strategy. When it comes to creating this strategy, Responsible AI is supported by three pillars: *People*, *Process*, and *Technology*. As we learned in Part Two, each of these three pillars has three different elements and an essential role in enabling Responsible AI. It was also in this part that we learned how to conceptualize the different categories of ethics solutions and how the solutions should interrelate to support overall value alignment for your AI projects. It is important to note that this part was focused on building a Responsible AI strategy on a project-level, not necessarily the overall, organization.

Finally in Part Three we took the practical conversation of Responsible AI from the how-to details to the high-level application for your entire organization. If the objective of Responsible AI is to create ethically aligned AI, then a Responsible AI-enabled organization is one that has the ethics resources necessary to achieving this alignment available and maintained at scale within the entire organization. To help you achieve this goal, the final part of the book took the same structure of pillars and elements from Part Two, and brought them to the high-level discussion of how to translate and execute this conceptual structure into a Responsible AI strategy on the overarching organizational level. We learned how to identify where your organization is in terms of Responsible AI adoption and what priorities should be prevalent at each phase. From there we broke down the different elements of Responsible AI into a three-stage plan of action for deploying your organizational-level strategy, highlighting along the way examples of successful Responsible AI strategies in industry, and ending with a look at who is going to be responsible for the execution of this strategy within your organization.

Pulling all three parts of the book together, you will find yourself with a comprehensive overview of how to operationalize Responsible AI for your organization, enabling an ethical approach to the build and use of your AI systems. You know your tool (ethics and its values), and you know how the tool works on the granular project level, as well as the higher organizational level. I may not have given you predefined ethics solutions for every challenge you may face along the way of your AI journey, but I have equipped you with the conceptual structure for operationalizing ethics, finally unlocking the door to successful Responsible AI for you and your organization.

The Two Things from This Book You Should Never Forget

If you were to sit down with a colleague after reading this book to discuss your main takeaways, there are two points I would hope you both not only agree on but plan to put into action.

The first is the Values Canvas. Responsible AI can be a complex and intricate field to navigate, let alone wrap your mind around what kind of solution is needed when and where. Translating abstract ethical values into hard-coded decisions for your AI systems can feel like a daunting task unless you have the ability to conceptualize the exact needs to fill and visualize where these needs sit within your organizational structure. The Values Canvas not only creates this map, but also becomes a tool to facilitate cross-organizational collaboration on building a robust and successful Responsible AI strategy. In fact, the Values Canvas is technology agnostic, as it can be extended beyond AI to cover the majority of technical solutions. Functioning on both the project and organizational level, the Values Canvas is the first takeaway from this book that I encourage you to bring back to your teams to exponentially advance your company in its journey to becoming a Responsible AI-enabled organization.

The second is the fact that Responsible AI is not primarily a technical problem to solve. Yes, there are technical solutions and a growing number of techniques to embedding specific ethical values in narrow use cases.

However, if you want to reach the full benefits of Responsible AI, you must embrace the fact that this requires organizational change, not engineering solutions. Our technology is the result of the decisions we take to build it, and those decisions are shaped by people and processes. If you are able to accept and internalize this point, then you are already well on your way to success in Responsible AI.

In Pursuit of Good Tech

Our technology is a reflection of our humanity, and ethics has always been core to being human.

We have all heard the saying "in pursuit of the good life," but did you know that ethics is an important practice in this pursuit? Although each and every one of us will have a different definition of what a good life means for our self, we can all agree that in general a good life is determined by our ability to fulfill our purpose. This is again a tricky definition, though, as what defines our purpose? I am no self-help guru, but as an ethicist who grapples with the existential questions of happiness, I can say that purpose is found in the values that we hold. For example, I personally value quality time with my loved ones. This means that a good life for me is a life in which I am able to spend that quality time I so desire with the people that I love. I hold a value, I find purpose in that value, and when I am able to live my life in accordance with that value I experience fulfillment of what I would define as my personal good life.

So what does this have to do with ethics? Ethics is the tool that we use to help guide us in the direction of our good life. Think of it this way, ethics can be roughly defined as the practice of analyzing our decisions for alignment with our values. In other words, if you have the choice between A or B and you use your values as decision-making factors to choose between the two, if A is better aligned with your values then in choosing A you are taking a step closer to your good life. Your values will define your good life, and ethics is the thing that helps you pursue that good life by aligning your decisions and actions with your values.

Let's bring this philosophical concept now into the world of AI. Just as we use ethics to help align our personal decisions with our personal values on a human level, so we can also use ethics to align the decisions around our technology with the values we hold within our cultures, societies, and global communities. Not only that, we also have the possibility to use technology to enable us as humans to better understand what we value in life and how our decisions lead us closer to or further away from those values. Without value alignment in our technology, AI becomes a blocker to the good life, as it becomes counterproductive and even destructive to this pursuit. If, however, we are aligning our technology to our values, then we have the opportunity to use AI to its fullest potential in this pursuit of this good life. This is called the pursuit of good tech, and I invite you, for even just a moment, to consider what this world would look like if this were the standard practice for innovation in AI.

What Next?

When someone first discovers that I am a professional AI Ethicist, I inevitably hear one of two comments.

First, that the person is scared of AI. This can manifest in many shapes and forms, from the founder who is fearful of what their new invention is capable of, to the enterprise executive who is overwhelmed with the speed of advancement and is afraid of falling behind, to the average individual reading about how artificial general intelligence (AGI) is going to take over the world. How quick we are to forget that we are the creators of this technology, and that it is completely within our power to bring it back under control if we do not like the direction it is heading.

And second, I hear that the person cares. Let me tell you, it is very easy to care about the values our technology is being built on, to care that ethics is embedded in our business practices, to care that we develop AI responsibly. But there is a wide gap between care and action, and we have reached the crux in AI advancement that action is of the utmost importance. So allow me to emphasize, I do not care that you care. I care that you act.

The great thing about action is that it helps conquer fear. There are so many things we can be doing here and now to help embed ethics into AI, and it is through these initiatives that we are able to defeat the growing fear of AI.

It is my hope that this book has been the spark you needed to stop caring and start acting.

REFERENCES

Chapter 1: Defining Ethics in AI

Bojinov, I. (2023) Keep your AI projects on track, *Harvard Business Review*, hbr. org/2023/11/keep-your-ai-projects-on-track (archived at perma.cc/9DCM-UA6A)

Dittmer, J. (2023) Applied ethics, *Internet Encyclopedia of Philosophy*, iep.utm.edu/ applied-ethics/ (archived at perma.cc/L4YV-REYS)

Fayyad, U. (2023) Council post: Why most machine learning applications fail to deploy, *Forbes*, www.forbes.com/sites/forbestechcouncil/2023/04/10/ why-most-machine-learning-applications-fail-to-deploy (archived at perma.cc/ N2JJ-WE7D)

Gustafson, A. B. (2020) Normative ethics, *Encyclopedia of Business and Professional Ethics*, pp. 1–5. DOI: 10.1007/978-3-319-23514-1_1222-1

Sayre-McCord, G. (2023) Metaethics, *Stanford Encyclopedia of Philosophy*, plato. stanford.edu/entries/metaethics/ (archived at perma.cc/6HUJ-GUGU)

Chapter 2: Know Your Values

European Commission (2019) *Shaping Europe's Digital Future: Ethics guidelines for Trustworthy AI*, digital-strategy.ec.europa.eu/en/library/ethics-guidelines-trustworthy-ai (archived at perma.cc/FX9F-TC8E).

Frede, D. and Lee, M.-K. (2023) Plato's ethics: An overview, *Stanford Encyclopedia of Philosophy*, plato.stanford.edu/entries/plato-ethics/ (archived at perma.cc/ HCU7-CZEF)

Google (2022a) Classification: Accuracy | machine learning | google for developers, developers.google.com/machine-learning/crash-course/classification/accuracy (archived at perma.cc/9JC2-LYTR)

Google (2022b) Classification: Precision and recall | machine learning | google for developers, developers.google.com/machine-learning/crash-course/classification/ precision-and-recall (archived at perma.cc/8YMV-46GL)

Hao, K. (2022) How Facebook got addicted to spreading misinformation, *MIT Technology Review*, www.technologyreview.com/2021/03/11/1020600/ facebook-responsible-ai-misinformation/ (archived at perma.cc/MK2A-SNXX)

Lang, A. F. (2020) Constructing universal values? A practical approach, *Ethics & International Affairs*, 34 (3), 267–77, doi: 10.1017/S0892679420000453 (archived at perma.cc/G6VS-P4ZW)

OECD (2019) Forty-two countries adopt new OECD principles on artificial intelligence, www.oecd.org/science/forty-two-countries-adopt-new-oecd-principles-on-artificial-intelligence.htm (archived at perma.cc/DWR3-LRWY)

OECD.AI (2023) National AI policies and strategies, oecd.ai/en/dashboards/overview (archived at perma.cc/RC6M-C9E9)

Chapter 3: The Duality of Ethics

Acar, O. A., Tarakci, M., and Knippenberg, D. van (2019) Why constraints are good for innovation, *Harvard Business Review*, hbr.org/2019/11/why-constraints-are-good-for-innovation (archived at perma.cc/CQ5A-KB2V)

Blanchard, A. and Taddeo, M. (2023) The ethics of artificial intelligence for intelligence analysis: A review of the key challenges with recommendations, *Digital Society*, 2 (1), doi.org/10.1007/s44206-023-00036-4 (archived at perma.cc/KV9W-UFZD)

Boden, M. A. (2018) 7. *The Singularity: Very short introductions*, Oxford University Press, doi.org/10.1093/actrade/9780199602919.003.0007 (archived at perma.cc/5Q3J-QCMA)

Colt, S. (n.d.) Tim Cook has an open letter to all customers that explains how Apple's privacy features work, *Business Insider*, www.businessinsider.com/tim-cook-published-a-letter-on-apple-privacy-policies-2014-9?r=US&IR=T (archived at perma.cc/WF37-6HMP)

Francis, R. D. (2016) Ethical risk management, *Global Encyclopedia of Public Administration, Public Policy, and Governance*, pp. 1–5, doi.org/10.1007/978-3-319-31816-5_2385-1 (archived at perma.cc/H7TB-NRNL)

Guan, H., Dong, L., and Zhao, A. (2022) Ethical risk factors and mechanisms in artificial intelligence decision making, *Behavioral Sciences*, 12 (9), 343, doi.org/10.3390/bs12090343 (archived at perma.cc/4U25-EVMD)

Komal, B., Janjua, U. I. Silva Rampini, Anwar, F., Madni, T. M., Cheema, M. F., Malik, M. N., and Shahid, A. R. (2020) The impact of scope creep on project success: An empirical investigation, *IEEE Access*, 8 (1), 125755–75, doi.org/10.1109/access.2020.3007098 (archived at perma.cc/H79R-SBSK)

Lauer, D. (2020) You cannot have AI ethics without ethics, *AI and Ethics*, doi.org/10.1007/s43681-020-00013-4 (archived at perma.cc/BA4G-YAPW)

McKendrick, J. (n.d.) Ethical artificial intelligence becomes a supreme competitive advantage, *Forbes*, www.forbes.com/sites/joemckendrick/2019/07/07/ethical-artifcial-intelligence-becomes-a-supreme-competitive-advantage/?sh=722df87f1a8f (archived at perma.cc/CY63-4YVN)

Murray, F. and Johnson, E. (2021) Innovation starts with defining the right constraints, *Harvard Business Review*, hbr.org/2021/04/innovation-starts-with-defining-the-right-constraints (archived at perma.cc/AFN6-5TYK)

Petrozzino, C. (2021) Who pays for ethical debt in AI?, *AI and Ethics*, doi.org/10.1007/s43681-020-00030-3 (archived at perma.cc/XFD2-EKHG)

Satell, G. (2017) The 4 types of innovation and the problems they solve, *Harvard Business Review*, hbr.org/2017/06/the-4-types-of-innovation-and-the-problems-they-solve (archived at perma.cc/TF96-295U)

Sculley, D., Holt, G., Golovin, D., Davydov, E., Phillips, T., Ebner, D., Chaudhary, V., Young, M., Crespo, J.-F., and Dennison, D. (n.d.) *Hidden Technical Debt in Machine Learning Systems*, proceedings.neurips.cc/paper_files/paper/2015/file/86df7dcfd896fcaf2674f757a2463eba-Paper.pdf (archived at perma.cc/6QTJ-JMFW)

Silva Rampini, G. H., Takia, H., and Berssaneti, F. T. (2019) Critical success factors of risk management with the advent of ISO 31000 2018 – descriptive and content analyzes, *Procedia Manufacturing*, 39, 894–903, doi.org/10.1016/j.promfg.2020.01.400 (archived at perma.cc/UAA9-DFMY)

Stahl, B. C. (2021) Ethical issues of AI, *Artificial Intelligence for a Better Future*, 35–53, doi.org/10.1007/978-3-030-69978-9_4 (archived at perma.cc/GT8D-52D7)

Stokel-Walker, C. (2020) How Skype lost its crown to Zoom, Wired UK, www.wired.co.uk/article/skype-coronavirus-pandemic (archived at perma.cc/DRL5-LL62)

Chapter 4: Calibrating the Compass

Hamilton, I. A. (n.d.) WhatsApp is trying to get users to agree to its new privacy policy again, a month after it sent people flocking to Signal and Telegram, *Business Insider,* www.businessinsider.com/whatsapp-asks-users-to-accept-new-policy-after-privacy-panic-2021-2?r=US&IR=T#:~:text=WhatsApp%20will%20start%20asking%20users (archived at perma.cc/GWC8-XWSB)

Narvaez, D. and Mrkva, K. (2014) *The Development of Moral Imagination: The ethics of creativity*, pp. 25–45, doi.org/10.1057/9781137333544_2 (archived at perma.cc/W3J6-J6GN)

Chapter 5: Five Reasons Why You Shouldn't Invest in Responsible AI

BBC News (2022) Volkswagen to pay out £193m in "dieselgate" settlement, May 25, www.bbc.com/news/business-61581251 (archived at perma.cc/AT6Q-C7Z2)

Mills, S., Singer, S., Gupta, A., Gravenhorst, F., Candelon, F., and Porter, T. (2022) Responsible AI is about more than avoiding risk, BCG Global, www.bcg.com/publications/2022/a-responsible-ai-leader-does-more-than-just-avoiding-risk (archived at perma.cc/5VRN-A3DP)

Renieris, E. M., Kiron, D., and Mills, S. (2022) To be a responsible AI leader, focus on being responsible, *MIT Sloan Management Review*, sloanreview.mit.edu/projects/to-be-a-responsible-ai-leader-focus-on-being-responsible/ (archived at perma.cc/3YVG-66UD)

Shekhar, R. (2022) Responsible artificial intelligence is good business, *LSE Business Review*, blogs.lse.ac.uk/businessreview/2022/08/30/responsible-artificial-intelligence-is-good-business/ (archived at perma.cc/C5N3-RERD)

Stackpole, B. (2023) New report documents the business benefits of "responsible AI," MIT Management Sloan School, mitsloan.mit.edu/ideas-made-to-matter/new-report-documents-business-benefits-responsible-ai (archived at perma.cc/VL5B-XHA6)

Stanford University (2023) The AI Index Report – Artificial Intelligence Index, aiindex.stanford.edu/report/ (archived at perma.cc/E9HB-36MJ)

van Maanen, G. (2022) AI ethics, ethics washing, and the need to politicize data ethics, *Digital Society*, 1 (2), doi.org/10.1007/s44206-022-00013-3 (archived at perma.cc/98NX-HPPU)

Chapter 6: The Responsible AI Blindspot You Didn't Know You Had

Mills, S., Singer, S., Gupta, A., Gravenhorst, F., Candelon, F., and Porter, T. (2022) Responsible AI is about more than avoiding risk, BCG Global, www.bcg.com/publications/2022/a-responsible-ai-leader-does-more-than-just-avoiding-risk (archived at perma.cc/8ZK2-4CBK)

Stackpole, B. (2023) New report documents the business benefits of "responsible AI," MIT Management Sloan School, mitsloan.mit.edu/ideas-made-to-matter/new-report-documents-business-benefits-responsible-ai (archived at perma.cc/SL53-5D2P)

Chapter 7: Who Is Building Your AI?

Stackpole, B (2023) New report documents the business benefits of "responsible AI," MIT Management Sloan School, mitsloan.mit.edu/ideas-made-to-matter/new-report-documents-business-benefits-responsible-ai (archived at perma.cc/47EG-4GKA)

Chapter 8: How Is Your AI Being Built?

Chowdhury, R., Rakova, B., Cramer, H., and Yang, J. (2020) Putting responsible AI into practice, *MIT Sloan Management Review*, sloanreview.mit.edu/article/putting-responsible-ai-into-practice/ (archived at perma.cc/V8E2-BMEK)

Expert Panel® (2021) Council post: 11 ways to ensure your company policies are beneficial, *Forbes*, www.forbes.com/sites/forbeshumanresourcescouncil/2021/08/19/11-ways-to-ensure-your-company-policies-are beneficial/?sh=6f767b903650 (archived at perma.cc/W3V7-S8QE)

Stackpole, B. (2023) New report documents the business benefits of "responsible AI," MIT Management Sloan School, mitsloan.mit.edu/ideas-made-to-matter/new-report-documents-business-benefits-responsible-ai (archived at perma.cc/VME2-2RHJ)

Vartak, M. (2022) How to scale AI in your organization, *Harvard Business Review*, hbr.org/2022/03/how-to-scale-ai-in-your-organization (archived at perma.cc/645W-S263)

Chapter 9: What Are You Building into Your AI?

Broussard, M. (2019) *Artificial Unintelligence*, MIT Press, mitpress.mit.edu/9780262537018/artificial-unintelligence/ (archived at perma.cc/4VLF-SAMP)

Chawla, N. V., Bowyer, K. W., Hall, L. O., and Kegelmeyer, W. P. (2002) SMOTE: Synthetic Minority Over-sampling Technique, *Journal of Artificial Intelligence Research*, 16 (16), 321–57, doi.org/10.1613/jair.953 (archived at perma.cc/7D3F-CBYB)

European Commission (2023) A European approach to artificial intelligence | Shaping Europe's digital future, digital-strategy.ec.europa.eu/en/policies/european-approach-artificial-intelligence (archived at perma.cc/6ZFW-CQ3M)

Fernandez, F. (2023) Bias mitigation strategies and techniques for classification tasks, Holistic AI, www.holisticai.com/blog/bias-mitigation-strategies-techniques-for-classification-tasks (archived at perma.cc/X7N4-6ALA)

Intersoft Consulting (2013) General Data Protection Regulation (GDPR), gdpr-info.eu (archived at perma.cc/Y6F7-HNE9)

Micheli, M., Hupont, I., Delipetrev, B., and Soler-Garrido, J. (2023) The landscape of data and AI documentation approaches in the European policy context, *Ethics and Information Technology*, 25 (4), doi.org/10.1007/s10676-023-09725-7 (archived at perma.cc/7V93-NPES)

Nassar, A. and Kamal, M. (2021) Ethical dilemmas in AI-powered decision-making: a deep dive into big data-driven ethical considerations, *International Journal of Responsible Artificial Intelligence*, 11 (8), 1–11, neuralslate.com/index.php/Journal-of-Responsible-AI/article/view/43 (archived at perma.cc/7QS8-D4LA)

Omar, M. (2023) Council post: The growing need for human feedback with generative AI and LLMs, *Forbes*, www.forbes.com/sites/forbestechcouncil/2023/05/25/the-growing-need-for-human-feedback-with-generative-ai-and-llms/?sh=138846c0250e (archived at perma.cc/DLX7-99EW)

State of California Department of Justice (2023) California Consumer Privacy Act (CCPA), oag.ca.gov/privacy/ccpa (archived at perma.cc/UY2R-VYSB)

Chapter 10: The Different Phases of Responsible AI Adoption

PwC (n.d.) Responsible AI – Maturing from theory to practice, www.pwc.com/gx/en/issues/data-and-analytics/artificial-intelligence/what-is-responsible-ai/pwc-responsible-ai-maturing-from-theory-to-practice.pdf (archived at perma.cc/2X3Y-TUUC)

Ribeiro, J. (2022) A quick introduction to responsible AI or rAI, Medium, towardsdatascience.com/a-quick-introduction-to-responsible-ai-or-rai-ae75fad-526dc#:~:text=The%20implementation%20of%20AI%20requires (archived at perma.cc/4KWH-M2GR)

Chapter 11: Becoming a Responsible AI Enabled-Organization

Apple Newsroom (n.d.) Apple announces powerful new privacy and security features, www.apple.com/newsroom/2023/06/apple-announces-powerful-new-privacy-and-security-features/ (archived at perma.cc/8LUL-R52K)

Boone, M., Pope, N., Xiao, C., and Anandkumar, A. (2022) Enhancing AI transparency and ethical considerations with Model Card++, NVIDIA Technical Blog, developer.nvidia.com/blog/enhancing-ai-transparency-and-ethical-considerations-with-model-card/ (archived at perma.cc/C9AJ-7BV7)

Firth-Butterfield, K., Heider, D., and Green, B. (2022) Responsible use of technology: The salesforce case study, www3.weforum.org/docs/WEF_Responsible_Use_of_Technology_Salesforce_Case_Study_2022.pdf (archived at perma.cc/YF4V-3FWJ)

Ivanov, O., Molander, K., Dunne, R., Liu, S. V., Masek, K., Lewis, E., Wolf, L., Travers, D., Brecher, D., Delaney, D., Montgomery, K., and Reilly, C. (2022) Detection of sepsis during emergency department triage using machine learning, *arXiv* (Cornell University), doi.org/10.48550/arxiv.2204.07657 (archived at perma.cc/M2AU-5MPN)

Linux Foundation – Training (n.d.) Ethics for open source development (LFC104), training.linuxfoundation.org/training/ethics-for-open-source-development-lfc104/#review_module (archived at perma.cc/4ZGX-4D2G)

Raghunathan, A. (2022) EAIDB: Ethical AI Ecosystem Database, Medium, medium.com/@abhinavr2121/the-ethical-ai-ecosystem-market-map-39779a9ea4ce (archived at perma.cc/LYZ4-7YCC)

Rolls-Royce (n.d.) The Aletheia Framework 2.0, www.rolls-royce.com/~/media/Files/R/Rolls-Royce/documents/stand-alone-pages/aletheia-framework-work sheet.pdf (archived at perma.cc/F5KH-AFM6)

Rolls-Royce | It's not what you think: a developer's guide to The Aletheia Framework v2.0, YouTube, www.youtube.com/watch?v=gzaMB-BLPOG0&list=PLk-17K0buHIu4wYKAW_KmpXonc_nhRaDX&index=6 (archived at perma.cc/9P4S-5Z57)

Marketing Artificial Intelligence Institute (n.d.) The Responsible AI Manifesto for Marketing and Business, www.marketingaiinstitute.com/blog/the-responsible-ai-manifesto-for-marketing-and-business (archived at perma.cc/XY79-2PPS)

Chapter 12: Who's Responsible for Responsible AI?

Edelmann, C. M., Boen, F., Broek, G. V., Fransen, K., and Stouten, J. (2023). The advantages and disadvantages of different implementations of shared leadership in organizations: A qualitative study, *Leadership*, 19 (6), doi.org/10.1177/17427150231200033 (archived at perma.cc/4K2H-3S6K)

Goncalves, A. R., Pinto, D. C., and Rita, P. (2023) Artificial intelligence and its ethical implications for marketing, *Emerging Science Journal*, 7, www.researchgate.net/publication/368521468_Artificial_Intelligence_and_Its_Ethical_Implications_for_Marketing (archived at perma.cc/W25N-UHPQ)

Heskett, J. (2023) How should artificial intelligence be regulated—if at all?, HBS Working Knowledge, hbswk.hbs.edu/item/how-should-artificial-intelligence-be-regulated-if-at-all (archived at perma.cc/GEY5-LAU9)

Lauer, D. (2020) You cannot have AI ethics without ethics, *AI and Ethics*, doi.org/10.1007/s43681-020-00013-4 (archived at perma.cc/45BR-FH3S)

Lu, Q., Zhu, L., Xu, X., Whittle, J., Douglas, D., and Sanderson, C. (2022) Software engineering for Responsible AI: An empirical study and operationalised patterns, IEEE Xplore, doi.org/10.1109/ICSE-SEIP55303.2022.9793864 (archived at perma.cc/8MYE-8JSJ)

Lupton, T. (1991) Organisational Change: "Top–down" or "Bottom–up" Management?, *Personnel Review*, 20 (3), 4–10, doi.org/10.1108/EUM0000000000788 (archived at perma.cc/P4M4-9H6R)

Verbeek, P.-P. (2008) Morality in design: Design ethics and the morality of technological artifacts, *Philosophy and Design*, 91–103, doi.org/10.1007/978-1-4020-6591-0_7 (archived at perma.cc/F6Z6-MF56)

Chapter 13: The Responsible AI Professional

Blackman, R. (2022) *Ethical Machines: Your concise guide to totally unbiased, transparent, and respectful AI*, Harvard Business Review Press, Boston, MA, amazon.com.be/-/en/Reid-Blackman/dp/1647822815 (archived at perma.cc/JK26-8NGQ)

Gambelin, O. (2020) Brave: What it means to be an AI Ethicist, *AI and Ethics*, doi.org/10.1007/s43681-020-00020-5 (archived at perma.cc/36DV-J9NH)

Hickok, M. (2020) What does an AI Ethicist do? A guide for the why, the what and the how, Medium, medium.com/@MerveHickok/what-does-an-ai-ethicist-do-a-guide-for-the-why-the-what-and-the-how-643e1bfab2e9 (archived at perma.cc/QAB3-A38A)

IBM (n.d.) AI Ethics, www.ibm.com/impact/ai-ethics (archived at perma.cc/
    TT7A-85JN)
Polgar, D. R. (2020) Building the Responsible AI pipeline, Dataiku, blog.dataiku.
    com/building-the-responsible-ai-pipeline (archived at perma.cc/QG5Z-TTZG)
Statt, N. (2019) Google dissolves AI ethics board just one week after forming it,
    The Verge, www.theverge.com/2019/4/4/18296113/google-ai-ethics-board-ends-
    controversy-kay-coles-james-heritage-foundation (archived at perma.
    cc/5QDH-EBA8)

Chapter 14: In Pursuit of Good Tech

Agrawal, A., Gans, J., and Goldfarb, A. (2023) How large language models reflect
    human judgment, *Harvard Business Review*, hbr.org/2023/06/how-large-
    language-models-reflect-human-judgment (archived at perma.cc/JGC4-Z6PM)
IBM (n.d.) What is a neural network?, www.ibm.com/topics/neural-networks#:~:-
    text=Neural%20networks%2C%20also%20known%20as (archived at perma.
    cc/43MY-37HP)
Nast, C. (2019) Can data be human? The work of Giorgia Lupi, *The New
    Yorker*, www.newyorker.com/culture/culture-desk/can-data-be-human-the-
    work-of-giorgia-lupi (archived at perma.cc/D2NL-JPEY)

INDEX

NB: page numbers in *italic* indicate figures or tables

accountability 205
active listening, AI Ethicist 222
AI-driven business 10
AI Ethicist 220–22
    active listening 222
    bravery 223
    critical thinker 222
    ethics 223–24
AI Ethics board 230–32
Aletheia Framework 192
Apple's *Data* strategy 188
applied ethics 10
architectural innovation 49
artificial general intelligence (AGI)
        13–14, 40
artificial intelligence (AI) 6, 9, 14, 17, 67
    adoption 167
    data science 22
    development life cycles 7, 68, 115,
        115, 205
    equation, human in 112
    Ethicist 236
    ethics (*see* ethics in AI)
    existential ethical risk 39–40
    humanity 11
    human values in 234–36, 239–40
    investment 69
    model cards 194
    moral imagination 54–55
    philosophical concept 239–40
auditing process 136

balance striking 53–54
Barnes, D. 68
bias-mitigation technique 113–14, 136
blue-washing *see* ethics-washing
bravery, AI Ethicist 223
business model 48–49, 209, 235
business, Responsible AI professional 225

cancel culture 72–73
care ethics 9
carpentry teachers 3–4
centralized/decentralized team 226–28
Change Instigator Spectrum 212–13

change management
    advantages 211–12
    government regulation 212
    responsibility structure 212
    single *vs.* shared spectrum 213–14
    top-down *vs.* bottom-up
        spectrum 212–13
clarity, Responsible AI strategy
        175–76
codes of conduct 25
Communicate solution
    in action 103–4
    description 101
    designing 102–3
    purpose 101–2
    strategy 185, *194*, 194–5
community/communal leadership 213
ConnectAI 169, 171–72, 173, 174
Cook, T. 45
critical thinker, AI Ethicist 222
cultural values 27

data privacy regulations 52
data science 21–22, 32, 83, 114
Data solution
    in action 142
    description 139
    designing 140–41
    purpose 140
    strategy *185*, 188, 193
decision-analysis tool 11, 15, 45, 47,
        63, 64, 67, 68, 75, 158, 176,
        220, 235
deontological ethics 9
designing structure 189
Digital Ethics 197
direction, Responsible AI strategy
        175
disruptive innovation 49
Document solution
    in action 145
    description 143
    designing 143–44
    purpose 140
    strategy *190*, 193

Domain solution
   in action 148–49
   description 146
   designing 146–48
   purpose 146
   strategy *195*, 198
duality of ethics
   decision-making process 36
   dumpster fire, cloud nine 37–38
   innovation tool 43–49
   purposes of 37–38
   responsible AI strategy 36
   risk mitigation 39–43
   value-aligning analysis 49–50

Educate solution
   in action 96
   designing 94–96
   ideation 96
   knowledge gaps 94–95
   purpose 94
   workforce 94
equal quality of service 89
Ethical AI Database (EAIDB) 198
ethical debt 41–42
ethical decision making 82
ethical drift 41–42
ethical innovation 44–45, 47–49
Ethical Intelligence 15, 64, 113, 136, 186
ethical risk management 39–41
ethical risk mitigation interventions 42–43
ethical values 205
ethics-by-design 15, 45–46, 209
ethics in AI
   see also Responsible AI strategy
   advisory firms 15
   business 10
   conceptual blockers 19
   critical decision-making factors 8
   decision-analysis tool 11, 15
   hammering 4–5
   history 9–10
   humanity 239–40
   investment 6–7
   profession of carpentry 3–4
   Responsible AI profession 223–24
   risk-and innovation-based approach 16
   risks and opportunities 14
   silent killer 5–8
   technical knowledge 15
   unintended consequences 8
ethics risk and innovation
      framework 55–56, *56*, *62*
   best case scenarios 58–59, *59*, *61*

   focus 58, 60–63, *60*
   worst case scenarios 56–57, *57*
ethics-washing 210
EU AI Act 156
Evaluation, Responsible AI
      adoption 170–71
   testing and connecting 176–177
existential risks 40
Expansion, Responsible AI
      adoption 172–75
   standardizing and scaling 177–78
Exploration, Responsible AI
      adoption 168–70
   clarity, direction, and support 175–76
external audience 210
extracurricular values 29

Facebook 31
fairness metrics 82
Fortune 100 bank 113
Foundational Value Finder
   alignment of values 27–28
   columns 24
   defined 23–24
   framework *24*, 29
   government value set 24–25, *25*
   industry value set 25–26, *26*
   location 28–30
   organization value set 26–27, *27*

gender bias 79–80, 82, 83
Glazier, L. 193
government value set 24–25, *25*

Hao, K. 31
Head of Data Governance 171
HireAI 57, 58
The Hobbit 88
human-centric values 4–5, 8, 12, 44
humanity, reflection of AI 233–34
hyperfocused value 30–31
Hyperfocus Value Challenge 31

IKEA 196
image generators 6
Implement solution
   in action 123
   description 120
   designing 120–22
   foundational values, AI project 122
   purpose 120
   strategy 187, *190*, 192
industry value set 25–26, *26*
innovation approach 36

ethical innovation 44–45
ethical interventions 47–49
ethics-by-design 45–46
misconceptions 46–47
risk management 43
transitioning traditional strategies 44
video calling 44
Instrument solution
    in action 126
    description 124
    designing 124–27
    purpose 124
    strategy 187, *194*, 197–198
Intent solution
    in action 118–19
    description 116
    designing 117–18
    purpose 116–17
    strategy *185*, 187, 189
international messaging apps 51
investment costs 73–74

knowledge gaps 94–95

laissez-faire approach 207
LanguAI 215, 216, 217, 218
Large Language Models (LLMs) 215
Leadership Spectrum 213–14
Linux Foundation's Educate Solution 196

Malmros, A. 75
Mednition 199
meta-ethics 9
Meta's ad-based revenue model 48
model cards, Model C++ 194
moral imagination 54–55
moral philosophy 10
Motivate solution
    in action 100
    description 97–98
    designing 98–99
    purpose 98
    strategy 185, *189*, 189–91

NatWest 32–33
normative ethics 9
NVIDIA 194

organizational culture 52
organizational structure placement 228
organization-level strategy 16, 164
organization's responsibility structure
    bottom-up and shared 217
    bottom-up and single 216

right balance striking 218
spectrums 214
top-down and shared 215–16
top-down and single 214–15
organization value set 26–27, *27*

People Pillar 84, *92*, *181*, 224
    in action 107–8
    Communicate 101–4, 185, *195*, 195–96
    Educate 93–96, *185*
    elements of *95*, 105
    finalizing 105
    impact of 112
    Linux Foundation 186
    Motivate 97–100, 185, 190–91, *190*
    Responsible AI adoption *169*, 172–74
    Responsible AI teams 229
    risk *vs.* innovation approach 110–11
    synchronizing 105–7
pillars of Responsible AI
    ethical decision making 82
    fairness metrics 82
    gender bias 82
    People Pillar 84, *171*, 172–74, *181*,
        183–84, 202–3
    Process Pillar 84–85, *171*, 172, *174*, *181*,
        183–84, 202–3
    Technology Pillar 85, *171*, 172, *174*,
        181, 183–84, 202–3
policy, Responsible AI professional 225–26
primary values 28–30
privacy 45, 53
privacy-by-design 38, 51
Process Pillar 84–85, 128, 131, 224
    in action 129–30
    bias-mitigation technique 113–14
    card fraud detection project 130, 131
    elements of 115–16
    fairness implementation 113
    finalizing 127
    impacts 133–34
    Implement 120–24, 187, 191–3, 198
    Instrument 124–27, 187, *195*, 197
    Intent 116–19, *184–85*, 187, 191, 197
    performance and tracking progress 133
    Responsible AI adoption *169*, 172, *174*
    Responsible AI teams 229–30
    risk *vs.* innovation approach 132, 133
    structural sportive trunk 114–15
    synchronizing 127–29
    technology 134–35
product quality 74–75
project-level strategy 16, 164
pursuit of good tech 239–40

Quality Assurance of Fully Autonomous
    Safety Critical AI 192–93
Quiñonero Candela, J. 31

radical innovation 49
reputational/legal risks 42–43
Responsible AI adoption 167, 237–38
    ConnectAI 169–71, 173–74
    Evaluation 170–72
    Expansion 172–75
    Exploration 168–70
    journey of 167–68
    People Pillar *171*, 172–74, *174*
    Process Pillar *171*, 172, *174*
    Technology Pillar *171*, 172, *174*
Responsible AI-enabled
        organization 164–65
    AI *vs.* Responsible AI adoption 167
    Aletheia Framework 192–93
    decision-analysis tool 176
    designing structure 189
    ethical resources 166
    foundational values 183
    IKEA 196–97
    large enterprises 200–1
    Mednition 199
    NVIDIA 194
    organization's size 200–3
    Rolls-Royce 192–93
    small organizations 201–3
    Values Canvas 166–67, 168–70, 175,
        181, 200, 238
Responsible AI Manifesto for Marketing and
        Business 187
Responsible AI professional
    AI Ethicist 220–21
    business 225
    ethics 223–24
    policy 225–26
    team 226–28
    technology specialization 224–25
Responsible AI software solutions 198
Responsible AI strategy
    adoption 16
    change management 211–14
    clarity 175
    communication 210–11
    conceptual structure 237
    costs financial and human capital 69–70
    creating support for 176
    designing 177, 208–9
    development life cycle 7
    direction for 175
    dual impact 38

ethical values 205
ethics 67–72
execution 29, 209–10
external communications 72–73
high value and human-centric values 4–5
immediate not existential 13–14
innovation 36
internal blockers 33
knowledge gathering 211
long-term and short-term market 66–67
operational structure 8, 12
organizational-level approach 164
organization's responsibility
        structure 214–18
pitfall 206–7
practitioners 15
project-level approach 164
risk-forward approach 36
roles 207–11
services 64
strategy building 208
structure not substance 12–13
subjectivity of ethics 34–35
universal values 20–21
Responsible AI teams 226
    centralized/decentralized team 226–28
    organizational structure placement 228
    People Pillar 229
    Process Pillar 229–30
    Technology Pillar 230
Responsible Tech company 191
Responsible Technologists 224–25
risk-based approach 36, 42, 44, 51, 52, 53,
        54, 110, 132, 155, 156–157
risk management 39, 42, 43
risk mitigation 36, 38
    cyclical process 39
    ethical debt and drift 41–42
    ethical interventions 42–43
    ethical risk management 39–41
risk tolerance 52
risk *vs.* innovation approach
    organizational culture 52, 53
    People Pillar 110–11
    Process Pillar 132, 132
    Technology Pillar 153–56
    value-alignment 53
Rolls-Royce 192–93
routine innovation 49

Salesforce's Motivate solution 191
scope creep 41
secondary values 29–30
self-governance 212

Signal's innovation approach 52
singularity problem 40
small and medium enterprise (SMEs) 201–2
social networking app 91
speech-to-text systems 57
strategy building 208
subjective ethics
    data science 21–22
    vs. objective factors 19
    responsible AI strategy 20–21
    technical-minded individuals 20
Synthetic Minority Over-Sampling Technique
        (SMOTE) 152

team, Responsible AI 226–28
technical debt 41–42
technical teams 209–10
Technology Pillar 85, 137, 151, *181,* 224–25
    in action 152–53
    Data 139–42, *184,* 188, 198
    Document 143–45, *190,* 193–94, 198
    Domain 146–48, *195,* 198
    elements of 138–39
    finalizing 150
    intangible results 158
    Responsible AI adoption *171, 172, 174*
    Responsible AI teams 230
    risk *vs.* innovation approach 153–56
    synchronizing 150
    tangible results 157
technology specialization 224–25
techno-value blindspot 80–82

transformational change 64

Undefined Value Risk 32, 33
undefined values 31–33
unethical behavior 40
universal values 20–22
utilitarianism 9

V2MOM 191
value-aligning analysis 49–50
values
    AI ethics strategy 18
    conceptual blockers, AI ethics 19
    ethics practices 18
    Foundational Value Finder
        framework 24–30, *24, 29*
    hyperfocused 30–31
    securing buy-in 33–34
    selection process 19, 23, 34
    sources 23
    subjective ethics 19–22
    undefined 31–33
Values Canvas 81–82, *87,* 166–67, 168–70,
        175, 181, 200, 238
    see also People Pillar; Process Pillar;
        Technology Pillar
    overview 87
    tool 86–88
    use case 88–89
virtue ethics 9

World Economic Forum 191

Looking for another book?

Explore our award-winning
books from global business
experts in Digital and
Technology

Scan the code to browse

www.koganpage.com/digital-
technology

More books from Kogan Page

www.koganpage.com

Printed in the USA
CPSIA information can be obtained
at www.ICGtesting.com
JSHW070617290524
63780JS00010B/13